Transformations
By Erik L. Welchoff

Tales of a Methonian Warrior
The Chronicles of Anton Seven
Book 2
Transformations
ERIK L. WELCHOFF
WO
WELCHOFF
ORIGINALS

Contents

Truth is the foundation of a Warrior,
and *logic* is the essence.
A *conscience* changes everything …
It is the *soul* of humanity.

PART ONE:

"Transfor-mations"

CHAPTER 1
City of the Humans

EVERYONE STOOD LOOKING AT THE portal. Anton unexpectedly hesitated after taking that first single step toward the unknown. The transformation of the portal from a vacant hole to a storm of energy caused by seemingly natural forces mystified him, and he vacillated; he was unsure of what would happen if he entered it, or if he should enter it at all. There were so many things he simply didn't understand since arriving in Peruvious, and he wished to have his world of science and technology returned to him, if only to be able to understand how everything functioned, and to once again feel confidence in his decisions. He didn't comprehend the moon's influence over the portal and the unending practice of magic controlling everything he'd witnessed. Technology was all he knew, and he missed its familiarity.

As everyone watched the opening of the portal, something else occurred. From the ground on either side of the pathway of stones, unusual plants appeared. "*Perhaps,*" Anton thought, "*in response to my first step?*"

The plants, which were roughly the height of a man, appeared to be some type of fiber optics, but they clearly were organic. They reminded Anton of the pictures he'd seen of sea anemones on ancient Earth, but these were above ground, not below water, and they were much larger. They were round and tiered in three levels, each tier smaller than the one below it. Each organic optical strand glowed, just like the technological counterpart that was more familiar to him. The strands of the lowest tier lay nearly flat, stretching from what looked like a bulbous vertical rhizome. This held the second tier like an arrangement of flowers; they were shorter than the first tier, and they stood bent at a forty-five-degree angle. The strands on the upper tier were even shorter and barely leaned from upright. The center stem, where all the strands converged, generated a beautiful violet light that fed the entire plant with color. The whole effect was mesmerizing. It held Anton's attention, but it left him with an uncomfortable feeling of trepidation, and he didn't want to continue down the path.

Together, the little faeries and these unusual plants lined either side of the path, lighting it so radiantly that it seemed nearly as bright as day. The result seemed to tempt anyone to walk through the portal of stone; they showed no fear whatsoever.

"Stand aside, my young friend, I'll lead the way," Vim huffed as he touched Anton's shoulder and gently nudged him aside. "You don't know what to expect, but I *do!* There is nothing to fear, especially for a big Warrior like you … "

Without hesitation, Vim headed straight down the stone path as if he'd walked this path his whole life. With a youthful spring in his gait and a smile on his face, he eagerly marched toward the opening, but then stopped just one step short. He turned around to make a farewell gesture to the Queen.

"Thank you again, my Queen," he said. "Your service to Peruvious is without measure! As of late, I've gained a new perspective of many of my old *friends*." He remembered Drôgän's revelation only days before; two of his old allies had kept important secrets from him with no explanation as to why, and it both disturbed and delighted him. Now that he knew the secret identity of the second piece of *One*, he unquestionably understood who the third piece must be.

Vim bowed stiffly to the Queen, then turned to face the portal once more, unsteadily grasping the staff with both hands. Then he gave Anton a beckoning glance and pointed with his head toward the portal, urging him to follow. "Come along," he said with a smile. "We must go *now*. The portal only exists for *very* short time, a few minutes at best, and its time is nearly spent!"

Anton immediately started down the stone pathway after his friend. He looked over his shoulder just long enough to wave a brief goodbye to the Queen, then returned his attention to Vim. Tania flew closely after him, never drifting more than an arm's length away.

"What will happen when we pass through this, uh—*gateway?*" Anton asked. His question was insistent, and he expected an immediate answer before he would take a single step further. As committed as he was to follow Vim, he still didn't wish to enter until he knew what to expect.

"Fear not, my young friend, it's perfectly safe," Vim said. "I appreciate your concern, but I assure you, no harm will befall us. This portal is magically enhanced, yet it's a natural occurrence of nature. It will take us to, shall we say, *another aspect of Peruvious*. I realize it was concealed with magic, and that you're uncomfortable with that, but it's necessary to disguise it from the enemy's watchful eyes, and anyone else who wishes to do harm."

Vim's reassurance helped calm Anton, but it didn't satisfy his curiosity. As he looked more closely at the portal, he noticed how strange the lighting inside seemed. The roiling gaseous fog and strange lighting defied physics in the sense that the light didn't radiate outward beyond the ring, but simply glowed inside it. The light was bright enough to hurt his eyes as he approached and gazed upon it. He again looked quizzically at Vim, hoping for a reasonable explanation.

"I understand you're confused, but as I said before, it's *natural*. Please accept that, and let's be off!" Vim offered little clarification, and he showed little patience for Anton's inability to simply trust him rather than analyze things at the last minute.

"Your answer doesn't satisfy the *logic*," Anton said. He was tired of everything being magic, or existing without a reasonable explanation. He desperately wanted things to make sense and magic simply didn't. His knowledge of magic was limited, and it frustrated him. Now, more than ever, he wished to have technology returned to him so he could make decisions based on what he knew. It seemed impossible for him to accomplish even the most fundamental tasks without it, and he hated relying on others for everything.

Suddenly, Anton remembered the words Amilius had given him: *Take your new apprentice to the City of the Humans and introduce him to Trepid Tantamount so that he can begin his journey to maturity. There, he will finish his education.*

Anton was only just beginning to understand the magnitude of this statement. It was obvious he needed to learn more about magic, and perhaps this was what Amilius meant. Or maybe not. Certainly, he required no other form of education; he'd already acquired all he needed.

He also recalled Drôgän's words: *If you should choose to follow the path set before you, your victory shall be glorious, undeniable and righteous; people will call you The Savior, and The Champion of One. If evil should tempt you and persuade you, if you step aside from your true path, the victory you achieve will be the undoing of everything. The thing that you desire most of all, the release from Peruvious, the return to your own world, you will never achieve.*

So far, it seemed to Anton that he was following his true path, the path to knowledge and perhaps a way back to his world. It seemed inevitable he needed to step through the portal in order to move forward.

"Fine, let's get this over with," Anton said, grasping Vim's arm and giving it a tug to let him know he was ready to proceed. "I've decided that trusting you and entering this portal is the best thing I can do."

Tania seated herself on Anton's shoulder just as he hastily stepped into the portal. "It's safe," she said, trying to reassure him. "Trust Vim, he knows!" Then they slipped neatly through the portal's opening.

Heaving a sigh of relief, Vim rolled his eyes and quickly followed after Anton. He was beginning to think he would have to spend time arguing with him and trying to convince him at the last minute, and he was relieved to see Anton's sudden and surprising acceptance. Still, it bothered him how his new champion had so many peculiarities and attitudes, and how it required him to work twice as hard to accomplish each step he faced even as time ran out. Anton was completely unpredictable.

Immersed in blazing bright light, it was impossible for Anton to see. He stood just inside the portal's entrance and waited for Vim to follow. When he did, he took the lead and motioned for Anton to accompany him. With each step forward, the light diminished substantially. After taking a few more steps, the light seemed to disappear almost entirely, and after the last few steps they suddenly took an abrupt step down and found themselves on a flat stone surface with the portal behind them.

Anton turned around to get a quick glimpse of the portal's exit. He saw a ring of stone identical to that of the entrance, but the terrain behind and around the exit was quite different. The exit shined brightly in its core, yet it cast no light and held no image; its center boiled and churned a maelstrom of fog just as the entrance had before the moon had somehow activated it.

Igniting his staff, Vim cast his magical radiance amidst the three friends, allowing their eyes to adjust to the changing amplitudes of luminosity. Somehow, the magical light assuaged the discomfort they'd experienced while traveling through the portal.

After their eyes adjusted to the dim evening light, Anton noticed they were not alone. Four men stood around them as if waiting for their arrival, and it was easy to see that they were awaiting acknowledgment. Vim looked around and smiled at each of the men. He obviously recognized them as friends.

"Vim has arrived!" one of the men yelled, before quickly running off shouting: "They have arrived! They are here!" as if to warn the entire vicinity of the visitors' sudden yet expected appearance.

"Welcome, you old wizard you!" said a second man. "It's good to see you, my friend."

"As always, it's a pleasure to be back in the city with my comrades," Vim replied. "Is Trepid ready for us?" Vim got to the point immediately, not wanting to waste a single moment.

"He *is* of course, expecting you, but don't be surprised when you see him; you may not recognize him," the man answered. "Now then, who's this fine-looking young boy you've brought for us to meet?" He looked at Anton and smiled.

"I'm Anton Seven, Methonian Warrior, and Vim's friend," Anton said, reaching out to offer his hand for a shake. But the man simply looked at him and disregarded his gesture.

"*Another* Methonian! I hope this one fares better than the last one you brought here. Just keep him away from that infernal beast! Boris didn't fare too well around him!" The man's face turned serious, and it occurred to Anton he must be referring to the Dragon Master. It was obvious nobody there knew Anton had already encountered him.

"Oh, dear me," the man said. "I'm forgetting my manners! My name is Eädwyn, but people here call me *The Incorrigible.*" He laughed heartily as did the other two men standing beside him.

"Pleased to meet you, sir." Anton replied formally. He didn't see any humor in Eädwyn's comment, and clearly it was some inside joke. Bowing in Methonian fashion, he put his right palm over his left fist, his eyes never leaving Eädwyn's. "There's no need to fear the Dragon Master," he said. "I've … *resolved* the issue."

The three men looked at each other with puzzled expressions and then at Anton. They didn't seem to believe what they'd just heard, or perhaps they were guessing at his meaning. Suddenly, they all burst into laughter.

"I see that you've had more than a *simple* run-in with *something* or *someone!* Why has your leg been encased in Vim's magical stasis? Perhaps you and the Dragon Master *have* met." Eädwyn smiled slyly at Anton, but his tone revealed sarcasm. He then pointed directly at the golden aura around Anton's leg, bringing the question to everyone's attention. They immediately wondered who Anton had battled, or what had caused him such damage that it required Vim's special assistance.

Tania darted around and stopped to look at each of the men in turn, giving them a scrutinizing glance. They simply ignored her as if she were no more than an insect. After completing her inspection, she flew back over to Anton, landed on his shoulder, and whispered in his ear: "They don't believe you. But don't worry, *I* know what you did!"

"Ahem, my name is Aëlfwyn," said the third man. "They call me *Trepid's Right Hand.* I'm pleased to meet you, Anton." He smiled and bowed slightly in a poor attempt to mimic Anton's Methonian greeting.

"How is it possible you've *taken care of the problem,* as you say?" He looked directly at Anton's leg as he asked the question and then into his eyes with a look of skepticism.

"I've eliminated him," Anton said. "The beast is dead. You are more than welcome to investigate this if you so please. His body still lies within the Barren Mountain, and you can find it there."

Anton's reply surprised everyone; they hadn't believed he'd actually met the dragon. All three of the men looked at him with puzzled expressions and then again laughed outright.

"He lies!" Eädwyn announced boisterously, and everyone laughed heartily once more. "He's pulling our legs! Get it? Legs! Or is it *his* leg *we* should pull?" He continued to laugh as he poked fun at Anton.

Finally, still chuckling, the fourth man introduced himself. "I'm known as Grëyfwyn. People call me *The Organizer*. I like to make sure everything's orderly and done *correctly*. I make the plans. You may have *taken care of* the Dragon Master, as you say, but it would appear that he got a piece of you as well?" He bowed slightly, quickly mocking Anton's Methonian bow, and again chuckled lightly. "Apparently, they've made *tremendous* improvements in cloning in the past fifty years. The last Warrior, Boris, was little more than a tasty treat! At least that's how the story is told!"

Another round of laughter filled the air as the three men pointed at Anton's leg and made comments to themselves. The humor was at Anton's expense, but it lacked any of the vicious intentions that he'd experienced at the King's castle. It merely belittled him, and he didn't like it.

With a forced smile, Anton again bowed in Methonian fashion. "Yes, they *have*, and I *will* prove it, in time."

"Enough of this!" Vim shouted. He tapped the ground with his staff, and a gentle roll of energy shook the stone beneath everyone's feet. "We're here to see Trepid. Please take us to him!"

"Patience, wizard! Cuðbwyn will return shortly to inform us of Trepid's wishes." Grëyfwyn gave Vim a respectful glance as he tried to calm his impatience.

After bowing his head to Vim, Grëyfwyn stared at Anton and then nodded once as if to accept him as a friend. "All of us here are proud to meet you, young Anton. We mean you no harm." His response was stiff and formal, yet he seemed to speak for everyone, and they all nodded in agreement. "You'll tell us of your umm, *victory*, is it?"

"There will be time for that later!" Vim interjected again then turned upon Grëyfwyn with an angry frown. "His so-called victory cost us. There is an increased imbalance between the upper and lower lands, and there's evidence the great seal is broken. We had a visit from Lord Agonia and, I might add, Anton quickly defeated him too, if only temporarily. We are not sure. I think Trepid should hear the telling of both of these tales." Vim made sure the men knew he intended to deliver the information as soon as possible to Trepid, and that the story wasn't for casual public discussion.

"Very well, wizard. You are most wise," Grëyfwyn said, nodding and accepting Vim's pronouncement without further question. "We are aware of the change in balance and the breach of the great seal; we have deployed the katrahs to investigate."

Vim nodded thoughtfully to Grëyfwyn and replied, "Very good. Taun will discover what we need to know."

"Who was the other man who left a minute ago?" asked Anton. He looked at Grëyfwyn and pointed in the direction the man had gone.

"That was Cuðbwyn. He's Trepid's *Eyes and Ears*. He will return shortly and greet you with a message. In the meantime, have a look around. I believe you will see many points of interest."

Grëyfwyn was gracious and formal, and now treated Anton with a degree of respect, something Anton appreciated. Nodding that he accepted Grëyfwyn's explanation, Anton again bowed.

Scrutinizing Anton very carefully, Grëyfwyn wondered how such a young, skinny man could kill the massive Dragon Master single-handedly. It was an impossible challenge even for the best of soldiers at the Great Castle of Amilius, and it was well beyond the abilities of anyone in the City of the Humans. It would take an army. The prospect that Anton had been able to do what all others feared even to discuss aroused his interest, but most of all, he wondered how Anton was able to do so unaided.

"When the time is appropriate, we'd greatly enjoy you telling us of your adventures here on Peruvious. We're always most interested to hear news from the outside," Grëyfwyn said. He looked at Vim as he spoke to Anton, wanting to inform him of his intentions.

"Thank you, I will," Anton said, bowing again, before accepting Grëyfwyn's offer to look around and examine his surroundings.

The ground beneath their feet was a solid sheet of stone—smooth, perfectly flat, and highly polished. The moonlight reflected off it as if it were a mirror. Looking past the portal platform in the distance, Anton saw the pyramid-shaped structure imaged in the entrance portal. He recalled Vim telling him about a Crystal Pyramid used by Vile the Necromancer, and he wondered why a large structure that seemingly resembled it existed here.

Turning around, Anton looked back at the portal. He wondered if the exit portrayed an image of the Queen, but it looked the same as the entrance had, and he was surprised to see that it resembled it only in its size and shape. It had the same boiling turmoil of fog that stung the eyes, yet cast no light. Its stone appeared perfectly shaped, as if manufactured by machines—and much more recently. This was in direct contrast to the entrance ring that had a rough appearance, as if chiseled by hand from stone and seemed far more ancient.

Continuing to look around, Anton noticed the men's clothing. They all wore heavy leather pants, and leather jerkins that were covered in light chainmail. Atop their heads, they wore knightly helmets. The resemblance to the four men they'd encountered on the high plateau near the portal was unmistakable; the only difference was these men lacked the same gauntlets and studded armor.

Suddenly, just as Grëyfwyn had predicted, Cuðbwyn returned and promptly interrupted everyone. "Trepid is prepared to speak to Anton," he said, "but he asked that he be healed prior to his visit. He said it's necessary." Directing his attention to Anton, Cuðbwyn smiled and bowed slightly, then waved his hand, beckoning Anton to follow.

"We'll require food and rest as soon as possible," Vim said. "Our day included far too much activity, and we're both quite hungry." Vim wanted to make sure Anton received a proper meal before long. He recalled his discomfort at the Castle of Ambrosias and the mistaken harvest of the fruit atop the plateau. He wanted to avoid any of Anton's impertinences. This unquestionably wasn't the time or place for them.

Suddenly, from behind them, two more people stepped out of the portal, and Anton stared at them with utter disbelief. They were unlike anything he'd ever seen: half-human and half-animal, they resembled a cross between humans and large cats. Anton stood there speechless, looking at them.

The first creature was unmistakably male, large and muscular with a lion-like face and the requisite head of hair. Unconscious in his arms he held what could only be a female. She was quite lean and resembled a human-like cheetah. They each wore nothing more than a modest loincloth. Both had cat ears, a short cat-like tail and short cat-like fur that covered their entire bodies, which were more human in shape than feline.

Collapsing to his knees, the male let out a mighty lion-like roar, exposing huge feline teeth. Blood oozed from multiple wounds all over his body and from the corner of his mouth. It was obvious they had been in a battle for their lives just moments before and had somehow barely escaped.

"The katrahs have returned!" Cuðbwyn announced. "This is unexpected. They had left only minutes before you arrived. That's why you conveniently found us here."

"They need help!" Eädwyn shouted. "Aëlfwyn, bring the medics!"

Gesticulating toward the distant pyramid, Aëlfwyn used hand signals to alert a group of men stationed near its entrance, With the light of the portal behind him they had no trouble seeing him, and they instantly scrambled into action and disappeared inside the pyramid.

Instinctively, Anton sprang toward the fallen creature. He didn't know what care he required, but it was obvious the female was an encumbrance, and he quickly offered to relieve the struggling male of his heavy burden.

Without a moment's forethought, the katrah gently placed the female into Anton's arms and then collapsed. "She's yuninjured, but she hit yer head; she's yust yunconscious," he said in a clumsy, strained manner, as if human speech was difficult through his feline teeth. Then, he too lost consciousness.

The katrah's injuries were severe, and Anton knew from experience he wouldn't live long unless he received immediate medical attention.

It also would require special medical equipment, which Anton knew did not exist.

Tania fluttered around and quickly inspected the katrah's wounds. Landing on his abdomen, she placed both her hands on a large gash and then cried silently, just as she'd done for the Queen. The open wound began to heal, but it would take time. It wasn't a simple prick in a finger, it was an extensive and deep laceration.

Raising his staff, Vim joined in the effort. Placing the globe against the katrah's forehead, he mumbled unintelligible words in his wizard's tongue. Electrical fingers of energy danced and licked around the katrah's head, and magical potency poured into him from the staff.

"It won't be enough," Vim said, after a moment. "His wounds are too extensive, and I can sense his life energy is fading. I can only prolong his life for a short time before the inevitable. The katrahs will produce no offspring; the last of their line is Deidra." He nodded at the feline woman Anton held gently in his arms. Quickly he looked up at Vim with interest; the information surprised him, and left him feeling a little disappointed.

Confused, Anton quickly looked down at the half-human woman he held. She was beautiful in her own way and more human-like than he'd first noticed. "Where can I take her?" he asked Eädwyn. "She needs medical attention."

"It appears she has a head injury," Eädwyn said. "Lay her down carefully; we'll attend to her after we've helped Taun." Eädwyn showed little concern for Deidra and focused his attention on Taun; this too surprised Anton and left him confused.

Kneeling on the stone, Anton laid Deidra down slowly and gently placed her head in his lap. Nelda had done the same for him on the afternoon of his marriage, and he decided to comfort this unusual creature in a likewise gesture. For some reason, he felt a connection to her, but he didn't understand why. It seemed only natural to treat her tenderly and with compassion; he was enchanted by her obvious genetic modifications. Somehow, oddly, this unique genetic difference spoke to his heart and his nature in a way he didn't understand. It was as if it spoke to his base instincts.

With Vim and Tania's help, Taun's worst wound had nearly healed, but Tania's efforts seemed to lose impetus. Golden faerie dust covered the injury, shimmering and glittering as if it were alive. Suddenly, Tania flew into the air, took a deep breath and landed on Anton's shoulder. With a sad look on her face, she whispered in his ear. "That's all I can do. His life is fading. Something is wrong deep inside of him, but it's strangely concealed from me. I feel like I should know what it is, but I don't."

Suddenly, there was a thumping from inside Taun's chest, as if his heart was trying to burst through his sternum. Unexpectedly, a pool of blood puddled just below his ribs, and from the nearly sealed wound in his abdomen a small creature emerged.

"Fracknoid!" yelled Vim. "I should have known!" Instantly, he enveloped the tiny creature in his magical stasis and raised the field of energy into the air.

Not completely contained by Vim's magic field, the creature fought for release. Roaring and shrieking, it wrestled so hard it nearly broke free. Tugging at the magical energy from the staff, it looked like a fish on a line flying around in the air. But it couldn't escape Vim's magical grasp. Struggling with all his might, Vim chanted loudly and swung his staff back and forth attempting to maintain control. The fracknoid jerked him around like a dog on a leash, but Vim held the staff firmly with intense determination. He continued the tug-of-war and angrily yelled his archaic words ever louder.

The fracknoid was small—not much larger than Anton's two fists put together—but it seemed to have the strength of a titan. It was black with short fur, four short limbs with long talon-like claws, and a score of razor-sharp metallic teeth that gnashed incessantly. It let loose a hideous shriek that tore at the atmosphere and made Anton's nerves sting like claws scratching his skin. Vim's magical stasis had held four humans motionless, but this creature seemed nearly unaffected by it.

It pulled at the field of energy so hard it nearly tugged the staff from Vim's hands.

It appeared Vim wouldn't be able to contain the fracknoid much longer, and Anton wondered if it would break free. Without another thought, Anton's Methonian reflexes kicked in. Carefully resting Deidra's head on the ground, he swiftly produced his Blue Flame Sword. A four-foot length of fire shot into the night air and a golden conflagration burst from his crystal ring that enveloped his body, and encircled the fiery blue blade. Unable to reconsider, he thrust the empowered sword directly into Vim's magical stasis. Golden energy met golden energy and blended into one. Blue fire sliced neatly inside Vim's containment field and struck the center of the strange creature, killing it instantly. In less than a heartbeat, it was over.

All eyes fell upon Anton, and no one, including Tania, was able to speak. The little faerie fluttered from one side of Anton, hesitated, and then fluttered back to the other. She clapped her hands and smiled as if watching a spectacle.

Vim looked at Anton with wide eyes, his mouth agape. "Unbelievable," was all he said.

"Impossible!" Grëyfwyn interjected.

"Our savior is amongst us!" Eädwyn proclaimed.

"The medics arrive!" announced Cuðbwyn.

Aëlfwyn directed two men carrying a stretcher over to Deidra. Stunned, they glanced around at the gathering for a moment, then proceeded to place Deidra gently onto the stretcher. When they finished, they turned their attention to Taun.

It was obvious to everyone that Taun was dead. Looking down at the katrah, Vim knelt next to him and examined him more closely. Placing his hand over Taun's eyes, he gently closed them, then grasped his staff in both hands and used it to help him stand. Leaning heavily on his staff, he heaved a sigh. "Good-bye, my old friend," he said. "We've lost the *bravest* of *all* men."

"Oh, dear, that unfortunate katrah," Tania suddenly remarked. "Poor Deidra is alone!" Landing on Anton's shoulder she again whispered in his ear. "She needs someone to help her. She is alone now! You must help!"

Not entirely sure what Tania meant, Anton looked down at Deidra, who lay on the stretcher, still unconscious. Then she rolled her head around as if she were about to awaken. She growled quietly, as if in pain, then opened her eyes and sat up part way. When she saw Taun lying on the ground in a pool of blood, tears began pouring from her eyes.

"Rowwerrrr!" she roared with a strain, and then cried outright like a human child.

"Be still, Deidra," Aëlfwyn said gently. He placed his hand on her shoulder and tried to comfort her. "You're injured. You must rest! There's nothing you can do for him."

Brushing Aëlfwyn's hand aside, Deidra placed her hand against her forehead, gasped in pain and lay back down on the stretcher. "Nowwerr at least I donnn't have to mate with *himmm*." With her eyes closed, she pointed in Taun's direction. "Still, I didn't want it to ennnd like this; he *was* good to mmmeee, rowwerrrr." Her words were stiff, as if human speech was an imposition. She let out a quiet growl and passed out again.

"What an odd thing to say," said Grëyfwyn.

"Indeed," Vim responded. "Taun was … *different*. He was special."

Aëlfwyn turned to Anton and spoke. "If you would follow us, I'll lead you to the healer. Vim has some, well, *business* here. He'll catch up with you later."

Anton glanced sidelong at Vim with a perplexed look. He hadn't parted from him since the Dragon Master had taken him into the crater of the Barren Mountain, and he didn't relish separation. "What business do you have?" he asked suddenly. "Why are you staying here?"

"This is *not* your concern," Vim replied sternly. "Please, do as Aëlfwyn asks, and I'll catch up with you shortly," he continued, trying to reassure Anton and then he heaved a sigh. Turning his attention to Taun's body, Vim effectively dismissed Anton.

"You should go," Tania whispered in Anton's ear. "He only wishes to *say good-bye* to Taun. They were friends. This is difficult for him. It isn't your place here now."

Nodding his head, Anton indicated he understood Tania's counsel. He now realized what the Queen meant about Tania's sensibility and, strangely, he felt as though he *needed* her advice. "You're right, Tania, I'll go."

Smiling to herself, Tania was pleased Anton was accepting her guidance. She knew how vital her influence was to him, and she was increasingly more confident of their growing relationship.

Offering his help, Anton took one end of the stretcher, and he and Aëlfwyn carried Deidra down the stairs from the portal platform. Somehow, he felt as though she needed him. It was an odd impression, one he couldn't explain. The perception came from deep inside his heart and spoke to him in a way that was new and unfamiliar. It was much the same feeling he'd had when he sensed the opening of the portal, but somehow different.

"You're a good man, Anton," whispered Tania. "I think Deidra will benefit from your support. She's alone now; she *needs* someone."

"How did you know what I was thinking?" Anton asked.

"Silly man! You helped her! Anyone can see your thoughts by your actions!" Giggling, Tania launched into the air and circled around Anton's head. "Humans can be *so* silly!"

"Really," Anton said, adding, "You're cute when you giggle." Anton smiled at Tania and then looked at the next stair leading down from the portal platform toward the pyramid; he didn't want to have a sudden misstep. Thankfully, the stairway's steps were long, each nearly two meters from one rise down to the next. This allowed two men plus the stretcher between them to fit conveniently on each step.

Ahead of them, the stone path led directly toward the pyramid, past a series of long rectangular ponds, five to each side. On either side of the ponds stood two monoliths nearly a hundred feet tall. Pyramidically shaped, and capped with a proper pyramid point, they had enormous runes that glowed iridescent green, as did the points at the top. They reminded Anton of the monoliths in the troglodyte's cavern, except there was no fire burning in a hollow space under the point.

The pyramid, which Anton estimated to be more than three-hundred feet tall and equally wide at the base, was still a good distance away. The pyramid rested atop three stair-stepped platforms that elevated the smooth-sided pyramid perhaps another sixty feet. It looked as though an Egyptian pyramid was resting atop a Mayan pyramid as a base.

Noticing Anton's interest in the pyramid, Aëlfwyn described its purpose. "We call that Neo-Kukulcan. It's Trepid's purview, his temple, his *domain*. We'll enter it and take you and Deidra to the chamber of the healer. When both of you are healed, you'll proceed directly to an audience with Trepid. It's there that he will *see* you."

The way Aëlfwyn said *see* made Anton's skin crawl. There was undeniably a hidden meaning behind the word, and Anton tried to determine its significance. All the answers he was seeking were in the temple of the pyramid. Anxious, he continued to hold up his end of the stretcher and marched ever closer with anticipation.

"Can you tell me what Vim is doing? Why wouldn't he discuss his activities with me?" Anton couldn't let the issue go, and his curiosity overcame his discretion.

"He'll give the katrah a *suitable burial*, if you please—nothing more," Aëlfwyn said. "Let it go, this doesn't concern you."

Aëlfwyn showed little concern for Taun's death, in fact, he seemed entirely cold, almost as if he disliked him. This seemed odd even to Anton who had scarcely any concern for such matters. But now, for some reason, it bothered him. He shrugged his shoulders and continued following Aëlfwyn.

The glowing runes on the monoliths illuminated the stone stairs and path as the two men carried the stretcher between them. Anton looked up at the runes and tried to decipher their meaning, but he had little knowledge of the archaic hieroglyphs. The symbols covered all four sides of the monoliths. Each side clearly stated a separate message—eight messages in all—but their significance was lost on him. The one thing that unified them was that at the top of each side there was an image of an eye with lines projecting all around it like a shining star.

As Anton passed the ponds, he looked into the water and saw various subsections. He sensed each one was full of a different type of fish or aquatic life and that there were hundreds in all. He realized it was an aquaculture. A breeze blew the strong, salty smell of seawater into his face, and it burned at his nose ever so slightly. It reminded him of Methonias, which had massive oceans covering nearly two-thirds of it. He'd visited them often during training missions, and most recently just a couple of years ago.

"Are these fish for food?" Anton inquired. "Or perhaps you raise them for some other purpose?"

"We believe that one day we can replenish the oceans with life. We have provided for thousands of different species, and we keep them safe and ready here. For now, that's all you need to know."

Aëlfwyn's responses seemed distant, as if he didn't wish to reveal anything to Anton, and this only disturbed Anton more. He wanted answers, and he wasn't getting any; what little information he did get he had to work at to extract. Everything on Peruvious seemed decidedly wrong. There was secrecy with everyone he met. Even Vim hadn't told him *everything,* but he did answer anything Anton asked, and Tania seemed to be more than helpful.

"They're going to repair the world someday, you'll see!" Tania told Anton. Her help was invaluable to him, and she surprised him more and more every time she spoke.

Overhearing the little faerie, Aëlfwyn huffed to himself, but tried to hide his reaction. For generations beyond even his knowledge, the City of the Humans had preserved all the species of sea life that they could;

nobody had a clue when and if there would ever come a day when the Prophecy of One would come to pass, and Aëlfwyn was skeptical of the success of their purpose. Tania just reminded him of the hopeful goal they all worked toward, yet nobody knew if it was in vain.

After passing the aquaculture ponds, they passed through a heavy portcullis in the side of the subjacent tier of the pyramid. From there, the path led directly down a steep incline into a lower level. The ceiling of the passageway was just inches above Anton's head. A tall man would have to stoop to walk through the stone corridors. Inside, it was dark. The way was lit by an occasional torch hanging from the wall, but the torches were spaced far enough apart that the illumination was barely adequate. Fortunately, they didn't have to travel far.

"The healer's chamber is here," Aëlfwyn said. He pressed his hand lightly on a section of wall and it shifted, revealing a hidden chamber behind it. "Please, you and the katrah will remain here. The healer will attend to both of you shortly."

As Aëlfwyn and Anton placed the stretcher on the floor, Cuðbwyn, Grëyfwyn and Eädwyn entered the healer's chamber behind them. Having heard their hastened footsteps, Anton wasn't surprised when they suddenly appeared. Cuðbwyn held a torch and used it to light several others that hung on the walls around the laboratory. The chamber quickly became well lit, allowing them to see quite well.

The first thing Anton noticed was how extensive the laboratory was. It had many vials, beakers, jars, and test tubes full of strange liquids and powders. Some of the beakers contained liquids that boiled on Bunsen burners, others sat prepared for use. The chemical smell in the chamber tickled his throat and he had to clear his throat to keep from coughing.

The next thing Anton noticed were several cots prepared for medical emergencies and wounded patients. The most interesting thing was the height of all the tables and workbenches—they were half the size that was comfortable for human use; they seemed to be made for children.

"Please, lie down on one of the cots, and the healer will attend to your broken bone in just a moment," Grëyfwyn said. Meanwhile, Cuðbwyn and Eädwyn carefully moved Deidra to a cot next to him.

"We'll leave you now, we have *business* to attend to," Grëyfwyn said, giving Anton a sideways look as the four guards left the chamber. At this point, everyone seemed completely indifferent to him.

"Vim will be here soon," Cuðbwyn called over his shoulder. "He's on his way now." He smiled, attempting to reassure Anton, then added: "It didn't take him long to finish his, well, *task*."

As if on cue, Vim hastily entered the chamber with his staff aglow. He had a dark look on his face, as if he'd just done something he despised. It was the same gaunt look he'd had after killing the four guards earlier in the day, and Anton remembered it well. Intuitively, he knew Vim had vaporized the katrah's carcass.

"Ah, good, you're to be healed, and Deidra will be feeling better soon," Vim said, forcing a smile as if trying to forget something that was bothering him. "I'll remove the protection I placed around your leg as soon as the healer arrives."

Vim sat down on a nearby stool, heaved a sigh and closed his eyes. His exhaustion was conspicuously visible. "I'm pleased we're finally here," he said. "I just wish we didn't have to wait for your *repair*. Your little walkabout caused us another setback. Do you realize our time grows ever shorter?" Vim scolded Anton through the slits of his eyes. Then he opened them and gave Anton a very serious look.

"Furthermore, we can't afford any more deaths! It's undisputable you shouldn't have killed the Dragon Master. By so doing, you broke the great seal. This especially shortens our time—easily tenfold by my estimation—and there will be other complications as well."

Slowly stroking and combing his beard with his hand, Vim looked at Tania. "As for you, I hope your meddling improves his decision making. Lord knows his decisions need improvement." Huffing, he grasped his staff with both hands and again closed his eyes.

Suddenly, a second door opened on the opposite side of the chamber and in walked a tiny man, a primord. He wore a tattered and stained lab coat similar to the ones the clone masters used, and he had an unusual apparatus resting on his head. It was made of a light plastic and had two sets of lenses, which marked where his eyes should be. Evidently, the device gave him some type of unknown visual enhancement.

"Ahhh, my dear Deidra, you've returned—and injured, I might add! And you, Methonian, welcome to my lab!" Bowing like his primord brothers, he suddenly ran over to Anton. "Forgive me, my name is Lorca, and I'm glad to meet you!" Again, he quickly bowed the way Beelif had, and then stood face to face.

"I see Vim has placed his magical protection on your leg. Wizard! Please remove your static photons, they preclude my work!" Smiling at Vim, Lorca crossed his arms, tapped the toes of one foot, and waited.

"Very well!" Vim said. "And thank you for the hello!" Rising, Vim touched the globe of his staff to the golden aura surrounding Anton's leg. In a loud voice, he said the word "disolemiate!" Instantly, the stasis disappeared. "Static photons indeed," he mumbled and then huffed.

Suddenly in pain, Anton gasped as he felt the full effect of the damage he'd incurred. He'd grown comfortable with Vim's protection on his broken leg and the abrupt rush of reality forced him to inhale suddenly, instantly taking his breath away.

"Now, let me take a look at the extent of your damage." Adjusting the lenses on his headset, Lorca leaned over Anton's ankle. "Clean break. All I need is a simple elixir. This is going to hurt, but it will pass swiftly. Prepare yourself, Warrior!"

Moving quickly, Lorca went to his bench, picked out a scalpel, and then selected a vial full of a purple liquid. "I prepared this a short time ago, so it's *fresh*! You're lucky, because it will work extra fast!"

Standing over Anton's ankle, Lorca carefully examined it in more detail. Next, he dipped the scalpel into the elixir, and then with great care, he placed it over the damaged bone. With a quick flick of his wrist, he neatly sliced deeply into Anton's leg and then poured the remains of the elixir over the cut. The wound healed instantly.

Unexpectedly, Anton's ankle began to bubble under the skin and his leg vibrated against his will. Purple fingers of luminescent color crawled around the damaged area and tingled, making him want to scratch. Reaching for his ankle, he tried to relieve the sensation.

"Don't touch it! Whatever you do, don't touch it!" Lorca warned Anton. He grasped Anton's hand and held it away as best he could, although he knew Anton could easily overpower him if he so chose. "It will *all* be over in a minute!" he said. "Just wait!"

Just as suddenly as it began, the vibrations ceased, and the iridescence disappeared. It was over.

"Can I stand?" Anton asked.

"Be my guest. It's as if you'd never damaged yourself. Well, there will be a scar from the incision. I am sorry about that. Serves you right for not taking proper care of yourself!" Lorca smiled and quickly turned his attention to Deidra.

Putting his full weight on his leg, Anton stood up. It held with no pain. All he felt was a slight tingle around the ankle. "Very good," he said. "It'll do."

"Now, for the *katrah!*" Lorca said. He returned to his table of vials and beakers and traded the one he'd used on Anton for another. "I can see from here she has a mild concussion. That's a simple fix." He then ran back to Deidra's side.

Gently stroking Deidra's long human hair, Lorca acted as if he were comforting a child, and Deidra abruptly awoke with a start. "Be still, my dear, I'm going to give you a potion," he said, smiling. Lorca motioned for her to sit up and said, "Please, *drink* this!"

"Rowwerrrr," Deidra purred, and then cautiously took the container from Lorca. Sniffing the concoction, she made a funny face and then took a tiny sip and made an expression of disgust. "Awww-full-rrrr," she growled. Rrrrrroowwwerrrr!" she roared.

"Finish it," Lorca insisted. "There is precisely enough." Lorca motioned for her compliance. "I realize it's an *acquired* taste, but you must finish it *all* for it to work."

"Rowwerrrr," Deidra growled, giving Lorca an angry look before quickly polishing it off in one quick swallow. "Yourrr smelly waterrr taze baaad," she drawled in her unique way.

Within moments, Deidra relaxed, slowly lay down on the cot and fell fast asleep. To Anton's surprise, she purred quietly like a content kitten, and the sound fascinated him. He looked around confused at the others as if to ask: "Why does she do that?" but everyone ignored him.

With great interest, Anton watched the entire event. He was somehow attracted to how Deidra reacted to Lorca. Her cat-like differentiations intrigued him. He found her to be captivating in a way he didn't yet understand.

"You *like* her, don't you?" Tania whispered into Anton's ear, trying to draw a response from him. "It's true! You think she's *special!*"

"I-I don't know. I've never seen anything like her," Anton said, shaking his head. He had a hard time discerning and accepting his own feelings.

"Oh, enough, you two! We need to go," Vim said. "Test your leg again, and let's be gone." Vim huffed and stood up as if he'd seen enough. "Good job, Lorca, as always. We're all forever in your debt."

"Your Warrior is healed, let me assure you!" Lorca said, looking at Vim and then at Anton, grinning from ear to ear. "Go ahead, do as he says. Test your leg. It's even stronger than it was before. It will *never* break *there* again!" Pointing at Anton's ankle, he expressed complete confidence in his work.

"Alert the four 'Wyns! We're ready!" Vim insisted that Lorca allow them to leave. The time had finally arrived for their visit with Trepid.

"I must attend to Deidra," Lorca said. "She'll follow after you when she awakens. I believe Eädwyn will be here shortly."

"Harrumph," Vim huffed. "Very well, but more time lost," he grumbled loudly. "Drôgän was right—time *does* grow short and shorter yet, I might add."

Not a second passed and Eädwyn entered the chamber. "Follow me," he said. "Trepid awaits you." Motioning for them to follow, he looked at Anton and then nodded at Vim. "It's time."

As they left the chamber, Lorca called after them: "Oh, Vim, don't forget the berrybrew! It will aid you!"

Perplexed, Vim looked back at Lorca. "How did you? Oh, never mind, thank you. I nearly forgot." Vim reached into his robe, produced the two bottles of the rare liquor Beelif had given him and handed one to Anton. "Drink!"

Unsealing the bottle, Anton put it to his lips and finished it quickly. The familiar flavor caressed his tongue, and it warmed him from inside as it traveled down his throat. He smacked his lips and wiped away the final drops from his lips with the back of his sleeve. Suddenly, he couldn't restrain the inevitable smile, and he grinned from ear to ear as the berrybrew performed its peculiar job.

Vim followed Anton and polished off the bottle he'd reserved for himself. Smacking his lips, his smile also stretched across his face undeniably proclaiming his consumption of the beverage, and then he wiped his lips with his sleeve.

Tania giggled at their expressions. "You look handsome when you smile, Anton. It does you well!" Flying around in circles, she giggled her tiny laugh and then returned to Anton's shoulder. "Your heart *is* pure!"

"Enough! Let us go!" Vim insisted, and the company quickly left the chamber.

"Follow me," Eädwyn said. "We've adjusted the labyrinth to allow you quick access to Trepid's chamber." Eädwyn motioned for them to follow, and the three men walked down the corridor in anticipation.

The Truth Behind the Alias

EÄDWYN LEAD THE WAY THROUGH an extensive labyrinth of corridors down into the depths below the pyramid. The low ceiling and narrow passageways gave everyone a sense of claustrophobia.

"We're almost there," Eädwyn suddenly announced. He stopped abruptly and looked back to see everyone's reaction, then continued.

Anton smiled incessantly and was just beginning to hear everyone's thoughts. The berrybrew worked wonders on his mind and gave him a pleasant yet very slight feeling of euphoria.

Sitting on Anton's shoulder, Tania shifted her position and huffed time and again as she attempted to wait patiently. She'd never met Trepid directly; she didn't need to. She seemed increasingly excited and fidgeted around more and more as they traveled deeper into the lower levels. Anton knew intuitively by her restlessness she'd never been there before.

Taking up the rear, Vim too shared the thoughts of those around him. He was more familiar with the berrybrew's effects and didn't give its mild intoxicating sensation much notice. On the other hand, he seemed quite impatient. He'd been waiting for this opportunity since leaving the castle, and the moment was nearly at hand. However, it was more than that. It had been fifty years since he'd visited the City of the Humans, and even then, he hadn't visited Trepid. He didn't know what to expect after being told he may not recognize him.

As they rounded another corner, it unexpectedly came to a dead end. "This is it," Eädwyn announced. Carefully placing his hand in the precise spot, he pushed against a wall near the end of the passageway and it slowly shifted aside. "All three of you are invited. I will remain behind. Go ahead, enter!" Pointing inside an enormous chamber, Eädwyn encouraged his guests to proceed.

"Finally, we made it," was all Vim said. He heaved a sigh as if a mighty weight was lifted from his heart and then entered the chamber, swiftly leading the other two and burning with curiosity.

Anton entered the chamber with mixed feelings of anticipation, curiosity, and trepidation. Nothing inside was as he'd envisioned it. The chamber was huge, easily more than two-hundred feet in all directions. A giant white globe, seemingly suspended in midair, lit the chamber. It floated freely, with no apparent form of support. The globe rotated slowly on its axis and looked like a moon or a distant star observed from a spacecraft. A layer of clouds covered the entire globe, masking the features of its surface. It took up a large portion of the enormous chamber, and Anton estimated it to be at least forty feet in diameter.

Standing motionless, Vim bowed his head as if preparing for prayer. Holding the staff in both hands, he closed his eyes and waited silently. "We are here, but where is Trepid?" he mumbled to himself.

Whispering in Anton's ear, Tania offered him her special advice. "You must speak when you're ready. But be very gracious—*you're* the one invited here!"

"Thanks, Tania," Anton whispered back. Taking one last grand look at the globe, he then addressed the atmosphere. "Hello! I'm Anton …"

You are Anton Seven. Welcome, my son, a deep full voice boomed. It seemed to be emanating from the sphere, but it wasn't auditory.

Anton heard the words clearly, as if they had been spoken aloud, but they were only in his head. Suddenly, the cloud layer cleared from the globe, and Anton realized it looked like a planet, with vast oceans and continents marking its surface. It continued rotating on its axis at approximately one revolution per minute, thus allowing the onlooker a quick yet complete view of the entire circumference.

You were told that my name is Trepid Tantamount. That is an alias so that I may remain concealed from those that oppose life. To you, due to your intellectual limitations, I am the 'Eye of One, or the All-Seeing Eye of God' but to those of the past and again those of the future, and as I have said unto Moses, I AM THAT I AM. I am the Lord God. In these latter days, as we approach the possible end of humanity and existence itself, all will know me as the ONE GOD. I AM ONE. When you are asked who sends you to either lead them or oppose them, say unto them: ONE has sent me!

The thought communication continued inside Anton's head. It was pure and crisp, as if the voice spoke directly into his ears, and he had no trouble hearing it. Anton suddenly realized the rotating blue sphere was a representation of the Earth. Gradually, it transformed again. It stopped rotating and became a single enormous human-like eye. Then the eyelid slowly opened to reveal the pupil beneath, and the eye looked directly and piercingly at Anton. It felt to him as if he had no secrets, that all of his thoughts were transparent to the eye.

Instantaneously, a searchlight-like beam of light shot from the *Eye of One's* pupil, striking Anton. He felt as if his legs could no longer support him, and he started to fall backward, but he didn't—the light held him suspended. His flesh felt as though someone had filleted it from his body, but there was no pain and no damage. It was more like the *Eye of One* could see through his flesh, but he wasn't sure. He felt the beam of light shine through him, as if he were somehow transparent to the *Eye of One.*

All of your questions will be answered, Anton heard inside his head. You need not ask them, I KNOW them, for I am *all* knowledge. This is the time of many transformations. All of you who stand before me will experience a personal and profound change. This is necessary so that the future may continue.

Anton's thoughts raced as questions filled his mind like a computer accessing its stored memory. He wondered what changes the *Eye of One* portended.

The katrah must be brought before me now! She must be present for this benefaction to continue. My words are to be shared.

As if summoned, Deidra immediately appeared and entered the chamber on her knees. She clasped her human-like hands tightly together, and her eyes were closed in complete terror. Stopping just behind Anton, she froze, peering around from behind him, attempting to use him as a human shield. Distress marked her face, as if she expected punishment—or worse.

Anton, I say unto you, I know your questions. You want to know who I am, you want to know where you are, you want to know why you are here. But most of all, you want to know what your purpose is here and why you are the one chosen. I will answer this and much more. *Prepare* yourself. You may find the answers disconcerting.

Since the time of Moses, I have existed here, inside this dimension, an aspect of what is now called Peruvious. This dimension exists in tandem with the world from which you came. It is the part of the world where human life began, the world I created eons ago. It is part of the *Earth.*

"Earth. Peruvious *is* the Earth, just as Drôgän had inferred when he recited the *Prophecy of One.*" Anton was surprised, but now everything was beginning to make sense. Still, he thought, "How is this possible? My Masters taught me the Earth no longer exists!"

I *see* confusion in you," the voice continued, answering Anton's unspoken questions. "Yes, the Earth *does* exist. It was destroyed by a previous event in history, but it did not perish from existence—it cannot. Peruvious is the post-apocalyptic name given to the Earth. It refers to the remains of the Earth. Your Masters taught you much about the Earth's past, but little of it has relevance or meaning to you, therefore I set before you a task: You will seek out the KACATU and use its inestimable knowledge to enhance your own. There you will receive all the noesis necessary to complete your mission. Our meeting today is insufficient for this transference; though I control time in this circumstance, the Prophecy precludes such interference. All events must continue without interruption. This is the time of transformations.

"Cockatoo?" Anton didn't understand. "An exotic bird?" he wondered.

Suddenly, an image of a destroyed city entered Anton's mind, as if the memory were his own. In its center, a single large structure still existed. It had a half-spherical field of energy surrounding it, protecting it, as if it preserved the structure for the future. He didn't know where it was, but he suddenly recalled Vim's story about Celestra. An unexpected feeling of warmth filled him, as if he'd made the correct correlation.

Your enhanced biology serves you well, but it too is insufficient. Lothendus improved and enhanced many of your capabilities, but he couldn't complete the effort; this I will complete. It is beyond any single human's capacity to fulfill all that I ask of them, therefore, I will enhance your biology so that you can withstand more than is humanly possible, and I will augment your tools to improve their capabilities. Later, when you have found the KACATU, received your final transformation, and assembled all the tools you will need, then and only then can you attempt to defeat Vile.

The voice continued to answer Anton's thoughts, and with each word, he felt his misgivings fall away like the peeling of a banana, leaving only the resulting fruit of knowledge behind.

Lothendus? Don't you mean my Masters? Anton asked quizzically inside of his mind."

Lothendus IS your Master! This you MUST realize, you met him prior to your arrival here; you know him as The Ruler of the Council. By using the knowledge and technologies of THIS world, he created all that is YOUR world, the world you know as Methonias. He created all that you are and he did so under MY directive. However, do not be deceived, he too has experienced a transformation and is no longer my tool. Corruption has taken his turn as is required by the Law of Balance.

The revelations sparked a series of insights in Anton and he castigated himself for missing the many connections he'd witnessed. Why hadn't he recognized these associations? Why hadn't his advanced Methonian intellect served him here? He'd felt something, a familiarity, or a correlation of the events he'd experienced over the past few days and he should have deduced this. Yet again, he'd failed.

Luthian had said, "*Where do you think they came from? Do you know? Did they tell you about themselves at that Temple of yours?*" In addition, Boris Three had posed issues about the Masters and their purposes. He had also posed many questions that the people of the various human colonies had tasked, and about their many misgivings. Now it all made sense. Anton finally had the answers he'd waited for, the answers to the questions he'd set aside to be answered later.

Still your thoughts and listen to mine. From this point forward, while you stand before me, only my thoughts shall be your thoughts. The mighty *Eye of One* continued to stare unblinking. *His* thoughts dominated Anton's and washed his feelings of failure away as if he stood under a mighty waterfall of purification.

I have told you who I AM, now I will tell you who YOU are. The *Eye of One* narrowed His view, as if straining to see beyond Anton's flesh and deeper into his spirit. He felt his body melt away as if it no longer existed. He felt as though he floated in midair, as if the law of gravity no longer bound him to the Earth.

This Law of Balance exists due to the battle between The Intelligence of Non-Existence and ME. It is a perpetual struggle of two equal and opposite forces. In ages past, beyond the existence of time, I created the heavens, the universe, and the Earth. Lastly, I created humanity for a single purpose: to fight the battle that determines the fate of the universe and all that I created. This is in accordance with the Law of Balance. Our agreement is to see whether humanity will choose to accept HIM or ME, existence or non-existence. Humans have the right to cast out this evil, and send Him back to His own universe, or to cast it into ruin and choose oblivion, to give up the struggle and the suffering of life. However, as long as one human being remains alive here, on the Earth, on this Peruvious, the final decision remains unfulfilled until my messenger proclaims his choice at the end of the age of man's first reign upon the earth.

Humans have the gift of free choice; they may choose in life whatever they so desire. If they choose evil, they become evil, they serve evil, and therefore, accept and produce evil and in turn accept the end of everything. If they choose the side of good, they serve good, they are good, they accept eternal life, and they serve ME. To each side, good and evil, the armies grow.

Furthermore, only those of human birth, and born ON the Earth, fall within the confines of the Law of Balance and thus are subject to the confines of this struggle. You stand outside of this agreement by the virtue you weren't born, therefore you are free of the confines of the birthright that a human mother and father give you. Most importantly, you didn't come to life HERE on the Earth, yet you are a part of humanity. As a result, you fall outside of the confinement of the Law of Balance. It doesn't bind you to the agreement, but you retain the right of human choice; you are free to make your own decisions, and you can act upon those choices. Since you are human, and present upon the Earth, you qualify to decide the outcome of humanity and existence unbounded by the Law of Balance. There is more to this, but that will wait until the end of the first age of man when you make the *choice*.

Unwittingly, the Intelligence of Non-Existence agreed to the terms of the Law of Balance. He didn't conceive the possibility that humans could evolve to manufacture themselves on another world thus escaping the confines of the Law of Balance; this moment I have waited for throughout eternity. You are the human not born of man and woman, the human not born on the Earth, the manu-factured man with a human soul that has the right to choose. You are the one spoken of in MY PROPHECY. Your brothers, those other Warriors that Vim summoned here before you, are impotent of value for MY purpose. You are different, you have a conscience, emotions, and are capable of understanding right from wrong, good from evil. You are the chosen one, the savior of humanity, or the destroyer. It is by your choice—not by theirs. They were altered only to serve another purpose and are of no use to ME.

Be not concerned that you are somehow different than your brethren, or are considered imperfect because of your emotions; these emotions are the identifier of a soul with the freedom of choice. Discount the ignorance of those who refute this truth.

For a moment, the narration in Anton's mind ceased. His thoughts remained interrupted and suspended, yet he was aware of the passage of time. He could see the enormous *Eye of One* staring at him and continued to feel ethereal, but by increments, the sensation slowly changed. He watched the *Eye of One* transform again into a repre-sentation of the Earth. Gradually, he felt himself drawn toward this exemplification; it seemed to be absorbing him. Suddenly, he felt as though he stood above the Earth and watched time regress at high speed below him. He could see everything.

Observe, you stand before the Earth of eons past! As the *Eye of One* spoke, it again transformed to the representation of the Earth at an earlier age. Its continents were of two solid masses rather than those that were so familiar; they were the supercontinents Gondwana in the southern hemisphere and Pangaea in the northern hemisphere.

Mesmerized and completely enthralled, Anton watched Gondwana and Pangaea split apart forming into other continents that gradually moved around the Earth; slowly the landmasses broke into smaller pieces creating Laurasia and Gondwanaland, and gradually they became the more familiar ones of a more recent Earth.

He observed life begin and then evolve as the continents moved; ancient creatures and dinosaurs lived and died violently and eventually they changed and evolved into other beasts. He witnessed the process of phylogenesis. The entire scene played out in a matter of moments, yet the information remained transfixed in detail in Anton's mind.

Long before man was as you know man to be, the Earth contained endless species of creatures that you have named dinosaurs and many other names; this you are well aware of. These creatures were the building blocks of so-called evolution. For an eternity, by human perspective, they gradually changed in form. The purpose of the faeries was to carefully select and alter these creatures and guide the changes. Their magic touched their building blocks, their DNA, turned on or off various genetic aspects, and generated mutations, thus altering them from one species to the next. As time passed, these creatures incrementally progressed from one form to another and then to yet another. You comprehend this process as evolution. Let all know that the labors of the faeries guided these steps, this evolution, and that they were the ones that ultimately engineered the human form. Once the human body reflected MY image and likeness, the process of melding a human soul with the human body was possible. Prior to this, all of life's energy came from the pool of life. The human soul is a very different thing: it came from ME.

Anton watched the process of evolution occur in front of him. He watched the little faeries perform their service altering DNA, and he saw the changes occur in nature that subtly converted one species to the next. The faeries seemed to know where to be and when to be there to perform their obligation. Some altered plant life, others the animals and yet others the insects; each effort moved the process ever closer to the desired result.

Ultimately, these creatures evolved into the various hominids, the human-like ancestors of man. Finally, Anton watched as Australopithecus afarensis climbed out of the primordial jungle trees and took his first bipedal steps. This entire process he'd learned about as a child on Methonias, but now he observed it firsthand in its entirety in a matter of moments, as if he too were a part of it.

Everything that Anton observed soaked into his memory, and his Earth cognition grew exponentially as the information flooded his mind. He became replete with a base portion of the knowledge he needed to fulfill his quest. He felt an insatiable need to obtain this information, but the reason for it still eluded him; he simply understood intuitively that it had an invaluable purpose.

Evolution is the correct method of genetic alteration. Other forms devised by human imagination are an abomination if used selfishly as manufactured slaves! This is an important fact you must consider in the future. I now return you to your physical self. These lessons, and soon many more, are necessary for your success. Now that you've received this gift, I have another small yet crucial transformation to perform—the coupling of your devices.

As if nothing had happened, Anton felt his spirit reunite with his body and again he stood on solid ground. As if compelled, he reached into his tunic and retrieved from its pocket his EHD. Reaching into it, he withdrew the katana he'd placed there when he was aboard the

Pleceivious before leaving the Methonian system. Returning the EHD to his tunic pocket, he quickly snatched the Blue Flame Sword from its scabbard and then removed his ring from his finger. Without a second thought, he offered them to the *Eye of One.*

Having once again changed from an image of the Earth to that of an eye, the *Eye of One* cast *His* gaze upon Anton's offering. Instantly, a beam of dazzling white light energy shown like a searchlight from the *Eye of One's* pupil and struck the three items in Anton's hand. They instantaneously floated into the air and remained static and suspended there.

These items are insufficient in their present separate state; they require improvement, they require melding, like the human soul to the human body.

As if commanded, Anton's Blue Flame Sword burst forth its blade of fire, and then the katana aligned itself parallel to it, matching the length of blade. The two items seemed to become translucent and then the blue flame absorbed the katana. Blue fire took on the substance of metal, and the metal took on blue fire. It was as if the katana's blade burned. The blue flame hilt lengthened but retained its original look, and the supergrip tsuka now marked its surface, blending into a new combined design. Finally, Anton's crystal ring erupted with golden fire and then grew in diameter. It slid over the tip of the newly formed sword and slowly moved downward toward the hilt. Blue flame turned to golden fire as the blade passed through the ring. When the ring reached the hilt, it again increased in diameter, stretched around it, and then completed its pass over the entire sword. As it cleared the end of the hilt, it returned to its proper size and slid over Anton's right ring finger—it had changed hands. With the golden flame still burning, the combined sword then placed itself in Anton's hand.

Behold! The Sword of Eternity! You will find this amalgamation to your liking. It will serve you well!

Consciously, Anton extinguished the fiery blade, and it disappeared leaving only the hilt just as it had always done. Again, he summoned forth the golden fire, and the double-edged burning steel sprang into the air with a whir of energy. The hilt lengthened simultaneously allowing him to hold it with both hands, and the supergrip tsuka allowed him to grip it firmly. He couldn't lose possession of it without conscious effort. The sword felt just as light as its Blue Flame counterpart prior to the melding, yet it seemed to carry the weight and inertia of the katana. Anton was pleased with the improvement; it had the best properties of both items.

This is my gift to you in accordance with the Law of Balance. Lastly, your heart was cleansed by the Faerie Queen and all of your prior sins forgiven. However, your mind and body require cleansing as well so that you will be free from your youthful proclivities. Therefore, I command you to step into the pool of liquid light you see below ME and absorb its qualities and its purity. Drink from it, and your body will be transformed.

Below the *Eye of One* Anton saw a pool of radiance appear; it looked as if it was pure light, yet it was as fluid as water. Compelled by the *Eye of One's* command, he stepped forward and smoothly slid into the pool. Immersed over his head, he swam in the purifying liquid. It was so intensely bright he couldn't see anything, yet it didn't harm his eyes. Taking an enormous draft, he drank from it as instructed. It felt as though life energy poured into his body, as if his body and spirit had absorbed eternal youth. Anton could only take a few swallows before it seemed impossible or unnecessary to consume more.

Time seemed as though it had stopped. Anton felt as though he floated in space, weightless and supercharged with energy. All of his hunger disappeared; it was as if he'd never felt hungry, and might never again. After bathing in the pool of liquid light for an unknown length of time, he finally returned to the surface and popped his head into the air and braced himself on the edge of the pool preparing to climb out.

Suddenly, unexpectedly, Anton's bracers started to glow; yellow fire emanated from them and enveloped them. Expanding, they quickly covered the entire length of his arms and they didn't stop there. Soon the bracers covered his entire body and the fire changed from gold to argent. Somehow, they became a new epidermis, a protective exoskeleton, and then melded into his skin. He touched himself; his skin felt entirely unchanged. It remained as supple as it had always been, yet somehow it felt invulnerable and impervious to damage.

Climbing from the pool, Anton returned to his comrades. It was evident an enormous change had come over him; his entire body glowed as if he too were an entity like Amilius. Light seemed to explode from every nerve and cast its radiance throughout the chamber. His skin was as white as a sheet and his eyes and fingertips fired beams of light like lasers. Most strikingly, his irises had turned golden, as gold and metallic in appearance as the element in its purest form. His hair too had transformed: it was as golden as pure metallic gold, and as silky as cashmere. It hung straight and long and reached the middle of his back. Lastly, the brandings on his arms he'd received at graduation were gone; his skin was smooth and featureless.

Tania returned to Anton's shoulder and smiled from ear to ear. "Our hair is identical! We are one. We belong together!"

Deidra covered her face; Anton's radiance hurt her eyes, and she had an expression of both fear and awe as she gazed upon him.

Vim bowed his head as if in respect. "Our deliverer is here, Pervious shall be redeemed!"

The *Eye of One* then turned *His* attention to Tania. The beam of light narrowed and its intensity softened. The time has come for you to fulfill your intended purpose; this is the culmination of your existence. When the time is right, when love it true, you'll perform your final destined calling. In the end, your greatest purpose will ensure the golden age of man.

Tania curtsied toward the *Eye of One*. Smiling, she then flew in circles around Anton's head as if she too had received a gift. "I am chosen! It will be me to fulfill the greatest service!"

Once more, the *Eye of One* adjusted *His* attention toward Deidra, held it there for a moment, and then returned *His* attention to Anton. *He* then addressed him about the other.

Deidra is of the same temperament as you; she has a true human soul, has a conscience, and is emotional. She exists without a true human body, yet has the spirit of a human. This is unique among katrahs, and it is to be admired and rewarded; it is a consequence of MY interference and has purpose. In accordance with the Law of Balance, she must prove herself worthy to retain this spirit and earn her entrance into the kingdom of heaven. You're to protect her and provide this opportunity; it is necessary. I can tell you no more.

Finally, the *Eye of One* directed *His* attention to Vim. Wizard, your service to ME is unprecedented. The time has come for you to rest. You must perform one final onus, and then you'll live forever in MY kingdom. You'll know what to do when the moment presents itself.

Bowing his head, Vim heaved a sigh. So soon, my lord? I'm always here to serve you, just tell me what you desire. I'm not ready to leave, but I cannot refuse you.

In your heart, you know the answer. You have now received this communication thrice. When the time arrives, you will know it, and then you will return to ME; no others may claim you, you have proven your worth to the side of good.

The *Eye of One* then closed and reformed into the grey cloud-covered sphere the travelers had first seen when they entered the chamber, and everyone slowly stood and looked around at each other. Without a doubt, they all felt inside their hearts that they knew what to do— everyone but Deidra.

Shivering with fear, Deidra looked at Anton. As she slowly stood, she put her arms around him, and then gave him a hug. "Rowwerrrr, you arrrr the *chosen* one-rrrr." Struggling to speak, she looked up into Anton's still radiant eyes, and she shivered fearfully. She then placed her cheek against his chest just as the Faerie Queen had done, and hugged him tighter. "Thank you forrrr helping me-rrrrrrr," she purred.

"This is not the time Deidra, we must go," Vim said aloud. "Our time grows ever shorter, and the enemy awaits us. War rages at the castle. Taun's death evidences that the great shield is broken, as does the presence of the fracknoid that killed him; you too bore witness to the invasion. There's obviously more you need to share with us, and soon!"

Anton suddenly looked at Vim. His radiance abruptly dissipated and he looked again like himself, save the color differences of his hair, eyes, and skin; his transformations were permanent. "We need to rest before we can begin our campaign. We need sustenance and a plan. Do we have time?"

"We do not, but you are correct. Our hesitation will cost many lives if, in fact, the castle stands besieged, but I agree with you. Let us receive aid from the 'Wyns and make plans before we begin our fight." Vim looked at Anton and motioned for all of them to exit the chamber. "They await us now."

Quickly leading the way, Anton assumed the leadership role; he felt as though he were in charge. Something fundamental yet substantial had changed in him, and he didn't feel like the confused and uninformed youth that he had been just hours before; he knew what to do and he was ready to lead. His confidence was indomitable, and everyone could see it.

Departing the chamber, the four 'Wyns awaited the four companions. "We'll take you to the city; there you will find friendship and rest." Aëlfwyn bowed toward Anton as he invited his guests. "It's a bit of a journey through the labyrinth, but it won't take too long if I lead. Follow me."

A look of awe marked the faces of the four 'Wyns as they beheld Anton's transformations; they seemed to have a different attitude toward him. He noticed the change in their demeanor, and he felt somehow relieved. Finally, he'd received the respect he'd desired, yet had never attained, even if only in a small way.

Vim lit the globe on his staff and provided all the light they needed to see. He couldn't wait to eat and to rest. It was too long since he'd had an opportunity; nearly half a day had elapsed since his last meal.

As much as an hour passed as the company traversed the narrow stone passageways through the tri-dimensional labyrinth, but soon they arrived on the far side of the pyramid. They stepped out on a wide ledge that overlooked a deep valley. Several circular structures surrounded by fog stood seemingly suspended in midair, but it was obvious they had a central support like the trunk of a tree that ran down to the valley floor far below. It was early morning, and the sun was just beginning to rise behind the pyramid in the east, a fitting moment to exit Trepid's domain.

Taking in a deep breath of the cool morning air, Anton put his hands on his hips and looked around inspecting the area thoroughly. Everything appeared well. His inner senses seemed somehow heightened, even more than his genetically engineered improvements provided him, and he could *feel* the area was secure, not just see it. "All is well," he announced with a commanding confidence, and all eyes fell upon him.

Of Man and Beast

"**T**HIS WAY, THE SUSPENSION BRIDGE is over here!" Aëlfwyn pointed to the southwest edge of the canyon and set off in that direction. "It's just over here," he repeated and pointed at the supporting posts. He wanted to make sure everyone could see them, because they were just barely visible in the fog.

"Breakfast will be ready when we arrive. The women have prepared a feast!" Grëyfwyn spoke directly to Anton; everyone knew that he was in command. "We have special quarters prepared for you as well. I'm sure you'll find them acceptable."

"Ahem, very good." Vim too felt the change of command; he wasn't sure he was ready to relinquish it, but knew he must. He was unprepared to adjust to Anton's transformation, yet he accepted it, knowing he must. However, there was something more significant,

more fundamental that disturbed him. The words of Drôgän, Amilius, Agonia, and finally Trepid left him disgruntled about his own
future. The replete inferences of his life ending soon left him feeling
unsettled. He wasn't ready to relinquish his life's work; death was too
permanent, it didn't allow him to see the outcome of everything he'd
ever worked for. He'd spent over a thousand years working toward this
goal, the salvation of mankind, and it was about to bear the fruit of his
efforts. But just as he was to achieve the reward of all he had done, he
was also about to relinquish his right to participate in that outcome.
He intended to make the most of the time he had left, regardless of
the inevitable.

Cuðbwyn was the first to walk across the suspension bridge as if
to declare it safe for passage. As he reached the far side, he waved for
the others to follow. "All is well, and the food awaits us!"

It was true: Anton could smell smoke coming from wood fires, and
the aroma of food cooking in the air caused his stomach to suddenly
growl in response. His young physique required sustenance, and it
didn't take long for him to race after Cuðbwyn across the bridge.

Flying alongside Anton, Tania giggled her tiny laugh and happily
followed him, quite delighted. "They eat well here, they have *exceptional* food! You'll see!" she snickered to him.

Deidra ran across the bridge like the wind; she was at home, her
home, the only home she ever knew. After she crossed the bridge, she
quickly disappeared, leaving the others behind. Within a heartbeat,
she was gone, and nobody knew where she went or even paid much
attention to her disappearance.

Anton was preoccupied with studying the structure they headed
toward. He could see there was a deck that surrounded a gigantic
inner trunk made of steel; it had the look of a lofty gazebo floating on
a cloud. There was a door and several windows positioned at intervals
around it, and as he looked inside the nearest window, he saw a large
room with a spiral staircase in its center that went both up and down.
The room contained all the domestic tools one might expect to see:

beds, chairs, a table and a wood stove. The circular deck had a handrail for safety wrapped all the way around except where the suspension bridges hung. There were four bridges in all, positioned at ninety-degree intervals to each other, and each bridge led to other similar tree-like dwellings in a daisy chain design. Each of the trunks had levels of circular dwellings both above and below of varying sizes. It wasn't clear how far up or down these structures went; the fog prevented him from seeing any further than one additional level in either direction.

Eädwyn pointed to a second circular building that was much larger than the first. It sat behind the first and a suspension bridge connected the two together. "Over there is the community commons. That's where we will eat. Follow me!" Waving for everyone to follow, he quickly traversed the bridge and entered the door.

Everyone followed and quickly entered the commons. Deidra was already there and was busy helping the other women; she assisted them at setting the tables and serving the meal. Over her shoulder, she smiled charmingly at Anton in a feline way as he entered the room.

Deidra's cat-like eyes seemed somehow alluring to Anton; she had a strikingly beautiful human figure, a woman's figure, with all of its sensual attributes, and if he ignored her feline differences, he found her captivating. Her feminine qualities were enticing, and he recalled Nelda and the young women of Tooloo as he gazed upon her.

Watching as the preparatory work unfolded in front of him, Anton also noticed that the women here were all entirely human; Deidra was clearly the last katrah. He wasn't sure, but suspected there were more half-humans somewhere. Why else had the soldiers at the castle called him a pig-human, and a hogtrah?

Looking out a nearby window, Anton was suddenly surprised to see clearly in all directions. Somehow, the windows removed the fog layer from view, allowing anyone to gaze freely into the distance, and this astounded him. Obviously, the glass panes were made of some high-tech material that he had never seen, and he wondered how a seemingly primitive village might have such technology available.

"Sit, Anton, you're our most *important* guest!" Grëyfwyn pulled a chair away from a table and motioned for him to comply. "Everything is ready, eat!" He smiled widely as if to say, "you are most welcome" and "you'll be impressed."

"Everyone, find a seat! The meal awaits us!" Cuðbwyn announced, and then sat down himself looking every bit as hungry as Anton felt.

Sitting on Anton's shoulder, Tania didn't seem interested in food and ignored it completely. "Everyone likes the food here. It's the best!" she whispered in his ear, and then looked around to see if anyone noticed her comment. "At least that's what everyone says," she continued.

Vim looked exhausted, but he was more than eager to eat. Selecting a little of each item, he hungrily ate some fruit, nuts, fried eggs, fried cured meat, cheese, and bread.

Anton also took a healthy portion of each item offered; he hadn't had a decent meal since leaving the primord village, and he appreciated the opportunity to assuage his hunger with the many delicacies offered him. As he ate, he noticed that everyone watched him closely. It was as if they expected him to do something, but he didn't know what.

"Perhaps you have something to say about your visit with Trepid? You obviously had a *most* unique experience there, Anton!" Grëyfwyn seemed the most curious and implored his response. He desired to know more details of what had transpired during his visit and probed him for answers for everyone to hear.

Still chewing, Anton stood. "I'm not sure what to relate; I saw the Earth in its formative years, learned of the involvement of the faeries with evolution, and took a swim in a pool of radiance. Is this what everyone wishes to know?" Looking around at all the faces, it was apparent that it wasn't. The women all seemed dumbfounded and the four 'Wyns seemed less than satisfied.

"Perhaps you'll tell us about the change of your hair, eyes, and skin? This is a most interesting tale indeed!" Eädwyn coaxed Anton further.

"Nobody has ever received a gift of such a magnitude throughout all of human history! The tale requires telling!"

Smiling, Anton looked sheepishly around the room; he then understood what everyone was needing to hear. "I swam in a pool of liquid light, and I drank of it as I did so. When I exited the pool, my bracers stretched over my body; they became fused to my skin. I have little else to reveal." Sitting down he continued to eat.

Silence filled the room. Somehow, Anton's explanation seemed inadequate, yet everyone remained speechless; several mouths hung slightly open, and people looked around at each other in confusion. Obviously, he wasn't the best rhetorician, and it showed. Dissatisfied, everyone accepted what little explanation he offered and continued with their meal; mumbles and quiet conversation filled the air, and one lady shook her head and laughed quietly. It felt awkward, and an uncomfortable tension was obvious.

"It would seem our friends are exhausted, perhaps their need for rest was greater than we'd anticipated; we shall hope for a proper account of your visit with Trepid after you've revitalized ." Grëyfwyn offered his graciousness; it helped to alleviate the expectations of Anton's inadequate explanation.

After everyone had their fill, Cuðbwyn stood and tapped his fork against an empty glass to draw everyone's attention to himself. "I want to extend a warm welcome to our savior, Anton, to our friend Vim, and to this unprecedented visit from Tania, a faerie; it's been many years since one of your sisters has visited here; this is the first visit in my lifetime. Now that all of you have eaten, we've prepared a nice suite for each of you to rest in. Afterwards, when you are fully refreshed, we'll talk and make plans. Anyone needing a bath or any other service, just let me know and your needs will be fulfilled. Let this be a time of relaxation and preparation; it is clear that a war is to be fought and is only a few hours away."

Standing, Vim too addressed the gathering. "Thank you, we'll all rest shortly." Vim looked at Anton and Tania. "There will be time for other activities afterwards." He looked at them as if making sure they complied. "Don't spend your time foolishly. Get some rest, we need you at your best!"

Flying into the air, Tania circled once around Anton's head, and over to Vim, stood in midair in front of him, and offered her agreement. "You're right, wizard, all of you need rest! I can see it!" Looking at Anton, she flew back to him and then spoke to him. "I'll be there while you rest, I won't leave you!"

"What about Deidra, is she going to rest?" Anton asked. He looked across the room where she sat. "After your injury it seems, well, prudent."

"Rowwerrrr, I'm home-rrrr, I will rrrest in my rrrooom; don't con-cerrrrn yourrr-self." Deidra looked sideways at Anton in a cat-like way and wondered why he had such a peculiar interest in her. She smiled timidly and began to gather the dirty dishes, as did the other women.

"You like her! I can *see* that you do!" Tania giggled and again circled around Anton. "She lives here silly boy! You needn't worry about *her*!"

Cocking one eye at Anton, Vim then rolled them and shook his head. "You should be concerned about yourself and the future of humanity; prepare for battle, it awaits all of us. Is that not what a Methonian lives for?" Shaking his head again, he carefully stood. "Where's this room you spoke of; I would greatly enjoy a soft bed; I have a great deal of sleep to catch up on, please excuse me."

Quickly, Aëlfwyn stood and pointed to the spiral staircase. "The rooms await you below, follow me." He abruptly left the commons and led the way.

"The rooms are just one level down," Cuðbwyn also responded and offered to show Anton. "The women have prepared a small but separate suite for each of you."

On the platform below the commons, and encircling the central spiral stairs was a series of tiny rooms; Vim quickly opened a door and found a small space with a bed and a tiny table and a small stool. Resting his staff against the wall, he removed his robe, sprawled on the bed, and immediately fell asleep; his snoring was noticeable almost instantly.

Anton too lay down on his private bed; he needed sleep, real sleep, not meditation, but he continued to stare at the ceiling of the tiny chamber. Too many thoughts preoccupied his mind and he couldn't simply drift off. His entire body buzzed with anticipation and various thoughts that preoccupied him. He still felt energized from the pool of radiance, even though more than a day had gone by since he'd last slept.

Tania stood on the small table next to the bed and smiled at him. "Go ahead, sleep! I'll be here with you, but if you don't mind, I'd like to have a quick look around first. I'll return before you notice I've left, never fear!" She quickly flew off and disappeared.

"Umm, sure, that's fine with me," Anton called after her. Sitting up, he then decided that maybe it *was* a good opportunity to meditate; he had many things to consider and needed this opportunity to cleanse his thoughts of all his recent experiences. Without any difficulty, he quickly reached into himself and found that new place inside himself; as he delved deeper inward, he suddenly felt as though he had escaped the confines of his body, just as he'd done aboard the Pleceivious and again outside the Castle of Amilius a couple of nights before. It seemed much easier to find that special place now that he had done it several times, and he was thankful for that.

Stepping outside of his room, Tania was there looking at the spiral staircase as if expecting something to occur. Suddenly she turned around and smiled at Anton.

"I see you! You're a clever man! Very few people know how to travel this way, follow me!" Begging him to follow, Tania flew around in a circle and then off over the edge of the outer platform. Waving her hand, she beckoned him further. "You can fly, just like me! You will see, come!"

Without giving it a thought, Anton followed her. It was true, he didn't need to walk, he only needed to concentrate and he could travel alongside her. In his ethereal form, he could quickly go places that would require a great deal of effort and time otherwise; this method of travel helped him explore swiftly and invisibly, and Tania knew where to guide him, yet it left his body vulnerable back in the sleeping chamber.

"Come down here, there are hogtrahs below, come see!" Flying at an incredible speed, Tania quickly left Anton behind.

"Wait for me," Anton called after Tania and concentrated on keeping up with her; it didn't take long for him to catch up. "What's a *hogtrah*?" he asked. "I heard that word used at the castle, it sounded derogatory."

"They didn't tell you about them, did they? These are the last of the half-human half-swine hybrids from ages past. *Humans* changed them; they needed to build an army so that they didn't have to fight and die in battle. My sisters and I had no hand in this! Creating them is an abomination! You should make friends with them, they need redemption; they crave it, but they won't ask for it, they will demand it! You *need* them!"

Within a moment, they stood on the valley floor and Tania pointed toward the south. "They live very close, you will see. Come, follow me!" Waving her hand and smiling, she again encouraged Anton to accompany her.

There was no fog on the valley floor; it hovered nearly fifty feet above and completely masked the elevated human dwellings in the overhead; it was a convenient and effective camouflage. The valley was quite narrow near the pyramid too, but widened quickly as they traveled further south. Within a minute or two, they came upon a small village of shabbily constructed wooden homes; they were barn-like in appearance but diminutive for their designed intent.

Wisps of fog blew down from above, mud covered the ground, and few plants of any kind grew; those that did were wicked looking weeds and gnarly trees. Scattered all around were ugly human-like people dotting the landscape busily practicing melee combat. They had pig-like faces with a prominent pig-like snout, and two tusks that protruded upward two inches from their lower jaw. Strong, immensely muscular, and quite human in shape and proportion, they snorted and huffed and sniffed the air as Tania and Anton arrived.

"Faerie!" huffed the first one; "I smell *faerie*! She's alone, but *something—snort—feels odd*! Something else is—*snort—around*! It *sees* us!"

"Look quickly," Tania whispered to Anton. "They've discovered us! We must go! They don't like faeries!" Hurriedly, she flew up into the fog layer and left the hogtrahs behind. "I should've disguised myself."

"Wait, I want to hear what they say!" Following along behind Tania, Anton looked back at the unusual creatures below; he didn't know what to make of them. "Do they associate with people?" he asked her.

"Sometimes, when they need to talk about things, they are *very* demanding; they are … *friends*." She said friends as if it were conditional. "The humans and the hogtrahs, *help* each other, when they need to. The rest of the time they remain separate."

Intuitively, Anton grasped her meaning. Obviously, any human would consider these creatures unpleasant and would limit contact. It would seem the separation, but close proximity, was necessary for them to live harmoniously together.

"You said you can disguise yourself? Do it! I want to know what they're up to." Anton returned to the ground, he knew they couldn't see him.

Waving her hands, Tania suddenly changed into a dragonfly. Her wings looked the same as before, and she was still the same size, but her body appeared different. Diving out of the fog, she rejoined Anton.

"Look!" one hogtrah said, pointing at Tania. "It just dragonfly—*snort*—see!" The second hogtrah placed his hand over his eyes to shield them as he too gazed at Tania, but a look of puzzlement covered his visage. "That not—*snort*—faerie!" He too then pointed at Tania.

"It *was—snort*—faerie! I *saw* it. I *smelled* it!—*snort*. The humans are *planning* something. Faeries—*snort*—don't come here; there is—*reason*; there is—*purpose*!"

"I tell others—*snort*." Running toward the nearest barn-home, the second hogtrah proceeded to alert more hogtrahs about what he had seen.

Anton returned to the fog layer and Tania followed him; he looked at her with a puzzled expression. "They're obviously suspicious of you, and I don't want them to discover us. I'd like to stay, but I need to return; is this all you wanted me to see?" Anton needed to rest and he'd seen enough; he felt as though he grasped the significance of what Tania wished to reveal.

Changing back to her faerie form, Tania responded: "there's more, ask the 'Wyns, they'll tell you!" Tania continued to offer her best advice and she was pleased that Anton listened to her and respected her.

"That I will, I see a need. There *is* something about them, something I should remember, something I learned on Methonias in class several years ago; I'll think about it." Smiling and nodding, Anton gratefully accepted Tania's advice.

Traveling back through the fog layer, Anton returned to his room; he needed to make sure he rested properly before the inevitable council and planning later in the day. Tania flew along with him and they returned together. As quickly as he could he reentered his body; he'd had more than enough adventure for one day.

"I will watch you. Rest at ease." Attempting to comfort him, Tania watched as Anton lay back, and then closed his eyes.

"Sleep," was all Anton said as he restlessly attempted to doze off; he tossed about for a few minutes before he could relax.

Seeing Anton's struggles, Tania waited for a few moments for him to drift off, and then with a wave of her hand, she provided him with her special succor; almost instantly, he fell into a deep restful sleep. She then curled up on the end of the bed and rested; she didn't require sleep, but she closed her eyes, relaxed, and listened.

LATE AFTERNOON CAME IN THE blink of an eye; Anton arose refreshed and looked quickly around. Tania had remained faithful to her word; she stood poised on his big toe watching him closely just as she said she'd do. When she noticed he had awakened, she spun in a pirouette like a ballerina on her tiptoes.

"Good afternoon!" she announced, and smiled warmly at Anton. She seemed excited and giggled with delight. "You slept *deeply*, I could tell!"

"Good, I need a fresh mind. Is anyone about?" asked Anton.

"Vim awoke a short time ago; he is *bathing*! Can you *believe* it?" giggled Tania. "He *never* bathes; he just uses his magic to suffice his need. The women here insisted, and he didn't like it. Now they're washing his clothing; he didn't like *that* either! I think they're repairing his robe; it *needed* it! I don't know how he could wear a robe that worn out! The women here are *so* helpful! They do the *important* things! They're not like *men*, they work hard!"

"That's good, Vim should take better care of himself." Pinching his nose for a second, Anton smiled and winked at Tania. "Where are the 'Wyns? Do you know?" he inquired.

Tania giggled at Anton's humor. "You're *hungry*! I can tell. I believe there's food in the commons, let's go see!" Flying off ahead, she led the way.

Tagging along as best he could Anton ran after his tiny friend; he was enjoying her companionship much more than he'd anticipated. He chuckled to himself as he raced up the stairs trying to catch her, but she remained just out of reach.

As they entered the commons, Anton saw the four 'Wyns sitting together talking; Cuðbwyn stood as he entered the room.

"Good! Both of you are up. Are you hungry?" he queried. "As you can see we are preparing for a meal; the women have nearly completed cooking dinner." Pointing toward the very large woodstove on one side of the chamber, Cuðbwyn directed Anton's attention to their activities.

"Where's Deidra? Is she going to be here? Tania said Vim is bathing; will he be here soon?" Anton had many questions and nodded in turn to each of the 'Wyns acknowledging them as he asked his questions.

"Yes, and yes. Deidra is about her duties, somewhere; Vim will be here shortly." Eyeing Anton, Cuðbwyn studied his transformed body; he was impressed with his clean appearance, it gave him the impression that he had become an entity.

Directly, Aëlfwyn stepped up behind Cuðbwyn. "We've discussed your attire, and we wondered if you'd like some new clothing. Your transformation, that is, your pure clean appearance seems obscured by your old attire."

Quickly examining himself, Anton felt taken aback. He didn't consider his Methonian garb to be inappropriate, it was traditional, and he was comfortable with it. "I'm not sure what you mean." With a confused look, he questioned Aëlfwyn. "I *like* my clothes, I *earned* them."

"That is good; we simply think that something reflecting your transformation would make a bold statement, that is, it would impress people more if you changed your overall appearance." Trying to alleviate Anton's discomfort, Cuðbwyn smiled and explained. "We've duplicated your clothes, but adjusted the color and material; would you be kind enough to don them and see if you *like* them?"

As if summoned, Deidra appeared carrying a stack of folded clothes; smiling, she offered them to Anton. "Rowwerrrr, we made these while you rrrrrested; let us see you-rrrr in them." Shoving them into Anton's hands, she smiled in a feline way and then abruptly turned around and left.

Smiling, Anton's eyes trailed after Deidra as she left; her small tail stuck out below her loincloth and twitched slightly as she walked away. "I guess I have little choice." Looking at them, he realized she'd spoken the truth; they were new, identical in every sense to his own clothes, and pure white with golden piping outlining its various edges giving it a clean look. "I'll be back shortly," he called over his shoulder as he left the room.

Leaving the commons, Anton returned to his private room. He quickly changed and gathered his belongings from his old clothes, distributed them in the pockets of his new clothes, and then placed his old Methonian clothes in his EHD. "Good enough."

When Anton returned to the commons, he saw Vim sitting there; Deidra sat next to him looking around impatiently; her eyes instantly fell upon him as he entered the room. All of the 'Wyns sat around the same table and they'd left an empty seat next to Deidra for him.

Everyone turned around to watch Anton as he sat. His golden-blonde hair, golden eyes, and perfect, pure milky white skin encased in the new pure white clothing gave him the appearance of an apparition; it was almost as if he himself glowed. Obviously, his transformation made him quite different from everyone else, and most importantly, different from who and what he was before he'd stepped through the portal.

Flying over to his shoulder, Tania whispered in his ear. "They think you're special; they think your better now, you should thank them! The women worked very hard for you!—*they* work harder than the *men* do here!"

"Umm, I want to thank you for the clothes, they're quite … *helpful.* They look nice." Stiffly, Anton accepted his gift. He was genuinely pleased with it, and he smiled awkwardly as he looked around the table. Stretching out his arms, he examined himself accepting the melioration, and unconsciously nodded his acquiescence. "It's an improvement; I believe I understand why you wish me to look this way; it's symbolic of purity; it will help with leadership. I like them."

"Bravo, young man, you are quite astute." Eädwyn clapped his hands, smiled, and stood up. "We too are pleased; your appearance must intimidate those whom you encounter; they must *feel* your transformation, not just see the difference; appearances can have as significant an effect as your skills, if done correctly. Now, let's eat!" Waving to the women, he ushered them along to serve the meal.

Anton was hungrier than he'd realized. Breakfast was many hours earlier, and he hadn't eaten at proper intervals for days. The food smelled incredible; he salivated unexpectedly in anticipation, and hunger pangs announced his need to everyone.

Tania sat on Anton's shoulder; it seemed as though she'd made this her place to be. Nobody gave her much notice and never spoke directly to her; the ways of the faeries held mysteries that few comprehended, and not everyone trusted them implicitly even though they had never been given reason to doubt them.

On the other hand, Deidra watched Tania frequently; she wished to know exactly what her role with Anton was, and she somehow wished she were as close to Anton as the little faerie. She didn't particularly like Tania's propinquity, and kept an eye on her. Inwardly, she hoped she'd be the one to maintain Anton's attention.

Taking a fair portion, Vim loaded his plate with meat, a variety of vegetables, and a large piece of bread. "I'm pleased with the efforts of the ladies here in the city, as always; they're perhaps the best cooks in all of humanity!" Smiling politely at each of them, he gave them the credit everyone else seemed to ignore.

Pleased, the women each thanked him in return for his graciousness and then went about eating their meal separate from the men. The act seemed somehow distinct and odd to Anton. In particular, he traditionally gave women's efforts little if any notice. At the Great Temple on Methonias, women remained completely excluded; few, if any, had ever laid eyes on the Temple and he was sure none had ever set foot inside. As a result, he had little interest in their activities other than to accept their service on those rare occasions that he encountered them. But something fundamental had changed in him since saving Celeste from the *Lapillusaurus*, his marriage to Nelda, his experiences with the young women in Tooloo, his meeting with the Queen, the advice and friendship of Tania, and his transformation in the pyramid. Recognizing Vim's politeness, he decided to acknowledge them as well, this time without any prompting.

Standing, Anton addressed the women directly: "I want to show my appreciation to each of you for your help; the clothing you tailored fits perfectly, and your cooking has pleased me greatly. Thank you again. I am at your service." Bowing in Methonian fashion, he accredited each woman one at a time, and then returned to his meal.

The 'Wyns seemed surprised at his gesture, and they looked at each other nodding their approval; it pleased them that Anton showed manners, be they given awkwardly or not; this was something they hadn't expected from a Warrior, a trait that no other Warrior preceding him had offered to anyone.

Taking particular notice, Deidra smiled and purred. "He's a grrr-reat man-rrrr. This is good!" She didn't speak to anyone in particular, but shared her thoughts aloud, and then sheepishly went back to eating quietly.

"My dear Anton, you surprise us unendingly. We see in you true nobility in the making." Cuðbwyn stood and raised his glass into the air. "A toast to Anton, our savior! May he be blessed with respect by everyone he encounters, and feared by all of our enemies!"

A cheer of acceptance and the clanking of glasses followed; Vim too showed his respect and accepted the toast.

"That was very nice of you, Anton. You're a great man!" Tania smiled proudly, knowing that her influence was partially responsible for his sudden change of attitude. "You'll receive honor and respect, you will see!"

As the meal concluded, Grëyfwyn stood and addressed everyone. "I hate to bring up the subject of business, but there are lives at stake, our lives and the lives of all living things; we must hold a war council, now, before the portal opens tonight. Everything is prepared and awaits us in the meeting room; please, let us retire there and discuss this issue." Leading the way, he immediately left the commons.

Everyone, including Deidra, quickly finished what they were eating and followed Grëyfwyn, only the women remained behind to attend the cleanup chores. Traveling down the spiral staircase one level, they then traversed three bridges to the north and entered a large meeting room. It had more than enough seats for all present, and

Anton noticed several other men he had yet to meet were already there; they were dressed like the guards Vim had killed outside the portal.

A podium stood near the center of the room and Grëyfwyn positioned himself behind it. "Please, everyone, take a seat so that we may discuss the future of Peruvious." Waving for everyone to sit, he quickly looked around watching everyone arrive and waited for their compliance. "Very well, let us proceed," he continued after everyone had seated themselves.

Looking directly at Anton, Grëyfwyn continued to speak. "We have among us, our savior; he's the hero spoken of in the *Prophecy of One*! May all who are present know his name, Anton Seven; he is a Methonian Warrior!" Motioning for Anton to stand, Grëyfwyn encouraged him to turn around so that everyone could see his face.

Bowing in Methonian fashion, Anton embraced the moment. "I'll try to uphold Grëyfwyn's kind words; I have yet to prove I can save humanity, I'm not yet your savior as you presume. It is my wish to live up to your expectations." Humility was new to him, but he felt it in his heart to share his sentiments.

"As the tale goes, he claims to have removed the Dragon Master from Upper Peruvious single handedly; only a true champion could honestly make such a claim. I'm confident he'll surprise us even more, and prove my assertions are accurate." Grëyfwyn continued to share his respect; he hoped it would gain everyone's trust and support as he offered his praise.

Before Anton could sit, he spotted an old friend; Beelif sat to one side of the room, a significant detail he'd somehow missed when he entered. Nodding an acknowledgement, he smiled and then returned to his seat.

Then suddenly, the door to the meeting room burst open as a guard rushed in. "Pardon! Sir, there is an angry hogtrah demanding entry; he wants to have an audience with all of you; he claims to have seen a *faerie*." As he said faerie, he noticed Tania sitting on Anton's shoulder; it was obvious he had been unaware of her presence.

"The hogtrahs were *not* invited, but given the peculiar circumstances of our future, and theirs, I will permit it. It's true, they *should* be here." Grëyfwyn motioned for him to leave. "Escort the beast in, but only under guard." Looking at Aëlfwyn, he encouraged him to oversee the effort.

Following the guard, Aëlfwyn quickly disappeared. The door remained open as two more guards stood ready for the arrival of the hogtrah.

"I'm sorry for the delay; it shouldn't take but a moment." Grëyfwyn stalled trying to smooth the sudden tension in the room.

Almost at once, Aëlfwyn returned with the hogtrah. "Yor wishes to speak to the council; he claims to have important words to share, and he has a demand to make."

"He *always* has a demand to make," replied Grëyfwyn.

Locking eyes with Grëyfwyn, Yor delivered his message.

"Me speak *now* to humans—*snort, not* wait!" Yor yelled as he abruptly appeared through the doorway; he easily pushed the guards aside as if they were merely children. With an angry scowl, he hastily looked back and forth scrutinizing everyone in the room, and he appeared eager for an argument or a fight.

Standing, Cuðbwyn watched as Yor crossed the room. "We allowed you entry, but that doesn't mean you're allowed to have your way! *Sit!*" Cuðbwyn ordered, and pointed at an empty chair on the far edge of the room; he continued to stare at Yor until he complied.

Snorting loudly, Yor stood his ground, looked swiftly around and noticed all eyes were turned upon him, Then, in a huff, he took the seat offered him, snorting loudly as he did so. "Me speaks soon!—*snort.*" he called over his shoulder as he tersely sat down.

"You were given permission to enter, you'll get your turn to speak later. Be patient!" Cuðbwyn ignored Yor's attitude and returned to his seat, yet he kept an eye on him watching for any sign of trouble.

"Now, unless anyone objects, we must discuss current events, and as you may have guessed, most are quite unpleasant. Since all of you have now met or seen Anton, you know that the circumstances in Peruvious are changing; the end of time as we know it is upon us, the final battles are eminent." Grëyfwyn looked around the room to see everyone's reactions and found both fear and concern in each face he observed.

"For those of you that haven't yet heard, it's with great displeasure that I must formally announce the death of Taun; he was killed by a fracknoid after returning abruptly from an assignment to the Towers of Tor. This can mean only one thing, the compromise of our security; the Great Seal is broken!"

Suddenly Yor stood. "You say nasty katrah dead? This *good* news!—*snort*. Only that one left now!—*snort*." Pointing at Deidra, Yor intentionally made everyone aware of his intense loathing of the katrahs.

"You will sit and remain silent, or you *will* be removed! No more outbursts!" Grëyfwyn pointed at Yor and ordered his compliance. "There will be no prejudice expressed at *this* council!"

Two guards quickly moved nearer to Yor in order to enforce Grëyfwyn's command. They positioned themselves, one to each side of the hogtrah. Several more guards arrived and lined the walls of the room anticipating trouble; the room was absolutely packed full of them.

Feeling uncomfortable, Deidra suddenly changed seats and sat closer to Anton; she tried to be as discreet as possible. She knew that if trouble broke out, he would be her best protection.

"As I was saying, the katrahs visited the towers only to find that they were under siege by a sea of fracknoids. This signifies only one thing, it's obvious that the great seal is broken, for as you know they exist only in Lower Peruvious. We believe this tragedy is a result of Anton's killing of the Dragon Master which he and Vim reported immediately upon their arrival." Grëyfwyn looked at Deidra, Vim, Anton, and then held his gaze upon Tania.

Feeling uncomfortable, Tania stood on Anton's shoulder and walked around behind his head grasping his hair for support. She then peeked back at Grëyfwyn like a child anticipating a reprimand.

"Beelif also arrived here just one day earlier for a visit; he too brought current news. All of the primords have recently moved their hamlet to a new and still undisclosed location; he needed to let Lorca know of the situation. It would seem our young champion compromised the hamlet's security through the use of a crystal ring." Scrutinizing Anton, he gave him an objurgating look.

"We sent four of our guards to guide Vim and Anton here, but unfortunate luck befell their efforts; the break in the great seal allowed Lord Agonia to enter Upper Peruvious; as a result, he captured them and enslaved them for his evil purpose, and it gets worse! Vim vaporized the guards when the lord attacked them as they waited for the portal to open. Because of their close proximity to the portal when this occurred, it's believed the two of them may have compromised its secret location." Grëyfwyn pointed at Vim accusingly as if admonishing him for his carelessness.

A sudden gasp filled the air as most of the attendees learned of the many crimes the two had unwittingly committed. Guards looked around disapprovingly; the news didn't set well with them.

"There's one positive event, Anton defeated the evil lord in battle, but this was at the price of Vim's actions to save him by vaporizing the guards. It would seem our new champion is quick to fight; he did so with the Dragon Master and the evil lord; it's hoped he'll learn to use the proper restraint when the need requires it now that he's received his transformation from Trepid." Taking a deep breath, Grëyfwyn slowly looked around the room and carefully scrutinized everyone's face; he wanted to know their reaction to his listing of Anton's crimes.

It felt to Anton as though his Masters were interrogating him back on Methonias. The list of accusations grew quickly, and he wondered what the verdict would be. Nervously, he looked at Vim for support.

Placing his hand on Anton's wrist, Vim looked at him and squeezed it as if to say: *"restrain yourself."*

"If it weren't for Trepid's approval, I would ask for this young man's incarceration; his crimes have cost us too much, although it would seem we've little choice but to trust him regardless." Glaring at Anton, Grëyfwyn made sure he understood the magnitude of his choices and he wanted everyone present to know who he genuinely was.

"As I said earlier, he's the one spoken of in the *Prophecy of One*. He's human, with faults, and has yet to learn our ways and what is right and wrong; even in his transformed state, he remains capable of free choice and the capacity to make mistakes." Grëyfwyn hesitated and looked around the room through the slits of his eyes.

"Who here has never made a mistake or a bad choice? Who here is innocent of a crime, be it big or small? Who here can claim to be a savior of humanity? I pose these questions so that you'll understand we support a man, imperfect, yet chosen by the *Almighty One!*" Continuing to glare, but not at Anton, Grëyfwyn again looked quickly at each face around the room.

"I for one stand by this Warrior of Methonias. I beg that everyone here do so as well, including," Grëyfwyn looked directly at Yor, "our neighbors." Pointing, he made sure the hogtrah noticed his gesture.

"Me speak *now*! You speak too *long*!—*snort*. You say nothing important!—*snort*" Standing quickly, Yor stared at Grëyfwyn. "You humans let *me* say to *you* now!"—*snort*.

"Very well, have your *say*, and then we'll make *our* plans. Fear not, they *do* include the hogtrahs." Looking at the guards surrounding Yor, Grëyfwyn then stared directly at the half-human beast. "Do you require the podium? Or are you comfortable speaking from there?"

"I say from here. You stay there!—*snort*. For long time, we live with humans, not friends, but not fight them. We *angry* at humans, they good friend with katrah, not hogtrah!—*snort*." Yor looked menacingly at Deidra; it was obvious to everyone he loathed her.

"We want no more katrahs, but you do—*snort*." Pointing at Grëyfwyn, Yor emphasized his argument. "You get rid of katrah, we be friends, we fight together like *friends*!—*snort*. They old enemy, we fight them; we kill most all of them, this well for us. Humans *make* hogtrahs, we not like this, but we okay with this, now, not before!—*snort*."

The tension in the room increased, and Deidra cowered in her seat. She wasn't a fighter, and she was the last of her species. Hoping to fulfill Trepid's purpose, she looked at Anton, her cat-like eyes pleading for protection.

With a slight nod, Anton returned her gaze as if to assure her she had nothing to worry about, and then he returned his attention to Yor and carefully watched him.

"We saw faerie, not like!—*snort*. We know you plan fight or no faerie here; we want new life, we want equals with humans!—*snort*. This I say.—*snort*." Again, Yor looked at Deidra, his eyes narrowed, and a smirk crossed his face as if to say: "I will kill you." Taking his seat, he folded his arms and snorted repeatedly to himself, as if satisfied.

"Thank you, Yor. We hear your words, and we appreciate your concerns. Furthermore, we accept your offer of support for our fight, and we offer our friendship." Watching the hogtrah carefully as he spoke, Grëyfwyn waited for his reaction.

Suddenly standing, Yor looked at Deidra. "You say katrah die! This good! We *friends!—snort*."

"Sit down, Yor, we didn't agree to your terms of trust; Deidra will remain alive. As you now know, she's the last of the katrahs, and we'll allow her to live out her life. Either way, there will be no more katrahs; you've already outlived your old enemy. Is this satisfactory?" As if offering an ultimatum, Grëyfwyn scowled at Yor. "Make your choice now, or leave!"

Quickly looking back and forth from Grëyfwyn to Deidra, Yor clearly didn't like the option. "She die, *now*! Then we be *friends!— snort*." Pointing at Deidra, Yor stood his ground fully expecting immediate compliance.

"No! She lives! And yes, we *will* work together, it's ordained; you must accept this." Grëyfwyn didn't back down and locked eyes with Yor.

Suddenly, Anton stood and looked directly at Yor. "Deidra is under my personal protection; therefore, I challenge you to a fight to the death! If I win, the hogtrahs must pledge their allegiance to humanity and fight alongside all humans willingly; if I lose, you hogtrahs can do with Deidra as you choose!"

All at once everyone in the room suddenly gasped and boisterously objected to Anton's declaration; they couldn't believe what they heard. Grëyfwyn raised his hand and a moment later, it was emphatically silent.

"*Snort snort snort!* You! Human! You kill great dragon? I *not* challenge!—*snort!* Unless ..." The hogtrahs eyes narrowed and a grin spread across his brutish face, "on *my* terms! I make *rules!*—*snort. My* way!—*snort.*"

"Anytime, anywhere, but the rules must be equal; they apply equally to both of us." Anton's hand hovered over his sword; he didn't trust the hogtrah and was ready for any sudden movement.

"Heh heh heh, this good, I *accept!*—*snort.*" Yor smiled and sat down snorting repeatedly to himself; he remained calm and smiling, as if he'd somehow succeeded.

Staring at Anton, Grëyfwyn motioned with his eyes for the Warrior to sit. "I would object, but our savior has spoken; it isn't my place to alter his directive. We seem to have strayed from the purpose of this gathering, the planning of our future, not the destruction of our own selves. I might remind all of you that fighting amongst each other is a waste of time and only reduces our chance of success." He continued to look at Anton as he spoke; it was obvious to everyone he disapproved of his sudden challenge, as if he was about to add another crime to the Warrior's docket; he, after all, initiated the disturbance.

"Now, may we return our attention to business; the evening wanes. It would seem we have several battlefronts; the king's castle is under siege, the compromise of the Towers of Tor requires immediate attention, the great seal requires repair, and Anton must again visit with Amilius, and then find a way to enter Celestra." Heaving a sigh, it seemed as though Grëyfwyn didn't have a plan; his eyes pleaded to the gathering. "Just one of these challenges seems beyond our capacity to accomplish, and yet we have five difficult challenges, now that our Warrior friend has added yet another."

Again, Grëyfwyn gave Anton his ire; his expression held disbelief and disgust. "We must choose the sequence of battle, and proceed immediately with the plan; are there any proposals?" Looking around the room, he hoped someone would share their ideas.

Nobody moved, even Anton seemed at a loss; he didn't have enough information to declare a proper battle plan, yet, but suddenly he spoke.

"I need more information," was all he offered. "I could formulate a *good* plan if I could see a map, or use a strategic battle computer; I need tools." He held his hands out palms up to show he had nothing in them.

"We have *no* such tools; they existed at one time long ago in another age in Celestra, but that time is gone! Use your head, Warrior!" Eädwyn suddenly stood and looked at Anton; he wondered why he made useless offers.

Standing, Anton returned Eädwyn's countenance. "Then I offer this: I'll return to the castle, free it from the grip of its enemy, visit with Amilius, gain the support of the humans there, and find a way to reach Celestra. In the meantime, Vim can take all of you humans, and the hogtrahs to the Towers of Tor. There you'll reclaim the towers from the enemy, and repair the great seal; I'm assuming Vim has the knowledge of how to repair it. There are only two battle fronts, and two extended tasks; I consider Yor a simple annoyance." Standing rigid, Anton expressed an uncompromising confidence and waited calmly for any challenge.

Yor snorted repeatedly and glared at Anton with a look of pure hate. He restrained his comments with great effort as if he had secretly made plans of his own and didn't want to act rashly or reveal them until he could carry them out.

Shocked, Grëyfwyn appeared speechless for a moment, and then offered his thought. "You think you can take on an entire army of fracknoids and who knows what else, including an unknown number of lords by yourself? At last count, there were five of them! The guards at the castle despise you, and you expect them to allow you to lead? Are you mad?"

Unwilling to back down, Anton pointed at Grëyfwyn and addressed his skepticism. "If your portal can set me inside the castle, I can gain their confidence and win; all I need is the support of Amilius. It's you people," he continued, pointing around the room, "who have the greater challenge. I *will* succeed, I must. It is the Methonian way. As for the issue of the hogtrah, I can't lose." He looked at Yor, and his eyes narrowed, his confidence was indisputable.

Instantly Yor stood and pointed an accusing finger at Anton. "*Snort—snort—snort—*you *wrong!* I *win!* Damn you humans, we hogtrahs *rule* Peruvious! We much *stronnnggg!—snort.*" He continued to stand and fidgeted as if he wished to fight right there.

Standing in ready stance, Anton's eyes carefully scrutinized Yor; he was prepared to respond instantly, his hand itched to grasp his sword. He hadn't liked the hogtrahs insistence to make the rules for their fight and he tried to provoke him into a rash response much sooner.

"No fighting!" Grëyfwyn pointed at Anton and then Yor. "There will be no *fighting* here! Both of you, *sit!*"

"Enough!" Vim stood up between the two; turning his back to Anton, he stared at Yor. "You will not fight, we need both of you! Not one more life will we sacrificed! Deidra will live, and fate shall choose her destiny; either way, she is the last of her people, and her fate is already sealed. Hogtrahs and humans must work together or all is lost for both!" Holding up his staff, he then lit the globe; the sight intimidated everyone, including Yor. "You'll choose to work together or there *is* no future." Pointing the globe at Yor it appeared as if he would strike him with his wizard's magic.

"*Snort—snort—snort.* Me thinks you wrong, *old* wizard. You die soon, I *seeeee—soooon!—snort.* You not kill me with that stick," he challenged.

Taken aback, Vim stood his ground; obvious anger and contempt filled his heart. "I accept my future, now make one for yourself!" Turning around, he looked at Anton and then returned to his seat, anger marking his face.

Silence again filled the room. Anton remained standing as if for no other reason but to defend Deidra; his eyes never left Yor. Grëyfwyn appeared speechless, opening and closing his mouth as if he had much to say yet refrained from doing so. The guards stood ready for battle. Vim continued to listen; he still seemed angry, yet also remained complacent.

"Very well, katrah lives—*snort*. Warrior lives. I live. Humans live. We fight together—*snort*." Sitting down angrily, Yor finally acquiesced.

"All in favor of our savior, our *leaders* plan, say aye!" Grëyfwyn called for a vote; it was time for action.

For a second or two the room remained silent, and then Vim stood once more. Raising his hand, he responded very loudly, "Aye!"

In response, everyone stood, raised a hand, and in unison shouted, "Aye!" Except for Yor, it was unanimous.

A moment later, Yor stood and then offered his reluctant response: "Aye—*snort*."

"Very well, the portal opens in a short couple of hours; we have just enough time to assemble on the platform. When it opens, we will leave to our respective commitments!" Grëyfwyn's words were final; the battle was about to begin.

"I gets hogtrahs, bring to portal—*snort*." Abruptly, Yor left the room; he seemed excited as he rushed to his home, snorting as he went.

Looking at Anton, Vim scowled at him. "You must learn to find another way to talk to people; threats won't earn you respect, not even with the hogtrahs."

"The only thing that *creature* understands is violence and strength. I had a plan." Standing his ground, Anton locked eyes with Vim. "Besides, it worked."

"Perhaps, but you'd better use a little discretion at the castle, or fail you will!" Pointing at Anton, Vim made sure he heard the magnitude of his words. "They already dislike you, and taking Deidra there only increases your problem—they dislike her even more. I believe your transformation will help, but diplomacy is the key; you'd better learn some, and quick!"

"Vim is right, you must persuade these men; they understand true leadership!" Tania whispered in Anton's ear and looked at Vim.

"Take our advice, please!" Suddenly Vim turned around and exited the room. "Get some food from the pantry, you've got a long journey to make. I think Deidra can show you where it is," he called over his shoulder as he strode out of the chamber.

Everyone else had already gone to prepare for the opening of the portal, everyone that is but Deidra. She stood next to Anton and looked at him as if she had something to say.

Noticing they were alone, Anton looked at her questioningly. "Is there something I can do for you, something you'd like to ask?"

"We go together-rrrr." Deidra said little, but her eyes pleaded with Anton.

"She wants to go with *you*! She *needs* you!" Tania whispered. "Ask her; ask her *nicely*, you've just *told* her so far. She is a girl, you shouldn't *dictate* to her!"

"I guess the two of you out-vote me. Very well, I had no intention of leaving you behind. You're under my protection and care. Trepid bound me to this, if this pleases you." Anton smiled at Deidra and tried to reassure her of his support. "Now, let's go. Is there anything of yours that you need to gather for the trip?"

"All I need-rrrr, I have. I will show you-rrrr the food supplies, come." Grasping Anton's hand, she led the way.

Escorting him quickly to the pantry room, Deidra packed a large knapsack full of water and food. Offering Anton a sample of several items, she made sure he approved of her selections. The smell of the room was intense and even though Anton wasn't hungry, his stomach growled in response. He'd never been in a pantry before and the olfactory overload stunned him with delight.

"Rowwerrrr, if we make it to lower Peruvious we won't find food-rrrr." Carefully selecting each item, Deidra worked at stuffing the knapsack full.

"You're quite thoughtful Deidra; your strategic preparation of supplies is most beneficial; I wouldn't have known where to find the food or given it much concern. Thank you." Smiling, Anton was pleased for her thoughtfulness. "It would seem I *do* need you with me."

"Rowwerrrr, you are a good man. I will work harrrrrd to help-rrrr you-rrrr." Returning his smile, Deidra finished packing the knapsack and handed it to Anton. "Heavy-rrrr."

Looking at Deidra, Tania whispered in Anton's ear. "See, you two *need* each other; it's good you're making friends!" Flying around them, she then spoke to both. "Don't be late, everyone has left, and you're last!"

Reaching into his pocket, Anton retrieved his EHD and placed the knapsack inside. "Better to carry it this way. The food won't spoil inside this device, and it doesn't weigh anything."

Amazed, Deidra watched Anton fold the EHD after placing the knapsack in it and then return it to his pocket. "How did you-rrrr do that-rrrr?"

"It's an EHD. You probably wouldn't understand the technology. Let's just say I placed the knapsack in its own dimension; time doesn't operate the same inside of it, therefore the food won't age or spoil." Anton was as short with his explanation as possible; he knew they needed to leave. "How do we get to the portal from here?"

"I can show you! Follow me!" Tania quickly left the storage room and flew toward the suspension bridge they'd arrived by.

When they had crossed the bridge, Deidra sprinted down a path toward the pyramid. Startled at her ability to run very fast, Anton worked at keeping up; her cheetah DNA gave her running capabilities that easily matched his own.

"Wait! I want to ask you a question!" Catching up with Deidra, Anton lightly touched her shoulder. "Can we talk? I'd like to know a few things before we go."

Pointing to the south side of the pyramid, Deidra indicated the direction they needed to travel. "This is the way-rrrr, and yes, you-rrrr may ask your-rrrr questions, I will answer-rrrr anything you wish to know-rrrr."

Side by side, they walked together in the direction Deidra had indicated. Anton could see the path she'd directed his attention to.

Landing on Anton's shoulder, Tania waited to hear what he had to say; she smirked to herself and placed her hand over her mouth as she giggled quietly. "It's good you are getting to know her," she quickly whispered in his ear.

"Enough, Tania, Please. I've heard enough about friendship. Don't worry. I like her—a lot!" Gently, Anton let the little faerie know he'd accepted her advice and needed no more nudging.

"Hmm, very well, I see that you do!" Surprised, Tania flew into the air and circled around Anton once. "I'm *pleased*," she called out, and again landed on his shoulder and stood there smiling with satisfaction.

As they continued to walk toward the platform, Anton asked his questions. "I'd like to know, in what way are the katrahs and the hogtrahs old enemies? I mean, why do you hate each other? Why do you fight?"

Suddenly stopping, Deidra looked directly into Anton's eyes. "They were-rrrr made for war-rrrr, we were-rrrr made for war-rrrr to fight them-rrrr. You humans no longer-rrrr fought each other-rrrr; you used us to fight for-rrrr you. Hogtrahs love to kill-rrrr, killing is all they know. The katrahs fought to surrrr-vive. We are smarrrrter-rrrr than they arrrr and they arrrr stronger-rrrr than we arrrr. In the end, they surrrr-vived better-rrrr." Looking disheartened, she lowered her eyes. "And now, I'm the only katrah left."

"Why did you say you were happy you didn't have to *mate* with Taun? Didn't you want the katrahs to continue?" Anton queried further, wanting to understand Deidra better.

"Be careful, you ask *very* personal questions!" Tania whispered in Anton's ear, as if scolding him.

"Rrrrrr, he was lion-rrrr blood, I am cheetah. I didn't want-rrrr my kittens to be mixed. I hoped for-rrrr *rrrreal* human children, not katrah kittens." A look of anger and despair marked Deidra's face and she slowly turned around and continued to guide Anton down the path. Shyly she explained further. "I want to be with a *real* man-rrrr, but this is forrrr-bidden; it doesn't work."

Shocked, Anton finally realized he had asked something very deep-seated in Deidra, something she may not have revealed to anyone before, but then he pressured her even further. "Have you ever told anyone this?"

"Rrrrrr, no! It is forrrr-bidden to have such thoughts, such feelings-rrrr." Her eyes pleaded with Anton to leave these questions alone. She'd revealed her inner most secrets, and it scared her.

"I'm sorry, I shouldn't have asked. Please forgive me." Anton apologized, hoping to comfort her as best he could. His curiosity went further than his restraint and respect.

Deidra looked directly at Anton, and her expression softened. "It's okay-rrrr, I like you-rrrr, it's okay that you asked-rrrr." Smiling stiffly in her feline way, she then looked away and heaved a sigh. A sudden spasm of sadness brought a tear to her eye. "You arrrr different, you didn't know-rrrr, and I feel safe with you-rrrr. I trust you-rrrr."

"Very well, I will protect you at any cost. I'm at your service." Bowing in Methonian fashion, Anton bound himself through his personal commitment: he would die to save her.

"Anton, you must think of the future! You must think of humanity! Be careful!" Scolding him, Tania reminded him of his duty and hoped to temper his commitments. "Silly man, your responsibility is to humanity! This *includes* Deidra!"

"They won't like you at the castle. Are you prepared for this?" Changing the subject, Anton prepared for the immediate future. "They didn't like me before either; they called me a *pig-human*. I hope they will feel different now, but it *will* be uncomfortable for both of us."

"This is nothing new-rrrr, humans always think this way-rrrr, it's nothing new-rrrr to me-rrrr." Shrugging, Deidra sounded indifferent. "As long as I'm with you-rrrr, everrrrything will worrrrk out, I'm confident-rrrr."

Suddenly sprinting, Deidra ran on ahead; she was done with Anton's questions, at least for now, and she was eager to get to the portal in time.

Running after her, Anton kept up without straining himself, but only just. Deidra was incredibly swift and easily matched Anton's best efforts. It took less than a minute to cover the final distance up the stairs to the platform, and they were the last to arrive. Even the hogtrahs, hundreds in all, had arrived and assembled. They stood in military formation, Yor was obviously in command. He shouted orders in a harsh sounding tongue that Anton struggled to understand, but as he watched, he could see they were an efficient, highly trained army, more so than the humans appeared to be.

The humans too had assembled a small army and waited beside the hogtrahs. Grëyfwyn commanded them and looked as though he was ready to leave. Both the hogtrahs and the humans wore their armor and held their weapons ready in military fashion. Each group had a style unlike the other and it seemed more like they prepared to battle each other than work as allies, yet together they stood in formation awaiting the portal's opening.

Standing next to the portal, Vim and the three other 'Wyns watched the turmoil boil inside of its magical circular ring. The moon was already rising and it was obvious it wouldn't take more than a few minutes before nature fed the portal with the energy it needed to open.

Anton and Deidra quickly made their way through the armies and stood next to Vim. Looking at the wizard, he struggled to express himself.

"I, I hope we're together again soon, I'll miss you. Don't fret—I *will* succeed at the castle." Trying to reassure Vim, Anton fumbled his concerns. "As you can see, I have plenty of *very* good council!" Looking at Deidra, Anton complimented Tania and acknowledged the katrah.

"And I have the upmost confidence in you, young man. You've surprised me continually, and your companions are available to help guide you. I have *always* trusted them; you're in good hands. Until we meet again, I wish you success." Patting Anton on the back in a fatherly way, Vim tried to reassure him. "Besides, everyone here already supports you." Pointing around, he urged Anton to look at the two small armies.

Quietly, Beelif walked up behind Anton. "I wish to go with you. Will you accept my offer to come along? I too may be of good council! At the very least, I can tell you a story!"

Taken aback, Anton lifted an eyebrow and looked at the tiny primord. "There will be battle. Are you prepared? You seem too small for such things! And, I doubt there will be time for a story."

Laughing outright, Vim looked at Anton. "His help is *always* indispensable. Take him up on his offer!"

"Very well, you're most welcome!" Smiling, Anton reached out his hand and patted Beelif's shoulder. "I'm honored!"

"I'll surprise you, trust me!" Returning Anton's smile, he danced a jig and kicked his heels together. "We will make a good team."

"You sound a lot like Tania when you say that," Anton replied.

The two small armies looked at Anton and at the portal. It was obvious they had committed to his plan and supported him completely. Everyone fell silent, and a sense of anticipation filled the air.

Moments passed, then minutes, and Anton and Deidra stood side by side and waited. Suddenly, a beam of light shot between the moon and the portal and its boiling fog cleared. An image of the Castle of

Amilius appeared. The image swiftly zoomed inside the inner walls and then Anton, Deidra, Beelif, and Tania quickly entered, leaving their friends behind.

Immediately the image changed and the Towers of Tor were visible. Yor yelled a command and all of the hogtrahs marched forth and entered the portal. The humans, led by Grëyfwyn followed closely behind. Vim stepped into the portal last with his staff brightly lit.

The three remaining 'Wyns watched the portal change once again; it returned to a boiling vortex of fog as it closed for the night, sealing everyone's fate. Looking at each other grimly, they turned around and silently headed home.

"Now we wait. All our best hopes are in the hands of our savior!" Eädwyn addressed his friends as they walked down the stairs.

"Aye, and a wizard, a faerie, a katrah, and the hogtrahs. Who would have known?" Cuðbwyn said.

"We'll prepare for the next step, we've only a day." Aëlfwyn reminded the others of their duty and urged them forward. "We must be ready."

CHAPTER 4
Annihilation

V IM WALKED THROUGH THE DAZZLING light and stepped out of the portal. The hogtrahs, humans, and Grëyfwyn preceded him and were already fully engaged in combat with a sea of fracknoids. Immediately, he turned around and raised his staff, chanted in his archaic wizard's language, and closed the portal exit that hung in the atmosphere. As a result, the midnight darkness enveloped everyone, and the ravenous fracknoids were nearly impossible to see. Only their bright, glowing red eyes marked where they were and the ground literally crawled with tens of thousands of the little red dots.

The two monolithic eight-sided Towers of Tor stood on the chiseled sheer edge of Upper Peruvious looking out over the vast expanse of the lower lands far below like twin lighthouses watching over the ocean to warn sailors of impending doom should they stray too close to shore. They stood intact, but someone, or something, had destroyed the giant crystal octahedrons inside the domes. They needed repair or they would never function again, and without them—both of them—reestablishing the great seal was beyond any hope or probability.

The allied armies of humans and hogtrahs blended together as they fought the sea of fracknoids that encircled them, and their efforts appeared dire and hopeless; even the impervious chainmail they all wore merely slowed the enemy's ferocious confrontation, and their swords were woefully inadequate for a proper defense or attack. Several of the humans and hogtrahs carried a wand-like device that discharged a stream of fire into the crawling sea of furry black creatures and melted them. These were their only successful weapons, and the only thing that stood between them and annihilation.

The moment Vim realized the danger he faced, he placed himself inside his protective sphere and levitated into the air. He had little choice but to do so, knowing he couldn't fight the enemy and defend himself simultaneously; the sheer multitude of fracknoids would simply consume him if he remained on the ground any longer. Considering his options, he decided to see what he could do to repair the obliterated lenses and prevent any more enemies from entering the upper lands. He hoped the allied troops would survive without his support.

The two towers stood nearly a quarter mile apart, and it would take Vim time to repair each one individually. Selecting the nearest tower just a short distance to the south, he levitated as quickly as he could to its balcony. As he landed, he couldn't see any evidence of fracknoids upon it or inside it; apparently, they were all engaged in battle on the ground. From this vantage point, he had an opportunity to work his magic against the enemy below and support the rapidly dwindling allied army.

Already there were hogtrah and human bodies littering the ground and hundreds of fracknoids ravenously consumed them. Their proportionally large mouths lined with razor sharp teeth gnawed and vibrated at more than a hundred chomps a minute, and even now most of the bodies were little more than bones being gleaned of every speck of flesh. A few more minutes of this slaughter and the humans and hogtrahs would all be gone.

Screams of agony from the humans, and squeals of angry pain from the hogtrahs filled the air. The effect demoralized the allies as their numbers quickly dwindled.

Raising his staff, Vim summoned forth an enormous field of energy that completely enveloped the entire top of the tower. Yelling archaic words in his wizard's tongue, he wielded his staff, and cast forth a seismic wave of golden energy. Lightning bolts fired off in all directions pounding the ground below as the wave of energy oscillated toward the densest mass of the fracknoid enemy. As it struck, it displaced them and tumbled them about as if a tsunami had washed over them. In swaths, the lightning bolts charred and burned those creatures that they hit. Hundreds, then thousands of them vaporized, giving the allied army a chance to defend themselves.

Sighting Vim's attack, the hogtrahs retreated and escaped the wave of energy. The humans were slower at responding, and Vim's attack killed a couple by accident. Only two thirds of the original army remained.

Grëyfwyn shouted commands and ordered a retreat. Then he looked up at Vim and yelled in his direction. "Damn, are you on our side or theirs? Take more care in your support!"

Sending a second wave of energy, Vim fought the enemy the only way he knew how; he used the power only he controlled. The second wave of energy struck to the far eastern edge of the fracknoids, the farthest away from the army; lightning bolts danced on the undulation of raw power and consumed every fracknoid in its path.

However, the fracknoids were fiendishly clever. Realizing from where the magical tsunamis emanated, they suddenly ignored the allied army and quickly ran toward the southern tower where Vim worked his wizard magic. By the thousands, they piled atop each other at an incredible speed and climbed the tower's side toward Vim; their ability to shift their tactics as if they were of one mind, and the swiftness at which they advanced to achieve their goal staggered him. Only moments remained before they'd scale the wall and reach him.

Fortunately, this shift in momentum gave Grëyfwyn an opportunity to redeploy his men toward the enemy's redirected tactics. They were less capable of defending themselves as they surged toward the tower, but many stayed to fight at the rear and protect the new front.

Hogtrahs and humans fought together successfully for a short time, but the fracknoids again changed their efforts. A group of a few hundred turned around and surrounded the allies, stifling their advance. Again, the fracknoids slaughtered the hogtrahs and humans by climbing them and covering them by the dozens like a blanket. They gnashed their teeth at them, chomped at their armor and sliced through it, chewed through their clothing with ease, and then ate them alive. Steadily, efficiently, they whittled away at the dwindling army. Wails of agonizing pain filled the air as the humans and hogtrahs fell to the ground squirming and writhing hopelessly in a final effort to save themselves, to no avail.

From somewhere, one of the hogtrahs produced a firebomb and heaved it deep inside the blanketing mass of fracknoids aggregated at the side of the tower; the distance was over a hundred yards, and everyone that witnessed it was dumbfounded at his incredible strength and ability to toss the very heavy object that far. By the hundreds, and then the thousands, the fracknoids caught fire, burned, and melted into a mass of black goo that covered the ground in a huge puddle of sticky toxic ooze. In the darkness, the dense black smoke rising off the burning fracknoids occluded the view of them climbing the wall, and the resulting vitriol smell was horrendous; it permeated the atmosphere, causing everyone to choke violently from the acrid vapors.

"Yor!" Grëyfwyn yelled, coughing. "More firebombs! The firebombs are working! Cast everything you've got!"

Smiling, Yor barked commands in his hogtrah dialect and ordered more bombs. Instantly, every hogtrah that had one tossed it into the sea of fracknoids.

Explosions and fire peppered the enemy and they burned and melted to the ground by the tens of thousands; the air thickened with smoke and the heavy vitriol vapor and brought many of the humans to their knees as they too succumbed to the attack's side effect.

As the smoke reached the balcony, Vim raised both arms with staff in hand and chanted in his wizard's tongue. Magical light and disrupted and controlled air swirled together as if in a blender and wound around the staff's globe; he then cast it downward, washing the black caustic smoky gas away and relieving the allies of the toxic fumes.

Suddenly, the fracknoids began a hasty retreat and ran across the sticky goop generated by their own dead. The first wave stuck as if glued to the goo, and they too melted in their own adulterate, but the second wave crossed over them and quickly escaped. They ran toward the northern tower as if it was a haven, or possibly, they had some other secret purpose.

Noticing the direction in which they ran, Vim encased himself in his protective sphere and levitated speedily toward the second tower. It was a quarter mile away, but he traversed the distance in seconds, well ahead of the pursuing enemy. Even so, he could see it wouldn't take them long to catch up.

Examining the balcony and quickly scrutinizing the destroyed crystal within the dome, Vim landed and prepared another magical assault—but his plans fell short of success.

Suddenly, from the east, an unseen enemy emerged from the lower lands far below the tower: two of the Lords of Ruin appeared and took an offensive position. They levitated into the air above Vim and stood to either side of and behind him. Naturally, he hadn't anticipated their sudden appearance, and he was completely vulnerable to their surprise attack. Just as he unleashed his wave of energy, they too unleashed their retaliatory response.

Lord Odious and Lord Sinister stood in midair a short distance apart behind Vim; as if they were of one mind, they simultaneously raised their arms over their heads. An aura of blue light surrounded them, and they lowered their arms and pointed them toward the wizard. A force of immense energy shot from each of them and struck him directly in the back. The impact instantly hammered Vim to the floor of the balcony, and he lay sprawled on the floor, unconscious.

"Success, Odious," said Lord Sinister.

"Indeed. The plan worked well. Unleash the nekelmuses," replied Lord Odious. "The inferior ones and the humans will be eliminated. Their position is indefensible."

"As intended," said Sinister. "The scales will tip to our advantage."

"Was there any doubt?" A smirk of confidence crossed Odious's face. "We *never* lose."

Levitating back toward the precipice, Lord Sinister signaled an unseen ally. Within moments, dozens of large, black, spherically shaped creatures, nearly six feet in diameter, floated up from below the edge of Upper Peruvious. They drifted slowly like hot air balloons and soon spread out high over the tower, and the humans and hogtrahs below. Each of them had one large demonic eye, one large mouth, and two prominent horns that stood erect to either side of the scowling eye.

Pointing to the remnants of the allied army, Sinister commanded his air force: "Attack and obliterate!"

Meanwhile, Lord Odious levitated toward the unconscious Vim. Placing him in a stasis of blue light energy, he raised his seemingly lifeless body into the air.

As quickly as possible, Lord Sinister returned to the balcony and placed the Staff of Balance in a second stasis field of blue energy. He then raised it into the air alongside Vim, but far outside of his reach.

In full sight of the small army below, the two lords looked like two blue entities. Their energy lit the sky over the tower as they levitated over the edge of the upper lands and disappeared, taking both Vim and his staff with them. The greatest power of the upper lands was now a prisoner of the Lord of Darkness.

As the two lords disappeared, the nekelmuses opened their mouths and launched dark red fireballs at the hogtrah-human army below them. The fracknoids had all taken a position around the northern tower and created an impenetrable barrier that barred any advance toward it.

"Yor!" barked Grëyfwyn, "retreat! We must outrun the nekelmuses!" Motioning to the army, he dodged and scrambled to avoid the pounding of the enemy's aerial assault.

Moments passed between each release of the nekelmuses' fireballs. As they recharged their furnaces, they slowly floated around, repositioning themselves for another attack. However there were enough of them to maintain a steady assault on the allies below. Fireballs the size of pumpkins pounded the ground all around the dodging army with deadly accuracy; the distance between them gave the hogtrahs and humans enough time to avoid much of the attack, but the distance quickly shrank as they floated purposefully to surround them and prevent their escape.

"The tower! Run for the southern Tower of Tor! It's our only refuge!" Grëyfwyn continued to command the troops and nobody questioned his logic. The towers were the only structures within miles and offered their only protection from the nekelmuses. The flat, dusty plains that surrounded them held no supplemental cover. They couldn't run forever trying to escape and had no attack to offer against them. Only arrows might reach them if they chose to come within range.

"I agree with human—*snort*; need cover!—*snort!*" Yor responded as he led his army around the gooey mass of melted fracknoids. "That tower is *trap!* We not last long there!—*snort*. We must *kill* them!—*snort.*"

"There's an extensive living area below the tower and it contains many other secrets. We must seek refuge within. The tower is more defensible than you realize!" Grëyfwyn shouted. He knew Yor was right. They couldn't last forever inside the tower, but there was no alternative. "There are weapons stored in a secret chamber! If we can get to them in time, we may have a fighting chance!"

"Weapons *goooood!* You show!—*snort.*" Excited, Yor hastened toward the tower, and the hogtrahs effortlessly outdistanced the humans.

It only took a couple of minutes for the entire army to enter the stronghold and close the huge stone barricade behind them. Even the pounding of the nekelmuses' fireballs couldn't breach the massive ten-foot thick stone door. Nevertheless, just as Yor had determined, their fate was sealed, there was no escape; the enemy had effectively trapped them inside and only had to outwait them or destroy the tower outright to win.

"We must guard the upper balcony of the tower! They can find a way in from there!" Grëyfwyn directed Yor's attention to a flight of stairs that circled upward.

"You show weapons, we defend!—*snort.*" Glaring at Grëyfwyn, Yor was convinced the humans had lied about them as a ruse to persuade them to retreat.

Looking for the right spot, Grëyfwyn placed his hand against a nearby wall, and suddenly a secret stone door slid slowly downward, revealing a very tiny room filled with ancient and dusty weaponry.

"Behold your past! These are leftovers from your ancestor's war they fought over a millennium ago." Holding up an electronic rifle that none of them had ever seen before, Grëyfwyn switched it on and it began to charge; little lights blinked all over it displaying its functions. He then offered it to Yor. "There are only a few—maybe a dozen or so—take them, and put them to good use!"

Smiling slyly, Yor snorted like laughter and quickly turned them on as he handed them one by one to the other hogtrahs. "Human *goooooooood!*—*snort.* We *know* this weapon!—*snort.* We *remember* this!—*snort!*"

Slapping Grëyfwyn mightily on the back, Yor quickly ran up the stairs with a gun in his hand. He intended to be the first to use it to defeat the enemy and claim all the glory for himself.

"I'm not sure how long these ancient plasma rifles will work, but they should get us through this. Now we have a real fighting chance!" Grëyfwyn yelled up the stairs trying to encourage Yor and the other hogtrahs. He knew in his heart that their chances of success were minimal, but with the firepower they now had, he also knew the hogtrahs would find a way to win.

Tiny multicolored lights flashed on and off and a subtle whirring sound slowly escalated in frequency as the weapons continued to charge themselves. It was an incredible testament to man's past knowledge that they still functioned after a millennium in storage. It took a few minutes, but the weapons managed to energize completely as the hogtrahs quickly took a defensive position on the balcony.

As if in chorus, all of the hogtrahs snorted loudly, and a few squealed as they prepared to fire their freshly charged weapons. They relished being reunited with their past, a past their ancestors had always shared with them and they had never forgotten. Quickly, they took aim and opened fire on the nekelmuses.

Red fireballs unleashed by the nekelmuses and rapid-firing balls of argent-red plasma energy promptly filled the air. The plasma rifles easily pounded and pulverized the nekelmuses, deflating them and sending them crashing to the ground as the hogtrahs systematically coordinated their fire on the enemy. Fireballs fired back and hammered down on the dome of the tower causing it to fragmentize. Chunks of debris spattered and struck the hogtrahs as they worked feverishly to whittle the enemy away. One by one, the nekelmuses fell to the ground in piles of deflated, leathery ooze; one by one, the hogtrahs fell dead from the striking fireballs and were removed as another hogtrah quickly took his place to maintain the attack. The sound of plasma rifles firing and the whir of them self-recharging filled the air with the deafening sound of their forefather's ancient high-tech weaponry.

Then, just as suddenly as the fight began, it ended. The last nekelmuse fell to the ground and the hogtrahs cheered themselves in victory, but there were many casualties. Fewer than half of the original allied army remained.

"Weapons *very* good! Weapons *gooood!*" screamed the hogtrahs in triumph. "*We* win the battle!" With a chorus of unending snorting, it was obvious to everyone that the hogtrahs were in complete ecstasy as they embraced both their past and their designed intent. War was what they were created for, and they reveled in the fever of battle and their small victory.

Suddenly, a flood of fracknoids poured over the edge of the balcony; the hogtrahs had forgotten them as they celebrated their initial success. Within a trice, every hogtrah on the balcony, including Yor, had a blanket of fracknoids covering them, and they struggled hopelessly to survive in the confined space. Soon all of them were dead.

Bolting the heavy wooden door leading to the balcony, the fleeing hogtrahs regrouped and held the entrance closed. It was ultimately futile, as they couldn't maintain the effort indefinitely, but it was all that stood between them, and extinction. Now that Yor was dead, the remaining hogtrahs looked to Grëyfwyn for leadership.

"What we do now, *human?—snort.*" asked one of the hogtrahs. "You have more weapons?—*snort.*"

"There *is* another secret chamber below here that may contain more, I don't know for sure. Hold the door and we'll investigate!" Grëyfwyn yelled up the stairs trying to reassure the hogtrahs.

As quickly as he could, Grëyfwyn opened a sealed passageway that led downward to the lower levels. He wasn't sure what he'd find, because many years had passed since he'd been to the tower, but he knew the structure had another secret cache, and he knew approximately where to look. He had learned everything about the tower during his school years in the event of an enemy attack. He was solely responsible for this secret knowledge.

Followed by several humans, Grëyfwyn hurried down a second flight of stairs and passed by many rooms designed for extended living in the tower. The two towers combined could house a small army for just this predicament; they were as much a fortress as a device to generate and maintain the great seal over Upper Peruvious. Over time, the need to maintain a human presence at the towers became obsolete, and they had remained uninhabited for centuries.

It took time to locate the door to the secret cache, but finally, Grëyfwyn found it. He placed his hand against the wall and the door opened and slid slowly down to reveal a tiny room filled with explosive munitions. But the weapons would be either useless or decidedly fatal in their present dilemma due to the close quarters. The explosives needed to be launched at the enemy or it would be suicide.

"Seismic bombs, and a large plasma cannon. Both are completely useless in these close quarters. I think they were intended to be used on Lower Peruvious if needed." With a look of despair, Grëyfwyn's hopes dissipated. "All that is left is to blow ourselves up or be eaten alive! If we blow ourselves up, the great seal will be lost forever, but the enemy will be completely obliterated."

The other men looked back and forth at each other and then one of them spoke. "Let's take as many of those *things* with us as we can. What choice do we actually have?"

"You suggest suicide?" another man hollered. "We can't afford to lose any more human life! This only plays into the hands of the enemy!"

"We've little choice. We're dead either way, there is no escape. The worst of it is that there will be no way to restore the great seal! Our lives are already forfeit!" announced a third.

"Didn't you see? The Lords of Ruin captured Vim! Only he has the ability to restore the great seal; all our hopes went with him into the lower lands," said a fourth man.

Everyone stood there for a moment and looked at each other in silence. They all knew that every choice led to the same result. All choices were permanent no matter which they made. Only self-destruction could afford any form of victory.

After a moment, Grëyfwyn heaved a heavy sigh. "Do all of you concur? I believe all of our hopes are in the hands of our savior. We've little choice here but to take as many of the fracknoids with us as possible." Looking at the rest of the men, he waited for their response.

Reluctantly, each man nodded his head and accepted his fate; the hogtrahs all snorted without a word as they mulled over their extinction. A look of despair marked each face, both human and hogtrah. Quickly, they prepared the seismic bombs for detonation and pulled the plasma cannon out of storage. Wheeling it up the stairs, they placed it in front of the door held by the hogtrahs. Snorts and squeals filled the stairwell as they saw the mighty weapon, and then the humans enlightened them about the explosives.

Switching the plasma cannon on, they all waited for a few minutes as it gradually charged. The gnawing and scratching sounds became louder and louder as the fracknoids chewed their way through the massive wooden door. Only moments remained until they'd breach it.

"Prepare yourselves! We'll blast the door off of its hinges," ordered one of the humans. "The cannon is fully charged," yelled another man.

Looks of horror and dread marked every man's face. The hogtrahs fell completely silent; every snort ceased.

Then suddenly, just as the cannon fired, the door burst open. A steady stream of plasma energy blasted through the fracknoids, devouring them by the thousands. Vitriol smoke filled the limited space and soon black ooze poured over the hogtrahs and humans operating the cannon; within seconds, it had killed every creature there and a subsequent toxic goop covered the plasma cannon, melting its outer casing and rendering it inactive.

More fracknoids poured in through the opening and filled every aspect of the structure. They ate the humans and hogtrahs both alive and dead. When they finally reached the lower level, Grëyfwyn ordered the detonation of the explosives. "Ignite!" was all he said.

The resulting explosion was massive, and it took out a half-mile section of solid rock in all directions, annihilating every man, hogtrah and fracknoid. The entire edge of Upper Peruvious sloughed away and slid into the lower lands in a mighty avalanche of broken stone, dust and rubble leaving behind what appeared to be a rock quarry. As a consequence, the restoration of the great seal could never occur; neither of the Towers of Tor stood to generate the defense, and without them, it was impossible.

Minutes went by, and then suddenly the ground heaved and vibrated violently as the two tectonic plates of Upper and Lower Peruvious again adjusted their balance like a scale weighing good and evil. Upper Peruvious first slid up, and then it sank to a much lower level as Lower Peruvious rose to a new altitude. The resulting shift was only by a few hundred feet, but the difference was significant; it changed the level of oceanic fluids that had covered Lower Peruvious for the past few days following the previous shift Anton had caused. The tides had again turned, and now it was possible to travel down to and traverse across Lower Peruvious.

CHAPTER 5

Reluctant Acceptance

Deidra held Anton's hand and Tania sat upon his shoulder as they walked through the dazzling light of the portal; Beelif hurried along behind them grinning from ear to ear, as if he'd just consumed a bottle of his berrybrew. As they stepped out of the portal, they found themselves deep within the Castle of Amilius, just outside of the throne room. Unsurprisingly, several guards suddenly surrounded them with their weapons drawn.

"Halt! What business do you have entering the castle unannounced?" One of the guards pointed his sword at Anton and began to interrogate them as the other guards pulled their swords from their scabbards.

"We're sorry for our exit point, we had no control over the exact location that the portal would deliver us. Amilius expects my return." Anton offered his best response. He felt uncharacteristically diplomatic, something he was unaccustomed to.

"We bring good tidings from afar, and we offer aid for your predicament!" Bowing graciously, Beelif too offered his response. "We're in need of your support, and we're willing to offer ours in exchange. Anton has received a gift of transformation from Trepid, and he wishes to help in your time of need."

Looking back and forth at each other, the guards seemed confused. Anton's unusual appearance intimidated them. Tania also held their attention as she sat upon Anton's shoulder. Beelif gave them little cause for concern, but Deidra raised an air of contempt; obviously, they would have a difficult time explaining why they brought her to the castle when they knew she would be hated; it was a dangerous decision.

"Send for Lord Vinicus, he'll decide what to do with these *intruders!*" One of the guards directed another sending him on his way. "All of you will remain silent and motionless until he gets here. The slightest move will have dire consequences."

"We have no quarrel with you," Anton said, bowing in his formal Methonian way, yet keeping his eyes on the obvious leader. "As Beelif said, we're here to help you. Please put your weapons aside!"

"They don't like *you*, and especially they don't like Deidra," whispered Tania. "It would be best if you didn't say anything, for now, it could aggravate them to violence."

Suddenly, Tania flew into the air, and then circled around Anton's head sprinkling faerie dust all over him, the overall effect somehow enhanced his transformed qualities. Even Deidra seemed surprised at the subtle change; he seemed different somehow, as if he'd become an entity.

"I said remain silent and motionless; I *will* slay you if I must!" The guard hoped to intimidate them further, but he sounded apprehensive as he did so.

"With all due respect, you've little hope of restraining us should we choose to disobey you. Make it easy on *yourself*." Not entirely sure why he said it, Anton surprised even himself. "It would be much better if you'd lower your weapons; there's no need for them. We've come to help you, not fight you."

For a moment, the guards' tenacity seemed to flounder, and then they lowered their weapons just as Anton had requested. In some surprising way, he had an unprecedented capacity to influence them.

Continuing to smile, Beelif danced a little jig and kicked his heels together. Deidra seemed particularly surprised at the guards' withdrawal; she looked at them and then at Anton, and her mouth hung slightly open as if she wished to say something. For no particular reason, Tania zipped around the room, stopping to look at each of the artful items hanging on the walls, sitting on the tables, and constructed into the ceiling and floor; it seemed obvious she'd never seen any of it before, or perhaps she was looking for something in particular that was missing. Anton wasn't quite sure what to make of it.

It didn't take but a minute until Lord Vinicus appeared, and he wasn't smiling. "How'd you arrive so deep into the castle? We're under siege, and you're able to penetrate our best defenses! Tell me now how you did this!" Pointing a sword menacingly at Anton and bringing it close to his throat, he scowled at him as if he were guilty of a heinous crime. "You're required by law to enter here *only* with an escort. You must be enemy spies! Put them in the dungeon!"

"Forgive us. we traveled through Trepid's portal, and we had no control over our exit point. I had no idea we'd arrive so deep within the castle." Anton offered a gracious reply and stood firmly with a look of confidence. "As you should know, I was requested by King Amilius to return here once I'd completed my so-called *training*."

For a moment, Lord Vinicus seemed at a loss for words. Anton's general appearance intimidated him. He recalled Anton's former hair and eye color, and the difference in his attire, and his new persona disturbed him. His Methonian brethren had changed too as they joined the forces of Vile, and Vinicus was convinced Anton was lying. One peculiar difference was his skin color: it was lighter; it was no longer the healthy tan he had seen before. Anton looked almost as if he were filled with light. On the other hand, the Lords of Ruin all had dark brown skin after they became Vile's tools. This left Lord Vinicus feeling uneasy and he hesitated for a moment.

"I see there are some *obvious* changes, and that you've fulfilled Amilius's command, but this unusual alteration in you warrants scrutiny, I don't trust it! Most of all, your *companions* were *not* invited," he snarled. Pointing his sword at Deidra, Vinicus continued his lecture. "Collect your, well, that little *faerie*, and I'll summon the King! We don't want *her* fluttering about as she pleases. Next time, keep both of your pets on a leash!" Looking annoyed, he frowned at Deidra. "This one is most decidedly *not* welcome! We have *rules!* We have *laws!* You shouldn't have brought … *it* here! Just like you, she's an abomination! We don't allow *them* inside the castle." Gritting his teeth, he made his prejudice both clear and obvious, and he was ready to back it up with both authority and violence.

"I'm sorry if we violated your rules, but my *friends* are under *my* care; I'll take complete responsibility for them being here." Anton stood resolute and defended his position. "They will *not* be any trouble to you."

"And they shouldn't. I say again, the King *didn't* invite any of your so-called *friends.* They shouldn't be here! I'll have them *removed!*" With a tone of disgust, his eyes narrowed as he glanced at Beelif. "Vim was to bring you here. Him we trust, with *reservations.* Why is *that wizard* not here? Did you *kill* him? I wouldn't put it past you, your kind kills everyone!"

"He had other concerns at the Towers of Tor," Anton answered. "I'm here to help you with your current predicament. In the meantime, I presume you'll allow my friends to remain with me. As I said, they're under my safeguard." Standing his ground, Anton was firm in his response. "As you say, they are my friends, and Deidra, *in particular,* is under my protection. Trepid *requested* this of me." Anton asserted his defiance as delicately as he could. He wouldn't allow Lord Vinicus to separate them.

For a moment, the two men stood their ground and glared at each other; Lord Vinicus then spoke: "*That* is not allowed in the throne room, we'll find a *suitable* place for her to stay." Exerting his absolute authority, he continued to stare at Anton. He wasn't about to back down.

"She stays *unconditionally* with *me.*" Anton said. Obstinate, Anton continued to defy Vinicus. He wasn't going to allow him to exert his authority over him, and he remained inexpressive, defiant, and resolute.

Looking around at his guards, Vinicus's indisputable authoritative expression ordered them to raise their weapons. Without hesitation, they complied and pointed their swords directly at Anton and Deidra.

Unexpectedly, a burst of light emanated from the throne room and a familiar voice echoed off the walls: "Enter, young Anton, and be welcome. All of your friends are my guests. They are equally welcome!" It was the voice of Amilius.

Surprised, Vinicus looked back and forth angrily at his guards and briskly gestured for them to lower their weapons. "Follow me!" he commanded angrily. "This isn't over yet!"

Leading the way, Vinicus escorted them to the throne room and offered Anton a place to kneel. Deidra held his arm with both hands as they proceeded. Beelif grinned from ear to ear and happily followed, skipping as he went as if nothing was amiss. Tania landed on Anton's shoulder and stood there as if mounted like an ornament.

Amilius stood in front of his throne with his hands on his hips looking like a Greek god. "You'll provide our guests—*all* of our guests—every comfort *my* castle has to proffer." Looking directly at Vinicus, he seemed displeased with his attitudes and actions. "Please, young Anton, Vinicus is a good man, even if he takes his job too seriously at the moment."

Thundaruss stood to one side and behind Amilius; he appeared staunch as if he were a statue. As Anton and Deidra knelt in front of the king, Thundaruss bowed stiffly to him, then fell to one knee, and lowered his head. "We honor thee," was all he said, but his inflection belied his words.

"You've seen greatness, and you've received even more—more than any mortal preceding you Your transformation is apparent for all to witness, and for this, I too *honor* you." Amilius then bowed graciously and fell to one knee mimicking Thundaruss, but his eyes never left Anton.

Ashamed, Vinicus quickly fell to one knee behind Anton's alliance and his guards abruptly knelt behind him. A feeling of uneasiness marked his face, and anger filled his heart.

Standing, and then pointing directly at Vinicus, Amilius spoke: "There's no place for prejudice in my court. Vinicus, unless you can release your hate, you must step down as captain of the guard. This I proclaim unto you." Amilius was firm, his eyes demanded instant compliance.

"Forgive me, my lord; I'm ashamed. We'll prepare and offer all the hospitality of your realm to these ... *honored* guests." Instantly, he arose and marched out of the throne room with his guards in tow. "Prepare rooms and a meal!" he ordered as they abruptly left.

"These are unfortunate times," Amilius said. "My castle is besieged by the Necromancer's minions. My time here on Peruvious is limited, and the time of the great decision is upon us all. You *must* prove yourself, *here*, if you're to find acceptance. Even my direct orders aren't enough to persuade the prejudices of old; the memories of the past run deep in the hearts of every one of my subjects. For this, I am sorry, and I apologize for them. Please, all of you, arise! It would be beneficial if you can find in *your* heart forgiveness for Lord Vinicus; he's a good man, but misguided by the events of the past and he is greatly concerned about the siege."

Standing, Anton bowed in Methonian style and stood in ready stance, as was his way. "I'm honored to serve you. I *will* defeat the enemy, and hopefully free your realm of evil."

"Free my *realm* of evil? You set your sights low! It is the choice, the reason for *humanity*, to free the *universe* from darkness! My realm indeed! This is but a triviality, a cog in the wheel. Set your goals higher; they fall short at merely this *realm*!" Amilius sounded surprised, as if he'd expected more from Anton.

For a moment, the king hesitated, and then he spoke again. "You were in the presence of *The Eye of One!* Your transformation is evidence enough. You received the education I requested—did you not learn from it? Indeed, you must free my realm, but it is *humanity* where you must set your sights; humanity requires liberation and salvation to carry forward the purpose of One!" Repeating himself, Amilius emphasized his point. "It is up to you to decide if existence will continue! That moment—that time of that choice—draws ever closer."

"A Warrior must achieve each step as a separate goal in order to accomplish the final objective." Standing resolute, Anton offered no emotion as he spoke; he simply recited his Methonian litany handed down by his Masters.

"Undeniable. Very well, your opportunity is upon you; stand prepared. This is our final meeting until after the choice is made. If you're successful at freeing the castle from the siege, I'll provide passage to your next objective. You've but to stand firm and proclaim your destination, and it will be granted. Now, I *must* return to the dimension from which I emanate, but before I go, I'll offer my utmost warning: if you fail, if you stray from your present course and intent, all is lost. Remain steadfast in your resolve or you will serve the enemy, either knowingly or unwittingly."

Instantly, Amilius disappeared. Thundaruss quickly stood and greeted Anton with apprehension. "I heed the words of my Lord Amilius. He is all wise, but there's nobody here who accepts you, or will succor your needs." Indignantly, he turned around and walked away.

Heaving a heavy sigh, Anton looked around at his friends, and then, for no apparent reason, his attention suddenly fell to the mosaic on the floor. He'd scrutinized it the last time he was here, but he didn't have enough time to determine the magnitude of its meaning. The depiction of the sword looked identical to his new hybrid sword; it was as if someone had seen it after its transformation, however, since that had occurred little more than a day ago, obviously, it was impossible. Yet, the ring was entirely obvious; it was absolutely his by shape, style, and color—but the shield left him at a loss. The most mysterious aspect of it was the symbol of the dragon and tiger that marked it: they were identical to the ones that his Masters had burned into his arms at his graduation.

Beelif stood next to Anton and smiled. "It's yours! Somewhere this shield awaits you! We must find it!" Reaching into his jacket pocket, he searched for a moment and then pulled out a tiny vial. "Maybe *this* will help!"

"What do you propose I do with that?" asked Anton. "I mean, how can *that* help me find a shield? Isn't it rather presumptuous of you to assume there's a shield here at all? And what would happen if I would simply take it, proclaiming it mine?"

Handing the vial to Anton, Beelif smiled and urged him on. "Go ahead, taste it, you only need a single drop!"

"Go ahead and try! You will find *yourself* in the process! I can tell!" Tania giggled, flew into the air, and then circled around the others laughing outright.

Watching Anton, Deidra puzzled over the tiny vial. "What is that-rrrr? Do you *drink* it-rrrr? I wouldn't, rowwerrrr. It is anotherrrrr smelly waterrrrr!"

"Go ahead! It doesn't taste like berrybrew, but then *I* didn't make it!" Smiling, Beelif urged Anton on. "I have used it before. It works! If you need to find something, anything, it leads you to it. We call this Spotter Drops! You can 'spot' anything!"

Watching Tania, Anton wondered what she meant. "I'll find myself? What are you trying to tell me, Tania?" With his hands on his hips, he insisted she enlighten him.

"Silly man, that shield is *you*! Can't you guess the meaning? It has your symbols boldly displayed upon it!" Tania stood in midair over the shield and pointed at the dragon and tiger. "See? *You* are the shield! It's *symbolism*. You're *so* silly!"

A sudden realization flashed into Anton's thoughts. Tania was correct. He wondered why it hadn't occurred to him. "Well, umm, thank you, Tania. Now I *know* I must provide protection for the people here; I'm to be their shield before the enemy."

Storming into the throne room, Lord Vinicus glared at the companions. "Just what are you up to? No good I'm sure! And just what is *that* in your hand there, one of that little creature's evil liquids? Give it to me! I'll dispose of it forthwith!"

"No! You will *not* command my actions!" Anton stood his ground and carefully stowed away the vial in his tunic. "You've no business demanding *anything* from us that doesn't belong to you. I'm here to help, and you choose to steal from me! For *shame*!"

Lord Vinicus ground his teeth together trying to contain his anger, and then he pointed at Anton. "I tolerate your arrogance only because Amilius has ordered our hospitality. But I say this: you'll refrain from using any of *his* liquids; all of them are *evil*." Vinicus stabbed an accusing finger toward Beelif as he delivered his ultimatum.

"Very well, I've no intention of doing so." Bowing slightly, Anton tried to alleviate the tension between them. "If you please, I'd like to assess the siege upon this castle; I believe I can negate it."

Stupefied, Lord Vinicus raised both eyebrows and his mouth tried to form a sentence. Nearly spitting, he stammered, "*I am* in charge of the castle's defense! Just who do *you* think *you* are? Your cohorts are sub-humans and faeries! In addition, you're of the same *blood* as those that hold us prisoner here! How could I *possibly* trust *you*? I should *banish* you! The only reason I don't is that you'd simply join *them* if I let you go! Or perhaps, you already *have?* You should be held prisoner deep within our dungeon!"

Taken aback, Anton realized that some of the Lords of Ruin, his Methonian brothers, must be outside. "How is it that you prevent the enemy from entering the castle? I hear no battle. Shouldn't there be a war in progress?"

"What?" Again, Lord Vinicus was confounded. "How do you *know* we're able to keep them out? Do you believe we have no defense? What do you already *know* that you aren't *saying*?" Overcome with suspicion, he shook his head in disbelief. "I think you're *already* working for them! Perhaps you'll tell *me* what *you* know!" Instantly, he placed his hand on the hilt of his sword as if he were about to draw it forth from its scabbard.

Tania quickly landed on Anton's shoulder. "He wants to kill you here and now! she whispered. Be careful what you say!"

Deidra stood behind Anton trying to hide; she tucked her arms together with her hands clasped below her chin attempting to become narrower and conceal herself as best she could behind him. "Rowwerrrr, you angerrrr him; please stop-rrrr!"

Reaching around behind himself, Anton patted Deidra on her hip. "Don't worry. I'm sure he won't do anything. He knows it'd be foolish." Guardedly, he attempted to reassure her. "There's no danger to you or anyone here, just Vinicus—if he should choose poorly."

Ignoring Anton, Vinicus continued his tirade. "It's obvious to *everyone* here that you consort with the enemy; you make friends with every *pig-human* you encounter! And, it's *my* belief that you've slept with that … *thing*." Pointing at Deidra, he hoped to provoke Anton; he desired to fight him and didn't care about the orders of hospitality Amilius had extended, even if he was jeopardizing his position.

"I know nothing of your current predicament, but I *do* know how to win a battle; it's my life's purpose, my designed intent, to *win* them." As politely as possible, Anton tried to avoid any further arguments with Vinicus. He didn't want the tension to escalate any further than it already had. "I'm at *your* service, command me, and I'll gladly serve you."

"Serve *me*? I don't require *your* service!" Vinicus nearly spat as he responded. His hand twitched on the hilt of his sword, the other hand on the scabbard, and with great effort, he restrained his yearning to draw it forth.

"If I could defeat your enemy, and release this castle from this siege that you are under, would you accept me and my friends?" Making an offer, Anton hoped to prove himself to Vinicus. "I offer my service, what have you to lose?"

"I don't accept *help* from a *pig-human!* It's your kind that I *fight!*" This time Vinicus did draw his sword and pointed it menacingly at Anton. "If you can defeat *me*, only then will I accept your offer. Go ahead! Draw that cute little sword of yours! It doesn't look like much! I don't even see a blade!"

"I have no quarrel with you. Besides, you wouldn't stand a chance." Spreading his arms wide and closing his eyes, Anton bowed, offering his head. "I'm yours. Kill me if you wish."

A sudden gasp filled the air as Beelif, Deidra, and Tania all stood there in shock. Vinicus too couldn't believe what he witnessed.

"You must not! Anton, you must not! Tania flew in front of his face and scolded him for his actions. "You're the *savior!*"

Suddenly, Deidra shed a tear; her feelings for Anton were evident to everyone in the room. "Rowwerrrr, I can't lose you, I *need* you-rrrr," she said before realizing her confession. "You're a good man-rrrr." Trying to recover, she put her hand over her mouth.

"My friend, this gains nothing; it plays into the hands of the Evil One! Refrain!" Beelif too scolded Anton and stood there aghast. His eternal smile had disappeared from his face.

Tossing his sword from one hand to the other, Vinicus looked at all of them. Suddenly, he slid his sword back into its scabbard, gritted his teeth, and then huffed angrily. "Very well, I accept your offer. Defeat the Lords of Ruin, *and* their army of creatures without the loss of one human life inside the castle, and I'll offer you every scrap of aid we can give you. If you fail, if just one human dies, you'll again offer me your head! Then, I *will* take it as a trophy! There's a very tall post outside I want to place it on. We'd all *love* to see it there!"

Standing upright, Anton smiled. "Show me your defenses. Take me to your enemy; there's work to do."

Smiling and nodding, Vinicus's eyes narrowed. "Heh heh heh, follow me! It's *impossible* for you to win. It'd be expedient if you'd simply offer me your head again! This time I would take it!" Quickly, he motioned for them to follow him from the throne room toward the outer hall. "Come."

Undaunted, Anton ignored Vinicus. "My friends will remain here; Tania and I will go with you." Falling in step behind Vinicus, Anton added his revision to the deal. "My friends are not to be harmed, or I'll have *your* head as *my* trophy."

Stopping suddenly, Vinicus turned around. "I wouldn't *dream* of throwing away an opportunity to watch them executed, *after* you've failed. I'd make you watch if possible. Don't worry, we'll take proper care of them. We'll provide every comfort they desire. After you're defeated by those creatures, they'll be mine to do with as I choose." Gesturing to his guards, he made sure they immediately carried out his will.

Beelif and Deidra followed the guards to an unknown destination within the castle, and Anton and Tania followed Lord Vinicus. It was only a matter of minutes before they could see the outer ramparts.

"As you see, we have a protective shield that is equal to the great shield that *once upon a time* protected Upper Peruvious, the one *you* destroyed! We wouldn't be in this *predicament* if it weren't for *you* and your *meddling!*" Pointing at the turrets and over their heads, Vinicus indicated a crystal in each one and a glistening sphere of energy that looked like electrified glass being generated by them. Shimmering and almost seeming to vibrate, the dome covered the entire castle, ending at the ground beyond the outer moat.

To Anton's enhanced Methonian eyes the shield was obvious to see, but he realized it would be nearly impossible for most humans to notice. Anton then looked more closely at the turrets. In the center of each one was a large crystal octahedron, easily Anton's height, that glowed brilliantly like a beacon. A beam of argent light shot directly up and sideways from each of its points, casting rays of energy from one crystal to the next, and creating the sphere of translucent energy that materialized all-inclusively over the castle. It appeared impenetrable.

Outside of the protective sphere to either side of the drawbridge, two of the Lords of Ruin stood in midair. With arms folded over their chests, they seemed to be waiting patiently, as if they anticipated something monumental. It seemed to Anton that they awaited his arrival.

Looking closer, Anton could see their eyes glowed blue, just as Lord Agonia's had when he'd battled him. Scrutinizing what little he could see through the outer gate, he perceived a sea of fracknoids just at the edge of the protective sphere, and dozens of other creatures that he didn't recognize both floating in the air and standing taller than a human amongst the fracknoid sea.

"Are there any hidden creatures that I can't see?" asked Anton. "What other enemies are present?" He looked at Vinicus, hoping to gain some information so he could calculate a battle plan.

"There are others. Why don't you go see for yourself! Remember, you must defeat *everything*, every creature, or offer me your head!" Vinicus smiled smugly as he answered Anton's question. "Just let me know when you're ready to bow before me. I wish to get this over with."

With an expressionless look, Anton stared at Vinicus. "So be it. Open the gate, and provide a way for me to exit beyond the protective barrier."

With relish, Vinicus laughed. "The gate will be opened for you. The protective barrier functions to keep these creatures out, it allows anyone to pass through it from the inside unhindered. Once outside, you can't return."

"Very well, I'll be unhindered." Quickly, Anton walked the final distance toward the outer gate. He had no idea what he would find beyond the outer ramparts, but he didn't hesitate to discover what awaited him. "Hang on, Tania, it's time for battle!"

"You must *not*! There are too many of them, you can't win!" Tears rolled off her tiny cheeks as she scolded Anton. "You're our only hope! This is suicide!"

"I *must* do this, I have *no* choice." Determined, Anton approached the gate and the guards opened it just enough for him to slide through, and then they quickly closed it behind him. He was outside, and only the moat stood between him and the magical barrier of the protective dome. Beyond that stood the vast sea of the enemy that stretched as far as he could see and beyond.

Looking over his head and around the ramparts, Anton could see hundreds of archers, both men and women, lining the walls, ready for battle. Many other weapons lay at their disposal, and he was confident they could withstand an initial assault, but their inevitable defeat was indisputable. Without question, the castle didn't stand a chance against the vast sea of fracknoids; there were easily a million of them, or perhaps two million, or three million; the numbers were beyond count, the ground literally crawled with them like sand on a beach in all directions.

As Anton looked out toward the drawbridge, he could see where the edge of the protective sphere ended just past the moat. The little creatures lined the edge perfectly, making its perimeter unmistakable. Looking beyond the spheres boundary, he could easily see the other creatures. In the air floated more than a hundred spherically shaped beasts with one large eye and one large mouth below it; he didn't know what they were but it was obvious if the protective sphere fell they would provide some sort of an aerial assault. Lastly, standing sporadically amidst the sea of fracknoids were giant creatures, nearly twice-human size, with bull-like heads, human-like bodies, and the rear legs of an ox. They were muscular beyond imagination and held no weapons, and it was unclear as to what they offered as a form of attack other than immense strength. Anton recalled the description of a minotaur in ancient Greek and Roman mythology. It seemed they measured up to that description with only slight differences.

The two Lords of Ruin stood motionless in midair at the end of the drawbridge, apparently waiting for Anton to cross. As they watched him approach, they turned toward each other, and it seemed they were holding a silent mental conference.

"You're correct, Tania. There are too many. I'm not sure what I can do to battle them and win." For a moment, Anton hesitated. Taking a deep breath, he let it out in a huff. "I can only hope my transformation offers me more abilities than I'm aware of. It appears hopeless. I don't want to just walk out there and die."

"Oh! I can see there are *many* differences, many *changes* about you. That's what faeries know best—how to recognize changes—but in your case, I can't determine the extent of your capabilities. I'm sorry." Offering little, Tania seemed displeased, if only for her own limitations. She no longer smiled, but her tears had ceased, as if she'd accepted Anton's decision to confront the enemy and was there to support him any way she could.

Then suddenly, a groaning sound of tectonic plates sliding against each other permeated the atmosphere. The ground shook violently and quickly pushed up under Anton just as it had done after he'd slayed the Dragon Master. A moment later, it receded and began to drop away from him. He felt weightless for a short time. A minute passed and then the ground came to a rest.

"Oh no! More life is lost! The scales have tipped again!" Tania shouted in Anton's ear. Fear marked her tone. "I feel as though our friends have failed!"

"Are you sure? Are Vim, Grëyfwyn, and all of the hogtrahs … *dead?*" Anton felt a sudden fear in his heart as he thought about his friends. Anger suddenly welled up in him, and he gritted his teeth and clenched his fists. He'd lost the entire village of Tooloo because of a poor decision, and now he faced losing a small army of friends to an unknown enemy. It was more than he could endure.

"I don't know precisely who, but there are *many* dead now! The balance of the Peruvian scales only adjusts after a monumental change in the life force of Peruvious!" Tania answered as best she could. She had no ability to see such things, but she could sense empathically the deaths of their friends.

With instantaneous reflexes, Anton grasped his sword from its sheath. Golden fire and a double-edged blade of steel burst forth from the hilt, lighting the area around him like a beacon in his hands. In response, his ring also burst into action. Golden fire enveloped his wrist and then spread until it covered his entire body. To everyone's perspective around him, he glowed as if he were made of pure energy, and as he held his sword high above his head, it accentuated the effect.

Tania stood motionless on Anton's shoulder seemingly unaffected by the energy. In fact, she seemed as though it empowered her as well. Breathing in the magical fire, her eyes turned pure gold, exactly the same color as Anton's following his transformation, and then her hair adjusted its color tone to precisely match Anton's pure metallic golden hue.

"I'm full of energy! I feel as if I'm impervious to anything!" Tania's little voice sounded amplified as if spoken through a small megaphone, and it blasted her words clearly for all to hear. "I feel your pureness of heart, your thoughts, your emotions, and your strength of will. You're … *indomitable*. Your training and abilities astound me."

Confidence welled up in Anton's persona; he knew unequivocally that he was ready to take on anything the enemy offered. Again, he looked fearlessly into the sea of fracknoids. Slashing his sword downward, he cast a conflagration of energy toward the end of the drawbridge. It flew at an incredible speed as if fired out of a cannon, and it escaped unhindered through the protective sphere and struck one of the minotaurs. Instantly, the giant creature exploded into a rain of hamburger that scattered over the sea of fracknoids. Immediately, they hungrily devoured the remains, and all evidence disappeared within seconds, as if the creature had never existed, save for a few bones.

Shocked and outraged, all of the nearby minotaurs screamed a mighty roar. Several slammed their hands together and opened them slowly. Blue fire erupted between their hands and in one palm, they raised a fireball of energy over their heads and then threw it directly at Anton, as if pitching a stone. The fireballs struck the protective barrier in front of the drawbridge, but caused no apparent damage. Obviously, the protective sphere was impervious to this form of attack.

"Anton, I feel abilities in you that you're unaware of! You can stand in midair just as your brethren do." Unable to whisper, her voice uncontrollably magnified, Tania continued to offer her wisdom. "Concentrate on where you would like stand, and you will levitate to that position."

Looking toward the two lords levitating outside the drawbridge, Anton wished to be at eye level with them. As if enveloped in Vim's golden sphere, he levitated into the air, and he too stood as they did. Golden fire, argent at the core, completely enveloped them, and they appeared as though they were a tiny star that slowly rose toward the heavens.

"Thanks, Tania, your guidance is invaluable. I would never have guessed." Anton's voice also sounded amplified, and he broadcast his words for all to hear.

The two lords unfolded their arms and stood in ready stance as if preparing to fight hand-to-hand like the Methonians they were. Ostensibly, as if of one mind, they looked at each other face to face, and it appeared to Anton as though they communicated, yet they didn't speak. After a moment, they returned their attention to their Methonian brother.

"We are the *Lords of Ruin!* You will submit to our directive and leave the protective dome. It's hopeless for you to delay the inevitable indefinitely, there are limited supplies contained within the castle. Time will do our work for us if you should choose to remain where you are." Speaking perfectly in unison, the two lords offered their challenge. "You have no hope. Approach us and end your suffering; you will join the *Lord of Darkness* and humanity's despair will end swiftly and mercilessly."

Anger again welled up in Anton. Raising his sword over his head, he slashed it downward, and a conflagration of energy fired instantly toward the lord on his right. The energy struck him mightily and pushed him far off into the distance, but it didn't kill or harm him. Faster than the eye could follow, he repeated the attack and struck the second lord with another conflagration, pushing him far off into the distance. The attack seemed futile, but it gave Anton an opportunity to make another tactical decision before the lords could return or retaliate.

"I'll have to deal with them directly; that didn't accomplish anything." Speaking to Tania, Anton revealed his thoughts, broadcasting them for all to hear. "I believe they speak the inevitable, there's no other way. I must leave the protection of the dome."

"You must not! There's no return once you have left!" Tania's tiny voice echoed mightily, and everyone nearby knew her thoughts and her feelings. "Find another way!"

"We'll fight together! Fear not, I *will* succeed." Concentrating, Anton levitated forward and up. Within a heartbeat he passed through the protective barrier unimpeded and stood in midair just beyond its security.

Instantly, the attacks began: the nekelmuses opened their mouths and shot fireballs at Anton; minotaurs slammed their hands together and threw their blue energy at him. Hundreds of balls of conflagration flew through the air from both close up and far away, many struck him, many missed. Buffeted about, Anton and Tania were attacked mercilessly, however they remained unscathed by this initial assault. Then, just as suddenly, the fireballs ceased. It was obvious even to the minotaurs and nekelmuses that their best attacks had had no effect.

Standing in midair, Anton awaited the return of the Lords of Ruin. It was inevitable they'd be the ones to decide the battle. It didn't take long. They levitated back and stood a short distance from each other in front of him.

"Your powers are formidable. They'll serve the Lord of Darkness well. Submit—it's your only hope for survival." Lord Bane and Lord Defeat spoke in unison, offering a final ultimatum.

"I'll not become a puppet of evil. Remove your army, return to the lower lands, and I'll allow both you and all of your creatures to live—for now." Steadfast in his convictions, Anton expressed tolerance. "Nothing you can say or do will convince me to join evil; I stand on the side of righteousness and justice. Unlike you two puppets, I haven't forgotten my Methonian training."

"We will remove these few remaining humans from the upper regions. All of your other friends have failed. It's a simple matter. Stand aside." Lord Defeat spoke independently as he slowly pointed across the protected castle indicating the humans within.

"We've waited your arrival and held back our attack upon this compound. You *will* join in our cause, you will become one of us, and you will help us to defeat the humans as a gesture of your acceptance. We'll work as one," Lord Bane said, pointing directly at Anton. "We'll begin by adjusting your little pet. She will provide the agency to persuade you to see that complete darkness rules all."

Facing each other, the two lords locked eyes. A beam of blue energy connected their foreheads, and then a second and third beam fired from their two heads directly at Tania, creating a triangle of light shafts. The laser-like beams struck the golden energy surrounding Anton and Tania, and then it narrowed, intensified, and slowly began to penetrate as it inched its way toward the little faerie. Paralyzed with fear, she was unable to escape and barely managed to hide behind Anton's neck, where she buried herself in his hair.

"Help! Don't let them do this!" Tania screamed. "They'll *change* me! They'll make me *evil*! We will lose!"

Realizing he had only a second to react, Anton swung his sword at the two lords, but it fell woefully short; they were just out of reach. However, the sword's blade sliced neatly through the blue energy, extinguishing it instantly. Even the shared beam of energy between the two lords dissipated as if dispelled. For a second, they teetered as if dazed, and it gave Anton another opportunity. Taking a step forward, he swung again and thrust his fiery blade toward Lord Bane's chest, but it missed him; at the last instant, the evil lord parried the attack. The lords were Methonian, too, and thus had equal training in combat, which they proved without fail.

"There are two of us, and you're alone. You have no hope to defeat us in combat!" Lord Defeat attempted to dissuade Anton, and prepared himself for hand-to-hand combat. "We've trained endlessly with our improved capabilities, you have not. End your misguided loyalties and join us, this is your last chance. Serving the Lord of Darkness is your true destiny!"

"You're unable to count. There are two of *us* as well." Anton's anger increased and he swiftly raised his sword over his shoulder and prepared to strike. "I have more true friends than you could ever know, and my friend has trained with abilities you have yet to understand long before humans even existed!"

"So *be* it. You and your friends—all of your friends—will *die!*" Together, the Lords spoke in unison. Instantly, they whirled around and prepared to attack, one in front of Anton, the other behind.

Anton's emotions and anxieties continued to escalate and, as a result, the golden energy around him boiled and churned like never before. Tania gasped as if in pain as the power increased in magnitude, but Anton knew she was adapting to the sudden intensification, and somehow it seemed to feed her own powers. Beyond that, he could hear, no, he could *feel* her thoughts and *knew* she too was transforming and becoming more potent with magic.

I feel different, thought Tania. I feel cosmic energy filling me with power! Just like you, I feel ... invincible!

Locked together mind to mind, Anton and Tania silently shared their thoughts. Anton's golden energy escalated, and it permeated both of them with indomitable power. Then, unable to contain the magnitude of Anton's intensity and fire, Tania started to shine like a small star upon his shoulder. She glowed so brightly the night around them seemed to peel away and disappear as if it were day. Subsequently, Anton too started to shine like a star. Both of them radiated light so intense it was impossible to see them through the glow.

Masked by pure light, Anton could maneuver inside his aura of energy as if cloaked; the Lords of Ruin couldn't see his attack. Blinded, they both covered their eyes in an attempt to shield them, and they struggled to defend themselves adequately. Anton's energy was beyond any shielding their hands could provide, and retaliation seemed impossible.

A sensation of calmness filled Anton's heart and then, at the speed of light, he thrust his sword directly into Lord Defeat. It pierced him directly in the center of his chest, and he exploded; it was as if he'd never existed.

Drawing back for a second attack, Anton swung at Lord Bane, but he'd already begun his retreat; he too maneuvered at incredible speed. As if sucked into a black hole, it appeared as if his body turned black, spiraled, and collapsed inside of itself. He simply disappeared. Anton's swing plunged through air and struck nothing.

We must remove the army surrounding the castle. Anton's determination was insuperable. I'll burn the region with fire and kill all of the fracknoids! he thought to Tania.

You must control your emotions! Do not harm the earth! Tempering Anton's anger, Tania reminded him of the need to restrain. You must find a way to preserve Peruvious!

Fireballs again pounded Anton and Tania as they exchanged their thoughts. The nekelmuses' and the minotaurs' attacks struck them by the hundreds and buffeted them about, and it was all they could do to maintain a stable position.

Enough! I must end this! Anton's thoughts struck Tania like a wave, and she had no trouble hearing them. I'm through with these annoying little creatures!

Suddenly, as if time stood still, Anton streaked toward a nekelmuse and thrust his sword into its mouth; the creature immediately exploded, and gooey, leathery fragments rained upon the fracknoids below. One by one, he attacked the nekelmuses, and one by one they exploded, littering the ground below; at his inestimable speed, it took him only a scant few minutes to defeat them all. As the last one fell, he stood in midair and looked at the vast ocean of furry black creatures below devouring the modest meal he'd provided them.

The minotaurs continued to attack, but Anton moved too quickly for them to strike him accurately with their fireballs and they quickly realized the futility of their efforts. After the last of the nekelmuses fell, they changed their tactics. Together, they concentrated their conflagrations at a single point on the protective sphere. Fireballs pounded it repeatedly in the same spot just in front of the drawbridge. Hundreds, then thousands of fireballs pulverized the same single point, and soon it took on a sustained aura of blue. Inexplicably, the minotaurs suddenly stopped, and then the fracknoids started to leap against the glowing blue discoloration.

Anton and Tania watched as the minotaurs and then the fracknoids attacked the protective sphere. However, neither of them expected anything to come of their attack, and they used the time to formulate a new assault. But their confidence was misguided. Just as the last fireball was thrown and the fracknoids began to pile against the pulverized surface, it was evident they'd somehow succeeded at weakening the defense.

The fracknoids gnawed at the damaged sphere. They annihilated themselves at first, but soon a puddle of sticky, black vitriol pooled against the destabilized surface. Black vitriol, surrounded by the caesious colored light of the minotaurs' attack, burned a smoking hole in the sphere. Immediately, the fracknoids poured through the breach by the hundreds, and as they did so, the hole grew steadily larger as the vitriol continued to melt the weakened energy of the sphere.

Alarmed and horrified, Anton shot like lightning toward the structural weakness. Standing over the entry point, he carefully lowered himself into the mass of fracknoids hoping to stop their advance. When his indomitable energy touched the tiny creatures, they combusted spontaneously. By the thousands, they attempted to pile against him and cover him, but it was futile. Any contact with his golden aura met with instantaneous vaporization.

You must seal the hole! They're entering behind us! Tania warned Anton and drew his attention away from the approaching mass of the enemy. The drawbridge is raised, but the Fracknoids are crossing the moat; there are thousands of them inside!

From the castle's ramparts, a sudden volley of burning arrows shot into the air and landed neatly and precisely in the moat; hundreds of fracknoids caught fire, but thousands more continued to cross. A second volley followed the first, and then a third, and soon a wall of black, acrid smoke billowed into the air.

How do I seal this damage? I don't know what to do! Anton pleaded for help. His knowledge of magic was still limited, and he struggled to determine its usage.

"Place your hands on the sphere and think about strengthening it!" Tania's voice echoed, amplified by Anton's magic. I will guide you! she thought. She too was learning to communicate with him by thought.

Locking her brain waves to his, Tania closed her eyes and concentrated, and images formed in Anton's mind. Placing his hands against the sphere, Anton visualized it intact, just as it was before the assault. Soon it began to strengthen and heal as his golden energy flowed into the energy dome, and then finally it re-formed. Moments passed, and then it sealed like new.

Turning around, Anton looked out at the minotaurs. They'd watched him work his magic and again they changed their tactics. Looking to each side, he could see they'd pulverized the sphere in several new places with their fireballs and were beginning to breach it again. It was impossible to repair the dome in multiple locations quickly enough to prevent the fracknoids from entering.

"I can't stop them from turning the dome into Swiss cheese! The fracknoids will enter on several fronts!" Screaming his outrage, Anton knew he needed to act quickly. "I must kill *all* of the minotaurs!"

Just as he had done with the nekelmuses, Anton flew like lightning toward the nearest minotaur; at the speed of light, he thrust his burning sword into the creature's chest, and it exploded instantly. One by one, he battled them, and one by one, they exploded—but it took time. Faster and faster, he fought them fanatically, and soon they were all dead, but they'd breached the sphere in too many places, allowing the fracknoids to enter in even greater numbers.

Concentrating, Anton controlled his anger; imagining himself as a sun, his energy boiled and churned with brutal intensity, and it started to expand around him.

Groaning from the escalation of energy, Tania squinted, clenched her teeth together, and held on tightly to Anton's neck. "Careful, don't harm the earth," she strained between her teeth, and her tiny voice, amplified as it was, echoed across the vast open range as if they stood inside a hollow chamber.

Pointing his sword directly in front of him, Anton shot a stream of energy like a flame-thrower into the sea of crawling fracknoids. They instantly caught fire and burned by the tens of thousands all around him. Running as fast as he could go, he sliced back and forth at incredible speed, melting swaths of the little creatures as he went. As he approached each of the breaches in the sphere, he stopped and healed them just as he'd done with the first. He was able to perform the repairs much faster now that he knew what he was doing and had practiced his technique.

I must finish exterminating the fracknoids! Too many have breached the defenses already! There must be tens of thousands inside now! Speaking his thoughts to Tania, Anton sealed the last of the holes in the sphere. I noticed something else. There are cracks covering the span between the damaged areas. This entire section of the dome is substantially weakened.

It was true. As if the sphere were made of glass, its surface appeared riddled with fractures between all of the holes he'd sealed, and he watched as fracknoids pushed against it in ever-greater numbers. As they made contact, the protective capabilities of the sphere annihilated them, creating a massive lake of vitriol all along the edge. Soon the liquid began to emit a heavy, toxic vapor. Smoke filled the air as the black, gooey substance burned and melted at the base of the dome, weakening it even further.

"They'll succeed at destroying it if I don't stop them!" Anton announced his alarm at the top of his voice. It echoed off the nearby mountains, and the ground vibrated beneath his feet.

Suddenly, his determination had increased ten-fold, and his golden fire amplified in magnitude proportionally; again he glowed like a small sun that expanded ever further around him. Concentrating, he imagined it reaching out into the sea of fracknoids, and it did. He concentrated even harder, and it expanded further. The little creatures boiled and melted by the tens of thousands, then by the hundreds of thousands, as Anton managed his ever-improving mastery of the magic he wielded. Then he started to run. Soon his fire covered more than a hundred yards of the creatures in all directions, and he ran and devoured the enemy with magic fire. After a couple of minutes, he'd succeeded in killing them all—millions of fracknoids were gone. An immense lake of vitriol marked the landscape staining the ground black with thick, tar-like goo; the vast acreage of farmland, the food supply of the people inside the castle, was gone forever. They'd never farm here again. The soil was permanently devastated.

Standing near the tree line of the forest where he and Vim had spent the night, Anton surveyed his work. He was displeased with the extent of the damage, but satisfied with his success. Still, he wasn't done; more fracknoids were inside the sphere and he needed to save the castle's people from them. Reducing his immense energy, he levitated into the air, and at an incredible speed flew back toward the castle. The protective sphere allowed him to pass through unimpeded due to his magical aura, surprising both he and Tania.

The humans are fighting the fracknoids! Some of them are dead! Both outraged and saddened, Tania made Anton painfully aware of his failure. *Vinicus will have your head!*

He can have it after I succeed at Celestra. Amilius has commanded I go there. Additionally, I must discover the fate of Vim, Grëyfwyn, and the hogtrahs. Finally, once Vile is defeated, I'll then freely forfeit my life, but not until I've accomplished that achievement. Undaunted, Anton dismissed her concerns. *All I care about right now is finishing this job and saving Deidra and Beelif from Vinicus's hate. I won't allow them to be murdered.*

Hovering over the outer rampart, Anton could see the fracknoids piling together and scaling the wall. They attempted entry at several locations, making it impossible to eliminate them in one fell swoop. He'd have to attack them in a series of aerial strikes and ground attacks—whatever it took.

The guards atop the ramparts fought feverishly as they tried to kill the little black creatures with torches. The men and women swung them like swords and had a modest amount of success, but the fracknoids outnumbered them a thousand-fold and were far more capable of killing. The situation appeared dire and hopeless, but they fought for their lives with fervent hysteria. Yet they failed to hold their ground against a much more formidable foe.

"I'll start with the breach near the main gate. That's where most of them have scaled the wall." Broadcasting his intent for all to hear, Anton sailed instantly there. *"Concentrate, Tania!"*

With their thoughts merged, Anton and Tania focused on their objective; the energy surrounding them increased in magnitude and enveloped the fracknoids. With Tania's support, they concentrated and controlled the energy with greater precision than before. Anton plucked the creatures in small groups or singly where needed. As the golden energy touched the fracknoids, it vaporized them, and this time he contained the vitriol soup they released long enough to dissolve the acidic goop into gas and then obliterate it, preventing its release into the atmosphere. One by one, pile by pile, Anton plucked, burned and destroyed the fracknoids. He feverishly struggled to save the lives of as many humans as possible, but still the fracknoids advanced; there were still thousands of them, and he couldn't just burn them away as he'd done outside the barrier without harming the people. It was too complex a problem, and it simply took more time.

Then suddenly, the fracknoids poured over the outer wall to the inner courtyard; they leapt out from the rampart and fell more than fifty yards to the ground uninjured. Hundreds of them vaulted like lemmings over a cliff, and ran straight toward the secondary inner moat.

It will take them time to cross the moat! Let's finish this job first. Continuing his efforts, Anton burned the fracknoids at an ever-increasing rate. "I must kill them *all* and *now!*" he yelled.

Golden fire turned argent and boiled around Anton. Slashing his sword, he cast huge conflagrations of energy toward the various concentrations of fracknoids upon the rampart walls. By the scores, they burned and melted. The humans ran from fear of both Anton and the fracknoids, and they took cover inside the turret housings just underneath the crystal octahedrons.

As more room atop the wall became available, Anton could safely cast his magic energy at the enemy below him. Again, he visualized his sword firing a stream of fire, and he slowly swept it across the wall burning every fracknoid he struck. Sweep after sweep, pile by pile, he burned and melted them and contained the vapors inside his fire, reburning it. Finally, the outer moat, the ramparts, the inner moat, and lastly the inner wall had no sign of fracknoids. It was over; he'd finally killed them all.

For a moment, there was silence, and then unexpectedly, a triumphant cheer filled the air as Anton and Tania levitated over the inner moat carefully surveying the defenses for stragglers. The humans ran down the stairs from turrets and fell to their knees to give their praise to the Methonian Warrior they'd despised only a short time before.

"All hail the mighty Warrior! All hail Anton!" they shouted. "Our savior is among us! All hail our savior!"

"I cannot accept your praise. My life is forfeit, according to my agreement with your Lord Vinicus." Anton's amplified voice echoed off the rampart walls, and it was impossible for anyone to miss hearing him. "I agreed to kill the entire army of the enemy and free you from the siege without the loss of one human life. In this, I have failed, and I'm truly sorry. Forgive me."

Bowing his head in shame, Anton landed lightly on the ground in front of the moat. Standing before the small army, he extinguished his magic fire and appeared more human-like than super-being, but his golden waist length hair, golden eyes, pure white clothing, perfect skin, and Tania sitting upon his shoulder gave him the appearance of an entity. Everyone kneeling before him fell silent in awe and confusion.

Suddenly, a voice from high atop the wall behind him boomed down into the crowd: "I cannot accept your sacrifice. I was, I was … *mistaken!* Forgive *me!*" Vinicus stood atop the inner wall beyond the moat in full sight of everyone. "I say to all of you here, you're all witnesses: I return to Anton his life. Furthermore, you're permitted to move about the castle unchallenged." Bowing his head, he then turned around shamefacedly and left his position upon the inner wall.

Unexpectedly, Thundaruss then took his place and stood upon the wall for everyone to witness just as Vinicus left. "I'm pleased to announce the will of Amilius, your king. It's with great pleasure I introduce you to our *friends.*" Motioning toward two figures, he pointed out their arrival.

Looking up at the wall, Anton watched as Thundaruss spoke. To his surprise, both Deidra and Beelif stood next to him; they smiled at the people below, and Deidra waved shyly in her feminine way at Anton.

"This is Deidra, the last katrah, and a friend of Amilius. She's Anton's consort, and we welcome her. Standing next to her, and many of you may already know him, this is Beelif, the leader of the primords. He too is a friend."

Abruptly, another cheer filled the air: "All hail Deidra and Beelif! All hail the king's friends!"

"From this day forward, there's to be no hate, no prejudice toward the katrahs, no prejudice against the primords, and most of all, we honor this Methonian Warrior, and the little faerie that saved all of us from certain demise. I introduce to you, Anton Seven and Tania!" Thundaruss motioned for everyone to stand. "Please, it is the decree of Amilius that they have free rein inside his castle and that we obey anything they might ask of us."

Then, just as unexpectedly, Thundaruss turned around and followed behind Vinicus. Deidra and Beelif continued to stand upon the wall looking down at Anton, Tania, and the crowd of humans.

It felt to Anton as if a new era had begun. The barriers between the different factions of the people inhabiting Peruvious were changing, and a new cooperation seemed possible. He felt as though humankind was worthy of salvation, and his determination to fulfill his commitment to save them strengthened. He was proud to be Methonian, and a humble servant of the people of Peruvious surrounding him.

Another round of cheers filled the air, and Anton grinned from ear to ear as if he'd just drank a fresh draft of berrybrew. Tania flew into the air and circled around his head and landed again on his shoulder. She smiled and giggled like only a tiny faerie could do.

Death and Devastation

THE EARLY MORNING SUN TINGED the eastern sky. Wisps of clouds swirled high in the atmosphere painting it with a smoky haze; red and yellow colors stretched as far as anyone could see. A sudden chill breeze brushed Anton's face, tossing his hair as he stood stoically regarding the people he'd saved from certain demise. He was satisfied with his accomplishment, finally a real win, not just an inadvertent kill or the removal of a tongue or pulling a small boy out of a pool of water. However, the realization that his friends may have failed fighting at the Towers of Tor tugged at his heart. Within a minute or two, Deidra and Beelif joined him in his moment of approbation by the people of the castle.

"You are-rrrr a good man-rrrr! Just-rrrr as I told you before-rrrr we left the city-rrrr!" Deidra also shared her appreciation; she'd had complete confidence in him since they had met, long before anyone else, including Vim. Somehow, instinctively, she could see in him what others missed entirely. She saw his heart.

"Well done, Anton! All of us believed in you, more so than you might think!" Grinning, Beelif bowed politely to him. "If only I had some *berrybrew* to share with everyone here, we'd *all* rejoice!" Nudging Anton with his elbow, he winked and smiled.

Suddenly, without warning, the ground shook violently, tossing people off their feet; anyone standing suddenly found themselves lying on the ground—that is, everyone but Anton. After a minute, the ground gave a heave and pushed up, rested for a moment, fell away for what seemed like an eternity, and then came to a rest; Peruvious had made yet another tectonic adjustment weighing out the balance of good and evil.

"Oh dear!" screamed Tania. "That was the biggest shift yet! You've destroyed a tremendous amount of evil!" She circled around Anton and watched the mayhem below her as the tectonic plates shifted, repositioned, and then finally realigned in a new balance again signifying his success.

Deidra lost her footing and Anton instinctively grabbed her, preventing her fall. Stumbling, she wrapped her arms around his chest and held on tightly. She looked deep into his eyes longingly, as if he'd embraced her out of love.

Adjusting his hold, Anton wrapped his arm around the katrah caringly, and then glanced at Tania and asked her a question.

"Are we in perfect balance, or is there still a difference in height between the upper and lower lands?" He held Deidra tight as if she needed protection as he spoke to the little faerie. "Can we cross easily into Lower Peruvious? Can the enemy enter the upper lands without effort?"

Putting her finger on her chin, Tania pondered Anton's questions. "I'm not sure … we'll have to go see! These things aren't easily revealed to me!"

"Then we'll go now! I must discover the fate of our friends, we need to know what other obstacles we face, and we must prevent any more beasts from entering the upper lands and attacking the castle. Who wants to join me?" Looking at his comrades, Anton posed the question to them. Calling out to the crowd, he addressed everyone present: "I will take anyone here who chooses to fight for the fate of humanity!" Looking into the faces around him, he waited for a response, but there was nothing but panic and trepidation in everyone's eyes.

A sudden gasp, followed by a mumble rolled through the masses, and then there was an abrupt silence. All eyes looked past Anton toward the bridge over the moat.

"*I* choose to come with you! *I* choose to support the survival of mankind." Thundaruss Rikin thumped his chest with his fist and then stood there stoically like a statue of a Greek god. He gripped the hilt of a large, two-handed long sword with the tip placed between his feet. "I will be the eyes of my Lord Amilius, witness all that is to unfold, and I will lend you my sword. However, if the enemy turns your loyalty to him, and it appears that you would join your brothers, I will fight you mercilessly until my last dying breath, and I will *destroy* you."

Surprised, grinning with satisfaction, and nodding his head in approval, Anton looked at the king's champion. "Very well, I *accept!* Your support is most welcome, and I assure you, I'm not so easily swayed to receive help from anyone." He was concerned with Thundaruss's conditional offer, but smiled and bowed in his Methonian way; he realized the significance of his proposal. "Is there anyone else?" Looking around, he proffered the question a final time, expecting the same results.

"I will never leave you, Anton. We are a team!" Standing in midair in front of him, Tania put her hands on her hips as if he'd forgotten about her. "I'll be with you until the end! And *don't* forget Deidra!"

"I too wish to be by yourrrr side-rrrr; I neverrrr want to leave you-rrrr." Deidra hugged Anton shyly; a tear ran down her cheek. "I want to help you-rrrr," she growled and purred in her feminine katrah way.

"I'd like to go as well, but my duties lie with my people, therefore, I bid you farewell!" Beelif grinned from ear to ear, bowed, looked at Tania as if to say good-bye, and then smiled at Deidra. "I'll miss all of you! Good luck!"

Reaching into his knapsack, Beelif pulled out several tiny vials and handed them to Anton. "These are potions of healing, they're potent, and they can heal the most severe wounds. Lorca gave them to me. Use them *wisely*."

Quickly Beelif moved several paces away from the others and then declared loudly: "I wish to be in my primord home!" Instantly, in a flash of brilliant light he disappeared.

"You must not leave yet, Anton." Thundaruss held up a hand forbidding the small fellowship to depart. "You must first rest, and you will need supplies. Please allow these people here to reward you for freeing them; they would be honored to help you in this way. Now, if all of you will follow me to the dining hall inside the castle, a lavish meal in your honor is being prepared as we speak!" Waving for them to follow, the king's champion endeavored to lead the way, but as he looked at Anton's expression he hesitated.

"We can't waste time. Our mission is to save the world," Anton said. "We will save our friends, well, if there is anyone left alive at the Towers of Tor. Our time grows short! I fear all will be lost!" Standing his ground, he resisted Thundaruss's proposal.

"None have survived, Anton, you will see." Tania floated in front of Anton, her eyes downcast; she sounded very solemn, very sober. It was something she hadn't done before. "Thundaruss is right; we need to prepare. We need to eat, sleep, and plan. You know this in your heart!" Supporting Thundaruss, the little faerie attempted to persuade Anton to accept.

Anton knew she was right, and he realized it deep inside his heart, yet he struggled with his desire to save his friends without hesitation; it was his Methonian servitude conditioning that persuaded his resolve. Departing the castle without a plan and facing an uncertain enemy could be fatal, a reality every Warrior faced, and most of all, he knew it might be a trap. Most of all, it was unlikely to change the fate of Peruvious if he did leave immediately. They did have a little time. "Very well, a meal and a brief rest, then. We will discuss our plan of action as we eat." Looking at Thundaruss, Anton conceded. "Your words are prudent, I therefore accept."

The companions followed Thundaruss past the ramparts into the castle formal. After a few short minutes, they arrived in the dining room. It was located behind the throne room, and as they entered Anton took in the magnificent architecture. Enormous arched columns of stone reached nearly one hundred feet above them and supported a glass roof; the far end of the chamber was made of stained glass depicting a garden paradise that Anton didn't recognize, and the floor of the chamber was completely covered by a mosaic of tiny square tiles depicting a lushly tailored garden path with tropical plants growing near the far end along the path. This reminded Anton of the garden dome of home in Mount Valde Domus. A long table, large enough to seat fifty people, sat in the center of the room.

"Please, seat yourselves wherever you wish, the food is on its way and should be here shortly." With great formality, Thundaruss proffered his hospitality, smiling at each guest in turn. He gestured for the companions to sit and then seated himself at the head of the table.

"We appreciate your cordiality; this meal is much more than required. Shall we get to business?" Anton got right to the point, completely ignoring any royal formalities or small talk. He had little use for any form of fanfare. "I believe we need to leave immediately following the meal. It is critical to get to the Towers *now*! It might save many lives, it might save all our lives, *even* the people here! We can't afford another army reaching Upper Peruvious." Looking at the king's champion, he implored his concurrency.

"We cannot fight on an empty stomach, and we need to be well rested, but most of all we need at least the barest framework of a plan. Please, eat!" Thundaruss insisted and pointed to a small army of waiters bringing a large meal of venison, many types of fruit, and a variety of vegetable dishes; they were obviously grown in the now-defiled gardens that had been the food supply for the community.

Anton looked at the small feast and nodded at Thundaruss. "As you say, we need sustenance." His stomach growled in response to the generous meal being set before them, and he looked to his companions urging them to proceed.

"Rowwerrrr, meat-rrrr, *venison*-rrrr!" Deidra responded with excitement. "Good food-rrrr." Her excitement was evident.

Looking at a strawberry, Tania flew over to it and picked it up. In her hands it was enormous, and she hefted it like it weighed well over fifty pounds, yet it wasn't any more than a large bite to Anton. "These are perfect berries! Have one!" Setting it on Anton's plate, Tania smiled shyly.

"That is very kind of you, Tania. Thank you." Anton smiled at the little faerie and looked from the corner of his eye at Thundaruss; he wanted to make sure he'd noticed the value of his friend, even if it was a trivial gesture.

Thundaruss did notice, and as he looked at Anton and then at Tania, his expression soured. He snorted, "Like a mother hen, or perhaps another girlfriend? You keep the most unusual friends, *Warrior*."

"Yes, and I value them as much as you value your friends, perhaps even more," replied Anton. "My friends genuinely like me, and I like them. How about yours? Do they like you?"

Irritated, Thundaruss responded: "I don't have to *like* you to understand your value to humanity and to the universe. I accept you. The Creator likes you and has sanctioned you; I, on the other hand, just have to help you so that you might save us all. This service is quite sufficient. Perhaps friendship will come later, after we have succeeded and have time to reflect upon that achievement." He looked directly at Anton and waited for a rebuttal, then continued. "Yes, I have good friends, friends I can trust, friends that would give their lives to save mine, and yes, we genuinely like each other." He then stared at Anton as if to say: "Enough about friends."

"Fair enough, we both have good friends, so try to understand how much I value mine. Now, about our plans. I want to see if anyone survived the battle at the Towers of Tor. Vim certainly *must* have, and I insist we offer him support as soon as possible. Our first duty is to make sure *he* survives; we need him, he bears the Staff of Balance, and he is also my friend."

"I agree with Anton-rrrr. Vim-rrrr needs us-rrrr," added Deidra. "We should go, *now*-rrrr!"

"Not until you have had a rest!" interjected Tania. "You have just fought a battle and used a great deal of magic, something that can drain you of energy! I can see in you the fatigue that you deny!"

She was right, and Anton knew it to be true, yet his loyalties tore at him. He was Methonian, and a Warrior, and he was obligated by this simple reality to offer his support to his friends and this prodigious cause. Conceding, he acknowledged Tania. "Yes, you are correct, both of you. I am tired. However, a few minutes of meditation and I will be as good as new!"

Unexpectedly, Lord Vinicus stepped into the room, bowed to Thundaruss, and seated himself opposite Anton. "I also offer my support. I have extensive knowledge of the region around the Towers, and I might be able to help." Slicing off a large piece of venison, he glared at Anton as he slid a large piece of meat into his mouth and began to chew it. It appeared as though he intended to make sure Anton's plans met with his approval.

Addressing Thundaruss directly, Anton attempted to elicit some information. "Unless you've spent time in the lower lands, you couldn't have any insight of what we'll find. Obviously, I haven't spent time there. Is there anything *you* can share?"

"I'm sorry, it's true, I haven't been to the lower lands as you say. Few have, since none return. You obviously realize that none of us here in the castle have. By now, even you should know that only *death* can be found there." Thundaruss emphatically answered Anton's inquiry and then added: "One point I do agree with you about, Warrior, is that the longer we delay, the less likely it is we can help your friends. And I do realize there is no way to know if we would be heading into a trap or if it is too late already to save anyone. There really is only one thing we can do." Looking at Anton, Thundaruss made sure he listened carefully. "We *must* go to Celestra, to the ancient city at the far end of Lower Peruvious. Only there will we be able to save the universe. We must find the KACATU."

"I concur!" added Vinicus. "You must forsake the towers and your friends in favor of a speedy outcome. It is our only hope for success!" A grin crossed his face as he supported Thundaruss; it was clear he would never support Anton unless he too agreed.

"I will never forsake anyone, even both of you!" Anton said. "If only to have a look below, and in the process to answer the question of survivors. I fear the enemy will take advantage of the situation and send another army over the tor now that the shield is destroyed. It would seem there is no defense of the castle if they send another army like the last and I am not here to help in its defense. You *know* that the castle's shield is insufficient against a vast army."

Lord Vinicus looked at Thundaruss, his mouth moving in anger, yet he couldn't utter a word. Suddenly he said: "This impudent child ignores both Drôgän's *and* Amilius's counsel; we *must* get to the KACATU *now!*"

Holding up a hand to Lord Vinicus as if to restrain him, Thundaruss stood and glared at Anton. "And just how do we travel through the wastelands of Lower Peruvious once Amilius has set us down at the tor? What protection do we have that would make the long journey possible? There is only one choice, Warrior: we must get to Celestra as quickly as we can! There is no other way! You have been offered instantaneous travel directly there! Only a fool would throw this unprecedented opportunity away!"

With confidence, Anton slowly stood to meet Thundaruss's eyes. "I will protect *all* of us," he smoothly replied. He then returned to his seat, giving Lord Vinicus a look of confidence. "I will find a way. I am a Warrior."

"Find a *way!* You, will find a *way?*" Thundaruss roared. "You are foolhardy! You are reckless! You are ignorant! I can't believe it possible you would ignore the advice of deities! Regardless of your vague explanation, *Warrior* or whatever, we don't have the time! The enemy moves even as we sit here arguing!"

"That is the very reason we should leave *immediately!*" replied Anton. "Now you should understand *my* point!" Taking a deep breath, he continued: "I will leave you behind if I must, if you don't agree to have a look over the lower lands *prior* to entering them. It is madness to simply appear inside the enemy's home without first knowing what traps you may encounter. It is crucial to have a better look at the battlefield *before* we enter into it. There is always a possibility that Celestra itself is a trap! And after so many changes of the balance between Upper and Lower Peruvious we have no idea what changes might lie in wait in the lower lands. We *must* have a look at them *first!*"

Taken aback, both Vinicus and Thundaruss hesitated. Looking at each other, there seemed to be something spoken silently between them, as if they hadn't considered the possibilities Anton proffered. What he had said was true, and they both knew it, yet they simply couldn't agree with him, regardless of his Methonian training and logic. They looked at each other for a couple moments, then Thundaruss sat down and returned his attention to Anton.

"Reluctantly, I agree. But only for now. If I think of *any* reason to dispute you, anything whatsoever, we will discuss this further. Now, if you're finished eating, let's get some rest for at least a few hours. Supplies will be brought to us prior to our departure."

"Then it's settled, we'll leave in the morning. I hope you understand I do appreciate the risk. It seems doubtful that any of us will return." Looking at Deidra, and then at Thundaruss, Anton made sure they absolutely understood both his commitment and concern.

Heaving a sigh, Thundaruss finished the last bite of food on his plate and looked at the three companions. "You will be shown your rooms. We will leave promptly at sunrise tomorrow. Use this day to prepare." Standing, he gestured to a nearby guard, waved for Lord Vinicus to follow him, and left the dining room abruptly.

Promptly, two guards motioned for the three companions to follow them. "Your rooms await. This way please," waved the first guard as he beckoned them to follow. "The rooms are small but comfortable."

"If it is no inconvenience, I would rather meditate at the end of the dining room by the stained glass; it reminds me of the gardens inside Valde Domus back on Methonias, and I would be comfortable there."

The two guards looked at each other and the second asked, "Is there anything you require during your meditation?"

"I need nothing. Just show Deidra her room." Anton looked at her as he spoke, wondering what she would choose.

"Rowwerrrr, I will stay with you-rrrr; a soft pillow-rrrr and perrrrhaps a blanket-rrrr is all I need-rrrr." Deidra looked at Anton as if to say: "I would never leave you."

The three companions moved toward the far end of the dining room and looked around. Within a moment, a cot, a light blanket and a pillow were brought to Deidra. "Thank you-rrrr," she responded, and then quickly lay down on it. It didn't take her long to fall asleep. After a few moments, she was purring like a very large housecat.

Meanwhile, Anton adopted the lotus position in the center of the stained glass facing the dining room table. Immediately he found his new place deep inside himself and began to feel the now familiar weightlessness, as his body floated two feet in the air.

"You are very unique, Anton Seven. I can see!" Tania floated back and forth, from one side of the Warrior and then quickly to the other side. "You can learn much this way." She spoke softly, not wanting to disturb him as he endeavored to master his unique skills.

Contemplating the enormous number of events he'd experienced since leaving The City of the Humans, Anton sifted through each moment again in his thoughts. His body floated over the floor, his mind seemingly in a trance to any outside observer, and several guards gathered at a short distance to see his peculiar Methonian ability. They wondered if he was genetically designed for this capability, or if it was an aspect of his magically enhanced body; either way they were stupefied by what they witnessed. After a few moments a small crowd gathered in the dining hall and they whispered quietly amongst themselves. After a time they left, leaving the three to their rest.

MANY HOURS PASSED, AND DAWN finally approached. Anton remained in his meditative trance. He'd maintained his meditation for hours as he floated; he never left his body, not wanting to risk any unforeseen circumstances. He wouldn't know where to go even if he did choose his new form of exploration. He contemplated very carefully the events following his arrival in Peruvious. He examined each nuance, each conversation, looking for more details than he'd grasped during the experience. He wanted to remember all details, no matter how small, so that he could pull from the knowledge if needed. He paid particular attention to those things said by Drôgän, the Queen, and Trepid. Vim also had many important things to share.

However, as the first rays of the sun tinged the eastern sky, Tania flew over to Anton's ear. "It's nearly time to go! You need to wake up! We can leave now!"

And just as she spoke, in walked Thundaruss; he wore his armor and weaponry, presenting himself every bit the knight he was. "Day breaks, the enemy awaits us," was all he said. Then he saw Anton floating in deep meditation. Awestruck, his words fell short. For a moment he didn't know what to make of the young Warrior, and his hand instinctively reached for the hilt of his sword.

Rolling over Deidra sat up and rubbed her eyes with one furry hand. "Rowwerrrr, gooood-rrrr rest-rrrr."

Slowly, Anton opened his eyes and returned his feet to the floor. Feeling refreshed beyond his expectations, he stood and faced the knight. "Good morning. I am ready," he responded, and then quickly offered a short but formal Methonian bow.

Nearly speechless, Thundaruss stood there for a moment more. "Shall we proceed? My sword is impatient! I might add that I still think you should change your mind. It would be more prudent to visit Celestra first, however, it is the will of Amilius that you be the one to make the choice."

As if summoned, several servants entered, placed some food on the table and quickly left the room. Everyone grabbed a handful and proceeded to eat the modest yet hearty breakfast of venison sausage fried in egg and potato, toast, apples and a large glass of water.

"Very well, and yes, it *is* my choice." Anton turned around and faced his companions. Quickly, he grasped an apple and a plate of the offered repast and consumed them as if he had no time to waste.

Deidra picked up a sausage and an apple and ate them greedily. She seemed particularly hungry, and it didn't take her long to eat a fair share. "Good sausage-rrrr," was all she said. She clasped Anton's left hand and waited.

Tania landed on Anton's shoulder and clenched his hair for support. "Good morning, Warrior! Time to leave! Remember, all is unknown except that all our friends have perished."

A moment later, another waiter brought ample supplies of food and water for the colleague's journey; Anton quickly placed all of it into his EHD with the supplies he'd gathered from the City of the

Humans prior to his departure from there. Thundaruss stood beside him, puzzled at seeing such a device.

After finishing his meal and loading the supplies, Anton quickly snatched his transformed flame sword from its scabbard and raised it into the air, igniting its golden fire. As it burst forth from the hilt he declared: "Deliver us to the Towers of Tor!"

Instantly, without a chance to reconsider, the four companions appeared atop an enormous pile of boulders and rubble. A strong prevailing wind blew, making their footing unstable on the uneven surface. Looking around, Anton surveyed the area for Vim, Grëyfwyn, and the others; his Methonian eyes searched for any form of life and any danger from the enemy—there was none.

"Strange, the Towers of Tor seemed to be missing. Everything is gone! It appears as if something horrendous has occurred," said Thundaruss.

Scrutinizing the surrounding area, Anton analyzed the huge cliff's edge that towered over them to the west. There was obvious damage from a recent catastrophic disaster. It appeared as though the entire side of the cliff had sloughed away, giving it the general appearance of a rock quarry. He then looked below them to the east toward Lower Peruvious. All he could see was a carpet of clouds that stretched forever, completely obscuring the lower lands. Very far off in the distance to the east stood one lone spire of a mountain: Vile's Spire.

"Where *are* we? Where are the two towers?" Anton directly questioned Thundaruss and then looked at Tania for an answer. He had no clear impression of what he was observing; there was only a ruined cliff wall and no obvious answers. He was completely unfamiliar with the territory and expected Thundaruss to inform him of all he needed to know.

"It would appear that this whole section of Upper Peruvious was destroyed. Only a massive explosion or a tremendous earthquake could have caused this much devastation." Thundaruss offered his educated assessment and then probed the rubble with the tip of his sword for more clues.

"He's right, the two towers are here below the rubble. I can sense them!" Flying unsteadily in the prevailing winds around Anton, Tania shared her knowledge. "We're standing in Lower Peruvious!"

The sudden revelation struck everyone like a sword piercing their flesh, and fear marked each face. It somehow now seemed obvious. The rubble appeared as though the edge of the cliff had met with an act of extreme violence. The rock and debris jutted haphazardly all around them, a clear indication of the recent disaster.

Shocked, Deidra suddenly hugged Anton and let out a roar. "Row-werrrr! We're-rrrr in danger-rrrr!" Terror marked her face and a shiver suddenly came over her. "There are-rrrr too many bad creature-rrrrs here! They'll eat us!"

"You wanted to be here, *katrah!* Accept your decision, accept your fate and settle down! We've no time for second thoughts and most of all, your fear!" Thundaruss scolded her, and shook his head with disgust. Looking at Anton, he addressed him too. "You shouldn't have brought your *pet*, you should've left her behind. It was unwise to allow *her* to come. Obviously, she won't live long, and she may even jeopardize *our* lives as we try to keep her safe. Don't expect *me* to protect her!"

Scowling, Anton retorted: "Mind yourself! *You* may not live long *either—especially* if you lose *my* support." Locking eyes, he watched Thundaruss's reaction. Extinguishing the blade of his sword, he wanted to demonstrate he didn't intend to fight him. He simply wanted to let him know who was in charge.

"Just for the record, I repeat, I won't waste my efforts trying to protect her. She's *yours* to protect." Thundaruss had no tolerance for the half-human katrahs, and he again made his prejudice clear. Continuing to poke around in the rubble, he seemed to be looking for something in particular. "I think your friends are buried here, see!" Pointing at what could only be a section of one of one of the towers, he drew everyone's attention to something buried below them. "We should give up on them and proceed to Celestra *now!*"

"Oh dear! The towers *are* here!" exclaimed Tania. Instantly, she flew down the enormous pile of rock and debris toward a section of the fractured remains. A sudden chill expression marked her face, and she abruptly gasped and covered her mouth. "Oh dear! Our friends *are* here! But we can't help them. They're all *dead!*"

"Rowwerrrr, we're-rrrr too late!" Deidra cried out as tears rolled down her cheek. "They're-rrrr gone! Tania knew it-rrrr! We need to go home!"

"Nonsense! We *need* to find any *survivors!* I can't believe Vim is among the dead." Disappointed with Deidra, Anton made sure she understood the enormity of their situation. "We're here to aid anyone who survived; set your feelings and fears aside for now, I need your reason and support, not your emotions." Awkwardly, he attempted to comfort her. He gave her a quick hug and then a stern look.

Returning his sword to its scabbard, Anton reached into his tunic and produced his EHD. He unfolded it and withdrew his old haori. Unfolding his Methonian garb, he offered it to Deidra and helped her put it on. "This will help keep you warm."

The haori was too large and hung loosely on her slender frame; it covered her just past her loincloth. "Thank you-rrrr, you're-rrrr very thoughtful-rrrr." The wind whipped her long hair around, and she continued to shiver in the brisk morning air even with the long jacket, but she pulled it snugly around her and it helped.

Dark, smoky clouds rested just below them in the rubble and ruins. They blanketed the lower lands with an obscure layer of dark cottony grey and looked more like an ocean than a layer of clouds. The sun rose in the east and lit the rubble. It couldn't penetrate the density of the clouds that stretched out below them, nor did it reflect off them, but it provided the light they needed to see with. It was intuitive they'd soon leave the sunlight behind when they descended into the dark and forbidding realm below: the domain of the Necromancer and his untold legions of mutated creatures.

"We can't stay here. Any thoughts as to which direction Celestra lies?" Looking at Thundaruss, Anton directed his question to the king's champion. "You should know approximately which direction we should travel."

Pointing to the east and north of Vile's Spire, Thundaruss gave Anton a look of antipathy. "It's impossible to travel there on foot, and it doesn't seem possible you could transport your pet and me inside that magic fire of yours. You should've requested we be delivered directly to Celestra as I advised—not here. We can't even see the terrain below. The smog layer is too dense! This *plan* of yours is a failure! Besides, I'm positive Vim wouldn't have gone down *there* by choice." Pointing down through the layer of clouds, he indicated the lower lands. "If you wish to find him, perhaps we should search around here. On the other hand, perhaps he's still in the upper lands returning to the castle. I don't think you *really* know *where* to look!"

"Can you *sense* anything, Tania? The staff maybe?" Ignoring Thundaruss's cynicism, Anton turned his attention to his faerie friend and asked for her guidance. "I trust *your* instincts," he said, completely dismissing Thundaruss.

"There's only *death* here, and I can't feel the presence of his staff. I definitely would if it was nearby, especially if Vim was, well, alive. The staff is *life* personified, it gives off a distinct signature I wouldn't miss." Smiling, she offered Anton the best advice he'd received since they'd arrived. Putting her fingers against her temples, she closed her eyes and concentrated harder. "Wait! There's a vibration below us to the southeast! It could be the staff! Its unique vibrations are obscured somehow …"

Suddenly, a look of shock struck Tania. She opened her eyes very wide, gasped loudly, and said: "It *is* Vim and the staff; he *is* alive! He's down there!" Pointing into the lower lands, she indicated the direction she sensed him.

"There's no time to waste! Let's go!" Brazenly, Anton marched forward. He held Deidra's hand and Tania sat on his shoulder. "Watch for any signs of life in this rubble. You never know what you might find, good *or* bad."

"This is madness! How do you expect to find a single *man* down *there* amidst a potpourri of inestimable *enemy*? Naturally, you don't expect to *survive*, especially while dragging a *katrah* along with you! And you're doing all of this on the intuition of a blasted *faerie*?" Thundaruss wasn't pleased with any of Anton's decisions, and he made his point emphatically clear.

"You're welcome to stay! I'll do what I must to save my friend. I'm bound to him in duty and honor. I've given him my bond of service. I *will* go!" Dismissing Thundaruss's pessimism, Anton climbed his way through the ruins and rubble.

"Stay? I wouldn't dream of it!" Heaving a sigh, Thundaruss followed behind the others. He wasn't pleased, but he had made a commitment and intended to fulfill the obligation, no matter what. "Consider Celestra. It's most imperative. Besides, Vim *knew* his fate. It achieves nothing to chase after him, we simply play into the hands of the enemy. Your decision is *unwise*. He's being used as bait!"

"Never mind that! If he *is* alive, I *will* rescue him—I *won't* leave him behind." Calling over his shoulder, resolute, Anton stood behind his decision and continued to ignore Thundaruss's advice and lack of support. He fully intended to go to Celestra, but his commitment to Vim surpassed any other choice.

"Very well, but you *will* comply once we've either rescued Vim, or discovered whatever fate has befallen him." Thundaruss likewise emphasized his perspective, and he insisted on having the last word. "We will continue—for now. I will, however, continue to remind you of your failures! They are adding up very quickly now!"

PART TWO

"A choice between good and evil"

CHAPTER 7

The Dark and Forbidding Lands

IT DIDN'T TAKE LONG TO reach the thick layer of smog; It appeared so dense that Anton felt as though he could walk across it. He stood at its edge, and the heavy stratum seemed to lap at his feet as if it were water. The dark grey puffy clouds ebbed and flowed like a layer of scum washing back and forth on an ocean rather than a condensed layer of vapor. He felt as though he needed a boat to sail upon it, or an Aerocraft to fly over it.

"Is it safe to *enter*? I'm not so sure!" Perplexed, Anton asked Tania for advice. "It looks, well, deadly."

Scrutinizing the thick smog, Tania shook her head. "I can't feel anything that will harm us, but it is obscured to my senses. There's no telling what it consists of. Maybe you and I should go first to determine its hazards?"

"Reasonable. Anyone disagree?" Posing his question, Anton looked first at Deidra and then sternly at Thundaruss.

"Rowwerrrr, I don't want you to leave me-rrrr, but I will do as you ask-rrrr." Deidra trembled both from fear and from the chill morning air. She looked at Thundaruss from the corner of her eye; it was obvious she didn't trust him and wanted Anton to know her feelings.

"Tania and I will return shortly. Prepare a little something to eat, we should top off before we enter." Indifferently, Anton ignored Deidra's fear. He had little time for her apprehensions and didn't believe Thundaruss would harm her intentionally. He realized she'd just recovered from her recent injuries in battle a couple of days prior, and had lost her only chance to perpetuate her unique species. As a result, now she needed him to comfort her. As much as he enjoyed it, the need could only lead to complete dependence should conditions worsen, and that was intolerable.

Being alone with Thundaruss troubled Deidra immensely even though she didn't show it. She relied heavily upon Anton for her much-needed emotional support, but right now he didn't have time to waste with her fearful apprehensions, and that scared her. She looked to Anton, and then to Thundaruss, then back to Anton with a look that implored him to reconsider.

"You should be nicer to her. She likes you, a lot!" Scolding Anton, Tania reminded him of his commitment and need to take care of Deidra. "She *is* important, more important than you realize as of yet, and I know you *like* her. I know *all* of your thoughts, *and* feelings."

"You're right, I do, but this is serious, and we haven't time to deal with the confinements of her emotions. Thundaruss has them, Deidra has them, and I'm trying to *shed* mine. Emotions will be our Achilles' heel. We must use our logic!" Grumbling, Anton appreciated Tania's advice, however, his concerns about the challenges he faced precluded bickering amongst his comrades; he simply wished to keep her safe for the time being by leaving her behind for a few minutes.

"I think she's beginning to *love* you, I can tell! I can *feel* it in her. Girls *know* these things!" Whispering in Anton's ear, Tania put the idea of love into his thoughts. She knew he wouldn't allow himself either to accept or express his suppressed emotions about the katrah. They were too dangerous for him to consider at present.

"Let it go, Tania, we've work to do." With a stressful huff, Anton focused on the current predicament. "It's time to get to work. Every second counts! I'm tired of everyone disagreeing with me and questioning my every choice!"

Bolstering his resolve, Anton snatched his sword from its scabbard and ignited its blade. Golden fire burst forth, permeating the atmosphere, and then his ring ignited, enveloping both him and Tania with his protective fiery magic. Instantly, the energy connected their thoughts together as if they were of one mind and consciousness.

"Stay here, I'll return in a minute or two." Looking at Deidra, Anton made sure she didn't try to follow, even though he knew she wouldn't.

Taking a step into the smog, he was surprised at what happened: the smog pushed away from his magic fire as if he'd intentionally parted it. Taking another step forward, he concentrated and his energy increased significantly. The smog divided even further and allowed him to see deep into the thick layer for quite a distance. Raising his sword with both hands over his head, he sliced downward and cast a bolt of energy into the thick layer of clouds. They parted and opened a fissure as far as he could see, and it held.

I think this opening is sufficient for everyone to travel through. If only I could extend my energy protectively around them. Is it possible? Will it harm them? Anton was unsure of the extent of his capabilities, he was still learning how to use his magic, and relied upon Tania's advice for each new trick he wished to attempt.

Unsure, Tania also hesitated. I don't know, but your power is molded and controlled by your need; it complies with your will. Therefore, I believe it should do what you ask of it. Think about protecting them and it should work.

I'll give it a try. Concentrating, Anton turned around to face Deidra and then smiled.

Cautiously, he imagined his magic enveloping her and shielding her from harm. Without a chance to reconsider, or for Deidra to realize his intention, it suddenly wrapped around her in an instant, and held her motionless. Unaffected, she stood paralyzed but expressed no fear. His fire soothed her, energized her, and most of all, it did just as he wanted: it protected her.

It worked! Honestly, I'm speechless! I can feel her with us, her emotions, and her pure heart! She wishes only to please people and to aid them when she can. Her thoughts are entirely free of human deceit and corrupt ambitions. It is refreshing! Tania felt delighted and shared her enthusiasm. We can travel safely, but we'll be seen. There's a drawback to using your magic, it attracts the attention of our enemy. They will know we're here and they will be able to track us and plan for our approach.

Standing alone, Thundaruss watched as the others floated down the landslide, he felt helpless as he ran struggling to keep up and he didn't want the portentous and possibly harmful smog to envelope him. He climbed and struggled at a torrid pace, vaulting across massive voids and leaping from uneven jutting stone, to loose dirt and jagged gravel, he put forth every effort he could muster to stay just behind Anton's magic fire as the three carefully floated downward ahead of him.

After what seemed like an eternity, they broke through the smog layer and stood a short distance beneath it. Instantly it closed behind them as if Anton had never parted it. Examining the fog from below, it appeared as though it was a canvas canopy, yet it was made of toxic gas, smoke, fog, and unknown vapors in a mixture so dense it defied reason. The morning sun scarcely hinted it existed at all through the smog layer, yet it painted colors of deep red and brown that barely tinged the undersurface.

Everyone stared at the implausible scene that lay before them. They witnessed a landscape of devastation beyond their imagination and were left in absolute awe. It was obvious this was an environment no mortal could hope to survive, and traveling on foot seemed entirely hopeless.

Thundaruss stood on a large slab of stone desperately trying to catch his breath. Speechless, he placed the tip of his sword into the defiled black soil just in front of him. The runes engraved on the blade burned gold and tiny sparks of energy scintillated from its tip. Jagged lines of electricity traveled across the top of the soil, and as he gazed upon the odd reaction, his eyes widened in surprise.

Floating motionless and enveloped in golden fire, Anton surveyed the terrain and then noticed the sparks from the corner of his eye. He then offered his opinion: "We can't walk safely here, the land is poisoned beyond anyone's capacity to tolerate. It's best not to touch *anything*."

It was true, and they all knew it. Thundaruss stood behind Anton's fire and clenched his teeth together knowing he couldn't go on without the same protection the others enjoyed, and he was physically incapable of maintaining the pace that Anton had set indefinitely. He stood there breathing heavily from his hours of exertion, and breathing in the noxious air, something his companions were free from.

"You *must* permit me the same aid you've given your friends! I'm here to help! Don't leave me to die meaninglessly from exhaustion and this poison air." Thundaruss implored Anton's aid. He knew he had offered minimal friendship, and perhaps was mistaken in so doing. "I, I'm sorry for my previous behavior. I support your decision and accept your command." For a moment, he hesitated, and then with great care, he knelt and bowed his head.

"Fear not, my friend, I've no grievance with you. Our disagreements only prove we both care for the same outcome, even if we struggle to work as a team. Be at one with us all." Facing Thundaruss, Anton smiled kindly, and cautiously made his offer of friendship. Then he carefully enveloped the king's champion in his aura of golden fire. "Now, we're a team. All for one and one for all, is it?"

Standing, Thundaruss drew in a breath of purified air. Anton's magic aura sustained him in many ways, and clean air was immediately the most notable. It quickly washed away his body's need to breathe rapidly after his exertion, and it removed the burning sensation in his lungs as if healing them. Within a heartbeat, he too floated along with the others just above the surface of rubble and defiled soil.

"It isn't much farther to the bottom. I'll take us there and we'll decide what to do next." Anton felt relieved as he accepted his final comrade into his protective care. He could discern Thundaruss's thoughts and knew his heart. "Behold, my friend, I'm true to mankind. Now you know my intentions are honest. I'll not betray humanity as did my brethren. My recent transformations preclude flipping to the dark side of evil."

Thundaruss couldn't perceive Anton's thoughts, but he could sense his honesty. Somehow, the energy surrounding them conveyed Anton's true nature, and it struck a chord within him. "It's true, I can *feel* you. How is this so? And how can I believe it's truly honest, and not just a magical ruse?"

"It suffices for now that you do perceive my intentions. Do not allow your distrust to govern your capacity to understand the truth." Anton was short. He needed to focus on the intensity of his magic and the safety it provided them all. He didn't have time to divide his attention by carrying on a full conversation.

As they reached the bottom of the lower lands, it was undeniable to everyone that it was impossible to travel any further without Anton's magic. The terrain was emphatically toxic. A shallow, giant lake of acid stretching as far as the eye could see covered a vast area in front of them. It washed over a solid sheet of smooth yet uneven stone that seemed to extend far into the distance, seemingly going on forever. Spires of what appeared to be rocks stacked upon each other rose high into the air like branchless trunks of dead trees. The spires were of varying size, some thin, some thick, some immensely tall, and others only a couple of yards high. They dotted the area randomly, like a sparse high-altitude pine forest. The spires defied physics. Some had larger stones that balanced impossibly atop smaller ones, some of the smaller stones sat impossibly balanced on edge supporting the larger stones. This seemed especially peculiar following all of the recent earthquake activity brought by the rebalancing of the tectonic plates, and the immense area of Upper Peruvious that had slid into the lower lands. It was completely inexplicable.

The stone surface they stood upon looked like mottled volcanic rock, twisted in swirls of cooled magma washed and etched smooth by acid for an indeterminable number of centuries. The overall effect gave it the appearance of lizard skin, or as Anton perceived it, it bore a striking resemblance to the skin of the *Lapillusaurus* he'd encountered deep in the Troglodyte caverns back on Methonias.

Multitudes of shallow depressions contained acid-bathed crystallized chemicals around their edges like acidic cinder cone volcanos made of basaltic magma and Miocene salt deposits. The depressions caused the tidal movements to ripple as the acid washed back and forth, yet they were no more than a few inches deep. The crystals were incredibly beautiful, but it was impossible to touch them safely.

Warm, acrid gases steamed in turbulent wisps from the flowing acid, permeating the atmosphere with deadly poison, and making it impossible for any normal creature to traverse the region. Only Anton's magic fire stood between the humans and a miserable, painful death. Ultimately, the atmosphere would melt their bodies from both inside and out.

"We can't stay *here* long! In addition, just how are we going to accomplish anything while we remain encased within your magic?"

Displeased, Thundaruss again grumbled and protested. "And, pray tell, just *where* do you believe your friends *are?* Surely you can see they wouldn't stand a chance trying to survive in *this* environment?"

"I can *feel* life, *human* life, far off to the east and south of here. It's *that* way!" Looking at Thundaruss, Tania pointed to the southeast as she answered his question, and then closed her eyes and pointed her nose in the air. Huffing, she continued: "Humph, *and* I can *feel* Vim's staff. It's in that same direction, and the sensation is getting stronger! I told you this *before.*" Turning around, she continued to point her nose in the air and then ignored him.

"I believe the atmosphere will improve eventually as we approach an ocean or mountain, or if a heavy wind blows this smoke and acidic air away. It *should* be possible to breathe the air further away from here. It's only logical." Speculating, Anton offered his thoughts, even though he wasn't entirely sure. "The most important point is that Tania says she senses life, therefore I believe we'll find life, and we'll find Vim. Furthermore, since she can *feel* his staff, and I know that only *he* can touch it, it therefore stands to reason it is in his possession or very near to him. Again, it is only logical, since nobody else can carry it." Supporting Tania, he looked directly at Thundaruss and waited for his response.

"Ahem, very well, we'll find out if she's correct, or wrong, but then I demand we continue immediately to Celestra as my lord and master Amilius stipulated. I repeat: it's my duty to make sure you fulfill his mandate. We must seek the KACATU." Returning Anton's stare, Thundaruss emphasized his directives, and he intended to see them accomplished.

"I've agreed to go to Celestra and find the cockatoo, I will comply! I never said I wouldn't. My word is my bond. I thought we'd put this argument to rest earlier." Standing resolute, Anton reaffirmed his commitment.

"Agreed, so be it. My primary responsibility is to make sure you do." Straightening his shoulders and standing confident, Thundaruss again emphasized his pledge.

"Then we're in agreement, yet again. If you help me find Vim, I promise I'll fulfill your request and proceed immediately to Celestra. Together we're strong, but if we continue to bicker, we will fail." Knowing they had no genuine argument, only a meaningless mistrust and disagreement, Anton let the subject subside. It was time to continue their journey, and he knew every second counted, even if they were headed for a trap.

Concentrating, Anton continued to carry his friends inside his protective energy. They skimmed the surface of the tortured terrain and meticulously watched for signs of additional unexpected hazards. The landscape was ominous. The spires towered over them precariously and the shallow lakes of acid gently rippled, flowed, and ebbed in thin waves, washing the entire volcanic area smooth. After they had travelled for many miles, the topography gradually changed. The acid lakes became less frequent and finally disappeared. The spires vanished entirely, and the scorched and mottled igneous rock transitioned into black and despoiled dirt. At first, absolutely nothing grew in the black soil, but soon that also changed.

"What's *that!*" exclaimed Anton suddenly. "It looks like, well, like *humans* growing in the form of *trees!*"

Tania gasped and began to cry. Her tears rolled down her cheeks and landed in tiny glittery silver drops on Anton's neck. "Those are the harvested souls of humans claimed by Vile. He collects the souls of anyone unfortunate enough to have ruined their lives by committing horrible sins and atrocities, or serving him directly."

The sight sickened Deidra, and she closed her eyes and silently started to cry. "I can't look-rrrr! There's too much evil, pain, and sadness here-rrrr."

"Your little *faerie* friend is correct," Thundaruss said. "Those are the lost souls of humanity. Apparently, they are kept here for some unknown fate in the same way they are kept in the level of suffering in depths of hell." It was apparent Thundaruss had some insightful knowledge of such things.

As they drew closer, Anton looked in more detail at the vast forest that covered many square miles. Individually, the trees were that of naked human bodies transformed into twisted, eerie trees, they were unmistakably both masculine and feminine. Their arms stretched upward and formed into branches, and their legs grew downward into the burnt black despoiled soil becoming roots that grew both deep and laterally along the soil's surface. Tortured, contorted human-like faces moaned painfully as huge black beetles the size of bread loaves crawled on their branches and ate their thick, crispy, black leaves. Every bite brought a wail of pain and agony from the trees, and drips of sticky black goo like thick honey dribbled slowly in long globules from their gaping mouths. The sight was intolerable and the smell was putrid. It resembled the stench of rotting flesh and vitriol. Incredibly, even the protective aura of Anton's golden fire couldn't protect them entirely from the horrendous odor.

"We can't stay here," Anton said. "The smell in the air and the sound of painful wails is inconceivable. Both the sight and the sound makes me ill." Anton felt overcome with disgust, his nerves grated at the sound of the screeching moans, and his stomach knotted. He wanted to vomit. "How is this possible? How could something so horrible happen to those that merely lived their lives immorally in some way?"

"It's decreed by *One*. Live your life in sin, choose not to accept *Him*, and you'll spend eternity in hell. These people have chosen poorly in life, now they're paying for those ill-made choices." Cold and uncaring, Thundaruss remained detached from the judgment of *One*. He didn't wish to become emotional the way Deidra and Tania had. He felt absolutely no sympathy or compassion for the condemned.

"We can't do anything for these tormented souls. They made their choices in life, and it is not for us to redeem them now. We must continue on!" Tania's tears continued to fall, and she trembled grievously from the sight. "Please, keep going. I can't *bear* to see this!"

"Yes, the *smell* is horrrrible; it's like the dead fracknoids-rrrr, only worrrrse!" Retching, Deidra also urged Anton to leave. "Please, go-rrrr!"

Suddenly, at the base of the closest trees near their roots, fracknoids emerged from the violated soil. It appeared as though the saliva that oozed from the mouths of the trees had created the evil little creatures as it fermented in the despoiled earth. The roots of the trees drank the acid from the nearby lakes, and their leaves fed on the filtered sunlight that sifted through the poisonous clouds overhead. The beetles' waste fertilized the dank soil with their own poison. It was suddenly obvious to all of them that the forest had a direct purpose: it was a fracknoid factory.

Without forethought, Anton quickly increased his altitude. He was unprepared for a fight with the tiny creatures, and he didn't have the time to waste in a pointless battle. He needed to find his friends, especially Vim, and that took precedent. Sailing over the top of the forest, he continued on his journey.

"Are we headed in the right direction, Tania? I can sense your feelings, but I want to make sure." Shaken, but not deterred by the sight of the forest, Anton needed to clear his thoughts. "I sense we're close, and I believe it would be prudent if we ate and drank soon so that we can face the next challenge. Any ideas?"

"I concur. We must rest for a while and refresh ourselves." For the first time, Thundaruss agreed with Anton. "But I don't see any place safe to do so either below us, or in the distance. It seems as though we must forfeit another meal, something I'd rather not do before an inevitable fight. If you are correct, then we are close to that fight."

"I'm hungrrrry too-rrrr. Maybe there-rrrr is a safe-rrrr place to the norrrrth or somewher-rrrr else. I think that Vim is in the most dangerrrrous place-rrrr. There may be safer places somewherrrr else."

Offering her thoughts, Deidra was both afraid and uncomfortable. "Can't we eat inside your-rrrr magic-rrrr?"

Unsure of how, Anton considered what steps he needed to accommodate Deidra's proposal. "I can't break my concentration. Perhaps if someone could reach my EHD and find the knapsack full of food?"

"Permit me." Reaching into his own supplies, Thundaruss produced a modest meal for everyone. "It isn't much, but I think it will suffice for now."

Deidra accepted the meager offerings of venison jerky and she fed Anton and herself small pieces; Tania didn't require sustenance, instead, she maintained her mental link to Anton, helping him maintain his focus on his magical energy and their objective. Their traveling slowed considerably while he divided his attention, but he managed to push forward steadily as he ate.

Once the meal was completed, everyone continued to examine their surroundings. The forest started to thin, and to everyone's relief it finally disappeared entirely, taking the stench and the screeches with it. The meager amount of sunlight that filtered through the dense smog layer above them dimmed even more, making it difficult to see clearly. It was obvious the day waned toward early evening.

"I'm surprised we haven't met any of the enemy, other than the fracknoids," Anton said. "It's as if we've been given free passage so far." Speculating, Anton reconsidered. Puzzling over the idea, he pondered the inevitability of a trap and that they were not simply expecting them, but eagerly awaiting their arrival. The simple truth was that the line of sight between Vile's Spire and their arrival at the tor made it unmistakable they were spotted the moment they had arrived from the castle. "It would seem that our friends fell into a trap at the Towers of Tor just as we're about to do trying to rescue them. I'm absolutely convinced Vim was brought here as bait and a battle is inevitable."

"So it would seem." Again, Thundaruss agreed and sounded as though he'd already considered this. "Why else would they have taken Vim and his staff down here alive but to lure you in? Wasn't it obvious from the start? I thought you Methonians recognized all the tricks and strategies of warfare!" Sarcastically, he poked at Anton verbally. "I question your schooling. All of you Methonians spend your entire childhood learning to kill and calculate battles, yet it's funny, *you* seem to be the least educated of your species. I find this … *strange.*"

"If you believe your insight exceeds mine, and you know the mind of our enemy, it would've been beneficial for you to share your concerns earlier. Next time, do so." Displeased, Anton scolded Thundaruss even though he knew the king's champion had warned him, even argued relentlessly not to come here at all. "I have many concerns, most importantly, how to keep all of you alive while I formulate a plan of attack in a region completely new and incomprehensible to me. This makes my job difficult, especially since nobody has shared any information with me about the environment of Lower Peruvious, not even Vim."

"You should've ignored Vim *and* your friends; you should've gone to Celestra as Amilius and Drôgän directed you to do—there lies the correct path of your *true* destiny!" Making his point yet again, Thundaruss countered Anton's scolding. "In the future, if we *have* one that is, if you'll do as *I* direct, perhaps we can avoid these little … *traps.* It would seem the four 'Wyns have given you all of their faith without questioning your capacity to formulate a successful campaign!"

"Don't listen to him!" Tania whispered in Anton's ear. "Vim is too important. Your loyalty to him is necessary too! If nothing else, we need to recover the staff!" Tania continued to offer her support. "I feel we're very close now! I know you'll succeed in the end! *I* have confidence in your judgment!"

Thank you, Tania, I appreciate your support. Frustrated, Anton sighed and ignored Thundaruss, and continued on his way. He was tired of the bickering, and it only slowed their progress as it divided his attention.

The forest of captured souls now was well behind them, and the topography had changed again to gently rolling hills that stank of death and decay. Anton had decreased his altitude shortly after eating and used the uneven terrain to his advantage. He levitated through the gullies and valleys hoping to hide his fiery magic as best he could, yet he knew the enemy could sense it and his approach. The soil beneath them was as black as night just as it had been where the forest grew. Gnarly bushes and the withered remains of black and seemingly life-less trees dotted the landscape. The trees had shiny thorns that oozed and dripped black poisons, and they were devoid of leaves or foliage. It was now evening, and the sunlight had all but disappeared. Only Anton's magic lit the ground below.

Unexpectedly, they burst forth from a shallow valley and abruptly flew into an enormous bowl-shaped depression. It looked as though it may have once been a small lake but the water had long since dried up. In its center, a single spire-like mountain rose high into the air. The enemy filled the entire region and every creature looked at them as if they'd prepared for their arrival. The trap they'd all anticipated and feared was sprung, and there was no hope of escape as they speedily flew deep into its core.

CHAPTER 8

The Mountain of Harvest

THE FOUR REMAINING LORDS OF Ruin levitated above the mountain. Their blue magic auras eerily lit the mountaintop, drawing everyone's attention immediately to them. Fracknoids covered the ground like a furry undulating carpet, nekelmuses rose into the air by the hundreds, minotaurs stood randomly in numbers too vast to count, and there was more. Two enormous creatures, easily three times Anton's height stood to either side of a pathway that spiraled up the conical spire-like mountain. These creatures looked very much the same as the minotaurs, but their heads were that of a snake, and each held a staff with a huge multifaceted ruby attached at the top. The staffs were the size of a small tree, but in the hands of the giant creatures, they appeared to be proportionally equivalent to Vim's Staff of Balance.

An overpowering feeling suddenly struck Tania, causing her to twitch and nearly lose her footing upon Anton's shoulder. They have Vim held prisoner at the top of that mountain, I can *feel* him! Her thoughts shrieked inside Anton's mind like a skewer piercing a slice of meat. The lords are going to sacrifice him! They've been waiting for our arrival! We're finished! And so is he!

I assumed so, Tania. They'll bargain first, and monologue their plans; that's the modus operandi of evil when they are confident they have won. Sounding as though he had no options, Anton seemed defeated, and his mind raced as he quickly tried to calculate a solution. I can't fight and protect Deidra and Thundaruss simultaneously, and these creatures know it. I'll have to set them down unprotected, it's what they're waiting for.

"Rowwerrrr, take us out of here-rrrr! They will kill us-rrrr!" Shaking and shivering with fear, Deidra wrapped her arms around Anton's chest and hugged him tight. "What are-rrrr we going to do-rrrr?"

"You must not bargain with them. We must retreat; the wizard is beyond our help. You should've gone to Celestra as was mandated by my Lord Amilius. There's no hope here! Your decision has led us to this absolute failure!" Again, Thundaruss chastised Anton for his choices and he scowled at him. "We may still have a chance if you leave *now!* Go!"

Regrettably, it was too late. The nekelmuses had maneuvered to surrounded them, and completely blocked an aerial exit. Minotaurs by the hundreds encircled them, and the two huge snake-headed creatures lighted the gems atop their staffs. A red burning bolt of electricity suddenly connected the two rubies, and from the conjoined center, a bolt of red energy abruptly fired at Anton and easily penetrated his golden aura. Swiftly, he dodged sideways, pulling his companions with him to prevent the bolt from striking anyone.

Suddenly, the four Lords of Ruin spoke together as if they shared a single voice. "We are the Lords of Ruin, and you have invaded our domain. This crime requires retribution! Your lives are now forfeit. You will bear witness the execution of our enemy, and then you too will join him in the harvesting of souls. The time has arrived, behold!"

Struggling to maintain his defensive powers, Anton's fire diminished significantly after the bolt of red energy had penetrated his magic. Focusing his concentration like never before, he bolstered his thought communication with Tania. A moment passed, and then the aura strengthened. His golden fire expanded, boiled, and intensified, and Deidra suddenly screamed from the increase of power. Thundaruss groaned through clenched teeth, his mighty muscles went rigid, and he struggled to catch his breath.

"Your defenses are useless. They will only harm your friends, and we still have the capability to collect their souls should you accidentally terminate them. Cease your defiance, and we'll grant you access to your wizard friend, and bear witness to the glory of the harvesting of his soul; he awaits you here, atop the Mountain of Harvest." The four lords continued to speak as one. Their magically amplified voices were bewilderingly persuasive and enticing; Anton felt a desire to see the harvesting for himself. They were attempting to compel Anton's DNA into their servitude, and the power of their will seemed insurmountable. "We will force your decision if you refuse to comply. You must choose immediately!"

Somehow, the petition of his Methonian brethren seemed to persuade and coerce Anton's self-control, even without speaking directly to his base DNA. It was a cold and piercing sensation, and it weakened his mental defenses. For a moment, he wavered, desiring to comply and join them. "I *must* do as they ask, there's no hope. I *must* submit." The golden fire surrounding the four companions again wavered. Ripples of energy loosely clung together, and then Anton lowered his sword as if it weighed a ton and he could no longer hold it.

Anton, no! You can't give in to them, they're trying to persuade you to ruin! This is what they do! Tania screamed inside Anton's head. Don't fail us now! Deidra, Thundaruss and I need you! All of humanity needs you! You are the one to make the choice to save or damn humanity and the universe! They are choosing for you!

Tania's words penetrated Anton's thoughts just as the lords' had done. She too spoke to him, persuading him, and reaching directly to his humanity and his heart, reminding him of who he was and the magnitude of the stakes involved. Shaking his head, for a moment he was bewildered and confused. The four lords' magical persuasion and the connection he and Tania shared were in direct conflict, and he struggled to sort out the truth of this predicament. "I must not give in to my brethren; I must comply with my friends' needs. Give in. Comply." Mumbling to himself, he prattled in confusion for what seemed like an eternity. His eyes clenched tightly together and a sudden feeling of anger erupted in his heart, anger that he couldn't calculate the correct response, anger that he might fail.

"I'll kill you now if you waver! You'll not become a puppet to the Necromancer as did your brethren!" Thundaruss threatened Anton and raised his sword preparing to fulfill his threat. One swift slice and it would be over in an instant.

"No! Rowwerrrr! Anton, no! I love you-rrrr, don't do this, I need you-rrrr!" Deidra pleaded for her life and his. She confessed her true feelings, hoping to reinforce his wavering resolve. She said it from her heart before she even realized her confession. "They want to kill me-rrrr! Don't let them! Save me-rrrr!"

Beams of blue energy fired from the foreheads of the four lords and connected them. A wide shaft of blue energy emanated collectively from them, traveled down the side of the mountain, and struck the remnants of Anton's golden aura, enveloping it completely.

"We'll give safe passage to your friends. Discharge your energy, and they'll be safe here with us. Their souls will reside eternally in oblivion! We've but to harvest them and their suffering of the flesh will end! We will be merciful and swift!" The Lords continued their magically enhanced persuasive techniques, attempting to reach Anton's fundamental Methonian servitude. "Join us, there is glory for us all! Methonians will rule the universe! You can lead us all to victory!"

However, Deidra's sheer horror and her feelings of love spoke to Anton's reasoning, dwarfing even the magically enhanced persuasive powers of the combined four Lords. Anton struggled for a moment or two to regain his composure, then his fortitude shifted and intensified, and a sudden explosion of power burst from his ring. Raising his sword high over his head, he thrust downward as if striking a blow and blasted a golden conflagration of massive energy directly through the core of the blue energy emanating from the lords, but it didn't reach them. Just as the golden energy blast launched, the giant snake-headed minotaurs fired their red energy and struck Anton's golden conflagration. A sudden clap of thunder resounded as red, blue, and gold energies connected. The earth beneath their feet shook as if a meteor had struck nearby. All of the magical powers exploded, casting a myriad of fragmented conflagrations in all directions, and the concussion detonated in the air, triggering a powerful gust of wind; Anton's golden aura extinguished as if a candle had suddenly been blown out. The protection supporting his friends disappeared.

Falling to the ground, Deidra and Thundaruss hit hard and were unable to stand. Thundaruss crumpled to his knees, Deidra landed awkwardly on all fours. Anton stumbled but miraculously maintained his footing, his Methonian skills prevailing. The fracknoids rushed over the top of them and covered them like an ocean wave rolling up a beach.

"No! You must save us!" screamed Tania. "Save Deidra, she must not die!" Pleading, she poured her heart and essence into Anton. Every feeling of love, friendship, and honesty emptied from her very being in waves of positive emotional energy, reinvigorating and reinforcing his resolve.

Feeling Tania's gift, a sudden intense anger again welled up in Anton. With his enhanced strength, he ignored the weight of the fracknoids covering him and raised his sword into the air as if it were as light as a feather. Fire burst from his ring, ran up his burning blade, and simultaneously enveloped the four companions once again. However, the fracknoids managed an attack of their own. In that split-second before Anton could re-summon his energy, they'd gnawed and chewed at Thundaruss and Deidra, inflicting hundreds of lacerations.

Thundaruss dropped his sword and struggled to free himself from the fracknoids that were gnawing at him, but they quickly chewed through his armor and all of it fell to the ground, leaving him completely unprotected. Deidra shrieked in pain as the fracknoids ate away Anton's hakama, her loincloth and gnawed her tender flesh. She bled from hundreds of gashes.

However, Anton's fire burned away the fracknoids and they instantly disappeared as if they'd never existed. Concentrating, he thought about healing. Golden fire staunched the flow of blood, and Deidra's lacerations mended. Thundaruss managed to regain a grip on his sword and he held it loosely in one hand, but the enemy had time to launch another foray.

A sudden burst of blue conflagration discharged from atop the mountain toward the four and struck Anton's golden fire. Again, it diminished in intensity, and it barely covered them in a wispy thin layer.

"Give in, we've already prevailed! You have failed! Join us. It's your last chance for glory! We will *destroy* you if you refuse!" The lords spoke in perfect symmetry, again attempting to speak to Anton's base DNA and compel him to comply with their will. "We are the Lords of Ruin, join us in victory! Join us, and be one with your brothers! The universe is ours to command!"

This time however, Anton didn't waver. Tania's thoughts had fortified his own, and Deidra had spoken to his heart. His resolve increased beyond measure, and he easily ignored the lords' attempt to persuade him. Inside his heart, he felt the same devotion for Deidra and Tania that they felt for him, and the determination to protect them empowered his resilience. Most of all, Drôgän had removed the key to enforcing his servitude, something that the Lords of Ruin couldn't know, and their best efforts fell short of the intended result.

Once again, golden fire enveloped him in full force. It grew in magnitude, turned argent in his chest and boiled like the surface of the sun. He radiated energy as bright as a star. At the same time, Tania began emitting energy so intense she was no longer visible.

Shrieking in pain, Deidra couldn't withstand the sudden increase in magnitude of Anton's energy. Thundaruss cried out in pain, and his eyes widened so much it appeared as though the lids had disappeared.

"You fool! You've blinded me!" he suddenly cried out. "I can't fulfill my service! You must spare us! Reduce your power!"

Nevertheless, Anton ignored his plea; the stakes were too high. All of their lives were in jeopardy. Listen to me, Tania! I have a plan, but it's risky. I must appear to give in to them! Desperate and out of time, Anton shared his strategy. Deidra can fit in my EHD for a short time, and I must allow Thundaruss to be captured. The distraction will give you and I just a split second to free Vim and then in turn save Thundaruss. The risk is sacrificing Thundaruss for Vim, but I will take that chance! If only I had more tricks, more abilities!

Unfortunately, Anton was too late. His plan was a failure before it began. The snake-headed creatures fired another bolt of red energy into Anton's golden fire, splitting it open, and for a moment, he was exposed and vulnerable. Simultaneously, a blue bolt of energy fired from the Lords directly behind the red bolt, and it entered the fissure striking him full force. The sudden impact broke his concentration and completely extinguished his magic, and everyone tumbled and fell to the ground.

"Spare them! Serpotaurs, deliver the enemy to us!" the lords urgently commanded their minions. "We'll crucify the humans atop the Mountain of Harvest along with the failed wizard! Our victory is at hand!"

Dazed, Anton fumbled while trying to regain his sword, which had fallen to the ground next to him. As he reached for it, a minotaur kicked him in the chest and he flew through the air and collided with a large stone, yet somehow, he'd managed to grasp his sword hilt in time, the supergrip tsuka providing him with a firm grasp. With a flick of his wrist, he returned it to his scabbard before anyone had noticed what he'd done. As he struck the ground, fracknoids covered him and gnawed unremittingly as if they couldn't wait to consume his flesh, but strangely, their teeth caused him no damage, and he seemed to be immune to their attack.

Tania flew into the air and circled around so quickly she was impossible to see. She was the only one to escape the attack and injury.

Unconscious, Thundaruss lay on his back with his sword tucked under his legs. Fracknoids surrounded him, but they didn't touch him. They gnashed incessantly, screeching their shrill sound and looked at him hungrily, as if they couldn't wait to tear into his flesh. Many bounced up and down fighting their insane need for flesh and the orders to the contrary commanded by the Lords of Ruin.

Sprawled on her stomach, Deidra too lay unconscious. The violence was far more than her fragile feminine katrah body could withstand. Blood oozed from her mouth and from hundreds of gashes all over her body. She'd incurred other unknown injuries and needed immediate care. Fracknoids surrounded her just as they did Thundaruss, gnashing their teeth and screeching insanely at the air. They craved to feast upon her but withheld, as the lords had commanded.

One of the serpotaurs grasped Thundaruss and Deidra, one in each hand, and slung each of them over a shoulder. The second serpotaur picked up Anton, slung him over his shoulder, and then reached for Thundaruss's sword. The moment he touched it, an aura of golden light emanated from the runes, burning his hand. He let out a reptilian-sounding hiss as if he'd expelled compressed air.

"Leave the evil artifact behind, it's of no concern," the lords commanded the beasts from atop the hill. "Bring the humans hither, their crosses await them."

The serpotaurs instantly obeyed, as if they existed only to follow the commands of the lords. Plodding up the mountain's winding trail, they slowly carried them toward Vim. To each side of the path, approximately a serpotaur's stride apart, lay small piles of eight or ten human skulls. Dried rotting flesh connected them and fused them together. Tiny candles that burned iridescent red and yellow lit each eye socket, giving off enough light to see the path clearly in the darkness. The moonless night was black, and the air was still and heavy with smoke and the odor of decaying flesh.

Slowly but steadily, the serpotaurs plodded along and wound their way up the mountain and eventually arrived at the top. The space there was limited, but there was plenty enough for over a dozen crosses that stood in a semi-circle. A large circular flat stone platform filled the gap between, providing a place from which the lords and serpotaurs could work. Laying the three prisoners on the stone slab, each in front of a cross, the serpotaurs stepped back and raised their staffs into the air.

The four lords floated into position high above the crosses in a half circle facing them; a beam of blue light connected their foreheads. Raising their arms in unison, including Lord Agonia's arm that Anton had obliterated, they began to chant in a deep, harsh, guttural language known only to them. Blue fire erupted between them, and then turned black at its core. In the center where all four beams connected, it appeared as though a black sphere appeared and it seemed to absorb all the surrounding light. The chanting increased and the tonality seemed progressively harsh. The black sphere soon positioned itself high into the air well above the crosses and the Lords, and then the chanting ceased.

"The destroyer of light, the Lord of annihilation observes. It is time to harvest these souls! Serpotaurs, mount the katrah, the human, and the Methonian!" The lords continued to speak perfectly in unison, and their voices resonated off the mountaintop as if amplified.

Feigning unconsciousness, Anton remained motionless on the ground near Deidra and Thundaruss as he prepared himself mentally for the next challenge. Concentrating, he could sense Tania's presence nearby, and he could hear her thoughts. He knew she was close, but she somehow remained invisible to the lords and the other creatures, and they ignored her entirely as if she were of little consequence.

The first serpotaur picked up Thundaruss and held him against a cross that stood mounted in the ground next to Vim; the second held an enormous hammer and a large spike. Placing the spike under his wrist and between his radius and ulna, he drew the hammer back and gave one hard blow against its head driving it through his arm and deep into the dense wood of the cross behind it. Thundaruss awoke with a scream and struggled futilely for freedom. A moment later, a second spike was pounded into his other arm, holding it solidly in place. Again, he screamed as blood poured from wounds below his wrists, down his arms to the elbows and dripped steadily on the ground. The serpotaurs quickly bound his arms and legs with thick thorny vines.

Opening his eyes just a smidgen, Anton watched as the serpotaurs nailed Thundaruss to a cross next to Vim. Vim was entirely naked, and his legs and arms were bound with thorny vines. His long hair was tied around the cross holding his head back, and atop it, he wore a crown of black thorns. As he continued to watch, the serpotaurs placed an identical crown atop Thundaruss's head and effortlessly tore away his clothing, stripping him naked.

"The Methonian awakes! Seize him now!" Lord Agonia spoke independently, entirely disconnected from his brethren, as if he desired revenge. "Serpotaurs! Quickly! Nail him to the cross!"

Anton knew he must act instantly. Rolling over, he lurched to his feet, grasped his sword from its sheath, and reached into his tunic to pull out his EHD. He then leapt toward Deidra and slid it over her.

She disappeared inside, and he quickly stuffed the EHD back into his tunic. He was so swift, it happened in an instant, and it appeared as though she'd simply vanished.

Together, the serpotaurs raised their staffs and a red beam of energy connected their rubies. They fired a secondary beam from the center of the joined beams toward Anton, barely missing him as he rolled, tumbled and parried the attack. Lurching to his feet, he whirled around and ignited his sword. A massive five-foot length of blade burst from the hilt in the shape of a two-handed longsword and fire erupted like an explosion from his ring, and his entire body instantly was enveloped in an aura of golden energy.

Again, the serpotaurs fired a bolt of light at Anton. This time it struck his fire and weakened it, but only for a moment. Spontaneously, Anton's fire regained its strength, but he couldn't sustain it before another shaft of red energy struck it and completely extinguished it. Miraculously, the golden fire continued to burn around his hand and ring and up the blade of his sword. Finally, he understood how to maintain control of his magic.

"Behold, the time of harvest begins!" The four lords again spoke in unison. "Summon forth the accursed staff!" Proceeding with their original purpose, they let the serpotaurs engage Anton so that they might complete their primary objective.

From the corner of his eye, Anton saw a long stick suddenly float into the air, seemingly from nowhere. As if in response, Tania flew at lightning speed and landed on his shoulder. Wrapping her arms around his neck, she gave him a quick hug, and reinforced her mental communication.

They will kill Vim! Stop them! she screamed inside his head.

Nonetheless, it was too late. The serpotaurs stood between Anton and Vim, and they fired still another red bolt of energy at him. Skillfully, he dodged the discharge and at blinding speed swung his sword cleaving the bolt. Golden fire struck red energy and deflected it. It appeared as though he'd deftly batted it back toward one of the serpotaurs, and the bolt struck him in the center of his chest. His ruby-capped staff flew into the air as he fell backwards, landing hard against Thundaruss. His momentum snapped the cross near its base and the two landed forcefully on the ground, the serpotaur crushing Thundaruss under his titanic weight.

Simultaneously, the lords held the Staff of Balance suspended inside an aura of blue energy. They chanted in their guttural language and an audio vibration caused the staff to vibrate rhythmically.

"*Save* him! They attack *now!* Tania's voice shrieked in Anton's ear. "Hurry, *save* him!" Her voice trembled, and tears flowed from her freely. "Saaaave himmmm!" she cried hysterically.

Golden fire erupted all around Anton, and his magic energy burned like the surface of the sun. Swinging his sword, he cast a conflagration directly at the serpotaur standing in his way striking him dead center in the chest. The serpotaur swung its staff reflexively in defense and neatly connected with Anton's energy. Golden fire struck the ruby and it exploded, shattering into thousands of fragments. The wooden shaft split lengthwise and flew out of his hands. Raising his sword for a second blow, Anton leapt into the air and struck the serpotaur, slicing deep into his breast. Golden fire detonated inside of him, and he exploded into millions of tiny fragments.

Unexpectedly, minotaurs by the dozens rushed to the aid of the serpotaurs. They launched themselves against Anton's fire, annihilating themselves as they buffeted him around. Nekelmuses by the hundreds shot fireballs at him and suddenly he was overwhelmed with a flood of the enemy's fire, and he struggled mightily to fend off their attack. Anger welled up in him and he quickly levitated toward Vim. Fireballs pounded him, minotaur arms reached after him, clawing viciously at him with hideous claws, penetrating deep into his magical fire, but they disintegrated nearly as fast. However, in the end, he was too late to save Vim.

A sudden guttural command shocked the atmosphere and the Staff of Balance launched like a lightning bolt toward Vim's crucified body. It pierced his chest and traveled neatly through him, splitting the cross in half lengthwise. The globe stopped just as it touched the remains of his sternum and exploded. White gas rose from the shattered remnants of the globe, and the crystalline fragments littered the ground and turned grey. The hair on Vim's head disintegrated in a smoky puff, releasing the wizard's head from the cross, causing it to slump downward. Vim's tongue fell to the corner of his mouth and blood poured down his chin.

The lords again chanted, and their blue aura stretched out like a long human arm that reached inside Vim's chest and snatched his spirit from his motionless body. For a moment, the magical hand held it in a vise-like grip. His spirit glowed silvery white and struggled to extricate itself, then abruptly turned black. The black sphere that hovered over the mountaintop sucked at his spirit and instantly consumed it like a black hole annihilating a star that had traveled too close.

"No! Damn you!" screamed Anton. "I will *not* fail in this!" Rage marked his face, and hate filled his heart. He couldn't accept defeat, especially by the hands of his Methonian brothers. It sickened him.

Immense power exploded from Anton, golden fire turned argent, and again Tania glowed like a tiny star sitting on his shoulder. Levitating high into the air, Anton's magical fire expelled beneath him as if discharged from a rocket's thruster, and he sailed at the speed of light toward the Lords of Ruin, stopping directly in front of them.

"You four are finished! I'll harvest *your* lives!" Anton's anger was immeasurable. He intended to make this his final battle with them, and his determination was indomitable.

Expanding his fire even further, he completely encompassed the entire mountaintop, and it easily enveloped the four lords in the process; they hadn't anticipated such an attack—never considered it remotely possible—and they fell victim to his rage. Trapped inside his magic, it was impossible for them to move, but they maintained an aura of blue energy around themselves as they struggled to extricate themselves.

"This is our domain! You've no hope of success, you cannot succeed! Give in to your destiny, and join us in glory!" Making a final appeal, the lords again attempted to sway Anton's determination, but this time it seemed apathetic, as if they feared for their own existence. "Your soul is in jeopardy! Let us remove your flesh and set it free! There is still a place for you among us! Give in and let us save you!"

Anton ignored their persuasive tactics. Somehow, it now sounded hollow and meaningless, and it only fueled his tenacity. His anger escalated, his fire boiled, and the sun-like vividness he pervaded obliterated the ubiquitous darkness. As if suspended at the epicenter of a nuclear explosion, the lords, in contrast, turned black and collapsed inward into nothingness. It appeared as though they too had succumbed to annihilation by a black hole.

The entire mountaintop lay waste. The serpotaurs evaporated, minotaurs turned to smoke, fracknoids by the thousands were gone as if they'd never existed. Thundaruss's body was vaporized, Vim's carcass was incinerated, and the crosses no longer existed. Everything was destroyed.

"You killed Thundaruss! Anton! You killed Amilius's champion!" Tania scolded him, as tears suddenly poured from her eyes.

"The *serpotaurs* killed him, he was *already* dead!" he angrily snapped at Tania.

"Your fire incinerated him! He may have lived! We may have saved him!" Shedding a tear, she again scolded Anton. "Withhold your anger! You bring us only ruin! You'll become as evil as the Lords of Ruin! Control your anger, don't become what you hate!"

Ignoring Tania, Anton still wasn't through. There was yet another fight that he intended to finish. Surveying the atmosphere around him, the mountaintop below him, the winding trail, and the base of the mountain, he could see more minotaurs, nekelmuses, and fracknoids filling the entire region. He didn't intend for them to escape, and he wasn't going to permit them to live. At the speed of light, he instantly flew toward the nekelmuses with his sword raised in front of him. Slicing and stabbing, enveloping and burning, he killed and killed and killed again, and in a period time he could not measure, he finally killed them all. Turning his attention to the ground, he did the same for the minotaurs. Slicing and hacking, stabbing and chopping, he eliminated them one by one at incredible speed. He moved so swiftly the eye could only see a blur of light pass from one victim to the next. A large number of the enemy attempted to retreat, and scattered in all directions, but he moved so rapidly they couldn't get away, and they too, in time, succumbed to Anton's voracious rage.

Finally, turning his attention to the fracknoids, Anton could see they'd successfully vanished. It had taken him too much time to destroy the nekelmuses and minotaurs and they had the opportunity to retreat and disappear—or perhaps prepare for another attack. Either way, they were gone and therefore of little concern, at least for the present.

Looking at the devastation he'd caused, Anton scanned the top of the mountain. Everything was gone, that is, everything but Vim's staff, which stood all by itself, the only thing left in sight. It stuck out of the black soil at an angle, pointing into the air. The globe had all but disintegrated, and the talons that contained it had disappeared during Vim's murder, but the wooden shaft remained. This stunned and mystified Anton, and for a moment he pondered the significance. There was a reason for this and he needed to know why.

"The staff is essentially intact! How is this possible?" exclaimed Anton. "It is logical to assume that it would be destroyed along with everything else. After all, it is only a small piece of wood! All of the crosses are gone, I destroyed them, and they too were made of wood, and they were much larger. Is this a remnant of Vim's magic?"

"There's more to this simple piece of wood than you can see. It contains some form of pure life's energy inside it, I can *see* it, I can *feel* it, but I don't know how it's possible." Tania offered her insight, but she didn't have an answer to the question. "It's concealed somehow to my perception. I only know the workings of fauna, some of my sisters are responsible for the evolution of flora. Perhaps they could tell you, but they aren't here."

"I *must* take the staff with me. There's a *reason* why Vim had it, and a *reason* why it still exists." Landing next to it, Anton extinguished his magical fire. "Maybe I should put it in my EHD … for safe keeping …"

Suddenly, Tania remembered Deidra. "Deidra! You *forgot* about Deidra!" she exclaimed urgently. "You must *release* her from that *EHD!*"

"*Damn* it, I hope she's okay!" Anton's eyes widened and he quickly reached into his tunic. Withdrawing and unfolding the EHD, he reached into it, fumbled around and then touched her. "She's still warm, but I can't tell if she is breathing!"

Carefully, he placed the EHD on the ground and reached inside it with both hands and pulled her free. He laid her gently on the ground, but she remained motionless and appeared unconscious. Feeling her chest, Anton could barely feel her heartbeat.

"Beelif's potion!" Tania yelled, landing on Deidra's head. "I will try to help!"

Laying her hands upon Deidra's forehead, Tania shed a tear and it landed between her eyes. It looked like a shiny silver drop of dew resting on her forehead. Suddenly, Deidra gasped and then she coughed. Her breathing was sporadic and strained, and her eyelids twitched but didn't open.

As Tania reminded him, Anton precipitously reached into his tunic and produced one of the potions of healing Beelif had given him before their departure from the castle. Unsealing it, he placed it against Deidra's lips and carefully poured its contents into her mouth. It was only a few drops, but the change in her was inexplicable. Instantly, she coughed, her eyes opened, and she sat up suddenly. The wounds covering her body seemed to miraculously disappear, slowly at first, but soon they were all gone.

"Rowwerrrr! Rowwerrrr! Where-rrrr *am* I-rrrr?" she asked. "What is that *taste-rrrr?* I don't like it-rrrr, it's, *sweeeet-rrrr!*"

"You're here with Tania and me. You're safe for now." Smiling, Anton tried to reassure her, and he felt a warm tenderness in his heart as he watched her recover. The anger he'd felt only moments before evanesced instantly. "How's your head? Does it hurt?"

"I feel, dizzy-rrrr, but I'm okay-rrrr." Unsure and unsteady, Deidra further considered how she felt. "What happened? What happened here-rrrr?" she stammered.

"Vim's gone. Thundaruss is gone—it's just the three of us." Clumsily, coldly, Anton tried to explain, but he was unable to convey a sense of reassurance. He didn't want to tell her too much until she felt better, however, his explanation sounded hopeless. Hesitating, he then added: "Too many things have come to pass. I, well, don't want to upset you."

"Rowwerrrr! *Gone-rrrr?*" Looking back and forth from Anton to Tania, Deidra started to cry and then quickly wiped the tears from her eyes. "How-rrrr?"

"We need to leave. I'll tell you later, *please!* We don't have time now." Standing up, Anton quickly surveyed the surroundings. He wasn't convinced they'd remain safe if they sat around talking. He expected fracknoids to reappear at any moment. It was dark—very dark—and nearly impossible to see anything at all with all the dust, smoke, and heavy cloud cover.

Walking over to the remnants of Vim's staff, Anton slowly reached out and touched it. The wood was charred, but it appeared to be in good shape, considering his destructive use of magic. Grasping it in both hands, he gave it a gentle tug and then pulled it free from the scorched black soil. Unexpectedly, it started to change. Mysteriously, its charred surface extemporaneously healed. A thin layer of new bark replaced the burned surface, buds grew from the wood, it bloomed blossoms, and then produced almonds.

"What the … what's going on?" Confused, Anton quickly ran over to Deidra and Tania. "Do you have any idea what the meaning of *this* is?" he queried the little faerie.

"The staff is still alive! I believe it has chosen *you* to carry it!" Tania's eyes widened as she spoke. "There *is* still hope left! You must take us to Celestra! We must leave!"

"I think there's more to this than meets the eye." Plucking the almonds from the staff, Anton cracked them open and offered a few to Deidra. He ate a few himself, and a sudden charge of electricity seemed to ignite every nerve of his body. "I feel, well, different. Something is happening to me, and I don't know what it is …"

Cautiously, Deidra sampled the almonds that Anton offered her. A sudden spasm shook her body, and she let out a scream. "Rowwerrrr!" she growled, and again, she fell unconscious.

"Oh no!" cried Tania. "You've *poisoned* her somehow!"

"Impossible! I ate a few of them too!" exclaimed Anton. "Something *else* is happening!" Once again, he placed his hand upon Deidra's chest. Her heart beat normally. "She's okay, I think. You're correct, we *need* to get to Celestra, and as soon as we can."

Picking up Deidra, Anton gently draped her over his shoulder. Tania landed on his other shoulder and gave his neck a tiny hug.

"Hurry, we're in danger here! Every moment we delay only increases our risk the enemy will return and attack us!" As Tania shared her concerns with Anton, she seemed somehow agitated or scared. "I can see you're *very* tired and you need food. I can feel it. We can rest in Celestra; it's not safe here."

Then the earth shook yet again. The ground lurched, and then lurched again. With enormous force, it heaved up under Anton and pushed hard into the air. Tremors shook the ground, and Anton laid Deidra back down and danced around as he grappled to maintain his footing. Then, just as suddenly, it stopped. The earth had once again reset the balance of the tectonic plates as it weighed out the change of good and evil left in Peruvious.

"Whew, I don't think I'll ever get used to that!" Wiping his brow, Anton carefully picked up the unconscious Deidra. "Time to go," he said coolly, and then added: "I can't believe Deidra slept through that."

Again, Anton gently lifted Deidra over his shoulder, and raised the Staff of Balance into the air. Hesitating, he considered what to do with it. "I want this thing to take us to Celestra. I wonder if I can use it the way Vim did."

Unexpectedly, his ring spontaneously started to glow. It touched the surface of the staff and suddenly a golden sphere enveloped them. Concentrating on levitation, they smoothly ascended into the air.

"I don't know where to go, I have no idea where Celestra is, and it's so dark I can't see where we're headed! What do I do?" Confused, Anton shared his apprehensions, hoping Tania could guide him. "How did Vim make use of this thing? How did he get it to do what he wanted it to do?"

"Relax. Maybe it will simply take us where you want to go, or perhaps, it will take us where we *need* to go." As always, Tania's advice was prudent and thoughtful. "I believe the staff can do more than we realize. Just allow it to do its job!"

"*This* I'm sure of: Vim could do things that defy both logic and principle, and he claimed it was all natural. He was inexplicable." With a tone of remorse, Anton seemed distant as he recalled Vim, but he concentrated on navigation. "I'm thinking about our need to visit Celestra. I hope the staff directs us there."

Exhausted, remorseful, and disappointed with the consequences of his choices, Anton took a deep breath and reaffirmed his tenacity. He wasn't going to let Vim's death deter him. He fully intended to succeed in his mission, no matter how exhausted he felt. Somewhere deep inside his heart he wanted to shout out in despair. Vim's death was an inexcusable failure—his failure—and he questioned his own capabilities as a Warrior. Even more, he questioned his Methonian heritage after witnessing what the Lords of Ruin had become. They were so determined to fight for evil that it seemed to defy the very reason and purpose of a Warrior. How could they so easily be swayed? He had managed to escape their fate, why couldn't they? It seemed as though they were even greater than he, not flawed with emotions and continual failures. They should have stood for justice!

"I shouldn't have failed. Vim should still be alive, if only … " Mumbling, he shamefacedly chastised himself to Tania. "I, I won't fail again. I'll plan better next time. There won't be any more … *mistakes*."

"Oh, Anton, you couldn't win, even *with* a plan! They'd set a trap for you, we didn't stand a chance. You can't blame yourself, it wasn't *your* fault." Trying to reassure him, Tania's feelings were quite evident. "Vim knew he was going to die, and I know you did too. You can't take responsibility for that."

"As you say. It's just that a Warrior *never* fails. We simply win, or die trying, and maybe I could've changed his fate." Anton continued to sort his grievances, but he appreciated Tania's support. "I *will* win *next* time, I have no choice … "

Unexpectedly, they floated down the side of the mountain to the valley floor below. A shimmer of light emanated from the base of the trail leading up the mountain. Lightly touching down, they stood next to Thundaruss's sword; it seemed as though it was waiting for them. The runes glowed brightly, and electrical energy discharged wherever it touched the ground. Retrieving it, Anton held it up and looked at the glowing runes engraved in both sides of the blade. They continued to glow brightly, and as he lightly rubbed his fingertips along them, the sword vibrated pleasantly in his hand as if signifying something important.

"*Amazing! Another* artifact of some sort! I'll put it in my EHD for now. I have no other way to carry it comfortably." Anton's eyes widened and he quickly stowed it away. "I wonder why the staff wanted me to have this."

"I'm sure we'll find out soon enough. Let's go, we need to leave!" Tania's voice sounded urgent as she encouraged Anton to press on. "Hurry! There's no time to waste!"

Encasing everyone inside the protective sphere, Anton again levitated into the night sky. An hour passed as they sailed upon the currents of air. Tania remained quiet; she understood Anton's need for concentration. She aided him as best she could by locking her thoughts to his, and adding her powerful faerie magic to help support his fatigue.

Suddenly, Deidra began to stir and abruptly aroused from her strangely induced sleep. "Rowwerrrr, where *are* we-rrrr?"

"I haven't a clue," Anton answered. "I believe the staff is taking us to Celestra, and I hope we'll arrive there soon." Offering her little, Anton slid Deidra from his shoulder and grasped her arm just as Vim had done with him during their travels. "I feel like we should be there soon, and I feel like we're doing the right thing. Somehow I just know it won't take much longer. It's just a comforting feeling I seem to have that gets stronger the further we travel."

Astonished with Anton's revelation, Deidra wondered how he could know. It made no sense to her. "I'm hungry-rrrr. I need to eat something-rrrr." Smiling, she ran her fingers through his hair and purred like a kitten. She admired his fortitude, and his ever-increasing skills, but most of all she desired his attention, and secretly she hungered for his affection.

Surprised, Anton faltered for a split second and the sphere scintillated and shuddered. Tania shared her raptness in Anton's thoughts and fortified his concentration.

"Please, Deidra, wait until we've landed. We don't need any mishaps at this point." Sounding strained, Anton gently scolded her. "I am sorry, but this isn't the time."

"Rowwerrrr, I'm sorry. I'm still hungry." Looking dejected, Deidra rested her head upon Anton's shoulder and gave him a small hug. "What were-rrrr those nuts you gave me-rrrr?"

"Those were *almonds,* silly girl. Haven't you eaten *almonds* before?" giggled Tania. "We wondered about you after you tasted one. It put you to sleep!" Giggling heartily, she shared her cheerfulness, hoping to distract Deidra and free Anton's concentration.

"We're here. Celestra's below us. I can *feel* it," Anton said. "The question now is: how do we penetrate the shield surrounding it?" Shuffling, Anton seemed unsure. "I need to land, and then maybe we can pass through it like we did at the castle."

"I'm sure you are right. Find a suitable place and we'll try." Tania sounded excited, and she again fortified Anton's concentration. "I can feel what you feel. I know what you know. It *is* below us!"

A sense of revitalization charged Anton as Tania continued to fill his mind with hers. The omnipresent darkness seemed to peel away to some degree, and the protective dome surrounding Celestra was unmistakable in his mind. Adjusting their altitude, he carefully attempted to pass through the dome. Slowly, he directed his ascent, however, the staff's golden sphere gently bounced off the dome, preventing their passage through it.

"I just *knew* that would happen," Anton said. "I'm going to land over there." Nodding toward the ground, Anton indicated a place near the southernmost point of the dome. "It looks like the entrance to Celestra used to be there."

Within moments, they landed where Anton had indicated. The ground was as black as midnight, the atmosphere was heavy with the smell of rotting flesh, and dense smoky clouds filled the night sky, precluding any light from the heavens. The darkness permeated every aspect of the region and seemed to suck away everyone's energy the moment the protective golden sphere dissipated.

"It's funny, I can *feel* the torment of the ground under my feet when I hold this staff. I can sense the hideous cruelty, the death, and the agony of all who suffered here." Anton shivered for a second as he drew in the revulsions of the past. His stomach ached from both hunger and horror, and his body hummed with exhaustion. He was sure he'd have nightmares after perceiving indirectly, yet intimately, the tragedies of the past and recalling the unbearable events of his own day. "Let's figure out how to get inside. I can't *stand* it out here."

Unsheathing his sword, Anton launched a three-foot length of burning blade into the night. Fire erupted from his ring, surrounded his arm, and then traveled up the blade. Somehow, after the battles he'd fought, it now seemed second nature to Anton to summon forth whatever magic he needed. It wasn't like just a day before when he didn't understand what to do with his sword and ring. Putting his arm around Deidra, he held her tight. Tania hugged his neck as the golden fire quickly enveloped them. Within a heartbeat, they levitated effortlessly through the protective dome and landed just inside. Releasing Deidra, he took a step back and inhaled deeply.

"The air is better in here. It's relatively clean, and it doesn't smell bad. There must be some sort of filtration system in place. Let's have a meal before anything else happens." Reaching into his tunic, Anton pulled out his EHD and opened it. "Here are the supplies—make yourself useful." Looking at Deidra, he handed her the knapsack of food.

Surprised, Deidra looked at Anton. "Rowwerrrr, as you wish-rrrr!" Deidra happily obeyed, even if Anton had casually assigned her the mundane task. "Where-rrrr will we rest-rrrr? You should find a safe place-rrrr!" Smiling, she offered her reciprocate request.

Returning her smile, Anton nodded his head and started to search for shelter. Ruins lay all around them, and he quickly climbed up a large pile of rubble nearby. He then raised the staff into the air, and it mysteriously aided his enhanced Methonian vision. He discerned the only structure left standing inside the dome was the tower housing the celestial eye.

"That's where we'll sleep. I'll tell Deidra." Turning around, he climbed back down the debris pile for his meal. "We can fulfill our task as soon as we've eaten," he said.

A Moment's Peace

QUICKLY UNLOADING THE ITEMS FROM the knapsack, Deidra set them out and prepared a piecemeal dinner for Anton. She too was very hungry, perhaps a side effect of the healing potion she'd drunk just a couple of hours prior, or perhaps a result of eating the almonds. Either way, her stomach protested fiercely. At first, the potion had energized her, but then it put her to sleep, and now she was famished. Her stomach growled relentlessly, reminding her of the most fundamental mortal need. Presently, Anton and Tania returned from their short excursion.

"Ahhh, *food!*" Anton gave Deidra a wide smile and sat next to her on a weathered broken slab of concrete. "We can see the observatory containing the celestial eye. I think it would be safe to sleep there if we can find a way in." Looking at the food spread out haphazardly on the rocks and debris, his stomach rumbled in response.

"Wow, even those field rations look good!" Offering casual conversation, Anton tried to draw Deidra's attention away from the events of the day. Hungrily, he ate the food she'd prepared for them.

"You're sure-rrrr it's safe there-rrrr? I'm tirrrred, and I want to rest-rrrr, but I'm afraid-rrrr." Shivering, Deidra ate as quickly as Anton. Neither of them had consumed much in the last two days, nor rested properly, and the fatigue showed.

Still sitting on Anton's shoulder, Tania's attention seemed detached; something seemed to be disturbing her and she intentionally withheld her thoughts from Anton. She placed a finger against her chin in reverie, but Anton ignored her while he ate and talked with Deidra. Nonetheless, Tania didn't like Anton ignoring her. Suddenly she stood up on his shoulder with her hands on her hips and spoke loudly. "How are we going to get inside of the observatory? I mean, do you think it's open and unguarded? I think it's sealed and it won't let us in, or even worse, there may be some *magic* protecting it." Trying to draw Anton's attention to her, she intentionally distracted him. She knew he needed to improve his relationship with Deidra, but most importantly, he needed to press forward and find the KACATU. "I think I'll go see if it's open!"

Impulsively, before Anton could either object or agree, she flew off toward the observatory as quickly as she could go, and in less than a minute, she was there. Flying around the dome in circle after circle, she stopped here and there lingering for a moment or two, and then continued to examine the structure systematically for an entrance, a crack, or some other type of opening. Other than the heavy front door that was intact and perfectly sealed, she found nothing. Satisfied, but not pleased with her discoveries, she returned to Anton to inform him of what she'd discovered.

Lightly touching down on his shoulder, Tania reported: "I don't see any way in other than the front door, but the building is perfectly intact. We'll have to find some way to open the door. It's sealed, and I don't know what to do. I know little of Celestra's buildings, You're more of an expert than I, I'm sure."

"Your scouting is most helpful. Thanks, Tania. We're through here. Let's go see what can be done to gain entry." Standing, he offered Deidra his hand, raised Vim's staff, and enveloped everyone in a golden sphere. Within moments, they stood in front of the heavy front door.

The instant the sphere disappeared, lights suddenly turned on and lit the meager remains of what was once an elaborate veranda. The building started to hum as if it were powering up and preparing for use.

"Identify." Surprisingly, a soft feminine voice spoke. "Identification required for entry. Place your palm on the identification circle."

Quickly scrutinizing the door, Anton looked for the palm identification circle. To the right side of the door, he saw a tall slender diamond-shaped slot in the center of a circular shape. Placing his palm upon it, he held it there for a moment. Spontaneously his ring began to glow white. It was as if the circle had somehow activated its unique circuitry. Anton knew this was something only his Masters' computers were capable of.

Abruptly, the soft voice spoke again. "Scanning. Programmed crystal device detected. Software detected. Identification complete. Security clearance required. Scanning. Lothendus's security code found. Security code accepted. Prime directive activated. Downloading software." A moment passed as Anton's ring glowed ever brighter. "Please, do not remove your hand during the download process."

Anton remembered well the unique sound of the soft feminine voice: it was identical to the one he'd heard on the shuttle when he left Methonias and aboard the Pleceivious as he traveled to Saurian Five. "How is *that* possible?" he mumbled disconcertedly. "How could it be *that* voice?"

"What do you mean? What are you talking about?" Confused, Tania had no idea what Anton meant. "It's just a woman's voice, silly man! What's so *special* about it?"

"It's just that I've heard it before, and I've never *been* here!" he replied. "I heard that *exact voice* while being transported aboard the Aerocrafts of Methonias, and later aboard the Pleceivious."

"Download complete. Updating operating system. Installing advanced instruction sets. Installed! Prime directive updated. Welcome, Anton Seven! You now have permission to enter. Insert the master key for final authorization and entrance."

"Huh? Key? Insert what key? What *type* of key? Where's the keyhole? Is it electronic or mechanical?" Anton looked at Deidra and then gave Tania a confused stare. "Do you see a keyhole?" Anton removed his hand from the circle and shrugged his shoulders.

"This is *human* technology! *You're* the one that knows the answer. I'm just a *faerie*! *We* don't know *anything* about such things! Don't be so silly!"

"Rowwerrrr, maybe it's that slot-rrrr?" Pointing at the diamond-shaped slot, Deidra offered her supposition.

"Maybe, hmmm, perhaps you're right! However, we *don't* have the *key!* How are we to enter *without* it? I don't want to damage the building to get inside! I'm sure there are automatic defenses in place to discourage intruders, and it might decide that's what we are if we fight our way in." Shaking his head, and then taking a sudden step back, Anton put his hands on his hips, huffed, and stood there with a look of disgust on his face. "We came all this way just to be *locked out?*"

"That slot is the same shape as a scabbarrrrd. What about Thundarrrruss's sword-rrrr?" Again, Deidra proffered her opinion. "Remember, its funny marrrrkings glowed-rrrr!"

For a moment, Anton stood there. He looked deep into her eyes with a surprised look on his face. "How astute! You know, I think your *right!*" He was simply stunned. Deidra had easily surmised what he should have intuitively known. Impatiently, he produced his EHD and reached into it. Removing Thundaruss's sword, he held it in both hands and then carefully slid it into the slot. It fit perfectly.

"Unbelievable. He carried a *key* in the guise of a *weapon*. He never intended to do any *serious* battle, obviously. It was just a ruse, or perhaps it had a dual purpose." Dumbfounded, Anton stood there and watched as the circle began to glow.

"Authenticating. Verified! Key accepted," responded the soft feminine voice. "Permission to enter *granted*."

The sound of seals breaking free and of air escaping reminded Anton of his visit to the Clone Labs deep inside the depths of Valde Domus back on Methonias. With a hiss of compressed air, the heavy hermetically sealed doors slowly slid open, allowing the three to enter. Without a moment's hesitation, Anton removed the key, returned it to his EHD, grasped Deidra's hand, and slid through the opening. The moment they stepped inside, the doors closed and instantly resealed behind them.

"We're inside! *Unbelievable!*" Again, Anton was mystified. "Just like that …"

"You two make a good team! We're inside! Now what do we do?" As always, Tania had few suggestions when faced with human structures, technology, and techniques. She simply kept everyone focused on the mission by asking ordinary pertinent questions.

"I guess we find the cockatoo—at least that's what Amilius and Drôgän wanted me to do. First though, let's get some rest. Both of us are exhausted." Anton's expression supported his claim: his eyes were half open, and it was obvious his thought processes had diminished due to his prolonged exertion and lack of proper meals.

Anton quickly examined his surroundings. It was obvious there was nothing to succor their needs. The room was large enough to hold fifty people and was circular in shape. The only noticeable feature was an elevator platform to their left, but the device was in the raised position and it sealed the ceiling, making it unavailable for their use. Around the perimeter of the walls were dozens of antiquated holo-monitors. Upon entry to the chamber, they had turned on, and began displaying scenes of various aspects of the building and the

City of Celestra prior to its destruction. It was obviously a defunct museum-style exhibit.

"How do we summon the lift? Where are the controls?" Anton looked around hoping to learn how to use the facility. "One thing's for sure, this place is defensible. Everything is reinforced and built like a fortress. I believe we're relatively safe in here, for now, especially since this is the only building still intact in the city."

"Request accepted. Scanning guests. Katrah detected. Unknown insect detected." The soft feminine voice continued to inform Anton of its procedures. "The katrah is designated hostile and is unwelcome here. She will remain on the current level. Further access is therefore categorically denied."

"Unknown *insect!* I'm *not* an insect!" Insulted, Tania flew around in a circle and announced her anger. "I'm *not* an *insect*! Do you *hear* me?"

"Scanning database. Correction. Faerie detected. Identification of hypothetical creature confirmed. Updating database. Accessing KACATU records. Accessing etheric records. Accessing. The existence of faeries confirmed. Admittance to the upper levels granted with proper escort."

"Proper *escort?* What *proper* escort?" Confused, Anton wondered why the computer allowed him access yet forbade his friends.

"Executing battle mode. Anton Seven, you have command of the complex. How may I be of service?" queried the computer.

"*Battle* mode? Why *battle* mode?" announced Anton. "I want you to allow Deidra and Tania full access to this *facility!* I require their aid and I personally take responsibility for their actions. They shouldn't require any escort. *I'm* their escort." Making his demand, he made sure the computer unconditionally accepted his friends.

"Records of the final conflicts of humanity are recorded inside your ring. This information controls the actions of the master computer. You desired a defensible place of safety, a sanctuary. The complex is now sealed and in battle readiness. Armored shielding applied. Electronic shielding applied. You are in full command of the complex.

Battle mode is required to protect the structure during the re-education process and the preparation, and for all possible and or likely requests after the re-education process has completed."

"*Re-education? What* re-education?" Again, Anton wasn't sure what was going on. "Cockatoo, you mentioned cockatoo. Where is this, umm, *bird?*"

"KACATU: Knowledge Accelerated Computer Aided Transfer Unit. You are required to re-educate so that the facility can be of complete service to you, and aid you in the defeat of the Necromancer. The new prime directive of the complex is to save humanity from extinction. Lothendus has given you complete control of the complex. You now control all security codes. You are the advanced servant of mankind, but currently, you are unable to use the facility without knowledge of its capabilities. Your re-education is mandated both by need and Lothendus's prior command. This mandate cannot be superseded."

"Where is this … *KACATU?*" Perturbed, but intrigued, Anton angrily commanded the computer. "I need to know *everything* that's in this place *and* where to find it."

"All laboratories, computers, armament, hangers, cold fusion generators, and living quarters are housed deep in the ground below the complex. Do you wish to report to the KACATU immediately?"

"No, we require rest. We haven't rested properly for days. Where can we find a place to eat and sleep?" Anton was exhausted and wasn't ready to submit to the computer's agenda. "Certainly, all of us are allowed to use the facilities here? If nothing else, I'd like to have a turbo-shower!"

"The human habitation facilities are located on Lower Level One. You can access the level from Upper Level One. Please stand in the area marked 'waiting area' while the lift is deployed."

Unexpectedly, the lift unsealed from the ceiling, gently lowered, and came to a rest next to them. Then the door opened, allowing Anton and his friends to enter. Fascinated, Anton scrutinized the ancient lift. It was circular in shape and had transparent walls that allowed the passengers to view everything as they traveled upward. It reminded him of the platform he stood on aboard the space station orbiting Saurian Five during his abduction to Peruvious.

Excited, Anton looked at Deidra and smiled. "Excellent! Let's go!" Leading the way, he grasped the katrah's hand and darted off toward the lift. "Finally, I'm beginning to feel like I'm home on Methonias! This should be quite interesting."

"This is like you-rrrr *home-rrrr*? I have *neverrrr* seen anything like this beforrrr!" Deidra was at a loss. She'd never known anything other than a primitive lifestyle. She'd spent most of her life in the City of the Humans, which existed in another dimension without any sophisticated technology. This was her first experience with advanced applied science, and it confused her immensely and made her feel quite nervous. She looked at Anton with an expression of fear. "You-rrrr will have to show-rrrr me what to do-rrrr." Nervously Deidra put her arms around Anton, and her discomfort and distress became distinctly evident.

The three entered the lift and the door slid smoothly closed. The lift traveled silently, and effortlessly as it rose to the next level, reminding Anton of the ones he'd used frequently at the Great Temple. Within a few seconds, he stood in another large circular room with many inactive computers positioned in a seemingly random pattern. It wasn't clear to him what their purposes were, but he didn't have time to decipher their usage. The upper level was larger than the room below, and perfectly circular in shape. It was concentric with the size and shape of the outer structure. To the far end was another lift and he continued to guide Deidra and Tania toward it. As they approached it, the lift door quickly opened to admit them, and then sealed swiftly behind them after they'd entered. Traveling at an incredibly high speed downward, it required artificial gravity to hold them against the floor. The lift descended for a couple of minutes before it finally came to a rest.

"Wow, my ears popped several times. We must be a great distance underground." Looking at Deidra's reaction, Anton could see confusion in her eyes. "It's just like the subterranean levels under the Great Temple back home. I visited them just before I came to Peruvious."

"How-rrrr is this possible-rrrr? How-rrrr can we be so farrrr underground-rrrr?" Deidra's mouth hung open. She seemed even more scared than before, and completely perplexed by the technology around her. She took several deep breaths, and fidgeted about, personifying her increasing discomfort.

Reminded of a wild animal trapped in a cage, Anton watched Deidra act out her animalistic behavior. He didn't know what to say or how to comfort her, so he wrapped his arms around her and gave her a hug. "Please, concentrate on your breathing and relax. It's okay, trust me! No harm will come to us. Just think of it as if you are in a building on the surface."

"I've never been inside the Great Observatory before, and I've never been to Celestra. This is a remarkable place!" Tania too was overwhelmed, but she adapted readily to the circumstances and she had no choice but to follow Anton wherever he went. "I don't like being deep underground. It interferes with my natural senses, but I feel safe with you! You should too, Deidra!"

"Rowwerrrr," she roared. "I *do* trrrrust him-rrrr, but this thing is too-rrrr small-rrrr; I feel trrrrapped-rrrr."

As the three exited the lift, they found themselves standing at the end of a long hallway that stretched beyond their view. It was easily a quarter-mile long. To each side were doors of varying sizes and at varying distances. The design reminded Anton of the space station MB-1 he'd visited orbiting Methonias, only this hallway was straight rather than curved.

"Computer, where are the sleeping accommodations?" queried Anton.

Instantly, a nearby door slid sideways and admitted the three. "This room was prepared for you. It is fully programmable to suit whatever needs you have—just ask and they will adjust. What scenery do you desire to see on the holo-windows?" Seemingly more helpful than before, the computer responded instantly to Anton's inquiries.

"Something tropical would be nice," Anton replied. "I'm truly intrigued. I wonder how all of this is possible … " As they entered the room, Anton looked around and couldn't believe his eyes. Surprised, he nodded his head in approval. He was impressed at the level of technology for its ancient design; it could rival the luxury of the present. The room was huge and appeared comfortable enough to live in indefinitely. It had two bedrooms, a tiny kitchen of sorts, a large living space and a plush bathing facility with extravagant amenities such as a jacuzzi, turbo and standard showers, and a simple bath tub. "There's a turbo-shower!" Pointing to the oversized bathroom, Anton quickly headed toward it, discarding items of clothing on the floor as he went.

Following along behind him, Deidra wanted to see what he was doing. As Anton entered the shower, she climbed in with him oblivious to his motives and the purpose of the device. "What do we do in here-rrrr?"

Smiling, Anton chuckled quietly. "Would you like to clean yourself?"

"Take a bath-rrrr! Where-rrrr is the pool-rrrr?" Confused, Deidra didn't anticipate what was about to occur.

As Anton closed the door, jets of water instantly sprayed from all directions. They carefully adjusted to the exact positions necessary to systematically strip all the dirt and contaminates from both of their bodies. No matter how they shifted around, the multiple jets of streaming water adjusted to carry out their designed function. Soap, water, and special cleansing chemicals washed and sterilized their bodies in a matter of minutes, but Deidra wasn't impressed. For her, it was too strange and foreign, and she felt frightened.

"Rowwerrrr! You should have warrrrned me! This is smelly-rrrr! It feels strange-rrrr! What is that foamy stuff-rrrr? What is happening-rrrr?" She growled and complained repeatedly and covered her eyes and bounced around inside the four walls through the entire experience.

Then, just as suddenly as the cleansing began, it ended. Jets of air blew the water away and dried Anton's skin and hair, and Deidra's short fur. Anton smiled at her and put his arms around her trying to comfort her. For no particular reason, he pulled her against him and gave her a passionate kiss.

"*Rowwerrrr*! You're-rrrr a *rrrreal* man-rrrr!" she responded erotically. Returning his kiss, she purred like a kitten. "Rrrrrrr, wherrrr can we *rest-rrrr?*" she smiled seductively, as only a woman could do.

"I saw a room with a large bed over there." Anton pointed toward the nearest bedroom and smiled. "Let's go find out how comfortable it is." Taking her hand, he led her directly there.

"I want to explore. I'll leave you two alone while you, well … *sleep!*" Always sensible and understanding, Tania flew out of the room and down the hall. "I'll return when you … *awake*," she giggled over her shoulder as she left, and the door closed after her.

Smiling, Anton lay down on the bed and beckoned Deidra beneath the sheets. She quickly climbed up on top of him, and then bending down, she kissed him passionately and purred with excitement. "Ther-rrr's a first time for everrrryone-rrrr."

ANTON AWOKE GRADUALLY; DEIDRA LEFT him feeling both satisfied and content. Somewhere deep inside his heart he felt a bonding for her. It was the same feeling he'd felt for Nelda, only this time the drug-induced DNA-altering effects of the Virlaqueus didn't control his yearning for her pleasures. Deidra slept with her head upon his shoulder and her arm draped across his chest. Refreshed and gratified, he gave her a gentle kiss. "Wake up, sleepyhead," he whispered in her ear. "We need to go!"

"Rrrrrr, rowwerrrr," she purred. "I want to-rrrr sleep-rrrr; don't want to-rrrr go." Rolling over, she took a deep breath and opened her cat-like eyes ever so slightly. Looking into her vertical irises, Anton smiled coyly. Suddenly, she remembered the previous night's passion. "We *mated-rrrr*! We are *mates-rrrr*!" Wide-eyed and alert, she sat up suddenly.

"Oh, don't be silly. We shared our affections. More importantly, we need to eat. Let's ask the computer about breakfast." Disregarding Deidra's comment, Anton considered their fundamental needs and the importance of finding the KACATU. He wanted to discover why both Drôgän and Amilius sent him here for a re-education.

"Computer, where can we find an FRU?" inquired Anton.

"You require sustenance. Proceed down the hallway, the cafeteria is located to your right. The Food Replication Units are online. Tania, your faerie friend, is already there and using them. She has anticipated your requirements."

As if summoned, Tania abruptly flew into the living quarters. "I see you two have *slept* well. This is good!" She giggled and winked at them. "I found the cafeteria and prepared something *special* for both of you!"

Surprised, Anton smiled at Tania. "As always, your help and consideration are priceless. Thank you, Tania."

"Hurry, get dressed! You can't go wandering around without clothes forever! That's what *faeries* do!" Giggling, she quickly flew out the door and led the way.

Anton donned his clothing in a matter of seconds. His Methonian training prepared him for military swiftness and his ability to get dressed hurriedly surprised Deidra.

"I don't have any clothes-rrrr, and I don't like them much-rrrr, but I would feel betterrrr wearrrring something here-rrrr. It reminds me of my home-rrrr in the city, and my friends therrrr required me to wearrrr at least a loincloth-rrrr." Looking at Anton, Deidra implied she wanted him to replace the clothes the fracknoids had stripped from her. "Is there something arrrround here-rrrr I can wear-rrrr?"

"Computer, are there any clothes available for Deidra?" Quickly, he tried to fulfill her request. He wished to do everything for her that she asked of him.

"There is a uniform storage unit near the end of the hallway," replied the computer. "Special requests for specific garments require more time for tailoring. If the uniform storage unit doesn't provide what you desire, simply make your request and it will be delivered upon completion of its manufacture."

"Computer, manufacture one loincloth for Deidra," ordered Anton. "Oh, and one Methonian haori for me please."

Instantly, hidden lasers fired from multiple angles around the room, scanning and measuring both of their bodies within seconds. Even Anton was amazed at the sophistication of the device. He simply hadn't anticipated the convenience.

"Rowwerrrr! What is that-rrrr! I don't like it-rrrr! Stop-rrrr!" A wild look marked Deidra's face as she danced around unsuccessfully trying to avoid the lasers contact. Everything that happened was all so new to her, and she was easily frightened by the unfamiliar technologies. When the lasers completed their task, she instantly leapt into Anton's arms. "*Warn* me next time-rrrr. I don't *like* it here-rrrr! When can we *leave-rrrr!*"

"I still have to find out what this KACATU is all about, but first we need to eat, and then discover its location. Afterwards, we can formulate our next step. I don't know when we can leave. You're just going to have to get used to things here for now." Disappointed in her, but understanding, Anton tried to comfort Deidra as best he could, but politeness wasn't his forte. "Please, let's go eat. Tania's waiting for us, and she's prepared something special. We need to show her how much we appreciate her."

Grasping the staff in one hand and holding Deidra's hand in the other, Anton led the way. It didn't take long for them to find the cafeteria. It was a room large enough to accommodate more than fifty people. It had several long tables and all of them were prepared for use. The facility had a general sense of disuse and obviously had not been used for centuries.

Tania fluttered around impatiently and then quickly flew to Anton's shoulder when he entered the room. "It's about time! Look what I conjured up out of that box over there! It gave me some little white pills in a small bowl, but I altered them into real food. What do you think?" Proud of herself, she waited for their praise and approval.

Speechless, Anton looked at the meal. Placed elegantly on one of the tables was every conceivable breakfast food he'd ever known—and a few others he didn't. "You're simply amazing Tania, thank you!" Immediately, he sat down and served himself a healthy portion of as many items as would fit on his plate.

Sitting next to Anton, Deidra skipped most of the selections, but found several traditional meat dishes: sausage, bacon, and ham seemed to be all she had an interest in. "Rowwerrrr, good food-rrrr," was all she said as she nibbled and chewed her meat daintily, yet fervently in her cat-like way.

Anton watched as Deidra purred and devoured her food. Her behavior resembled that of a cat, and it disturbed him—yet at the same time, it intrigued him. He was captivated by her uniqueness. In some ways, her cat-like mannerisms shocked him, but his desire for her human femininity and distinctive qualities drove his fundamental male instincts wild with desire. He didn't understand why. It seemed somehow ethically wrong, yet he didn't deny his feelings, he simply gave into them. Eating hungrily himself, he quickly polished off his teeming plate in a matter of minutes.

"Well, you two really like my meal! You are most welcome!" Feeling ignored yet pleased, Tania made her point. "I guess I'll have to provide for you more often!" Giggling, she waited for the additional praise she'd anticipated.

"Thank you, Tania, you're invaluable. You continually astonish me with what you can do." Smiling as he chewed his last bite, Anton gave her the compliment she desired. "How is it you can alter food pills into real food?"

"Well silly man, for me, it isn't very much different than altering DNA, or adjusting one creature to another. I simply reconstructed their base elements and gave them shape—that was the hard part. It's just a little trick I figured out, an aspect of my purpose." Closing her eyes and raising her nose into the air, she sounded smug as she bragged. "I'm just glad that you *like* it," she said, looking through the slits of her eyes.

"Very much, and so does Deidra." Nudging her with his elbow, Anton encouraged her to respond. "As you can see …"

"Yes!" Tania laughed excitedly and spun around like a top in midair. Suddenly she came to a stop and bowed, spreading her arms wide.

As soon as they finished eating, Anton stood and immediately asked the computer another question. "Computer, which way is it to the KACATU?"

"The main computer complex is on Lower Level Two. Proceed to the secondary lift at the far end of the hallway. The loincloth and haori you requested will be delivered in two minutes. There was no pattern for the exact articles of clothing you requested, therefore designs from the historical database were used for the manufacturing of the two articles."

Cleaning up, Tania placed the dirty dishes and leftovers into the recycling unit located beside the FRUs. Just as she returned to Anton's shoulder, a small, automated robotic table on wheels entered the cafeteria and delivered the garments Anton had ordered.

Donning the miniskirt, Deidra smiled. It fit perfectly and draped halfway to her knees. It included a slit in the back for her tail with a zipper for modesty. "This is a skirrrrt, not a loincloth-rrrr! I *like* it-rrrr! It is short-rrrr!"

"Very good! I'd like to say, it looks *very* good on you! Now that we have *that* out of the way, let's go!" Excitedly, Anton hurried down the hall with Deidra in tow. He couldn't wait to see what he might find on the next level. The intuitively familiar feeling of the complex gave him the desire to show his friends around as if he knew exactly what to expect. A sense that he had returned to Methonias lifted his spirits, and as a result, he acted more like a schoolboy than the transformed super-human he had become since arriving on Peruvious.

Entering the lift, the three instantly traveled downward to the next level. The elevator's speed was slower this time; it took more than a minute to reach level two. When the doors opened, Anton nearly leapt out into the room with excitement, all but forgetting his Warrior's caution. To his surprise, he entered a vast chamber perhaps a quarter-mile square and easily one hundred feet tall; it was completely full of highly advanced CNC machinery, all of it powered up and functioning. Robots were busy producing every conceivable product imaginable and even more that Anton couldn't begin to fathom. Manufacturing and construction was not his expertise.

"What is this place?" he exclaimed suddenly. "It's, well, it's a factory!" Looking at Tania and then at Deidra, his expression went blank. "Where's the KACATU?"

"Proceed to section forty-three R&D. The research laboratory is located there." The computer continued to guide Anton toward his destination. "Section forty-three R&D is located down isle sixteen to your left."

Quickly scanning the room, Anton suddenly noticed a vast walled-off area. Beside the sealed door read the words: "Research and Development, Section Forty-Three."

"It's over there. I can just make it out." Pointing, Anton acknowledged his discovery. "Careful you two, the activity of the machinery and robots around here looks potentially hazardous."

Within a minute, they entered the walled-off room. Inside was a waiting area complete with chairs, a table, an FRU, and a lavatory. Printed beside an inner door was a warning that read: "KACATU Access restricted. Only authorized personnel allowed." Next to the door was another keyhole identical to the one at the building's entrance. Anton nodded for Deidra to sit as he pulled out Thundaruss's key from his EHD and slid it into the slot.

"Access to the KACATU is denied to the katrah and faerie," announced the Computer. "They are to remain in the waiting room during the re-education sequence for their own safety."

Looking at Tania, Anton huffed and shook his head in frustration. "Take care of Deidra. I'll go inside and have a quick look around. I won't be long, I hope."

Anton stepped inside the room and the door closed after him and sealed itself with a hiss of compressed air; Tania and Deidra looked at each other and for a moment both were speechless.

"Well, now what?" Tania exclaimed, putting a finger to her chin.

"Rowwerrrr, I don't like it here-rrrr. I want to go back to my room-rrrr."

"I think we will, if he doesn't return soon." Trying to comfort Deidra, Tania fluttered around as if she were searching for something to do. "I don't like it here either. I hope he's quick. This place scares me!"

"Re-education commencing. Subject receiving preparatory procedures," announced the computer. "Please return to the upper level until the procedure completes." Then the computer fell silent, leaving the two women alone.

"Humph, I think we should go. Anton is trapped in there and the computer doesn't want us to stay." Tania flew around Deidra and then motioned for her to follow as she flew toward the lift.

Looking at the door, and back at Tania, Deidra reluctantly trailed along after the little faerie. A single tear ran down her cheek. "He's not coming back-rrrr."

Forced Knowledge

THE DOOR SWIFTLY SLID CLOSED behind Anton. He stood there stunned as he gazed upon the vast collection of advanced indescribable devices held within the mysterious room. A gigantic glass sphere sat on a large circular pedestal in the center of the chamber like a giant crystal ball. It appeared as if it housed the universe. Encompassing its entire perimeter were ancient computer consoles, all of which were active. The consoles seemed to be similar in design to those he'd seen in the control room aboard the space station orbiting Saurian Five, yet that's where the resemblance ended. Their specific purpose was indeterminable, however, it seemed intuitive they must operate the functions of the sphere. Astonished, he slowly walked around the sphere with a look of curiosity on his brow and pondered its intended purpose. It couldn't just be displaying the universe for no particular intent.

"The re-education process is ready to initiate. Please remove your clothing and be seated on the reclining surgical unit," announced the computer. "The KACATU is prepared for you and awaiting your compliance."

A door opened into a tiny room just large enough to house a surgical table. Eyeing it, Anton raised an eyebrow and hesitated. "What procedures are scheduled?" Nervously, he inquired the computer suspiciously. "Just *how* am I to be … *re-educated?*"

"The computer aided education process is too complex for a quick explanation, and your current knowledge is far too limited. Please remove your clothes and seat yourself in the reclining surgical unit," replied the computer. "Once the process has concluded, you will comprehend the procedure."

"Only after my, what, *surgery*?" inquired Anton.

"The procedure requires your unconditional compliance. You must comply for the procedure to commence," the computer responded.

Reluctantly, Anton slowly removed his clothing and folded each article meticulously, and placed them on a nearby computer console. He then seated himself on the surgical table. This reminded him of his visit to the Clone Labs, a memory that still disturbed him. It was a memory he didn't wish to repeat, yet it seemed to him that was precisely what he was doing. Lying back, he put his arms on the armrests and adjusted himself for comfort. Taking a deep breath, he closed his eyes and waited.

Unexpectedly, restraining straps promptly immobilized his arms, legs and chest, and braces restrained his head completely. Panel doors in the walls slid open and mechanical cybernetic arms reached out and injected him with drugs. Instantly, he fell unconscious. It all happened so quickly he didn't have time to react to or consider his situation.

"Removing temporal bones. Exposing temporal lobes," announced the computer as it worked at an incredible robotic speed. It sliced with laser scalpels, clamped arteries and used healing lasers to cauterize bleeding. It performed each movement so quickly it seemed as if the robotic arms would collide, yet the device operated on Anton flawlessly. Next, the arms operated on his cranium, removing a small section of skull above each ear. "Inserting cybernetic computer net." Delicately, the arms inserted a cybernetic neural net underneath the skull, and wrapped it around his temporal lobes. Meticulously, the arms connected the net in a thousand places to his brain. This took a considerable amount of time, stretching the surgery to hours. When it had completed the installation, the robotic arms replaced the temporal bones, and advanced chemicals sprayed over the bone tissue and instantly re-fused them into place and completely healed his flesh covering the surgery. Finally, the computer announced: "Surgery complete. Neural net installed. Injecting stimulants. Complete. Subject returning to consciousness." All the restraints holding him in place returned behind the panels and disappeared from view.

The drug-induced sleep was completely dreamless for Anton. He was entirely oblivious to the operation being performed, and he remained suspended unconscious in this state for hours as the computer performed its advanced implementation of its programmed surgical procedure. Suddenly, his eyes flew open as the stimulants took effect, and he looked up at a single robotic arm with a syringe pointed at him. Slowly it returned to the wall panel beside him and disappeared.

In less than three hours, the procedure was complete. Anton slowly raised his head and looked around, trying to remember why he was lying down. He saw the giant globe and pondered what it was. The various computers surrounding the giant sphere provided the only visual activity in the room. They held his attention for a few moments as they silently blinked and processed incomprehensible programming. For a few moments more, he stared at the large sphere containing the universe and watched the slow movements of the galaxies. He was unable to grasp their purpose or meaning. Confusedly, he gently shook his head trying to remember why he was naked and sitting there on the operating table. His sense of identity seemed distant, and he struggled to recall what had happened. A moment passed, and then another, yet his thoughts seemed hindered at determining his circumstances.

"Computer, what just happened? I seem to have lost some time," Anton finally inquired. "I feel, well, I feel odd. My thoughts are numbed. I feel like I need to *know* something, and it *eludes* me. It's like my thoughts are empty."

"Surgery complete. Subject nearly recovered. Activating KACATU link to the neural net. Please return your head to the horizontal position while an upload connection is established."

Uncontrollably drained of energy, Anton gladly complied and relaxed. His hands trembled, and his head throbbed with pain.

"I have a headache," he announced. "I can't think clearly."

Instantly, a cybernetic arm sprang out from behind a panel beside him, injected him with a drug, then returned to its hidden position behind the panel.

"The discomfort will pass shortly. Relax and remain completely motionless while the upload is performed. If this is a problem, the restraints will be returned to hold you in place."

Anton continued to fidget and he rolled his head slowly from side to side. The drug soon took effect, but it left him agitated, and he wanted to stand.

"Initiating restraint sequence," announced the computer. Just as quickly as the restraints had disappeared after his surgery, they returned and held Anton completely immobilized. Immediately, two lasers struck Anton's head, one above each ear. His eyes suddenly opened wide, his mouth hung open, his fists clenched, and his entire body became rigid, as if they had paralyzed him.

"Upload connection established. KACATU accessing neural net. Transferring etheric records. Complete. Uploading universal physics and related photon knowledge base libraries. Complete! Uploading celestial eye operation and control functions. Complete! Uploading the corresponding usage libraries. Complete!"

For what seemed like an eternity to Anton, the lasers held his head in a stasis. Trinary code filled his neural net with information at trillions of geopbytes per second. In reality, it took less than a minute for the transfer to complete, but it felt to him like an eternity, as the newly installed memory accepted massive amounts of data, and then finally the lasers terminated. Anton's eyes and mouth slowly closed. The room seemed to spin in all directions as the neural net established billions of neural connections to his brain. More time passed.

"KACATU connection to the neural net terminated. Removing restraints. You may now move about the room freely," the computer finally announced.

Anton lay there for a few moments longer, and then in a sudden flash, images filled his thoughts. Suddenly, his eyes sprang open and again a wild expression covered his face. He sat up abruptly and looked intensely at the sphere in front of him and grinned.

"I *know* what this *is!* It's the Etheriscope!" he exclaimed. "I comprehend the meaning, the purpose, the reason—*the need!* Light! It's all about *light!* How could I have missed the *significance?*"

As quickly as he could, he stood up and walked over to the computer console that controlled the sphere. "I *know* how to use *everything* here! It's so *primitive*, so *simple.*"

"Re-education sequence complete. Anton Seven, the facility is at your disposal,"

announced the computer. "Preparations are needed for the final conflict. What are your instructions?"

"I need to process the information you've installed. The staff needs immediate reconstruction! It is missing the dragon pearl, it was destroyed. And I need advanced weaponry!"

"Compliance. Commencing manufacturing of weaponry."

Whirling around suddenly, Anton donned his clothing and grasped the remains of the Staff of Balance. Marching over to the far side of the room, he slid it into a matching hole on a computer panel near the entrance to the room. It fit perfectly, like a sword sliding into its scabbard. Operating the controls, he then activated the enhance-ment process, a process both Lothendus, and in turn Vim, had each performed over a millennium before using the same computer.

Pulling out his EHD, Anton removed the *Lapillusaurus* pearl. Placing it in a bowl-shaped depression next to the staff, he operated a few more controls and then walked over to the Etheriscope in the center of the room.

"Foreign object detected. Scanning for recognition. Software detected. Security codes detected. Advanced programming and instructions sets detected. A new prime directive detected."

Suddenly, every computer in the room lit up with increased activity. Previously unseen holo-monitors activated, and a flurry of computational activity unlike anything Anton had ever witnessed before seemed to possess every console.

"Advanced programming accepted. Security codes accepted. Downloading software. Complete! Commencing the reprogramming of the entire complex's computers. Complete! Rebooting. Complete!"

Inadvertently, a sudden overwhelming need to thoroughly com-prehend the data placed in his neural net made Anton's head spin. He suddenly felt dizzy again, and he desired to sit down. Looking at the computer terminals surrounding the Etheriscope, he recognized the KACATU's mental-link console. He sat down in a chair in front of it and rested for a short time.

"Reprogramming of the CNC machines is complete. Manufac-turing of new computers in progress. The entire complex is scheduled for a complete refit. Installation of new hardware projected in sixteen hours, twenty-three minutes. Complete refitting of the entire man-ufacturing complex with updated CNC technology projected in two days, three hours, five minutes. Manufacturing of updated designs contained within the *Lapillusaurus* Pearl will commence immediately following the refit."

Taking a mental note of its activities, and then ignoring the com-puter, Anton activated the laser-to-neural net link from the KACATU.

Two lasers, one to each side of his head, established an interface with his neural net, and his dizziness instantly faded. Placing his hands inside the console's input interface, he prepared to use the giant sphere for its engineered purpose.

"Brilliant design," he mumbled to himself. "If only I had *this* knowledge when I first arrived on Peruvious. Now I understand the reason Vim introduced me to Drôgän, Amilius and Trepid, and I understand the true purpose of photons, light, and universal physics." He hadn't mumbled to himself in days and the old familiar quirk seemed to comfort him.

"Photons," he continued to mumble. "Light waves, gravity, the illusion of time created by gravity or the lack thereof, multidimensional reality, advanced string theories, wormholes—it's all here. I can use it! The staff, the celestial eye! But first … "

Concentrating on the giant sphere, the panorama of the universe suddenly became active. Searching for a specific location, the galaxies suddenly expanded and passed from view as if Anton were looking through the front viewing screen of a spaceship as it traveled. It was as if he was navigating through space, yet the universe was housed in front of him. Faster than millions of multiples of light speed, faster than the Pleceivious could ever physically travel, Anton zoomed through the universe until he found the place he wanted to see: the Triangulum Galaxy.

"It would be nice to see home," he mused. "Unfortunately, this Etheriscope is incapable of viewing Methonias in real time. It would be nice to see what my Masters are doing."

Zooming in on his home star system, and then finally on his home world of Methonias, Anton searched for a glimpse of the Great Temple. Within moments, he located where it was supposed to be, but he was less than satisfied with the result. It was a view prior to its construction, and prior to the terraforming of the planet.

"This ancient contraption is amazing, but I need to use it purposefully," he mumbled.

Reluctantly, he zoomed out and began to search for the Milky Way. He then zoomed in on the star system of Sol and finally, Peruvious. Activating the etheric records, he viewed time at high speed; beginning with the formation of the planet and then moving incrementally forward to the present. He viewed the entire process of the formation of life, its evolution and the processes controlled by the faeries. History unfolded in front of him, and he manipulated the speed to observe everything carefully. He increased the pace to pass the events that held little significance, and slowed the pace for the specific points of interest and import he wished to observe. He viewed in depth the specific occurrences that shaped the development of the human race.

Then again, he returned to the beginning of etheric time. Once again Anton watched the formation of the earth. Battered by celestial debris, and hammered by an enormous collision with another smaller planet, the moon suddenly appeared driven from the earth by the impact. Countless meteors hammered both the earth and the moon, bringing frozen liquids by the megatons to the infant-earth. They covered the entire planet with water, filling it with the largest concentration of fluids in the entire system. Tectonic plates shifted and a single huge landmass rose from the primordial sea.

Then suddenly, in a flash of brilliant light, the earth changed. The specifics of the event were obscure, but Anton derived that it was the moment that *One* placed *Himself* upon the earth in *His* fragmented form. Soon afterward, life began, primitive at first, then, in time, it became more sophisticated and the variety and abundance escalated exponentially. Ostensibly, as if by magic, the faeries suddenly appeared and traversed the entire planet. They touched every form of life and altered it, guiding it through the slow process of evolution. Amazed by what he witnessed, Anton delved ever deeper into the details. He stopped to observe the mechanics of the alterations and then moved on to the next. The faeries cast an infusion of light, of photons, into the DNA of everything. They invoked the magic of divine power given to them to wield and control, dispensing it precisely in tiny amounts where it needed to go.

Hours passed as Anton studied the details of the etheric records. Meanwhile, robots brought nutrition pills and water to him as he devoured all that he witnessed. Soon a day went by, and he became exhausted. "I've just *got* to rest," he mumbled, and then left the room.

A cot lay folded near the lavatory, and he used it for a short nap. More nutrition pills and water arrived, then Anton returned to his work. Continuing, he watched as primitive birds evolved, and from them the dinosaurs. Countless species ruled the planet for eons. Creatures of every description were hatched and born, and they lived their lives in the horrible violent process of natural selection and DNA manipulation.

Gradually, over an indeterminable amount of time, the faeries guided the changes needed to achieve the ultimate biological design, that of the mammal. Eventually, this line of evolution produced a primitive human form, that of the hominids. In multitudes of slight tweaks and changes, the faeries eventually produced the australopithecines. The role of the faeries was unconditionally essential to guide nature to produce man.

Finally, after many changes and iterations, most of which branched off into extinction, the faeries altered the hominids DNA into homo sapiens, and the first of the human souls entered these early designs. They lived out a primitive existence in the early days, but their superior intelligence, opposable thumbs, and upright walking, ultimately provided them the tools needed to advance themselves toward their definitive purpose, to fight the Intelligence of Non-existence, Vile the Necromancer, and to return to paradise victors over evil. Naturally, at this early point in evolutionary time, humanity still had no concept of this objective.

Centuries passed, and then millennia. Anton continued to watch as primitive societies evolved, and finally, the first major inception of culture developed and ensued. Eventually, man learned to navigate the world's oceans in primitive sailing vessels, and finally, the first true development of technology transpired. Primitive airships, self-powered sea vessels, and high-rise buildings were constructed and used. People traveled the world and populated it on every continent and soon populated the entire planet. The first religion and communication with *One* provided a peaceful existence and man's knowledge increased. Prayer was a staple of the cultures of every society, and war became the staple of man's existence.

After several millennia, something significant occurred: the two *Intelligences* again battled, this time to claim the ownership of human souls. The powers unleashed were tremendous, and in the end, resulted in the complete destruction of the earth. The tectonic plate that provided man's first home fragmented due to a cataclysm of incredible powers, and the subduction of most major continents under the ocean returned them to the earth's mantle, expunging them and all evidence of man's earliest cultures permanently from existence. In the end, *One* banished the *Intelligence of Non-Existence*, but at a tremendous price—the creation of the multiple dimensions of hell and the loss of those souls that chose to live their lives in sin. They found themselves cast down to serve evil. The choice between heaven and hell, good and evil, was now man's to make. The armies of the two intelligences grew steadily as man's gift of the freedom of choice played its role in providing armies for each side.

"So that's the connection. That's why that horrible forest exists outside of Celestra." Anton's realization left him bewildered and disheartened. More determined than ever, he continued to study the etheric records. "I must have *all* the answers," he mumbled repeatedly to himself. "I must know *everything* that Vim knew. I must understand how to master the manipulation of light."

Again, hours passed, and then another day, as Anton carefully studied history. The etheric records unfolded their hidden secrets before his eyes as he directed what course he chose to follow, and what knowledge he chose to learn. He watched as cultures rose and fell—Mesopotamia, Samaria, Egypt, Rome, China—he studied all of them from beginning to end; his appetite for knowledge was insatiable.

Of all the significant events in human history, two particular events stood out above all others. The first Anton reviewed was the finer details of the Egyptian empire. He watched as the Hebrews were freed from slavery by a man. He listened intently to all of the conversations this man had with the Egyptian Pharaoh, and the conversations he had with Drôgän who appeared as a burning bush atop a mountain. He watched as he cast a staff on the ground in front of the Pharaoh, and watched it change into a serpent, and then when the man retrieved the serpent by its tail it incredibly transformed back into a staff, *the* staff, *Vim's* staff, and subsequently, now, Anton's staff.

Anton then followed the history of the staff, its burial, and finally its rediscovery by Lothendus. Using the Etheriscope, Lothendus was able to discover when and where it had disappeared in antiquity, and where it lay waiting for centuries for him to retrieve. He watched Lothendus meld a dragon pearl with the staff, and later, he saw Vim repeat this action when he claimed the staff after Lothendus's banishment. Both meldings happened here, in this chamber. Both men had transformed the staff, and now Anton realized that he too needed to do the same.

Most importantly, Anton continued to watch the events of a second man's life. He watched as a woman became pregnant without knowing a man. He watched the birth of a child, and he watched how Drôgän had appeared as if he were a star in the sky above the child's birth. He watched the life of this man, from childhood to adulthood, and finally his crucifixion. The similarity of Vim's death stunned him, but most of all, he was shocked how humanity had referred to this man as their savior, just as the people of Amilius's Castle had referred to him as *their* savior.

Sitting back in his chair, Anton disconnected from the Etheriscope. Standing, he walked over to the staff and the *Lapillusaurus* pearl. "This piece of wood is many thousands of years old, and it still exists. Most significantly, it produced nuts, and I ate them." Amazed and perplexed, he scratched his chin. "The staff is mine, but I don't have a dragon pearl, and *I* killed the *Dragon Master*."

Staring at them for a long time, he considered his options and how he could replace the Dragon Pearl. It seemed an impossible task. Then suddenly, a crucial realization entered his thoughts: serpent, dragon, *Lapillusaurus*, all of them are reptiles! Carefully, he removed the staff from the computer console, and then picked up the *Lapillusaurus* pearl. Placing the pearl on the floor, he cast the staff down on the floor. Instantly, it turned into a serpent just as it had several times before. Slithering, it opened its mouth and bit down hard on the pearl; its head transformed into a *Lapillusaurus* talon, and held the pearl suspended between the fingers untouched. Grasping the serpent by its tail, Anton raised it into the air and watched it transform back into the staff just as it had done for Lothendus, Vim, and the man from earth's ancient past.

Unexpectedly, the *Lapillusaurus* pearl began to glow, and then a voice emanated from it declaring: "*Behold, the Staff of Balance reborn, but this is no ordinary transmutation. From this day forward, this staff shall be known as the Universal Staff of Balance. Use it wisely, young Anton, it's more powerful than it ever was before.*" It was unmistakably Drôgän's voice.

Instantly, Anton's ring began to glow. Argent fire burned around his hand, ran up the staff, and enveloped the globe. Energy filled his body, and he too turned argent and radiated brilliant white light. For a moment, he stood there like a sentinel. Then suddenly, unexpectedly, a small golden cylinder on a chain dropped from the pearl and landed gently in his hand. It was identical to the ones he'd seen both Vim and the Ruler of the Council, Lothendus, use.

Placing the chain around his neck, Anton held the cylinder up toward the globe. Energy fired from the globe like a lightning bolt and struck the cylinder. It filled the cylinder with power until it glowed like his ring. Grasping it in his palm, he then absorbed the power into himself.

"I, I feel, *invincible!*" he shouted, and the tiny room echoed, as if his voice were amplified. "I sense cosmic power! I feel as though I have the energy of a star held within my hands, and I have dominion over all of Peruvious!"

Grasping the staff with both hands, Anton noticed it felt as light as a feather. Sliding it back into the hole in the computer console, he continued to hold it for a moment longer. As if in response, the computer suddenly revealed a new image inside the Etheriscope. It fluctuated and presented a new replication of the past. Fascinated, he released the staff and returned to his seat. Watching the scene, he observed the history of the twentieth century unfold before him.

"I wonder why it chooses to show me *this*," mumbled Anton. "What is the significance?"

The advent of man's humble technological beginnings divulged themselves in detail. Wars of all descriptions wreaked havoc across the planet one after another. Petty excuses for genocide drove man to destroy man at an ever-increasing pace. More and more officiousness drove mankind's ideology and justification to exterminate. Technology increased exponentially as the need to slaughter drove humanity to ruin. By the scores, human souls filled the dimensions of hell.

As the twentieth century concluded, the twenty-first century in turn revealed itself, and Anton witnessed the beginnings of mankind's first genetic experiments and alterations. The first true cloning and the first true splicing of human genes with those of lower life forms produced the hogtrahs. These hybrids fought the Eugenic Wars, killing most of humanity. One by one, each religion became a target and then one race after another. Eventually, the hogtrahs outnumbered the humans two to one. Their contempt for humanity and their own self-loathing drove them fervently to kill and destroy unimpeded and irrepressibly.

Sequentially, the twenty-second century unfolded, and the inception of the katrahs produced a balance that saved humanity from complete extinction. They fought to save mankind by augmenting their war with the hogtrahs. In time, these two factions nearly eliminated themselves, leaving humans once again as the dominant species.

Finally, in the twenty-third century, after the destruction of most of the earth, humans built huge intergalactic spacecraft and departed the earth. Those few that remained, a mere handful of what humanity once was, built the City of Celestra. It was a refuge, a place of higher learning and of peace, and once again, humanity thrived just as it had in its humble early beginnings. War was finally outmoded.

Now that he grasped man's entire history, Anton appreciated all that Drôgän, Vim, Amilius, and Trepid had revealed to him. He recognized the significance of what he was asked to do. He understood the role that the hogtrahs and katrahs had played in history, but most importantly, he realized the stakes of winning or losing the final battles. The universe itself was in peril, and he was the mere mortal *One* had chosen to lead the final conflict to defeat the Intelligence of Non-existence and to save mankind and the universe from irrevocable annihilation.

This realization left Anton speechless. He felt too small to do something so paramount, so profound. He wondered how one simple human could fight the gods! Much of this responsibility Vim had gone to great efforts to reveal to him over the past few days, but now that he witnessed the events for himself, he fully appreciated their significance.

However, he wasn't through learning. Adjusting the Etheriscope, he attuned it to a mere thousand years into the past. Witnessing Lothendus's history, he watched as he directed the construction of the Great Observatory and the creation of the celestial eye. He watched as he battled Vile and was ultimately defeated, and how the overlord had deformed him, wrecked his soul, and banished him from the earth. Finally, he witnessed Vim's involvement and the transference of the Staff of Balance into his hands. He witnessed the destruction of the City of Celestra, and the gradual decline of humanity. Speechless, Anton sat there staring at the Etheriscope for a time, and then one final question entered his thoughts.

"I need to know how Vim was captured, and what happened to Grëyfwyn and the hogtrahs." Mumbling, he felt the pain of humanity's failures, and of his own. Yet, at the same time, he felt his resolution to succeed increase. His desire to carry forth the fight to defeat Vile was his only option.

"I *will* win. I have no other alternative. I just don't know how yet, but I *will win*." Adjusting the controls, Anton searched for the Towers of Tor. He witnessed Vim's capture by his own evil Methonian brethren, the noble death of the hogtrahs and the mortifying choice Grëyfwyn made causing his own death, and the destruction of the two Towers of Tor.

Disheartened, he slowly stood, and retrieved the staff. The moment Anton touched it, the sphere radiated light and ignited his ring. Power flowed through his body, and his feet left the floor. Floating, he left the research room. His heart ached with despair as he tried desperately to formulate a plan to achieve the victory over evil, a task he felt somewhat hopeless to achieve.

As he entered the manufacturing environment, he couldn't believe his eyes: modern new equipment replaced the old, and manufacturing was at full capacity. Drones moved parts around and robots assembled them at a such a pace it appeared as though devices simply appeared as if by magic from nowhere. Surprised, he returned to the elevator and stood there looking at it. Replication printers filled the chamber, their lasers burning new parts of every conceivable design for completely unknown purposes. He stood there for a few moments and put his hope in the new computers to provide him with the tools he needed for success. He had no other hope at this time, and he reasoned that computers had an answer he couldn't know.

"I, I no longer require this primitive form of travel," he mumbled as he looked at the lift. Concentrating, he levitated and passed through the solid granite that encased the entire factory. Effortlessly, he returned to his room and found Deidra and Tania waiting for him. To them it appeared as if he simply materialized out of thin air.

"Anton!" Tania suddenly exclaimed as he mysteriously material-ized before them. "How did you get here? What *happened* to the *staff?*"

"Rowwerrrr, you've been gone-rrrr a long time-rrrr, morrrrr than thrrrree days-rrrr." Deidra too expressed her surprise. Her eyes bulged as she spoke. "I missed you-rrrr." Racing over to Anton, she threw her arms around him, embraced him, closed her eyes, and tipped her head back.

Holding her in his arms, Anton kissed Deidra passionately and returned her hug. Fire burned in his heart as he realized just how much he'd grown to love her. It was a passionate true love from his heart, a love he felt inside his soul, not one imposed. "I missed you as well. It's nice to be back with both of you." Winking at Tania, he acknowledged her as well.

"What have you been *doing* for the past three days? We were begin-ning to think something *awful* had happened, and we were about to go check on you, even if the computer tried to stop us." Pointing a finger at Anton, Tania scolded him. "Couldn't you at least have let us know how long you'd be down there? We were worried." Like a parent chastising a child, she admonished him further.

"There wasn't time, I had to complete the reconstruction of the staff and learn about earth's past. I learned *where* the staff comes from and *how* to use it. I just need practice … " Standing proud and gallant, Anton dismissed Tania's pertness. "As you know, time grows short."

Caught off guard, Tania suddenly gasped. She realized that for the first-time Anton sounded as determined as Vim, and surprisingly, he conveyed the old wizard's temperament too. "*You've changed.* What *happened* to you down there? And how did you reconstruct the *staff?*"

"That room—the KACATU—it forced information or, more accu-rately, knowledge into me. More importantly, it's the room where Vim's staff, the Staff of Balance that is, was originally constructed. The Etheriscope showed me what I needed to know to rebuild it." Mini-mizing his response as best he could, Anton intentionally ignored the surgical implantation of the neural net; he didn't wish to argue about its morality, or any other issues, but he was confident Tania would uncover the truth eventually.

"Rowwerrrr, what's yourrrr plan now-rrrr?" asked Deidra. She too could feel his change of temperament, and she wasn't entirely pleased with the differences. "Arrrr you-rrrr *hungrrrry-rrrr*?" Watching him like a cat stalking its prey, she changed the subject, hoping to ease the tension.

"You two give me the impression you don't trust me, why?" questioned Anton. "Everything is all right. The device in that room, the Etheriscope, it revealed a tremendous amount of history to me, and it took a long time to sit through all of it. I hope I've given you a sufficient explanation." Again, he didn't want to reveal the surgery, and it was difficult to do so without lying. He hoped they wouldn't inquire further, and he hoped Tania wouldn't notice some subtle change to his skull and brain, or see the net inside of him with her magical faerie insight.

Speechless, both Tania and Deidra seemed stunned, or perhaps simply perturbed. For a few moments, neither spoke a word, but their eyes communicated unspoken thoughts with each other.

"Well then, yes, I *am* hungry. All I've had for the last three days are nutrition pills. A real meal would be *most* satisfying." Answering Deidra's inquiry, Anton agreed that he required life's most fundamental need, that of sustenance, and he was glad to sidestep any further interrogation by changing the subject at this time. It wasn't that he didn't want them to know about his surgery, he simply didn't feel like discussing the details just then. He was still digesting the experience himself and didn't want them to worry needlessly. He promised himself he would enlighten them later when the time was right.

"Oh! Let me offer you a *good* meal!" Giggling like a small child, Tania quickly flew out of the room toward the cafeteria. Within a few short minutes, she'd prepared a pleasant meal as she had done before, using the nutrition pills and a little faerie magic to alter them.

Following soon after her, Anton and Deidra quickly made their way to the cafeteria, took a seat and watched Tania expectantly. The food the little faerie had prepared was extravagant, and Anton relished every morsel. Salad made of leafy greens and fruit, polenta sliced in rounds, cheeses, baguettes and sirloin tip prepared medium rare covered the table. It was easily enough to feed five people.

"Unbelievable. You're a *treasure*, Tania." As if he hadn't eaten for a week, Anton stuffed his face faster than he could chew. "This is the best meal I've had since leaving Methonias, no offense to the women of your city, Deidra!" he said with his mouth full.

Giggling, both Deidra and Tania watched Anton as he ate like a teenage boy, amusing them no end.

"You-rrrr funny-rrrr. You-rrrr should have rrrreturrrrned to eat a meal with us-rrrr." As if to say I missed you, Deidra teased him. "You-rrrr eat like a hungrrrry kitten-rrrr."

"So, what are your plans now?" Tania stood on the table in front of Anton with her hands on her hips. "You must have a plan after being … *re-educated!* What did you *learn?* You need to tell us *everything.*" She then pointed her finger at Anton and shook it as she asked her final question, as if scolding a small child, as if she knew he was hiding something.

"I learned about human history. I know about the faeries' role in evolution, I saw all of you performing your designed intent, altering DNA and guiding nature throughout time. I know about the hogtrahs and the katrahs, I saw everything your people did, the wars, the fighting. I understand the animosity you have for each other. However, the primary thing that I was able to accomplish was to put the staff back together. It's better than before. Most of all, I think I know how to fight Vile. But I need to see the celestial eye. The key to my plans lie there."

Anton was still formulating his strategy as he spoke, and he wasn't completely sure of how he would prove what he said. He knew light was the key, and he knew the celestial eye used light in a multitude of ways. He believed that he simply needed to practice using it, but he was concerned about what condition the overlord had left it in after he'd used it to destroy Celestra. Even the Etheriscope couldn't show him the finer details of a close-up, hands-on inspection.

"Let's get some rest, and then tomorrow I'll try to use it." Not entirely sure of himself, Anton speculated as much as formulated his plan, and it showed. "The celestial eye is the key to victory. I'm sure of it."

"It doesn't *sound* like you're sure of it. I think your *guessing!*" interjected Tania. "It *sounds* like you're just going to try to do something with it, but you don't know *what.* How come that KACATU didn't teach you to use it?"

"Well, perhaps I don't know exactly what to do, yet, but the KACATU gave me complete knowledge of its usage. I mean, the KACATU didn't teach me to use the device, it simply installed the knowledge into my memory. It placed the knowledge of the controls inside my head. Besides, the only other option would be to go to Vile's Spire and fight him directly. Therefore, the celestial eye is the only option left that I can try." Looking at Tania, he expressed his misgivings. Taking a deep breath, he sat back in his chair and hoped his explanation satisfied her discerning questions.

Shaking her finger at Anton again, Tania quickly responded: "Fighting Vile directly would be suicide. You can't *do* that! Lothendus tried it and look what happened to *him!*" Stating the obvious, she again chastised him for no other reason than to make sure he didn't attempt something rash and unplanned. She looked at him sternly and again put her hands on her hips. "I think you need help. There are only three of us, and Vile has a vast army, including all those other Warriors that came here. You couldn't possibly fight *that* alone! We can help you here!"

Huffing, Anton explained further: "On the other hand, this complex is preparing something for me to use. I think the factory below is manufacturing some form of weaponry, and it's at full capacity. Unfortunately, I don't have any real idea exactly what the machines are making. Until they've completed this, I need to use this interim to become more familiar with the celestial eye." Looking back and forth at Tania and then Deidra, Anton appeared as if he were even less sure of himself than before.

"The one thing I *do* know, this staff is more powerful than it was when Vim used it. At least I have a more formidable weapon than either Vim or Lothendus, *and* I have my ring and sword. Most importantly though, I have *you two*." Smiling, Anton used his limited charm to persuade Deidra and Tania's acceptance.

Blinking, Tania was speechless for the first time. For a moment, she hesitated, started to say something, hesitated again, and then she changed the subject. "Well then, okay, you continue to decide what to do. In the meantime, you two go and get some rest. Tomorrow you can show both of us what you're talking about." Skeptical, but trusting, Tania reluctantly acquiesced.

"Rowwerrrr, I think you-rrrr need to take a turrrrbo showerrrr!" Deidra winked at Anton, smiled in her feline way, and then put her head on his shoulder. "Maybe I need one too-rrrr!" Purring, she encouraged his next move. She wanted him to relax. She knew he'd been under a great deal of stress and it would help if she could distract him from his responsibilities, even if only for a few hours.

"Indeed. It's been a few days, and I sure would like some company … " Smiling, Anton recognized Deidra's subtle hint. "The last shower I had was the best one I'd ever had." He put his arm around her and hugged her.

"Oh, you two!" Tania giggled. "I'll clean up here. Go, go clean yourselves up!"

Like two teenagers, Anton and Deidra left hand in hand and quickly made their way to the turbo shower dropping clothing as they went.

THE MORNING CAME QUICKLY AND Tania woke Anton and Deidra from their slumber. "Wake up, sleepy heads, I've prepared your breakfast. Get dressed!"

Groggily, Anton sat up and quickly dressed. Assisting Deidra, he helped her with her skirt. Within minutes, they entered the cafeteria and enjoyed another of Tania's exquisite meals. Anticipation filled the air, and the two girls seemed eager to explore Anton's plan, but he seemed preoccupied in reverie and didn't speak much to them as he ate.

"You-rrrr so *quiet* this morrrrning. Is something *wrrrrong?*" inquired Deidra. "Did *I* do something-rrrr *wrrrrong-rrrr?*"

"Sorry, just thinking. I need to do so many things, and time grows short. I suspect the enemy has made plans too. I'm nervous." Again, Anton shared his misgivings. He expressed a particular lack of confidence, and both Tania and Deidra noticed and shared a look of concern between them. For a few moments, the room was categorically silent.

"Oh, *Anton*, we're *all* nervous, but we *believe* in you! There's no other hope!" Supportively, Tania expressed her trust in him, but she too sounded less than confident. "No matter what happens, we're safe, for now. You have time, just use it *wisely!*"

"Yes. You're correct. Let's get going." Abruptly, Anton marched out of the cafeteria with Deidra in tow. Tania quickly cleaned up the mess and caught up with them in their room.

"Time to use the celestial eye," Anton said. "Let's go." Leaving the room, they quickly proceeded to the nearby lift.

The three entered the lift and sped rapidly toward the surface, and within a couple of minutes, they were there. The door opened and revealed a circular chamber with what looked like a giant telescope encased in thousands of gadgets, including piping, robotic arms and various computers and electronics at its center. The ceiling had a semi-circular dome and a sliding door to allow the telescope a view of the outside. It was undeniably the celestial eye.

"That's it," said Anton. "It looks just like the etheric records I witnessed in the Etheriscope." Taking a step out of the lift, he headed straight for it.

Without warning, several lasers fired from all directions. Anton ignited the staff and placed a protective sphere around them, and then turned around to look at Deidra and Tania.

"Oh no!" screamed Tania. "That light beam killed Deidra!"

Lying on the floor of the lift, Deidra lay still with a hole in her chest. Tania landed on her and put her hands on the injury. Immediately tears flowed from her eyes as she silently cried.

Stupefied, Anton stood there for a moment with his mouth agape and his eyes wide open. "No! What the *hell* just *happened?* Computer, what did you *do? Damn* you!"

"Security defenses active. Intruder terminated."

"*Damn* it! Computer! Turn *off* the security in here!"

"Acknowledged. Defenses on hold."

Looking at Tania, Anton's eyes pleaded for a miracle. "Save her! I can't lose *her* too, I *love* her!"

"Anton, listen to me. She's barely alive, and there's only a few moments before she's gone! You'll have to choose between her life, and mine!" With a serious look, and a tone she'd never used before, Tania implored Anton to make an instant decision. "I can save her, but at the price of my *own* life."

For a moment, Anton faltered. Looking quickly between the two, he fumbled for words and found none. His eyes implored Tania to choose for him, but he knew she couldn't. "What do you mean?"

"Anton, choose! Choose now! Her life is nearly *gone!*"

"I have a potion!" Reflexively, Anton produced the tiny vial Beelif had given him; within a heartbeat, he poured it into Deidra's mouth.

Nothing happened.

"She's too far gone; that won't *work!*" Tears flowed freely from Tania as she spoke. "I'm barely holding her spirit here, and I feel it slipping away."

"*Save* her! I *need* her! I can't live *without* her! I, *love* her!" Speaking directly from his heart, the words flew uncontrollably from his lips. A second later Anton realized the levity of his words: he'd lose Tania.

Suddenly, Anton remembered the words of Trepid: "*She is the only katrah to have a true human soul, but it exists without a true human body. This is unique in all of nature and is a consequence of MY interference. In accordance with the Law of Balance, she must prove herself worthy to retain this spirit and earn her entrance into the kingdom of heaven. You're to protect her and provide this opportunity. It's necessary. I can tell you no more.*"

Gritting his teeth, Anton remembered what Trepid had told Tania: "*The time has come for you to fulfill your intended purpose. This is the culmination of your existence. When the time is right, when love it true, you'll perform your final destined calling.*"

Anton's thoughts whirled in his mind. Emotions filled his heart, and sweat beaded up on his forehead. Speechless, he watched Tania proceed with her plan. Instantly, she glowed like a tiny star. Floating into the air, she suddenly launched herself like a speeding bullet directly into the wound in Deidra's chest, entering her body as if she were made of air. A moment passed and then Deidra's entire body began to glow a soft shade of pink.

"Fear not, my dear Anton, this is my final transformation. I do it out of love for you!" Tania's voice emanated from Deidra's chest, and her words sounded like a final farewell.

Magic light encased Deidra's body. Her chest wound healed, and her katrah appearance altered and transformed. Her cat-like ears atop her head shrank and disappeared, and human ears replaced them. Her cat-like fur disappeared, and milky white human skin replaced it. Her cat-like teeth shrank and disappeared, and human teeth replaced them. A minute passed in silence, and then two. Suddenly, Deidra opened her eyes and looked up at Anton. They were blue and human, the narrow slits of her cat's-eye pupils had vanished. Tania's silky blonde hair replaced Deidra's, and her facial features ever so slightly resembled Tania as well. Blinking, she struggled to sit and swallowed dryly while trying to speak.

Kneeling, Anton supported her and gave her a kiss.

"Row-ww," she said weakly, sounding entirely human. "I feel strange. I feel dizzy. I feel … *tired*." Placing her hand beside her forehead, she closed her eyes and passed out in Anton's arms.

"Fear not, my love, I've got you, and I'll never leave you." Kissing her, Anton gently rested her head on his lap and lovingly petted it, just as he had done for her once before in the City of the Humans when they had first met.

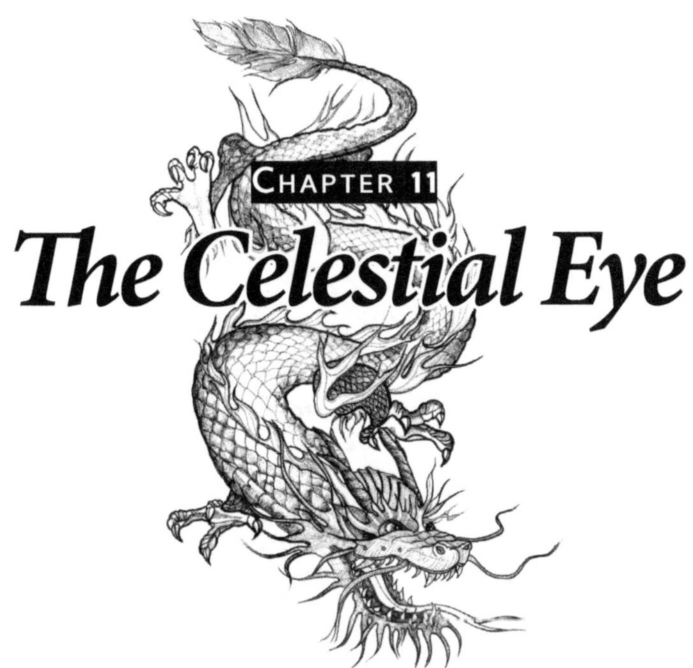

The Celestial Eye

FOR WHAT SEEMED LIKE AN hour, Anton knelt on the floor holding Deidra's head in his lap. He gently caressed it, massaged her shoulders, and combed her waist length golden blond hair with his fingers. For a time, her sleep seemed troubled, but gradually she relaxed and began to breathe smoothly. He didn't know what else to do. Tania had given her life for the katrah, and he no longer had her wisdom to help guide him. He already missed her. The time felt empty, and his heart felt lonely as he thirsted for her friendship. For the first time in his life, he felt completely helpless, and all of the problems he now faced seemed so far away. All the knowledge and power he had gained since arriving in Peruvious hadn't been enough for the magnitude of loss this decision delivered him. He couldn't understand how anyone could choose between one life to save another. It seemed so unfair.

Eventually, after a considerable time, Deidra awoke. She stirred her shoulders, her eyes fluttered and slowly opened, and then effortlessly she sat up as if nothing had transpired since the laser had nearly killed her.

"What happened? Where's Tania?" she asked. "I feel, well … *different*. I feel *really good!*"

Bewildered, Anton smiled at her, a confused expression marked his brow. A feeling of warmth filled his heart, yet he looked at her as if she were a familiar stranger. "Nice to know you're okay. I was, well, worried."

"Of *course*, I'm okay, why would you worry? Why was I asleep? I don't remember going to sleep here!" Surprised and oblivious to what had occurred, Deidra questioned Anton.

"Well, you won't like it if I tell you, but the defense system on this level determined you were an intruder and shot you in the chest. You were dead—or nearly. Tania saved your life, but sacrificed herself in so doing."

Appalled, Deidra's mouth hung open and she raised her hand to cover it in grief, and then immediately began to cry. "What? What do you *mean?* I don't *believe* it! How *horrible!* I can't accept that!" she lamented. "I feel *fine!* I don't feel *injured!* I feel *good!*"

"Look at yourself, listen to your speech! It's changed. Tania is part of you—you're completely human now! It's her gift to you, Deidra. Enjoy it. Be it. She would want it that way! It was, well, *necessary.*" Anton tried his best to both convince and console her, but expressing his deep-seated feelings wasn't his forte. "She'll always be there with you! You'll always be together, she's a *part of you* now! She's *inside* of you!"

"She shouldn't have done that! She's *too* important!" For a moment, Deidra sat there in a state of shock. A tear rolled down her cheek. Closing her eyes, she strained to feel the little faerie inside of herself. "Yes, it's true. It's like I can sense her thoughts. They're *my* thoughts, but they are *hers*. I know what she thinks, and I feel her *love* for you. It was *very* strong. That love is a part of *my* heart now. I remember the connection you two shared."

"Yes, I believe you. I too know how she felt. We shared all of our thoughts and feelings for several days. I knew what was in her heart." As Anton imparted his understanding, he reached out and took Deidra's hand and looked deeply into her eyes. "You're completely human now. Look at your skin, your fur is gone, your eyes and ears have changed, and everything about you is entirely human."

Astonished, Deidra looked at herself; her eyes darted around her body. "Oh my, you're right! I feel cold. I have no *fur!*" Hugging herself, she suddenly seemed at a loss. "I need *clothing?* Oh my! I've never needed *that* before! *Tania* never needed that before!" Goosebumps covered her skin and she suddenly hugged Anton looking for warmth.

"Computer! Provide proper female attire for Deidra." Anton quickly responded to her needs. "The computer will deliver something in a few minutes."

"Your request is too general. Please revise. Describe the proper female attire you desire."

"Computer, bring Deidra a tunic or, I mean, a *blouse?*"

"Affirmative. Delivery in three minutes."

"Oh! Computer, make it match the skirt she's wearing." Smiling, Anton winked at Deidra. "And computer, some undergarments please?"

Deidra returned his smile and giggled like Tania. "You seem to understand girls *better* now. It looks like we've had a positive influence on you!"

Raising an eyebrow, Anton looked stunned. "You said, we've. Do you feel like two people?"

Putting a finger to her chin, Deidra thought about his question for a moment. "In a *way*, I do! I guess it's kind of, well, like we're sharing our lives somehow. I seem to know things about Tania's life. I'm remembering things that she did, but only if I'm thinking about her. Strangely, it feels as if I've lived *her* life *and* mine."

"Interesting," Anton replied. "Who would've guessed this would happen? It makes me wonder about both of us. We've both been transformed into something very different. Obviously, there's some *purpose* behind all of it. I just don't know what that purpose *is* yet."

As expected, the blouse and undergarments arrived via robot. The little device floated out of the lift and dropped the clothing in Deidra's lap.

"Clothing delivered," announced the computer. "Are there any further instructions?"

"Not now computer."

Excited, Deidra was surprised to see such a beautiful ruffled blouse. "Oh my, this is *lovely!*" Giggling, she quickly put it on. "I've never worn clothes, I always hated them. But for some reason, this is fun! I seem to, *like* them now. I seem to *need* them now!"

"Very well. I'm glad you're comfortable. Yes, I remember how you said you hated clothing, and now look at you! You've changed!"

Giggling like Tania, Deidra got to her knees and hugged Anton. "Thank you for saving me. I feel good about the change, but I'll miss who and what I was. I'm still not used to it. I always wanted to be human. I felt so jealous. But now that I've finally become one, I feel a loss."

Cocking an eye at Deidra, Anton felt as though he needed to continue his mission. Standing, he abruptly announced: "I need to get back to work." Suddenly all business, he turned around and looked at the celestial eye. "I need to learn to use this thing. I really need to get back to work—time grows short."

"Yes, go ahead. I'll watch you!" Deidra giggled, expressing Tania's humor, laughter, and inflection impeccably.

Standing there for a few moments, Anton examined the outside of the huge device. Made of dye-infused tritanium, it was as black as the heavens at midnight. "Brilliant," Anton remarked. "Light can neither enter nor escape through the housing. It's entirely light absorbent."

Enthusiastically, he then climbed the platform stairs leading to the enclosed control seat below its eyepiece. Completely encased in a sealed egg-shaped compartment, it too was made of the same black tritanium. A small round hatch on its side was its only feature, and Anton quickly opened it, climbed inside, and found a very comfortable seat surrounded by a multitude of controls. The interior somehow reminded him of the cockpits he'd seen inside the Aerocrafts back on Methonias.

The stored knowledge the KACATU had uploaded into his neural net was unmistakably invaluable. Anton knew exactly how to use the multitude of levers, buttons, and dials, and operate the controls on the computers holo-monitor. The interface was nearly identical to the ones he'd used far below to operate the Etheriscope.

"Brilliant. I wonder what time of day or night it is," he mumbled to himself. "Computer, open the observatory door."

The large portal door in the dome slid sideways allowing the celestial eye to view the early morning sky. It was still dark, but sunrise was just a couple short hours away, and it would rise sooner than he wanted. Immediately, Anton turned the dome toward the south in the direction of Vile's Spire. He wanted to have a good look at the home of his enemy, but when he activated the view screen there was no image.

"What the heck? It doesn't work!" he suddenly cried out. "Damn, Vile must have destroyed it when he used it! I should've expected that!"

Angry, Anton opened the hatchway and stepped back out. Walking around the platform, he examined the exterior of the celestial eye, looking for any obvious damage.

"What's wrong? What happened?" exclaimed Deidra. What're you doing? What're you looking for?"

"Apparently, Vile rendered the eye useless. I'm looking for damage," Anton retorted angrily. It seemed as though all of his half-formulated plans lay waste and he was at a loss as to what to do. "I guess I'll have to *fix* it *somehow*, but I don't know what's *wrong* with it."

"Maybe you should ask the computer. Shouldn't it know?" Sensibly, Deidra offered her pertinent advice, sounding more like Tania than herself. It was clear that both their minds and their characters, had blended perfectly.

Unnerved, Anton stared at her. "You're right! Computer, run a diagnostic on the celestial eye. What's broken? I mean, what damage has it incurred?"

"Booting diagnostic computer. Booted! Running self-diagnostics. Scanning. Inconclusive results. Recommendation: reinstall or replace the holographic crystal."

"Holographic *crystal*? What's that? Where is it?" inquired Anton. "How do I *do* that?"

"The holographic crystal isn't responding. Therefore, the crystal is either missing, installed improperly, or damaged. Recommendation: reinstall or replace the crystal," replied the computer.

"I ask again, computer! Where's the crystal *located?*" Anton was impatient, and it showed. He'd come so far only to have another setback, and he'd lost his tolerance, allowing his emotions to flow freely. For some reason, he ignored the fact his neural net contained the information he needed and he should intuitively know where to find it. Out of habit, he relied upon the computer for answers, as his negative emotions controlled his decisions.

"The crystal is located inside the main view screen computer monitor. An exact replacement crystal is required prior to accessing the existing crystal. Access is currently denied."

"Okay, the next question is: where can I get a holographic crystal?" Taking a deep breath, Anton let it out in a huff. "Can you provide me with one?"

"No capable crystal detected inside the complex. All mined crystal resources are depleted. Manufacturing of a new crystal projected in thirteen days, seventeen minutes following the acquisition of raw materials. Artificially manufactured crystals are of limited use and capability."

"Thirteen … limited … damn! Wait! I have a *holo-projector!*" Producing his EHD, Anton remembered his crystallographic holo-projector. "I *have* a holographic crystal! Perhaps this will suffice? Where does it go?"

"Unknown crystal detected. Warning: attempting to install and use an improperly programmed crystal will produce unknown results. Access denied."

"Damn it! Computer, can the manufacturing complex alter this crystal? Where can it be examined to determine its compatibility?" Angry, yet hopeful, Anton looked around the room hoping to find a machine to examine his crystal.

"All manufacturing is performed at lower level two. The research and development room has the necessary equipment to determine said crystal's capabilities."

"All the way back down there? I don't have time! I need to use the celestial eye!" Anton's anger escalated. He was frustrated, and he had no knowledge of manufacturing processes. He was a Warrior. "I'm going to attempt to use *this* one! Computer, allow me access to the holographic crystal's compartment and allow me to plug this crystal into the celestial eye!"

"Access denied. Place the crystal into the Pneumatic Transport Tube. It will be sent to the Research Facility for further analysis. If determined to be compatible, it will be altered and programmed to the proper specifications."

"Pneumatic tube? What pneumatic tube?" he asked. Looking swiftly around the room, Anton searched for something that looked like a tube. Immediately he noticed a small cylindrical container atop a workbench at the far end of the chamber.

Quickly, he raced over to the workbench and opened the tube, placed the crystal inside, and then put the tube inside a small compartment. Instantly, it vanished in a whoosh of vacuum.

Looking at Deidra, Anton finally shared his thoughts with her. In his anger, he'd completely ignored her for the past few minutes. "I guess we wait," he said, "and while we do, I'm going to examine this device further."

"Is there anything I could do to help you? I don't know what you're doing, but it seems to me there are a lot of computers *here* that are busy doing *something*." Pointing at a nearby holo-monitor next to the Pneumatic Tube, Deidra directed Anton's attention toward it.

"You're right! The monitor is showing me what it's doing with my CHP!" Excited, Anton sat in front of the monitor. "Like Tania, you're forever helpful. Thanks."

Delighted, Deidra accepted her new role in life. She had a new-found love for assisting Anton in anything he needed, and felt as though there was an even higher purpose for her services. "Thank you! Anything to help!" Smiling, she stood behind Anton, put her arms around him and watched.

For a few moments, Anton sat in front of the monitor and observed the progress. He wondered why the KACATU had installed the knowledge of how to operate the celestial eye, but hadn't installed the knowledge of any of the other computers in the chamber.

Hovering like Tania, Deidra watched everything Anton did. He knew that if she had faerie wings, she'd be fluttering about looking at things, or sitting on his shoulder watching him up close. He was pleased she took such an interest.

On the other hand, Deidra had no concept of what she witnessed, but the past few days in the complex had given her a tremendous respect for technology and the subsequent comforts it provided. Everything she observed seemed to interest her. Tania's gift of life had given her a boost in her interest in everything new—all the wonderful and exotic things she had never seen before—and a desire to adapt and learn about them. But most of all, it gave her a higher level of bravery than she had ever known. She applied these new capabilities as an increasing talent.

Watching the holo-monitor intently, Anton could see what the computer was doing. It took the crystal into the KACATU room and placed it into a tapered hole in a console that fit it perfectly. "Amazing! Who would have guessed? It seems as though everything I've brought into this complex has a purpose here. I'm sure my Masters were aware of what my needs would be or at the very least, hopeful."

"Crystallographic holo-projector identified. Device software detected. Security codes detected. The new standard of programming and instructions sets detected. Programming accepted. Security codes accepted. Downloading software. Complete! Updating computer. Complete! Updating crystal's instruction sets for compatibility. Complete! Sending crystal to manufacturing department for reworking."

As Anton continued to watch, he saw the crystal placed inside a machine for remanufacturing. In a matter of seconds, it had shortened it ever so slightly and adjusted the taper. It then shaped the tip to fit the celestial eye's interface connection. Immediately upon completion, it placed the crystal inside the vacuum tube and sent it on its way back to Anton.

"Reconstruction complete! Returning the crystal to the celestial eye."

In less than ten minutes, Anton held the reworked crystal in his hand. "This complex is beyond words. It's obvious my Masters have these abilities too. That's something I never knew. Obviously, they can do everything at the Great Temple that's done here, and probably more." Excitedly, he leapt from his chair and climbed back into the celestial eye's control seat.

"Computer, instruct me on how to install the crystal. Where do I insert it?" Quickly probing around, Anton searched the smooth seamless surfaces looking for a panel to open, but he found nothing.

Unexpectedly, a panel did open, and a small cover slid sideways, revealing a row of unfamiliar circuitry. Amongst the circuits was a row of unknown crystals, and he noticed one of them was black and cracked as if something had burned it. It was obvious to Anton that the damage could only have occurred when Vile had used the celestial eye to destroy Celestra over a millennium ago.

"Wow, it must have received a tremendous jolt of energy," he mused. "Or perhaps some form of powerful magic. I guess those are the same thing really, they seem to be connected or intertwined somehow. I should review the etheric records and see if I can determine the exact cause when I have time."

Removing the damaged crystal, he tossed it aside and inserted his newly reworked CHP. The moment the crystal seated itself, the small cover slid sideways and closed, and the celestial eye powered up automatically.

"Repairs complete. Installing new instruction sets. Complete! The celestial eye is ready to deploy. What are the coordinates you wish to observe?"

"Computer, aim the eye directly at Vile's Spire. I want to see inside his tower." Anton immediately proceeded with his plan. He intended to finish what he'd started earlier, and he was becoming impatient. "I wish to view the *inside* of Vile's home, not the outside."

"Acknowledged. Complying with request."

Immediately, the computer took control of the eye's movement, and within a couple of seconds, it had targeted the objective.

"Focusing the eye. Vile's Spire targeted. Initiating electromagnetic wave shielding. Stealth mode activated. Photon separation filter active. Alert! Surveillance systems blocked at target site. Unable to view objective. Are there further instructions?"

"Damn! Now what? How could the view be blocked? Essentially, this device is supposed to see through *anything* at *any* distance!" Mumbling his anger, Anton's thoughts raced as he tried to calculate a solution. Suddenly he had an idea. "Computer, what type of shielding is inhibiting my view?"

"Analyzing. Gravity-time distortion waves are emanating from inside Vile's Tower. Logical conclusion: The Crystal Pyramid is active."

"Damn. Computer, change the eye's prescription. Activate enhanced refraction mode, and filter and deflect the gravity-time distortion waves emanating from the gravity well."

"Compliance! Changing the lens prescription per requested instructions."

Instantly, the celestial eye became active. Mechanical arms holding various sealed diamond-crystal lenses withdrew them from inside the maintube. Erector lenses, field lenses, the objective lens and the eyepiece ocular all slid from their respective alignment as another set of arms placed a new series of lenses into position.

"Reconfiguration complete. Filters in place. Refraction distortion filtration implemented."

The holo-monitor suddenly displayed an image of the tower. It appeared grey and out of focus, but the intense darkness caused by the gravity-well dissipated.

"Computer, measure the radiometry of the refraction distortion. Filter those photons required to see the structure down to less than one lumen per nano-second and enhance the image." The view continued to improve as Anton guided the computer's adjustments. "Computer, install the secondary viewing lenses in the secondary maintube, synchronize, and enhance the images."

"Compliance! Installing … installed!"

Just as before, lenses emerged from their storage compartments and small mechanical arms inserted them into the eye's secondary maintube, creating a dual-monocular scope.

"Synchronizing imagery. Multiple objective photon-interweaving active. Refracted light displacement redirected through the binary prisms. Activating computer enhancements. Image coefficient measures less than one billionth spectral distortion."

Finally, the image of Vile's Tower was perfect. It felt to Anton as though he stood directly in front of it and could reach out and touch it. Pleased, but still dissatisfied, he wanted to see through the walls of the structure. He wanted to see Vile himself. He needed to see the face of his enemy.

"Computer, add charged-particle enhancements. Calibrate to view the inside of the tower." Eagerly, Anton waited for the final changes, anticipating complete success.

Yet again, the mechanical arms installed a set of lenses in the tertiary maintube, and then added a magnetic field generator and a charged-particle apparatus behind them.

"Compliance. The magnetic field generator and the charged particle apparatus units are online. Activating computer aided enhancements. Complete! Synchronizing tertiary tube. Complete! Tri-ocular capabilities are online and active. Split-view capabilities stand at ready."

Immediately, the tower walls disappeared or, more accurately, became translucent, and Anton could easily see inside the tower. Operating the windage, elevation, eyepiece and field lens focus controls, he carefully sighted in the celestial eye to locate the enemy. He wasn't entirely sure who or what he would see, and he didn't know what Vile even looked like, but search meticulously he did. It seemed intuitive to him that he'd know Vile when he found him.

Searching for an hour, Anton didn't see anyone, or for that matter, anything at all. It was as if the place was devoid of all life and all objects. Finally, disappointed, he gave up and decided to eat and rest. Exiting the control seat, he looked around the observatory room for Deidra. She was sitting in the chair next to the vacuum tube controls slumped over the console fast asleep. Smiling, he chuckled quietly to himself.

Dim and filtered daylight seeped in through the observation doors of the dome and filled the room with subdued grey daylight. Suddenly, Anton realized that the additional photon activity of the sun, coupled with the toxic cloud layer over Lower Peruvious impeded the celestial eye's full capabilities. The smog obviously had an unknown detrimental effect on everything.

"That's *got* to be it," he mumbled. "The atmosphere is tainted, and it must be wreaking havoc with the celestial eye. I should've tried to screen that too. I'll make another attempt after dark. Perhaps it'll be easier then without the additional photon interference." A sudden realization entered his thoughts and he considered that perhaps the very reason for the cloud layer over Lower Peruvious was to diffuse the capability of the celestial eye, not just as a poison to deter humans from traveling in or living there.

Placing his hand gently on Deidra's shoulder, Anton woke her from her slumber. "Wake up, sleepy head. I need some food and some company. Care to join me?"

Still groggy, she replied, "Sure." As she tried to stand, she stumbled into Anton's embrace. "Hold me, my love."

Surprised, yet pleased, Anton supported her, drew her close to him, and held her tight. He hadn't anticipated her falling into his embrace, and yet he desired it immensely. Her sudden faltering pleased him. He knew she was completely dependent upon him for everything, and in some fashion, her vulnerability struck a primal instinct for his compassion and devotion within his heart. Holding her tightly for a moment, he breathed in her aroma. Her intoxicating feminine fragrance caused his passion to rage with inestimable desire.

Suddenly, Anton realized that he needed to focus on his work, and with great effort, he gently released her. "Let's eat, and then retire until nightfall. I must return to work as soon as the sun sets. I'm running out of time, but I'll always make time for you. It'll just have to be later."

Like two teens in love, they walked briskly to the lift holding hands, smiling shyly at each other.

"Computer, take us to the cafeteria on lower level one please." Anton held Deidra close, smiled, and then kissed her; his passion flowed, and his excitement conspicuously showed.

"After dinner … " responded Deidra and she smiled timidly, seductively, enticingly, and propositionally. She'd noticed his obvious excitement and her intentions were clear.

Hand in hand, they entered the cafeteria. The nutrition pills that Tania had used to create a meal were the only thing the cafeteria offered, and Anton stood there looking at them feeling disappointed. His whole life he'd used them to supplement his food intake when real food wasn't available, but for some reason, right now, they seemed particularly indigestible. Perhaps Tania had spoiled him with her faerie magic, or perhaps his youthful passion and his desire to please Deidra demanded he provide something real to enjoy.

"These simply won't do. I need *real* food." Looking at Deidra as if she could offer the needed knowledge, Anton's eyes pleaded for help. "These pills seem so inadequate right now. Do you have any ideas?"

"Use your *staff*, silly boy! Vim used it to provide for *you*, remember?" Offering prudent advice, Deidra continued to sound more and more like Tania. "I think you can figure out how to use it to do what Tania did! And, you might remember, we have a lot of food supplies in that EHD of yours too!"

"Hmmm, perhaps I *can* use the staff!" Grasping his staff, Anton held it high and offered a single command: "Transmogrify!"

The globe on his staff radiated energy, and a single burst of light instantly struck the pills on the plate in front of him. Magically, they transmuted into a gourmet meal of which even Anton hadn't imagined. Astonished, he stood there a moment and grinned at his accomplishment.

"Unbelievable!" was all he could utter. "This *is* as good as Tania's faerie magic! She'd be *proud* of me!" Grinning, he chuckled lightly as he looked at Deidra.

Deidra was utterly astounded. Anton produced an even better meal than she'd anticipated. "Wow, you can cook for me *anytime!*"

The food was exquisite, and they ate together enjoying every morsel. Anton couldn't remember a time when he was happier, not even the time he'd spent in the village of Tooloo with Nelda, and he believed Deidra felt the same way. It was as if time had stopped for them so they might share each other's company privately. It was clear to him that they both felt genuine love for each other, not the chemically induced love caused by the Virlaqueus he'd experienced just a few weeks ago. However, the sense of impending doom loomed over him and haunted him in the back of his mind.

After they finished eating, Anton again used the staff to clear the table just as he'd seen Tania do. "It's all about what I imagine in my head, and the power of the staff makes it happen. I will have to improve my imagination to utilize this magic to its maximum potential. I'm certain it's my best weapon and my best tool."

Amazed at Anton's ever-improving skills, Deidra smiled at him as he cleared the table. "I hope you learn to use your skills for something more important. It seems to me you haven't learned to use the staff as a weapon, just as a tool, but I'm glad I don't have to clean up here!" Offering her concern, she gently placed a thought into Anton's mind. She hoped he'd realize they needed to share everything, and she looked at his staff as if she expected him to grasp her point.

"I realize that. It's true. I don't know how to fight with this thing." With a grimace, Anton huffed as he considered Deidra's argument. His Methonian training hadn't given him any knowledge or skills to simply invent a magical attack with a staff. He wondered if the Etheriscope could enlighten him to Vim's usage and he could adapt his own knowledge to perhaps improve it.

"I was wondering how you're planning to use both the staff and your sword. Have you thought about that?" Deidra queried him further, asking perhaps the most pertinent of questions. It was obvious to her this issue needed addressing, and she wondered if he'd given it any thought.

"I'm not sure what to do about that yet. You're right. I can't wield both of them. And it's true, we'll probably need to use both of them." For a moment, he faltered and looked at her and then at the staff. "Hmm, two of us and two weapons … " He contemplated the point for a moment and then continued: "Yes, I'll give it some thought." More than ever, his thoughts raced to evaluate Vile's defeat. Deidra's point left him guessing. He knew what she was thinking but he wasn't sure about it yet. It would require that she fight along with him, and he wasn't ready to relinquish his responsibility for her safety, both for himself and his responsibility to Trepid's request, even though deep inside his heart he knew she was right. "Let's go. It's late morning, and I'm exhausted.

After eating, Anton simply needed to rest. The past few days had taken their toll on his fortitude and his earlier passion had waned. His body ached for some real sleep, perhaps a byproduct of his surgery followed by simply consuming nutrition pills. "Let's get some rest. I want my thought processes to be fresh and strong later."

"Okay, if that's *really* what you *want.*" Sounding a little disappointed, she forced a smile, and then suddenly hugged him. "Let's go, I'll let you sleep." It was apparent to Deidra he'd lost his previous interest, and he suddenly sounded distant. Disappointed, but understanding, she nodded her acquiescence. She appreciated his reasoning, but she still felt dejected.

Evening arrived and Anton awoke suddenly and launched himself from his bed. Looking across the room, he saw Deidra sitting at the vanity combing her long blond hair looking out of the corner of her eye at him. "I don't want to oversleep. It's time to get to work," he suddenly announced.

Quickly donning his attire, he hurried over to Deidra. She had thoughtfully prepared some nutrition pills and placed them on a table so that he could conjure a meal for them, and as he neared her, she looked at them and tipped her head in their direction to draw his attention to them.

"I thought ahead. Let's eat!" Hurriedly finishing her grooming, she waited for him to transform them. "I'd like something *meaty.* I guess my old tastes haven't changed much." Smiling wryly, she urged Anton further to perform his magic.

"Let's be quick." Emotionless, and sounding distracted, Anton quickly altered the pills base elements and produced a simple breakfast of fried eggs, hash browns and sausage. "Enjoy!" was all he said.

"Well, what's wrong with you? Are you always grumpy after you rest?" Deidra expressed her displeasure about his lack of comportment.

"Don't you have a little time to share with me before you go back to the celestial eye?"

"Sorry. I need to focus. I'm worried about everything. I'm worried Vile has set another trap and I've run out of time. I'm worried that the celestial eye isn't a sufficient weapon to battle him with, and I still feel inadequate against an enemy I *really* don't know. I'm sorry, but we need to get started."

Emotionlessly, Anton finished his meal and waited for Deidra. When she was done, he quickly left the room, and she followed a step behind him.

"I hope you complete what you're doing. I don't like you like this." With a huff, she folded her arms as they traveled up the lift. "It wouldn't have hurt to be together for a few minutes. I love you so much." Again, she felt dejected and she stood there looking at the floor.

"I love you *too.* I'm sorry. I'm just worried." With a sigh, Anton started to reach for her to give her a hug, and then suddenly the lift came to a stop and the door flew open. "Later," he said. "We'll be together later."

Deidra launched herself toward her seat next to the computer console and huffed. Disconsolate, she wondered what his problem was as she stared at the holo-monitor and watched the factory produce part after part of things she didn't comprehend.

Anton stood at the base of the platform stairs for a moment and gazed in her direction. "I'm sorry. I'll make it up to you later. Please, trust me. I need that." Climbing the short flight of stairs up the platform, he again turned around. "This is just so important, you know?"

Feeling a little guilty, Deidra quietly replied: "I know, but I need your comfort too. Don't you understand? I'm scared!"

"I know, and I need *your* comfort. I'm not scared, just nervous, but now it's time to get back to work." Quickly climbing into the control seat, Anton closed the hatch behind him and adjusted the controls to see inside Vile's Tower.

Settling in, he was delighted to see that the lack of sunlight gave him a clearer view of the tower, and it didn't take long before he found what he'd spent so much time searching for earlier in the morning. At the top of his tower, Vile stood on a platform gazing into his Crystal Pyramid, his index finger touching its peak.

A sudden shiver ran up and down Anton's spine. It seemed as though Vile looked directly at him, and he suddenly felt the thoughts of his enemy inside his head. A split-second later, his head throbbed with immense pain, and he abruptly passed out.

From Darkness to Revelation

WAVES OF PULSATING ENERGY FILLED Anton's head with excruciating pain. Devastating agony pounded it relentlessly. Time seemed to have stopped, or perhaps had never existed at all. He had no thoughts of his own, he had no memories to recall. There was only the omnipresent pain and misery inside his head. He sat in the control seat of the celestial eye completely oblivious to everything around him, and he felt as though he was no longer a part of the physical world. This was his new reality. His past was just a distant dream, or perhaps it had never been. He floated in a sea of grey emptiness, as if suspended in an unbounded dimension where nothing existed and never would, or ever could. The only reality for him was his imprisoned mind, his pain, and a vast vortex of darkness and desolation surrounding him.

Struggling, in agony, and unable to speak, Anton sought release from this tortured imprisonment. Desperately, he strained to remember who he was and why he suffered, yet nothing but pain filled his mind. Sharp, piercing misery tormented him relentlessly, holding his thoughts suspended. His self-identity faded deeper and deeper into oblivion.

Time passed unnoticed, but in reality, his body still existed in the real world, and after a while, a faint recollection entered his thoughts. For some inexplicable reason, he realized that his agony and torment wasn't the only thing he'd ever experienced. Somehow, he recalled that there was a time before the pain, a time without it, a time where he'd felt something else, but it eluded him as to what it was. Anger welled up in him, and hate and despair tore at his heart. Coupled with the unending, agonizing pain, these were the only feelings he could sense, and the more he struggled to grasp them, the stronger they became.

"Oh my god! Make it stop!" he thought. "Why am I *suffering*? Why *do* I suffer?" Unexpectedly, questions formulated in his mind. "Words, I remember words! I do have thoughts! I do, I do. What *are* they? What are *my* thoughts?"

Grasping for unobtainable answers, Anton feverishly fought to comprehend how everything had come to this timeless imprisonment of pain and torment, yet he couldn't recall anything prior to its inception. Then suddenly, faintly, he knew in his heart that there was something prior to the pain. Time did exist, real time, a time when he didn't feel this way. Why else was he struggling to free himself from the pain? Time. It existed … once.

"This *can't* be timeless, this *can't* be without end. Time exists. Pain isn't everything, it isn't the *only* reality. But what is reality?" He struggled with himself to remember. Straining his thoughts, questions and realizations formulated within his mind. "Why *am* I in pain?"

Searching deep inside himself, inside his heart, he began to feel something else, something warm, something strong, something real. It was familiar, yet distant, but it was growing, like a tiny sprout in a vast barren desert of scorched sand. Forcibly, he concentrated on the feeling and nurtured it. Slowly, he drew it forth and fanned it like an ember of fire. It was a feeling he couldn't deny, and not even the overwhelming pain in his head could suppress and eliminate it. It was a feeling he'd become familiar with—it was love. He knew this feeling. It was recent, and it was undeniably dominant, but something held it away from his grasp, something he couldn't explain, and it was something he loathed.

Pain! More pain! Intensifying pain! The harder Anton struggled to grasp the feeling, the more the pain amplified and pushed it away. Soon his head felt as though it would explode. Then, with enormous mental effort, he defied the pain. He blocked the pain, ignored the pain. He cleared his thoughts and imagined himself sitting in the lotus position. Consciously, with titanic effort and steadfast determination, he relaxed, and the ember of love he'd carefully nurtured began to burn like a small fire. Soon the feeling escalated, and then it expanded throughout his body. The more he grasped the feeling, the more the pain receded. Soon it succumbed completely to his indomitable strength and the fortitude of his Methonian will.

For what seemed like an eternity, Anton sat in the control seat of the celestial eye. His heart was filled with the burning fire of love. This feeling slowly and incrementally stretched to every limb, every cell, every molecule of his being, as if it coursed like lifeblood through his veins. It was all that there was, it was everything, and it was part of him, a personification of his true nature.

Then, with unrestricted ease, Anton opened his eyes and looked at the display screen in front of him. Reflexively, he turned it off with a flick of his wrist. Immediately he adjusted the windage and elevation controls of the celestial eye, and then the ocular focus. Finally, completely exhausted, he climbed from the control seat and exited the chamber. His mind was dizzy, his footing was uneasy, and his knees seemed uncharacteristically weak. Grasping his staff in one hand, he held onto the handrail with the other and supported himself as he carefully walked down the platform stairs.

From across the room, Deidra watched as Anton struggled to navigate his way. Surprise marked her face, and she suddenly leapt from her chair and raced over to his aid.

"What's wrong? What happened? Why are you walking so strangely?" she exclaimed. "Did something *happen* to you? Did you *hurt* yourself?" Her eyes darted from one eye to the other as she looked at him questioningly, and then suddenly she threw her arms around him.

"I'm okay. I'll be fine, now that I have *you* with me." Returning her hug, he held Deidra firmly in his arms, and then gradually loosened his hold and looked deeply into her eyes. "I love you," he said stiffly.

"Yes, I know, and I love *you*. What're you trying to tell me?" Still unsure of what was happening, Deidra's eyes entreated Anton to reveal his unspoken secrets. She needed to know why he was acting so strangely. "Are you going to tell me what you *saw*? Are you going to tell me what you *did*? Are you going to tell me what *happened*?"

Reaching out, she unconsciously grasped Anton's hand that held his staff as if to help support him somehow. Suddenly, unexpectedly, the globe on the staff ignited with power. An explosion of energy filled the room, enveloping the two in a colossal aura of golden fire. It connected them, and energy coursed through their bodies. Their eyes burned like golden fire, and they looked at each other in astonishment.

"I hear your thoughts. I feel your heart. I know you! It's as if I've always known you!" Deidra's voice sounded amplified, as if she were an entity. "I feel as though we've been together throughout eternity, and only now are we again reunited."

"Yes, I feel this too. It's like we've finally returned to each other after eons of separation." Anton knew Deidra's thoughts, her feelings, and her genuine love for him. He knew they shared a connection that seemed to span time itself, but he didn't know why or how. The meaning of it eluded him entirely.

"I can see what happened to you in there. Your strength and fortitude surpass me. I don't know how you managed to return to yourself." Admitting her vulnerability, Deidra was in awe of Anton's incredible resilience. "Oh my, I feel something strange is about to happen!"

Then suddenly, another transformation occurred. Deidra's aura glowed ever brighter, and golden faerie-like wings that burned like fire suddenly appeared from her back and stretched out as if she were about to take flight. Her blouse and skirt simply faded becoming translucent, then vanished entirely. She smiled lovingly at Anton with a look of complete confidence. It was as if she'd become an entity filled with knowledge, patience, and understanding.

Unable to maintain his grip on the staff, Anton's hand released it, surrendering it to Deidra. "It's *your* staff, not *mine*. I know in my heart it belongs to *you*. It was never intended to belong to me. All this time, through all of its transformations, it has sought you as its true owner." Relinquishing possession of the staff, he bowed in Methonian fashion and took a step back.

"Behold, I'm reborn again!" proclaimed Deidra. "Thank you for this gift. It fits my hand well." Reaching up toward the globe, her hand disappeared inside its brilliant radiance. A moment later, she withdrew a small vial attached to a beautiful golden chain. Placing the chain around her neck, she held the vial in one hand. Instantly, a bolt of energy fired from the globe and struck the vial. Golden energy filled it, she drew it close to her chest, and closed her eyes. Energy poured into her body and filled her with power. Taking a deep breath, she smiled, raised the staff over her head, and then extinguished its energy. Resting the staff's heel against the floor, she drew it close to her chest and embraced it like an old friend.

The illumination of the atmosphere instantly returned to normal as Deidra quenched the globe's energy. For a moment, she stood there motionless. Her stark beauty was virtuous, and Anton gazed upon her and smiled longingly, his heart filled with desire and passion.

"That solves the issue of how to use both weapons simultaneously." Crudely stated, his thoughts returned to the fundamental issue they both faced as he fumbled at humor. "You, umm, are more beautiful than ever! My desire for you, my love for you, is inestimable."

"Thank you, my love." For a moment, Deidra stood in front of Anton in her resplendent and majestic form. "I must abnegate my wings for now. They're unnecessary inside this structure."

To Anton's amazement, her fiery wings dissipated and faded away, and her blouse and skirt reappeared. It was as if the wings had never existed. For a moment, he stood there and silently pondered how she knew she could make them disappear at will.

"Astounding! Inconceivable! How did you *know* you could do that?" questioned Anton. "You've never had *wings* before, how could you *know* this?"

"I just knew. It was just … *familiar* to me. It was as commonplace as you donning or removing your haori. I sense that part of me that is Tania." Smiling shyly, Deidra stood there holding the staff and gazing into its globe. "There are more surprises held within this staff. I can *see* them, I can *feel* them, but I can't *explain* them, at least not yet. They will be available to me when needed."

"You can *see* the magic inside the globe? What? What do you mean?" Perplexed, Anton queried Deidra further. "I didn't *see anything* when I held it!"

"It's all here, inside, I can see patterns of energy and they mold to my thoughts as if they're ready to spring into action at a moment's notice. They swirl and coalesce, expand and anticipate, eager to do my bidding. It's almost as if the energy is about to explode to accomplish anything I ask of it. It's just on the verge at every moment."

"You can *see* all of that?" Anton asked again in amazement. It all seemed impossible to him. He hadn't felt or seen anything inside the globe and it left him disconcerted. "Obviously, the staff was meant for *you*, somehow. I don't understand, but I'm pleased that you know how to use it."

"I *will* know how, when I need to … I, I just know." Confident, yet puzzled, Deidra too was a bit surprised. "I feel it fits in my hand when I hold it. It's as if I've always held it, and it belongs there, it's supposed to be."

"It would seem that we're both supposed to fight Vile, not just me alone. Are you ready for the challenge? I mean, do you think you can defend yourself sufficiently without my constant protection?" Awkwardly, Anton probed Deidra to test her confidence. "I'm free to fight if I don't have to defend you at the same time."

"I'm sure there's nothing that can harm me while I hold the staff," Deidra replied with absolute certainty. It was clear she believed in herself. "I know we're a team, we're not just together."

"Very good! I am quite pleased. Now, I need to spend some time meditating. After that psionic mind blast I experienced, I need time to assess our options, and I want to travel to Vile's Tower unnoticed. Apparently, he could either see me or sense me when I used the celestial eye. I don't know how, but he *knew* I was looking for him. The next time I use the eye, I won't let that happen, but I need to gain some control over my thoughts, some sort of a defense—I need to meditate." Sounding unsure, Anton enumerated his concerns to Deidra.

"I need time to think, but we're running out of it, I just know it. I could sense the mind of Vile lurking, hiding somewhere when he attacked me. His hunger to finish this after millions of years is insatiable, and he knows the final conflict is nearly upon him! Most of all, I know he wants to capture me. He finds me useful in some way. Perhaps that was his intent just now, but it didn't work. I believe *love* is the answer, as silly as that sounds."

Deidra's face expressed concern. She knew he was right, and she knew the moment they left the protection of the dome surrounding Celestra they'd be completely vulnerable again.

"How do you propose to leave here unnoticed? You *know* he'll see us somehow. They have a clear bird's-eye view of us, and they're *expecting* us to go to his tower! There isn't anywhere else *to* go, and there certainly isn't any possible way to sneak in unseen! I don't think *any* plan will work." Skeptical and scared, Deidra started to cry, and a tear rolled down her cheek. "I hate what we've gotten ourselves into. I know that there was no other way, but I still hate it!"

"Don't worry. I'll figure something out somehow. Right now, like I said, I *must meditate!*" Reiterating his fundamental requirement, Anton attempted to reassure Deidra, as if some miracle would simply fall into place, but as usual, his initial proposals fell short. It was obvious he didn't yet have a solid plan. "Let's go below," he said. "I need some food and time to think."

"Okay. I hope you come up with something soon. *I* certainly don't have any ideas. *I'm* just *scared.*" Looking uneasy, Deidra stared at the floor, and then reached for Anton's support. "Even with this staff, I'm scared. Even with you near me, I'm scared. I just want to be safe and put all of this behind us."

Looking at Deidra, Anton responded coolly: "We will. Just you wait and see!"

Hand in hand, they entered the lift and proceeded to the cafeteria. This time Deidra used the staff to alter the food pills into a light meal. Ham, cheese, bread and fruit covered the table, and they ate together quietly. The tension between them was evident, but it wasn't toward each other. Moreover, they both knew their interlude of peace was ending, and they would soon have to fight the final battles for humanity, so they sat there struggling to converse. Real fear marked Deidra's face.

"Good food. Nice work. You seem to know what you're doing. It's, well, *good!*" With his mouth full, Anton fumbled again as he uttered his thoughts. "You should cook more often."

"Yes, I, well, have a good teacher, inside of me that is. I just *feel* what I need to do." Looking shyly at Anton, Deidra also fumbled for words. "I miss Tania."

With a heavy sigh, Anton stood up. "I better get going, I need to think, you know?" Looking at Deidra, Anton nodded toward the dirty dishes and then left the cafeteria.

Heading down the hallway, he darted into their room and immediately adopted the lotus position in the center of the floor. For some reason, it felt both strange and familiar to him as he finally returned to his fundamental roots. Taking a deep breath, he cleared his thoughts, and soon he drifted into the first level of meditation, where he found the solace and peace of mind he so desperately desired. It was something he'd missed recently. As he relaxed, his thoughts delved ever deeper into himself, and he entered into a purified state of mind where he returned to his special place he had first discovered onboard the Pleceivious, the special place that took him beyond the confines of his physical body.

Somewhere along the line, Deidra entered the room, sat in the chair next to the vanity, and held the staff close to her and watched Anton intently. Igniting the globe, she could feel him relinquish his emotions and the stress caused by the psionic blast he'd received from Vile. He seemed to cleanse himself in this way, and to her it was an astounding feat. Closing her eyes, she quietly tried to link her thoughts with his and drift along with him, but she didn't have the same experience or his incredible strength of will to mimic his mental capabilities, and it eluded her completely.

Intentionally oblivious to Deidra's presence, Anton blocked her attempts to communicate with him and continued to search inside of himself unabated. Soon his body began to float above the floor just as the power ignited in his ring. The energy was minimal at first, and his ring only glowed slightly around his finger. But the golden fire gradually increased, burning completely around his hand, and then crawled up his arm, enveloping it. After a few minutes, his entire body glowed, but it burned from within his chest, as if he were the source of the energy rather than his ring. As his fire completely covered his body, he lightly stepped outside of it leaving it behind. Traveling ethereally, he quickly left the tunnels below the Great Observatory and found himself outside in the City of Celestra. There, he unexpectedly discovered a flurry of mechanical activity.

"Oh my god, what's going on here?" he suddenly exclaimed. "The city is nearly restored! Or moreover, it seems as if it is some form of a device. I'm at a loss as to what though." Looking around, he could see hundreds or perhaps thousands of unique specialized robotic machines fast at work building everything. "How is this possible?"

It was true. The factory below the city had built robots to perform the task of constructing a new Celestra. At amazing speeds, they sailed in the air, raced across the ground, and dug into the soil installing gadgetry Anton had never seen or conceived of before. Everything was entirely unfamiliar to him and didn't resemble any of the technology of his past. Designs of things he knew nothing of filled the landscape. Every scrap of debris from the former devastation was gone, as if it had never been there.

"All of this was accomplished in the past few days! It boggles the mind." Confounded and bewildered, he watched as structures literally grew in front of him, as if they were living organisms rising from the ground. Then he tried to determine what it was that the robots were creating, and he realized none of the structures were for human habitation. They had a much different purpose. The entire city was the surface of something even greater, something hidden from view inside the ground. It was one gigantic device, stretching to the edge of the protective dome and deeper into the ground than he could guess.

Looking further to the edge of the city, he could see the glistening sheen of the protective dome where it reached the ground. At short intervals, small octahedron-shaped crystals sat atop short posts and glowed intensely, projecting energy into the dome and strengthening it. For the first time, Anton noticed from where the dome originated.

A tall tower that stood at the far northern end of the city held a much larger crystal that was identical to the smaller ones he now observed. The large crystal projected energy into the air, creating the dome. He wondered why he hadn't noticed it before when they'd arrived. It seemed odd to him he hadn't paid it any attention, or perhaps it was a more recent development. He wasn't entirely sure. He now understood why there were no crystals left to replace the damaged one in the celestial eye.

Looking through the dome, Anton then noticed what lay beyond the barrier. By the tens of thousands, creatures of every description surrounded it, watching, and waiting. They were agitated, and restlessly milled around anticipating the moment they could enter.

Curious, Anton wondered why they hadn't attempted to penetrate the dome. He suspected a plan was in place, and it was about to commence, but what plan? "I need to discover Vile's tactics," he thought.

Again, he looked at the barrier and the pattern of crystals fortifying it, and at the tower housing the primary crystal. He again looked at the flurry of activity below him, robots building at an ever-increasing pace. For a second time, he tried to guess the purpose of the construction, but it still eluded him. Then he saw new robots emerging from multiple locations out of the ground like ants leaving an ant hill. Whatever it was that was going to occur it would happen soon. That was unmistakable.

"I *must* visit Vile's Tower atop his spire to spy on his plans, but *dare I?*" he questioned himself. "The final battle is at hand. Do I have time? Furthermore, what will happen *here* if I leave? Do I have enough time to spy? I need to know what the enemy is up to!" Puzzled and confused, Anton weighed his options. "If I don't spy, I won't be able to discover what his plans are. If I do spy, will I be able to return in time to save myself and Deidra? Can she handle an attack on her own?"

Anton continued to look below at the inestimable size of the enemy's army and carefully watched their movements. It was impossible to see beyond the barrier in the darkness due to the multitude of extremely bright lights that filled the city.

"*Decide*, damn it! I'm going!" Instantly, Anton shot like a rocket in his ethereal form and quickly passed through the protective barrier, leaving the confines of the city behind him. The barrier had no influence on his ethereal form, and he passed through it without noticing it. Moments passed as he sailed across the countryside faster than an Aerocraft. It didn't take him long to project himself to Vile's Tower and ultimately, he found himself floating there looking at the portentous structure. If he'd had a body, a shiver would've run up and down his spine at the sight of it.

The spire was extremely tall. Its base had several hillocks that attached to it like the roots of a great tree, and they stretched beyond the spire for a mile or more. The spire's sheer straight sides stretched into the air more than three thousand feet piercing the dense smoggy layer. Near the top, it narrowed to half the diameter, a mere quarter-mile across, and it was entirely flat on top. At its center stood Vile's Tower, a stone structure rising more than three hundred feet, with a giant human skull carved from stone capping it. The sight was ominous, and even in his ethereal state, Anton could sense the dreadful evil held within. Waves of unseen energy emanated from inside the skull, and it seemed impossible even to approach the structure, let alone enter it.

"I can't do it, but I *must*." Fortifying his resolve, Anton concentrated, and then pushed forward. "I can't bear the sight of him again, but I *have* to." Inside, he saw the enemy for the second time. His horrendous visage was unspeakable, and it repulsed him.

Vile stood gazing into his Crystal Pyramid. It rested on a small table in the center of a dais, and it suddenly became highly active as Anton entered the chamber. The pyramid was nearly two feet tall, and it glowed with waves of deep-blue ultraviolet energy that surged in its core, casting waves of energy throughout the chamber.

"What is this?" Vile yelled. "The pyramid senses something … "

Anton floated unseen in the chamber, and for the first time, he got an accurate look at the enemy. The sight was undeniably repulsive. Vile was entirely black, as black as his ring was after the destruction of Tooloo. His eyes glowed a deep shade of red that seemed to pierce the atmosphere. He wore a red sash around his waist that was nearly identical to the one Drôgän wore, a detail Anton found perplexing. From the torso down, Vile had no legs, just black smoky fire that tapered to a point and fluctuated around like the tail of a tornado. This too was nearly identical to Drôgän, yet his fiery tail where his legs should have been disappeared into an urn. The similarities the two shared were astounding.

With a wave of Vile's palm across the pyramid's tip, the platform rose toward the ceiling, ascending to the highest reaches of the tower, yet it had no visible support or means of propulsion. Floating to the other side of the platform, Vile positioned himself for some unknown activity and gazed into the pyramid. As the platform reached the ceiling of the massive chamber, he looked up and waved his arm. In an instant, two jaw-like doors opened, allowing the platform to continue its ascension through the top of the skull where it finally came to a halt. From that vantage point, he could easily view the furthest reaches of Lower Peruvious. Only the dense, smoky clouds that covered the entirety of the lower lands obscured his capacity to do so.

Reaching inside a nearly indiscernible black vest, he produced a scepter and laughed hideously. The sound seemed to tear at the atmosphere. An enormous gem capped the two-foot rune-covered shaft of the scepter, and it emitted a dazzling vermilion glow. Bloody power radiated in all directions, wounding the atmosphere of the dark and cold night with its corrupt energy.

Again, Vile pointed at the Crystal Pyramid. "Reveal to me the activities of Celestra," his voice grated commandingly. At once, a tornado whirled inside the triangular prism walls of the pyramid. After a moment or two, the turbulence faded and an image of Celestra formed.

Stroking the side of the pyramid with his right hand, he adjusted the image. It zoomed in or out as he rubbed forward or back, and it moved from left to right as he stroked the pyramid's face. He continued until he could easily see the details he sought. Returning the scepter to his vest, he rubbed the left side of the pyramid, and the sounds of the region surrounding the protective dome increased in volume. Then, with a wave of his arm across the pyramid's peak, the image of Celestra vanished, and the platform slowly descended.

"Odious!" Vile bellowed as he descended. "Appear!" Instantly one of the Lords of Ruin materialized in the main chamber of the tower.

"How may I serve you my master?" Odious replied like an obedient slave, then bowed in Methonian fashion.

As the platform came to a rest, Vile paid little regard to Odious's formality. Waving his scepter, he snarled, "I have several important tasks to accomplish before we begin our campaign. Everything is in position, and we need to act before the completion of that accursed antigravity generator."

"Yes, my all-wise master. It *is* as you've predicted. I will tend to your minions." Odious replied thoughtlessly, as if he was merely a puppet, as if his mind was controlled absolutely, and he simply responded mechanically. Again, he bowed in his Methonian Warrior's modus, demonstrating his utter slave-like loyalty.

"Gather the other lords and bring them to the command chamber. We'll begin our assault tomorrow when the sun sets. I have a final assignment for each of you. Now go!" In an instant, Odious collapsed in a swirl of darkness and disappeared from Vile's chamber.

Then, without warning, the Crystal Pyramid again glowed intensely. Brilliant blue beams of light twisted around inside the device and ultraviolet beams danced throughout the entire chamber. Once again, Vile waved his arm across the pyramid's peak, and the platform began to rise into the air. The jaw-like doors at the top of the dome-shaped skull opened and allowed him to escape the confines of the tower.

"Clouds," rasped Vile, and the dense clouds that surrounded the spire parted, allowing him an unobstructed view toward the city of Celestra. "I must discover what the pyramid senses. Reveal it to me!" he commanded. His index finger touched the tip of pyramid, and once again, an image of Celestra appeared inside the heart of the pyramid.

Adjusting the image, he zoomed inside of the protective dome and looked closer at the activity of the robots. For a time, he studied their movements and gritted his teeth in anger at what he witnessed.

"They move too quickly, but I must wait for the fall of night tomorrow. It's now a contest of time," he stated clearly for no one to hear.

However, someone did hear. Anton floated in his ethereal form a short distance away. The energy of the pyramid tore at his spirit like fire burning his flesh, yet he had no body, and it did no damage, it merely assaulted him as if a thousand knifes filleted his skin. Ignoring the acute discomfort, he watched intently and gathered every fragment of information his enemy unwittingly revealed.

Minutes passed as Vile snarled and adjusted his view of the activity, and then with a wave of his arm the platform again descended. This time it didn't stop in the chamber inside the skull as it had before, but continued downward to another destination, a room about half the size of the first. Clearly, it was Vile's command chamber.

Following him, Anton continued to watch as Vile revealed his plans. He stayed far enough away from the pyramid to avoid the streaks of energy that emanated from it, yet close enough that he didn't lose sight of his enemy.

Ultraviolet-blue light silently radiated from the Crystal Pyramid, lighting the room in an eerie fluorescent bluish glow. Several torches lined the walls and blue fire burned from them, but their fire paled beside the intense malevolent radiance the Crystal Pyramid radiated. On the floor around the platform, a large black star in the shape of a pentagram was inlaid in the stone. It covered half the small room and appeared as though it depicted a black hole. Standing at four of the five points of the pentagram were the remaining Lords of Ruin.

Lord Odious, Lord Sinister, Lord Agonia, and Lord Bane all held a staff at arm's length with the heel touching the floor and the tip pointing inward toward Vile. A large ruby capped each staff, and they looked identical to the ones the serpotaurs had used, only on a human-sized scale. In unison, the lords chanted: "We come to serve oh mighty master of darkness." And then they all bowed in obedient Methonian modus.

Grinning, Vile responded with a snarl: "I have a special assignment for each of you. Recently, as you know, we harvested the accursed wizard's soul and we were able to destroy the despicable staff he carried. Without the existence of the staff, our plans are guaranteed success." Smiling broadly, he chuckled like the rumbling of an earthquake.

"According to the ancient *Prophecy* of the despised enemy, a Warrior, such as you, will use crystal to defeat me, but *I* am the Master of Crystal! *I* alone have the only significant artifact capable of fighting this battle, and as we know, it is *impossible* for *him* to *use my artifact!*" he shouted with a deafening tone. "However," he snarled, "that tiny trinket your brother wears *is* of concern, therefore, you *will* bring him to me! Together, we shall easily master this new Warrior and put his crystal to use for my purpose. All of you have failed thus far to conquer him and bring him hither. Your value is in question. If you wish to rule the universe beside me, it's imperative you bring him here, to me, *now!*"

"It *will* be done!" all of the lords responded in unison, and again they bowed as obedient Methonian slaves.

"I want him alive! Does everyone understand? As you can see, it takes five of you to complete the pentagram. Lord Defeat's demise has compromised our capabilities. Now, stand ready!" Raising his scepter, Vile ignited its crystal, and bloody red energy fired a beam of light that split four ways and connected with the four rubies atop the Lord's staffs. In response, they too glowed with immense energy and filled the room with red fire. "Now go!" Vile suddenly yelled. "Return with our enemy, and together we'll rule all of creation, *and* non-existence! Both universes will be under *my* domination!"

Dismissed, all of the Lords of Ruin twisted in upon themselves in a swirl of darkness and disappeared. Vile stood alone in his command chamber, and a malevolent smirk slowly crossed his face. He tipped his head back, stretched out his arms, and chuckled insanely. "Ha ha ha heh heh! My victory is at hand!"

Again, the pyramid pulsated and showed an increase of activity drawing Vile's attention. "What's going *on?* Something is amiss! The enemy is near! He's witnessing me! I thought I'd taken care of that!" Turning toward his platform, he flew toward the pyramid and quickly rubbed its side with his right hand. With a wave of his left hand over its peak, the platform ascended toward the uppermost level of his tower.

Quickly, Anton fled the tower. A feeling of revulsion filled his heart, and a sense of intense fear swirled inside his head like a storm. He traveled at lightning speed back to Celestra and as quickly as possible reentered his body. Gasping, his eyes fluttered and he looked at Deidra as he worked to clear his vision.

"How uh, how long was I *gone?*" Fumbling his words, fear marked his face, and he looked at Deidra with apprehension. "I *know* their plans, but even more significant, I've realized something I hadn't before, and it's been staring me in the face ever since I arrived on Peruvious, or actually, I've seen it my whole life, I just didn't put it all together until now. It was something Vile said and demonstrated."

Confused, Deidra looked at Anton and wondered what he meant. His words seemed disjointed. "Well, I don't know what you're implying, but in the meantime, are you going to tell me what they're *doing?* It seems to me I have a right to know!"

"They're preparing to attack at sunset tomorrow. The lords are coming here, now. They need to capture me and take me back to Vile's Tower. They're afraid of me and my crystal ring, and they need to remove me as a threat."

Unmoved, Deidra appeared speechless. For a moment, she didn't say anything, but then her mouth opened slightly as if she had something to say. "I guess it's about to start. I wish we weren't alone, I'm so scared." It was quite evident she was petrified with fear, and a shiver suddenly ran up her spine. "What else did you figure out, I mean, you said you thought of something? Tell me!"

"Yes, something fundamental, something simple, yet it would seem to be the key to everything. When I was a small child I was given this ring." Holding up his hand, Anton displayed his ring for Deidra to see. "I didn't realize it then, but *crystal* is the *key*, the one thing that connects everything together. My Masters knew it, Lothendus knew it, and now, finally, I *know* it." Watching Deidra's expression, Anton hesitated.

"What do you mean? We've seen the magic of your ring, but what do you mean *crystal* is the *key?*" Still not grasping his meaning, Deidra pressed Anton for more information.

"It's like this: The Staff of Balance used a Dragon Pearl, a piece of crystal that enhanced its capabilities. This is a product of a genetically engineered monstrosity. My ring is made of crystal. The computers use crystal circuitry. I acquired a *Lapillusaurus* pearl back on Methonias, and it is now part of the Universal Staff of Balance that you hold. Vile uses a Crystal Pyramid. The protective domes over the city, the castle, and formerly the two Towers of Tor all use crystals. Even the circuitry and lenses of the celestial eye are made of crystal. Do you understand where I'm going with this?" Looking at Deidra, Anton wanted to make sure she followed his logic before proceeding.

"I understand what you're saying, but I don't know why. What does crystal have to *do* with all this? It's just a piece of translucent mineral rock, or glass really, how could it be the key?" Confused, she urged Anton further. She followed his line of thinking, but she didn't yet grasp the profundity of his logic.

"Each of these crystals is a different shape, and it's obvious this is an important point. However, what really makes the difference is where the crystals come from. Some are mined from the earth, some are created by genetically altered creatures, and as far as the Crystal Pyramid is concerned, I have no idea exactly how it was manufactured or created, and that scares me."

"I still don't understand what you're trying to say. Okay, so everything is crystal. What difference does it make, and why is this important?" Deidra listened closely to Anton, yet she still didn't perceive his point. She appeared perplexed and shook her head. "What have crystals got to do with anything other than having some sort of magical powers?"

"Actually, they aren't themselves magical! This is the entire point! What makes the crystals special is light: they're a focal point, they refract, alter, and focus *light*." Looking at Deidra, Anton again waited to see if she was beginning to follow his logic. "The Creator, *One*, created the universe and light. The Intelligence of Non-existence, Vile, uses light from the furthest ends of the spectrum, both ultraviolet and infrared. He also uses the energy of extreme gravity, or to put it another way, the annihilation of light! This is where he derives his power. When gravity becomes too strong it emits gamma radiation and that is death! Black holes are death! They destroy light!"

Suddenly Deidra's eyes opened widely. "*I see!* At least I *think* I understand what you're trying to say! The crystals focus the Creator's energy somehow, if it's there. The Creator and light are synonymous. But I don't understand how your ring works. Isn't it manufactured somehow?"

"I've given *that* point a lot of thought. Its power is invoked due to the presence of the Crystal Pyramid and the Universal Staff of Balance. Both of these artifacts either use or are made of crystal, and they exist here, on Peruvious, and the hands of these supreme beings touched them in some way. This seems to have given all crystals that come into close range of them special magical properties. Since my ring is made of a type of *living* crystal, it has the ability to function independently, but still needs the divine artifacts to activate its potential.

Even more, since the Universal Staff of Balance has the same type of living crystal, and both my ring and the staff have sophisticated circuitry and programming installed in them, they should be able to function in tandem somehow. And now, the celestial eye has my crystallographic holo-projector inside of it—it too has crystal from a *Lapillusaurus!*" Anton smiled slightly and slowly nodded his head. "What do you think?" he asked.

"It makes sense. I think you're right!" Deidra's eyes lit up, and she smiled as she accepted Anton's logic. "What does that mean for us though?"

"Well, ultimately, light destroys darkness, but extreme gravity destroys light. It contains it and crushes it and won't allow the photons to escape. Kind of a stand-off, really. Outside, up in the city, I observed thousands of robots constructing an enormous device. Celestra is now an anti-gravity generator. When I was looking through the Celestial Eye, the computer informed me about some sort of a gravity well at Vile's Tower. I believe it was referring to the Crystal Pyramid, but I'm not *really* sure. Apparently, the computer here is building a device to negate that power. I just fear these two powers will destroy Peruvious in the process. Apparently, it's up to us to control that somehow."

Deidra was impressed with Anton's logic, particularly how he was able to determine something she never would have realized. She knew in her heart he was most likely correct. She'd gained an enormous respect for his opinion, but his revelation of Vile's plans scared her.

"We still don't know if we're strong enough to fight so many of them! There are *too* many enemies, and there are only *two* of us. How can we possibly win?" Her fear was evident, and she asked the most significant point that was on her mind. Still, Deidra didn't know what to do. She'd only followed Anton out of love, but now she had to share the burden of confronting the enemy, and she had no desire to fight, even with the aid of the Universal Staff. She trembled uncontrollably as she thought about using it.

"I've given that more thought than you might realize. I can't do it all by myself, it's true. I understand that you're terrified, and I appreciate your fears. As I look at you, it's more than *obvious* how scared you are. Well, frankly, I'm scared too. This whole thing is on a level I can't entirely imagine. However, I believe in *us*." Anton looked at her vacantly. He watched as she suddenly began to cry and covered her face with her hands.

"*You're* just *scared?* I'm *horrified!*" she said between sobs. "I can't go out *there*, I can't *fight!* We need *help!*" Crying outright, she buried her face in her hands.

"Don't cry. I *know* we can win. It's just a matter of finding an edge, and I need to think of a way to destroy the Crystal Pyramid. Besides, there's nobody else but us, and do you really want a lot of other people to die so that you don't have to face your fear?"

"No! I just don't want to *fight!* I want this to be over with!" Tears rolled down her chin, and Deidra shivered as if she were freezing.

Slowly, Anton knelt beside Deidra and gave her a gentle, caring hug. "Our love is precious, and it's important. There's something about it that gives us the edge we need, the edge I'm talking about. Trepid said as much. I just need to figure out what it *is*, and *how* to *use* it to our *advantage*. The celestial eye is important somehow. It seems to be the key, the center, the focal point. Don't worry, I'm not going to become one of those trees we saw, or be harvested the way Vim was, and I won't let *anything* happen to *you!* Obviously, Vim didn't know what to do either, and he paid the price for that, but *we'll* know what to do."

Anton continued to embrace her, and soon Deidra wiped her tears from her face with the back of her hands. She put her arms together between them, rested her head against his chest and closed her eyes.

"I love you. Let's be together. It may be the last time." Looking longingly up into his face, she looked back and forth from eye to eye and then glanced at the bed. "Take me."

Smiling, Anton gently, caringly, picked her up, carried her over to the bed, sat her down, and then slowly undressed them both. Tenderly, he kissed her lips and they embraced. They needed each other, more than words, more than love. They needed to share this moment so that they could face a horrifying and uncertain future, a future that was perhaps only hours away.

Cosmic Power

ANTON'S STOMACH RUMBLED WITH HUNGER, waking him partially from a deep sleep. As he rolled over, a sudden jolt rocked the bed and his eyes immediately opened. In a flash, he was acutely cognizant of his surroundings, and he focused his Methonian attention on the source of the jolt. As Deidra slept, her arms gently embraced him, and as a result, it divided his attention. He affectionately recalled their extensive intimacy just a few short hours earlier, and his body could still sense the pleasure it had experienced. Smiling to himself, he ran his fingers lovingly through her hair. Suddenly, another jolt shook the bed and he realized the significance: they were under attack, and he needed to react immediately. Lurching from his repose, he donned his clothing at incredible speed and prepared to confront the enemy.

"What's wrong?" Deidra asked groggily. She'd slept deeply through the first two shockwaves, and she watched Anton dress. "Why are you dressing so quickly? Why is the bed shaking? Did *you* do that?"

"We're under *attack!* It *begins!* Prepare for *battle!*" Adrenaline and his Warrior's training drove Anton's consternation. He yelled his response excitedly. "You'd better get your hands on that *staff* of yours. You're going to *need* it—*now!*"

Again, a heavy shockwave shook the entire room, cracking the ceiling, and dust sifted into the atmosphere and spilled on the floor. Deidra's eyes suddenly opened wide and fear marked her face as she realized the magnitude of Anton's words.

"I don't know what's going on up there, but it must be a bombardment of incredible powers in order to shake the ground so hard and so deep. Computer, give me a full analysis of the external shockwaves!" Anton needed answers and he didn't have time to wait. Drawing on his resources, he headed straight for the elevator with a reluctant Deidra in tow. She was still fastening her blouse, and she was undeniably terrified.

"Analyzing. Analysis complete. Multiple energy beams are firing at the protective dome. Warning: a dome breach is imminent. At the current rate of attack the estimated time of breach is five minutes, twenty-three seconds, and counting." Alarms suddenly sounded as the computer revealed its data.

"I'm *afraid!* Hold me!" Deidra bawled. "I'm not *ready!* I don't *want* to *die!*" Tears poured from her eyes as she pleaded for comfort. She was neither prepared, nor alacritous to fulfill her destiny. "I don't *want* to go outside! I can't *face* them! I'm too *scared!*"

"Well, it's no longer safe in *here* either! Ready or not, you *will* face them! Either you go to *them,* or *they'll* come to *you!* There *is* no other option!" Less than sympathetic, Anton's encouragement was harsh and direct. He didn't have time for her fear, and he needed her help. The world needed her help. Mankind needed her help. She was too important to the outcome, and he wasn't going to allow her to cower in fear without even attempting to support him.

The door to the elevator suddenly whooshed open, and Anton pulled Deidra in behind him. "Computer, seal the front door of the observatory! Take us to the celestial eye!" he ordered.

At incredible speed, the elevator raced toward the surface. Within a minute, the door again whooshed sideways and opened, and Anton literally flew from inside the lift toward the celestial eye. Immediately examining his surroundings, he could see the last vestiges of daylight through the dome's open doors. Obviously, it was either late evening, or the density of the clouds had increased significantly, leaving the chamber completely dark. Only the activity of the computer's consoles and holo-monitors cast any light into the chamber.

"Twenty seconds to breach. Nineteen, eighteen … " The computer continued its countdown.

Anton's emotions suddenly overcame him, and golden fire burst from his ring. Instantly it enveloped the two, and in response, the globe atop Deidra's staff ignited with power. Both artifacts were made of *Lapillusaurus* crystal, living crystal, and as a result, they acted in tandem. Another shockwave shook the ground, and Anton levitated into the air, leaving Deidra behind. Grasping the hilt of his sword from its scabbard, he raised it into the air and five feet of dual-edged steel covered with golden fire burst forth to support his impending combat. Like a streak of lightning, he sailed through the observatory door and flew like a fireball directly to the highest point over Celestra. There, he looked around for the source of the energy bolts that shook the city.

Straightaway, Anton saw the four Lords of Ruin busy at work—and they had a multitude of help. Serpotaurs with giant ruby-capped staffs, minotaurs, and nekelmuses all surrounded the entire city and augmented the attack. Together, the lords fired powerful bolts of red energy from their staffs, striking the protective dome. In a coordinated effort, the serpotaurs, minotaurs, and nekelmuses added their firepower to the melee. They all concentrated their energies at a single point near the apex of the dome, just above Anton's head.

To Anton's surprise, Deidra flew on her fiery faerie-like wings enveloped in a golden aura that radiated from her staff and quickly caught up with him. Her stark beauty distracted him, but only for a second. Just as she arrived, a loud popping noise echoed from the dome's generative crystal, and then the dome suddenly flickered and shut down. Another massive ripple of energy shook the ground, and Celestra was completely exposed. Without hesitation, the armies surrounding the city cried out in a triumphant chorus, and boldly advanced at a dead run. Fracknoids, minotaurs and serpotaurs surged forward by the millions. Nekelmuses floated on currents of air that hurried them toward Anton and Deidra, unleashing scores of fireballs as they approached.

"They must *not* reach the *celestial eye!*" Anton yelled. "I must *use* it to combat such an enormous attack force."

"Don't *leave* me! I don't know what to *do!*" Deidra hesitated, and hovered near Anton, dismayed. "You never *told* me how to fight and I'm too *scared* to do it *alone!*"

"Damn it! See if you can repair the crystal! At least do something!" With a wild look, Anton pointed at the large crystal inside the tower behind the observatory. "Just *heal* that crystal! You have the *power*, now *use* it!"

Like a rocket, he then streaked through the air back toward the observatory and levitated through the open doors of the dome. He sailed inside and hovered next to the celestial eye.

"Somehow, this must be used as a weapon. Vile did so and destroyed the city ages ago, and it's obvious the computer has made some changes to it. It looks *entirely* different now!" Pondering his options, Anton looked quickly around, trying to formulate a plan of action. "Computer! Question: what did the robots create outside in the city? I mean, what has Celestra become?"

"An anti-gravity generator was constructed. The globe of the Universal Staff of Balance provided the design and initiated the command to proceed. Construction completed thirty-two minutes and forty seconds ago. The newly augmented celestial eye is prepared for battle, observe!"

Promptly, the dome surrounding the celestial eye parted in the middle, slid downward, and disappeared completely, exposing the device to the outside and leaving the entire level exposed on all sides. It barely resembled the machine it once was. It looked more like a giant laser cannon atop a turret than an advanced telescope. It immediately became active, and small mechanical arms quickly removed the current set of lenses and replaced them with scores of new ones. The door to the control seat opened, inviting Anton to operate the controls.

"The enemy approaches. The controls are at your disposal. All systems active and powered-up."

As if on cue, the nekelmuses' fireballs suddenly pounded all around, pelting and hammering Anton and Deidra with conflagrations born inside their living nightmarish furnaces. Glancing upward, Anton could see they completely filled the sky. Thousands of black spherical creatures completely blocked the view and blotted out any hint of daylight.

Sliding into the control seat, Anton sealed the hatch behind him. The computer's controls were active, but the view-screen was out of focus. Surprised, he noticed there were two seats, not the single one he'd used before. Obviously, the computer had planned for Deidra to share the space with him if needed.

As Anton operated the controls of the celestial eye, Deidra flew toward the protective dome's cracked crystal housed in the nearby tower, hoping she could repair the damaged crystal as Anton had commanded her. It had a large fracture in it, as if someone had struck it a mighty blow with a giant jeweler's chisel. Dismayed, she struggled with her confidence in her own abilities, but she desired to follow Anton's instructions, so she raised her staff and concentrated.

As she worked, hundreds of fireballs launched from all around struck Deidra's golden aura. The attack buffeted her around as she hovered next to the tower, but her fear and determination drove her forward. Holding her staff in both hands, she concentrated on healing, and the power inside the globe grew stronger, brighter and more powerful. It stabilized her as she stood in midair, but she was too late to save the crystal.

Suddenly, four beams of red energy streaked past her, striking the crystal, and it exploded into hundreds of shards. The tower housing the crystal shattered and crumbled, hurling tritanium and stone fragments in all directions. The protective dome would never function again.

"You have no hope of success! Give up now, and we'll be *merciful!*" The voices of the Lords of Ruin spoke in unison. They cast their magically amplified voices toward Deidra, trying to influence her emotions and choices. "Lay down your staff. There's no hope of success! Give in to defeat! You'll share a role in the destruction of humanity! It *is* your *destiny!*"

Undeniable fear filled Deidra's thoughts, her entire body shivered, and she could barely hold the staff in her trembling hands. Bravely, she turned around to face the four lords, but her golden aura waned, as did her resilience, and the staff suddenly seemed to weigh a ton. Grasping it as firmly as she could in both hands, she closed her eyes and screamed: "I will *not* give in! I am the holder of the Universal Staff of Balance! You are nothing! Be gone!" The tone of her appeal sounded paltry and her voice trembled with terror, even in its amplified capacity, but she defied the lords nevertheless.

With a sudden thrust, Deidra then pointed the staff toward the lords and an enormous blast of golden energy fired from the globe as if it was a mega-cannon. Screaming, she swung it like a club over her head, and the energy swiped through the air, striking hundreds of nekelmuses that floated around the celestial eye and exploding them on contact. Opening her eyes, she saw them falling and littering the ground by the scores, and she saw the lords abruptly scatter, trying to dodge her powerful attack. They narrowly escaped, but quickly regrouped with exceptional Methonian skill.

Simultaneously, Anton operated the windage and elevation controls of the celestial eye, whirling it around to take aim. As the focus compensated, he zeroed in on Lord Bane and prepared to fire a bolt of energy. Using the eye like the giant laser cannon it now was, he fired a columnized beam of green energy, striking the Lord Bane's chest and instantly burning a huge twelve-inch diameter hole through him. Lifeless, he fell to the ground amongst the dead nekelmuses and the writhing masses of fracknoids. Lord Bane's staff flew through the air like a harpoon and struck a serpotaur in the chest, killing him. It eerily resembled Vim's death atop the Mountain of Harvest.

Red streaks of energy from the other lords' staffs struck the celestial eye, attempting to destroy it, but the dye-infused tritanium absorbed the light energy as if it didn't exist. Realizing it was futile, they quickly changed their tactics. Maneuvering evasively, they hoped to avoid another of Anton's attacks. Concentrating on Deidra, they raised their staffs in unison and jointly struck her golden aura with red beams of power.

Meanwhile, serpotaurs by the scores raised their staffs and joined in pounding Deidra with their bolts of red energy, completely enveloping her. Her golden power struggled to retain its integrity, and it fluctuated and weakened. Filled with the fear of dying, the fear of failure and losing her chance for Anton's love, her inner will empowered her tenacity. Suddenly her golden aura increased tenfold and as a result, the beams of energy that enveloped her astonishingly dispelled. Concentrating, she ignored the lords, pointed the staff toward the devastated tower, and focused her thoughts on healing it, just as Anton had demanded of her.

"Computer! Power up the anti-gravity generator! Activate the neural-net interface!" Anton yelled as his adrenaline levels continued to peak. His body twitched and he felt as if he needed to launch himself into battle, but the battle couldn't be fought hand-to-hand. "Locate and lock onto Vile's Spire!"

Instantly, a deafening hum resonated as terawatts of energy powered up across the entire city. Lightning bolts crackled and danced from structure to structure as the entirety of Celestra became active with electricity. Two small lasers fired at Anton's head, interfacing his neural net with the celestial eyes computer and allowing him to control the device with his mind. For a moment, he sat motionless as the computer transferred huge amounts of data into his neural net. Immediately, he was aware of the capabilities and usage of the enhanced celestial eye and the purpose of Celestra. He knew how to win, he had but to accomplish it.

"Raise the city," Anton commanded. "Power up the fusion reactors! Activate the secondary shielding!"

Immediately, the entire city of Celestra vibrated and slowly rose into the air as if it were a giant platform. As a result, those creatures confined to foot travel found themselves inherently barred from infiltrating the city, yet millions of them had already done so and remained inside the city, but were separated from the ground below. Quickly, they surrounded the observatory and prepared for their next offensive.

Computer, take aim at Vile's Tower. Zero in on the last known coordinates of the Crystal Pyramid! Anton commanded the computer with his mind and provided the images necessary to triangulate the trajectory. He no longer needed to speak to it verbally. The celestial eye quickly adjusted its aim and zeroed in on the stone skull resting atop Vile's Tower. Anton viewed it clearly in his holo-monitor.

Simultaneously, Deidra continued to repair the devastated crystal and its tower. She was completely unaware that Anton had already activated a secondary shield, and he was too busy to inform her. To her ultimate surprise, her magic slowly restored the crystal's housing, but she was still under attack from the three lords. They had surrounded her, and they fired their energy beams at her golden aura. The opposing energies abruptly negated each other and her reconstructive efforts ceased.

However, theirs weren't the only energies active. A plethora of serpotaurs continued firing their bolts at the tower, adding a multitude of firepower to the three lords' attack. Hundreds of red beams concentrated together, and as a result, the remains of the structure exploded. Deidra had no hope of stopping so many of them from working concurrently. Overwhelmed, frightened, and all but defeated, she quickly retreated.

Flying toward the observatory, she attempted to escape the onslaught of the lords. Her efforts had gone awry, and she felt helpless. She didn't know what else to do. Unlike Anton, she wasn't a Warrior. Always prepared for the next melee, he knew what to do, but she required his guidance in order to continue. Looking at the besieged observatory, she could see the serpotaurs, minotaurs and fracknoids surrounding it, and it was apparent he needed her help. Quickly, she swung her staff around and cast a golden blast of power into the enemy forces below.

Fracknoids by the thousands vaporized and turned to a pool of gooey black vitriol outside the observatory entrance. Minotaurs by the scores milled around trying to avoid the blast of energy, but not all were successful. Serpotaurs raised their staffs in preparation for another assault. It was certain they had a coordinated plan and that it was about to commence.

Suddenly, one serpotaur raised another upon its shoulders and leaned against the observatory wall. Shockingly, minotaurs climbed them like a living ladder, and fracknoids followed suit, easily outpacing the minotaurs. They flowed over the exposed level containing the celestial eye and quickly surrounded it. Minotaurs by the hundreds drew back their arms and threw fireballs at Deidra, striking her golden aura and battering her around, and she struggled to maintain her defenses.

Screaming, and with tears pouring down her cheeks, Deidra swung her staff around and over her head, unleashing a conflagration of immense golden energy toward the serpotaurs' living ladder, delivering a devastating blow. The blast flung nearly a score of the enemy head-over-heels through the air, and they fell silent upon the ground. Minotaurs fell alongside the serpotaurs and landed hard, killing many of them outright. Instantly, fracknoids by the hundreds feasted upon their damaged and slain bodies.

"Thou shalt not enter!" Deidra shrieked. "Forbear thou accursed beasts!" Her voice echoed as if amplified. The very sound of her words stung the multitudes of creatures, and they hesitated and grasped their ears in agony.

Every fracknoid within a hundred yards literally melted before Deidra's eyes. Both surprised and pleased, she raised her staff for another strike. Swinging it over and around her head, she fired a second blow at another living ladder of serpotaurs and obliterated it, but many more surrounded the observatory walls and they replaced the fallen with more ladders. She simply wasn't fast enough to strike them all. There were simply too many of them.

Anton could see every detail unfold from inside the celestial eye. After linking with the computer, it was as if the walls that surrounded him were transparent. The optical surveillance systems fed information to him from outside, making it possible to see everything simultaneously. He could see Deidra's struggles, her modest successes, and her failures. He knew the sheer number of the enemy would soon overwhelm her and overtake the celestial eye, and he could see the lords preparing another strike from behind her. Abandoning his aim at Vile's Tower, he whirled the eye around and instantly took aim at the advancing forces in an attempt to protect her. She'd failed to watch the lords behind her, and he knew he needed to act quickly if he was to save her.

As the minotaurs climbed over the top of the wall, Anton quickly spun the celestial eye around in a complete circle and fired a bolt of green energy just over the wall's edge. Every creature he struck exploded and littered the vicinity with their defiled flesh. Fracknoids vaporized on contact. Again, fracknoids feasted upon the fallen dead, their voracious unquenchable appetite was endless, and as long as they had flesh to consume—any flesh, it didn't matter—it occupied them for a short time and slowed their supportive advance.

You must tap the energy of the cosmos! thought Anton. He knew he could commune with Deidra mentally as long as they both wielded their crystals' energies, and he needed to use their shared resources as a communication tool before the lords unleashed an unseen attack from behind. Beware, the Lords are behind you!

I hear you, but I don't know what you mean! What energy are you talking about? queried Deidra. Scared and indecisive, her thoughts shrieked her response. What should I do? I'm so scared! With the back of her hand, she wiped streaming tears off her face and pleaded for Anton's ideas and assistance as she whirled around to face the lords' advance.

I know it sounds crazy, but relax, focus your thoughts, and remember the power you felt when you first held the staff. You knew then how to tap upon its energy. Just feel it, and tell it what to do! Anton knew she could do it. All she needed was his encouragement and support to give her a push. Think about stopping them, or smashing them, or burning them. Just don't damage the city in the process!

Closing her eyes, Deidra took a deep breath. Concentrating, she thought about immense power and in response, the staff vibrated in her hand, and the globe instantly burned like a star. It glowed so bright that the entire city lit up as if it were daytime. The sudden magnitude of light blinded all of Vile's minions. fracknoids closed their eyes and shrieked and froze in place gnawing purposelessly at the air, blindly trying to defend themselves. Minotaurs raised their arms and hands and shielded their eyes and roared. Serpotaurs stood motionless and hissed, and an inner eyelid closed to protect them from her luminosity. Nekelmuses closed their single enormous eye, and they floated around in circles completely out of control, bumping and crashing into each other.

All of the creatures were born from darkness, and the light from Deidra's staff came straight from the cosmos. Their eyes simply couldn't withstand it, and the radiance repelled them, or held them steadfast as if suspended in a stasis field. Even the three Lords of Ruin gasped and shielded their human eyes. They too couldn't behold such extraordinary power, and it left them without recourse.

Shielded by technology, Anton was entirely unaffected by Deidra's sudden radiance. He smiled and concentrated on his next objective. Aiming the celestial eye, he located Lord Agonia and fired a green bolt of energy directly at him. Instantly, the Methonian lord vaporized as if he'd never existed.

"All right! That's *two* of those accursed lords!" Anton cried out triumphantly. "Two down and two to go!"

However, forever linked together by thought, the last two lords knew they'd lost yet another of their brothers. Suddenly, unexpectedly, they combined their energies and somehow managed to fire two red beams that connected as one. The single beam adroitly struck the platform surrounding the celestial eye. Immeasurable power pulverized it, and the attack shook the device as if a bomb had exploded next to it. As a result, Anton thrashed around inside the control chamber and the platform surrounding it collapsed. The attack continued for several moments and obliterated the eye's rotational mechanism, rendering it motionless.

"Damn it!" yelled Anton. "I was just getting the upper hand! Computer, initiate the self-repair system! Get this thing moving again!" Desperate, he activated the only help he had. Mechanisms inside the eye engaged. Small robotic arms speedily removed damaged hardware, and from seemingly nowhere, new parts replaced the old, but it took time, time Anton couldn't wait for. He needed to act while the repair systems performed their service.

Lurching from the control seat, he ignited the full power of his ring, and levitated into the air. Grasping his sword, a double-edged fiery blade sprang forth, and he flew toward the two remaining lords, ready to do battle.

"It's time to fight mano a mano, Warrior to Warrior," he thought to himself. Protected and shielded by his ring's power, Deidra's blinding energy had no effect on his ability to see.

Lord Odious and Lord Sinister continued blindly firing their energies toward the celestial eye. In an instant, Anton flew toward the lords and swung his sword. Striking the combined beam of red energy, he deflected it back toward the lords, negating it, and subsequently, it knocked them out of control, head over heels. Instantly, he rocketed toward the two lords like a thunderbolt, and a deafening crackle permeated the atmosphere as he broke the barrier of sound. Swinging his sword, he then struck Lord Sinister, cleaving his arm that held his staff just below the shoulder. The artifact shot through the air as if fired from a cannon, and it skewered several nekelmuses, killing all of them instantly. Lord Sinister reflexively grasped his useless stump, attempting to staunch the bleeding, but he had little capacity to manage it successfully.

Meanwhile, Lord Odious had time to react. With Methonian swiftness, he too delivered a blow. Swinging his staff like a club, he struck Anton, but his golden fire protected him from the death blow. Odious intended to destroy Anton, but as his red energy met Anton's golden fire, a concussion of incredible powers exploded. Both Warriors flew uncontrollably through the air and landed hard on the ground amongst the fracknoids and other creatures.

Odious lost his hold on his staff, but the supergrip tsuka held Anton's grip steadfast on his sword.

The moment Anton hit the ground, and before he could re-ignite the full power of his ring, fracknoids completely covered him like a blanket. Gnawing relentlessly at his flesh with their razor-sharp teeth, they desperately desired to consume him, but they couldn't penetrate his transformed skin. Just as when they'd attacked him at the base of the Mountain of Harvest, his flesh proved impervious to their razor-sharp metallic teeth.

It suddenly occurred to Anton that the melding of Drôgän's bracers with his body, and immersing himself in Trepid's pool of liquid light had forever changed him. It enhanced his body's durability, making him impervious to the fracknoids' ravenous teeth. Shaking them off as if they were merely gentle kittens, he regained his feet, ignited the power of his ring, and slowly levitated into the air. From there, he expanded his power tenfold.

Not faring as well as Anton, Odious feebly groped for his staff. The explosion and subsequent fall had damaged him immensely, but as he recovered his evil artifact, he drew upon its magic to heal himself. Feebly, he ignited the ruby's energy and absorbed its malevolence into his body. His eyes glowed red, his flesh radiated bloody red light, and he slowly levitated into the air completely restored and filled with immense power. A look of confidence again covered his face, and he grinned maliciously.

Simultaneously, Lord Sinister searched for his staff. The stump of his arm bled profusely, but he managed to recover the artifact from inside a dead nekelmuse and quickly worked at healing his useless stump. Drawing upon its energy, he staunched his wound, and levitated into the air. He too radiated bloody red light. Both of the lords had had just enough time to recover as Anton approached, and they stood in midair enveloped in an aura of red energy like two sentinels awaiting his arrival.

Deidra continued to glow like a star, and multitudes of serpotaurs, minotaurs, and fracknoids milled about below her unable to attack; they were completely stunned by her brilliance. The nekelmuses drifted aimlessly in all directions, bumping into each other as if they had no purpose, firing their fireballs aimlessly and killing each other. Completely whisked aside by her cosmic powers, both the night and the dense atmosphere had vanished completely, giving the illusion it was daytime over the city. She stood there transfixed and motionless, concentrating. Not even her fiery faerie-like wings fluttered. Through her the energy fueled from the endless reservoir of the cosmos, gushed, intensified, and gained strength and momentum with every passing moment.

Soon the fracknoids began to squeal a horrifying sound neither Anton nor Deidra had ever heard. It was even worse than before. By the tens of thousands, their chorus of high-pitched squealing soon pierced Anton's ears, and his skin began to crawl as if insects covered his entire body, biting and stinging him. However, just as suddenly as the hideous sound began, it ended. Deidra's use of immense power impelled the change, and unexpectedly, the fracknoids simply melted into pools of vitriol that covered the entire surface of Celestra in a thin layer of toxic goo.

Then another sudden jolt shook the city, and a thunderclap resounded in the air. Just as it had happened after battles in the past, the ground began to shift and adjust, balancing the difference of good and evil in Peruvious, but there was more. Gravity itself seemed to increase, and unexpectedly Anton felt twice as heavy as he had just moments before as the tectonic plate of Lower Peruvious rose into the air at an accelerated speed, and then just as swiftly, the ground suddenly dropped away at an extraordinary rate leaving him to stand in midair.

Deidra seemed oblivious to what was happening. Her energy was immense, and it appeared as though she had transformed into the energy she emitted. The power flowed from her as if she were a star permanently affixed over Celestra, and nobody could attempt to approach her or gaze upon her. She took little notice of the increased gravity, or the movement of the tectonic plates as she seemed to move along with everything else, as if she were a light fixture in the sky.

The lords also seemed incapable of attacking Deidra. They eschewed her effulgence, regrouped, and connected their red energies as if preparing for another indescribable offensive—or perhaps in defense. Their strength and power also increased gradually in size and magnitude, and soon they stood at the heart of a glowing red sphere of fiery energy. They too seemed oblivious to the increase of gravity and remained fixed in position high over the celestial eye.

However, Anton noticed the adjustment. He felt as though the earth pulled and sucked at him, drawing him toward it like a magnet attracting steel. Realizing how Deidra and the lords seemed oblivious to the change, he too increased his golden aura, drew forth the Sword of Eternity from its holster, and unleashed its fiery dual-edged blade. Looking below him, he watched as the ground continued to descend, and then suddenly it started to elevate back toward him as the balance of good and evil continued to adjust and settle. He wondered if the city below would catch up with him and he quickly levitated higher into the air hoping to stay ahead of it as it quickly approached. As he reached the top of the secondary dome where Deidra stood, the sensation of weight seemed to change. Somehow, her energy negated its effects, and he wondered how she traveled along with the city and dome as if she were a part of it.

Concentrating, Anton attempted to join with Deidra's energy, yet somehow, he was unable to enter. She'd created a barrier not even he could penetrate. "I won't worry about her further," he thought to himself. Are you okay, my love? he asked her.

Fear not, I hold the Universal Staff of Balance. None who attempt to enter will endure! Behold! The lords are vulnerable, I can sense it. Use this opportunity while it lasts! Directing Anton's attention toward the two lords, she exposed an impalpable disadvantage.

Unable to perceive it for himself, Anton simply accepted her perception and seized the opportunity to attack.

You must strike now while they work to save themselves! The moment is fleeting! she continued to urge. The moment of opportunity has nearly lapsed!

Anton didn't falter. Without a second thought, he streaked through the air like a missile, sword first, and pierced the conjoined red aura they'd conjured. Golden fire met red energy resulting in an explosion of power that sent a concussion throughout the entire city. Every creature, every serpotaur, minotaur and nekelmuse died in an instant. The concussion was deafening. As a result, the two Lords of Ruin flew head over heels through the air and landed hard on the ground, unable to withstand Anton's assault.

Anton's speed was incredible, and he shot through them like a bullet through paper barely noticing his passage. Streaking through the air in a large circle, he circumnavigated the dome and then returned to Deidra. She was impervious to his explosive incursion, and continued to shine as bright as a star overhead as if nothing had occurred.

Verifying she was unharmed, Anton once again launched himself at the lords. His fury was as unquenchable as a fracknoid's appetite, and he didn't intend to quit until he stood over their lifeless bodies. Lord Sinister lay on the ground and appeared delirious. He groped aimlessly for his staff that lay well beyond his reach, but he recognized Anton's sudden appearance and clumsily regained his feet with great effort.

The ground still trembled from the movement of the tectonic plates, and Anton took a few uneasy steps as he acclimatized himself to the tremors. Previously, the shifting and balancing took little more than a minute or two before the motion ceased, but this time it seemed to continue much longer as more of Vile's creatures continued to die. As he adjusted to the shaking, he looked directly at Lord Sinister and spoke.

"I will fight you mano a mano, like a true Warrior, no weapons, just hand-to-hand." Holstering his sword, Anton stood in ready stance and watched Lord Sinister's eyes. Only a small spark of energy burned from his ring. "This is just between you and me, and when I'm done with you, I'll finish Odious."

Lord Sinister understood Anton well, but Vile's control over his thoughts precluded him from exercising the same chivalry that he'd once shared as a brother Warrior. A smirk marked the corners of his mouth as he slowly adopted the ready stance. Missing one arm, he was at an obvious disadvantage, but he knew Odious would aid him.

Their thoughts were forever linked, and he knew he had but to distract Anton long enough to attain his support and the advantage.

"Very well, you've chosen your method of defeat." Sinister's blue eyes were expressionless, but his tonality suggested treachery. "It's as you say, it's just between you and me!" he smirked sarcastically.

Lunging at Anton, Sinister attempted to strike the first blow, but he was too slow for Anton's enhanced reflexes. The melding of Drôgän's bracers had given him an advantage Sinister could never hope to match, especially with one arm missing, and he easily sidestepped the lord as he lurched forward.

The other lord approaches you! Deidra was well aware of what transpired below, she had a bird's-eye view of the fight, and she and Anton too shared their thoughts just like the lords. She quickly informed Anton of what he couldn't see. Beware, he attacks from behind, and his staff is full of energy!

Whirling around and stepping backwards, Anton faced both lords, one to the left and one to the right. It would be a fight between the three of them.

"Deceitful to the end! Neither of you are any longer true Methonians. You're merely pawns of that evil overlord!" Directing his promulgation toward Odious, Anton prepared for his attack. He kept both lords in view, one with each eye. "This fight is between Sinister and me. I'll finish you next!" Defiantly, he pointed at Odious and then leapt backwards into the air performing an acrobatic somersault the instant an energy bolt fired from Odious's staff. It narrowly missed him, but his enhanced body and Methonian skills made it seem as though he had an eternity to react.

"This fight is between Vile and you. We're the deliverers of his wrath!" Odious answered Anton's proclamation with his own wooden response. "Submit to your inevitable defeat and join us in glory! *Embrace* the darkness! It *is* your destiny!"

Then suddenly, Odious held up his staff and increased its energy. Firing a red bolt of power toward Deidra, he concentrated, and the energy rapidly increased in magnitude. Soon it began to oscillate randomly like a lightning bolt, and then it corkscrewed in a spiral. Dark energy poured from the core of the spiraling red power and pierced Deidra's aura of radiance.

The ground continued to tremble as the last stages of the tectonic plates shifted, but a new disturbance added to it and amalgamated the vibrations locally. It came from Odious's staff. As the incredible powers pouring through his ruby increased, the heel of the staff touching the ground conveyed harmonic tremors. The staff bucked, contorted, and writhed like the movement of a snake, and it was all he could do to hold on to it, but like any true Methonian, hold it he did.

Undefeated, Sinister regained his clarity of sight and quickly retrieved his staff while Anton stood momentarily frozen in place, completely bewildered by Odious's inconceivable use of energy. Whirling it around, Sinister powered up the staff's ruby and prepared to strike a blow.

Nonetheless, from the corner of his eye, Anton was aware of Lord Sinister's attack. With instantaneous reflexes, he retrieved his sword from its holster and a fiery length of blade suddenly shot into the air just as the lord discharged a red bolt of energy toward him. Swinging his sword, he skillfully deflected it away and turned to face his opponent.

Simultaneously, the vibrations resonating from Odious's staff shook the ground, progressively making it impossible for any normal human to stand, but Anton's Methonian skills held him glued to the ground like a magnet holding steel. Intensifying the golden fire from his ring, he leapt into the air and levitated over Lord Sinister who, for some strange reason, seemed completely oblivious to the vibrations.

"I've no time for ethical battle. This must come to an end!" declared Anton. Summoning every scrap of his incredible strength, his ring burst with inestimable energy. It appeared as though it had detonated from him in all directions, like a hydrogen bomb exploding, and it completely enveloped Lord Sinister, holding him frozen in place.

Raising his sword into the air, he swung at the ruby and struck it directly. "Join your brothers in defeat!" he shouted.

As if it were a lightning rod receiving a thunderbolt, Sinister's staff crackled and vibrated with Anton's golden power. Electricity flashed, oscillated, and danced around his body. His eyes widened, his mouth hung open, his hair sizzled and smoked, and he fell to the ground, lifeless, scorched black and smoldering like a barbequed animal fresh off the grill.

"Three down, one to go!" announced Anton. "I'll finish you next!" Whirling around, he looked at Odious and was shocked at what he saw. Looking up at Deidra, he realized she was in jeopardy. He could feel her anguish, and he knew she wouldn't last much longer without his intervention.

The power of Odious's staff had increased tenfold. It was well beyond Anton's imagination. A huge mass of darkness completely enveloped the evil lord as if he'd become a miniature black hole. Only the ruby jutted from the darkness, firing a giant corkscrew of red power surrounding a crackling core of electrical darkness like black lightning. The energy struck Deidra's star-like aura and slowly surrounded her with its obscureness. Unimaginable cosmic forces escalated, and they devoured each other midway between them. He couldn't comprehend how she was able to maintain her strength at all, and he couldn't conceive how he could overcome the sheer magnitude of the dynamisms he witnessed. Suddenly, he remembered the celestial eye, and at the speed of light, he shot like a bullet directly toward it.

"I hope the self-repair systems have completed their overhaul. It's my only hope!" he mumbled as he climbed into the control seat. Instantly the neural-net interface connected with his mind, and Anton immediately knew the repairs had indeed completed, along with additional shielding. "Amazing!" he thought.

Whirling the eye around, Anton quickly aimed it at Odious. "Power up the anti-gravity generators to maximum! Prepare to fire!"

A sudden shift in the entire city confirmed Anton's request. The shockwave added to the vibrations Odious generated, and a sudden lurch shook the entire region. Shockwaves of earthquake proportions rippled at an incredible magnitude, but Odious's aim remained steadfast upon Deidra as if nothing had occurred, and she was beginning to waver. Her light oscillated in magnitude, evidencing her strength and fortitude had faltered considerably.

"Fire!" shrieked Anton, and a massive bolt of green power struck the darkness surrounding Odious. "Take that, damn you!" he shouted.

Seconds passed and Anton watched as Deidra's energy vacillated, but the beam of power Odious produced also wavered. Anton was sure she was about to fail, and he felt somehow helpless sitting inside the eye unable to defend her directly, but he maintained his fire upon the evil lord and focused his attention. Moments passed, and then suddenly Odious's black energy weakened.

However, something else suddenly added to the mix. From the south, a huge second beam of dark energy surrounded by a corkscrew of blue light struck the secondary shielding. It was Vile adding his attack using the Crystal Pyramid from atop his tower. Again, the ground shook violently as new tremors bucked the entire city, but Anton sat in his seat resolute, not taking his eyes off Odious. Impatiently, he yearned to see the moment of his victory, he yearned to see the exact moment the evil lord vaporized, but it wasn't to be. Suddenly, Odious's darkness diminished, his beam of energy ceased, and he swirled in upon himself and disappeared as if he'd never been there, as if a black hole had annihilated him.

Just as suddenly, the secondary shielding buckled, and shut down, and Deidra's aura of light diminished to a mere flicker of what it had been just moments before. Only the globe on her staff continued to radiate light. Then, just as the shield ceased, Vile's beam of darkness struck her full force and she instantly disappeared.

Anton sat in the control seat witnessing the sudden change of events and involuntarily screamed. "*Nooooo!* What just happened?

I was just about to win!" Irrepressibly, a single tear rolled down his cheek. "Damn you, Vile! What have you *done* with my *love?*"

Whirling the celestial eye toward Vile's Tower, Anton prepared to fire at it, but then suddenly realized Deidra might be there somewhere, somehow. Confounded and angered, he raised two fists into the air and screamed.

"*Where is she?* What have you *done* with her?" Furious, confused, and uncertain, Anton leapt from the control seat of the eye and levitated into the air. "Damn! Damn you *all* to hell!" Pointing accusingly toward the south, he cursed his enemy.

"You're going to get what you wanted after all, aren't you?" Unwavering, Anton continued to point toward the tower. "So, it's between you and me, just as you wanted in the beginning," he continued to scream. His voice echoed throughout the city, amplified by his crystalline magic, but nobody heard.

In midair, Anton stood in Methonian ready stance. Golden energy exploded from him and surrounded him on a scale he'd never achieved before. It appeared as if a nuclear explosion had occurred, as if a hydrogen bomb had just exploded over Celestra. Golden energy vaporized every scrap of flesh, every pool of vitriol, every dead body lying within range, and at the speed of light, it poured out beyond the limits of the city far into Lower Peruvious, striking every serpotaur, minotaur and fracknoid. Instantly, it vaporized every creature within miles. Nekelmuses exploded and turned to smoke by the thousands. Not a single creature endured. He'd destroyed the entirety of Vile's remaining minions in a single blow.

Again, Anton raised his fist and shook it toward the south. "You're *next!* I'm on my *way!* Deidra had better be alive and safe!" Standing motionless in midair, he abruptly fell silent and stared toward the south, loathing what he saw. His lips formed words that went unspoken, his hand trembled over the holster containing his sword, and tears rolled down his cheek. "Mano a mano," was all he could say. "It's between you and me."

Then, unexpectedly, it began to rain. Enormous, dense clouds appeared from seemingly nowhere and covered the entire region. Huge raindrops pounded all around, creating vast puddles within moments—but that wasn't the worst of it. The rain was acid, and it sizzled and corroded everything it touched. Wrapped in an aura of golden fire, Anton was impervious, but he stood there watching as his anger slowly subsided, his thoughts finally cleared, and a real concern for the safety of the city formulated in his mind. He then returned his concerns back to the tower.

"I'm coming, my love. I'll save you." Falling silent, Anton streaked through the air toward Vile's Tower, but only for a moment. Grief conflicted with his Methonian training, and he stopped, turned around, and returned to the celestial eye. He needed to prepare and to be ready for the biggest confrontation of his life. It was time to fight Vile directly, on the enemy's turf.

CHAPTER 14

The Manichaean Conflict

As Anton returned to the celestial eye, he quickly interfaced with the computer. Every second was precious if he was to save Deidra, but more than that, he needed to prepare himself to confront an opponent that was well beyond any human's capacity to oppose successfully. Moreover, he knew Odious also would be waiting for him when he arrived at Vile's Tower. As quickly as possible, he gave the computer instructions to carry out after he'd left Celestra. He knew his chances of victory were minimal at best, and he knew he wouldn't be coming back if he didn't succeed. If he did fail, and it seemed inevitable that he would, he wanted the celestial eye to annihilate Vile's Tower and perchance the evil overlord as well, but logic told him that was impossible. Still, he maintained hope that his plan would be unprepared for.

For a few minutes, Anton sat there, breathing and collecting his thoughts, as he tried to formulate an invincible plan of attack. His emotions ran high, completely out his of his control, but he had learned how to bring them back into focus and under his control, and his thoughts finally returned to logic as the anger and hate dissipated.

"A plan, I need a plan. I need a good plan, I need a winning plan, but what?" he mumbled to himself, and then he had an idea, an idea he'd never considered. Why would he have? "I remember. prayer has the ability to invoke help from Trepid, Drôgän and the Queen. I, well, I don't know how or why it is necessary, however, I believe they might aid me in some manner."

Silently, Anton thought of his new friends, friends that had guided him with their wisdom, given him gifts, and had transformed him, then he prayed. "Please give me inspiration. Give me an idea that will save Deidra." No sooner had he completed baring his heart's desire, his pure, honest, unselfish feelings and his great need, he felt inspired. A sudden and devastatingly effective inspiration struck him like a blow to the head, and he began to instruct the celestial eye's computer. Time passed as he worked out the details and then finally, he completed instructing the computer and preparing the tools at his command. It was a good idea, but not without risks, risks he would gladly take. He would do anything to win.

Anton sat quietly and attempted to prepare himself mentally for a confrontation no Warrior could ever hope to win. Filled with anxieties, and the excruciating grief of having a second love, his true love torn from him, he felt frustrated and powerless. He knew his emotions would be his primary vulnerability if he couldn't clear his thoughts and focus on his objective. Consequently, he yearned to meditate, if only for a short time.

Minutes passed while he struggled to focus his thoughts. Time seemed to last for an eternity as adrenaline coursed through his veins and held his anxieties steadfast with a relentless grip. Finally, he gave up. He was unable to enter even the first level of meditation, and he sprang from the control seat and shot into the air like a bullet. A vast aura of golden fire surrounded him, and the Sword of Eternity ablaze in golden fire pointed the way toward his destiny. Covertness wasn't necessary.

"I'm coming, my love. I *can't* fail. I *won't* fail, not *this* time!" he mumbled to himself. He was irresolute. He didn't know if he'd simply deceived himself, or perhaps his Methonian determination simply suffused his fear of failure. Come what may, it was only a matter of moments before he'd face the dire predicament of rescuing Deidra and confronting this pertinacious enemy head-on.

It was difficult to see Vile's Spire in the darkness, and he knew his approach lacked any form of stealth. Wrapped in a sphere of golden power, he was as obvious as a firefly on a warm summer night, or a rocket leaving a trail of fire behind as it streaked through the sky. Either way, he had no hope of approaching unnoticed as he coursed toward his destination.

Time felt compressed, and it seemed to take forever, but Anton finally arrived at the spire about midway up. Anxious, heartbroken, angry, and desperate, he slowly floated to the spire's peak and then levitated outside the base of the tower, unmistakably wrapped in his golden fire, and obvious to anyone within the structure.

In the darkness, the tower looked ominous, foreboding and otherworldly. Blue light radiated from the eye sockets of the stone skull, and it seemed as though they were alive and watching him approach. He knew quite well someone did. He could feel the presence of the Crystal Pyramid's immense energy, and he looked upward toward it, anticipating his inevitable doom. Uncontrollably, a shiver ran up and down his spine, and an undesirable sensation of coldness stabbed at his heart like a frozen blade of a knife piercing it. The atmosphere was heavy and laden with an eerie smokiness that stank of rotting flesh.

"As expected, you're a little late for a *true* Warrior. Your brothers were far more anxious to arrive than you!" boomed a coarse voice from inside the stone skull. "Odious! Greet our … *prisoner*. Bring him to me!"

As Vile spoke, his voice seemed to shred Anton's skin from his body, and a sensation of insects crawling over his entirety irritated him immensely, as if he was being stung by thousands of bees. Anton hated the feeling, he hated insects, and his personal loathing for them only added to the discomfort. Then suddenly, from seemingly nowhere, Odious materialized between Anton and the tower. He stood in midair just ahead of him, expressionless, and unquestionably confident. Slowly, he lowered himself to the ground and stood there staring up at Anton with a look of certainty, as if he'd already won the battle.

"By your command, oh master!" Handling a heavy staff large enough for a serpotaur's massive grip as if it was of an appropriate size for a man, Odious bowed slightly and pointed the ruby capping the artifact menacingly at Anton. Red power shone brightly in the darkness and cast rays of scintillating energy in all directions. Its shaft writhed like a giant serpent in his grasp as if it had a mind of its own and Odious held it back from eagerly attacking Anton.

"Finally, you choose to fight *me* rather than a *girl!* No *true* Methonian would *ever* fight a *girl!* Lay down your staff and we'll settle this like two Warriors!" Anton attempted to disarm him and shift the odds in his favor. He knew he had strength and agility far beyond that of Odious, but it seemed insufficient as he prepared to fight on Vile's home turf. He knew that the serpotaur-sized staff was a formidable weapon with unknown powers and capabilities, and he felt less than confident as he gazed up at its scintillating red gem.

"The time of choice is *now!* Submit, or your soul is *forfeit*, and the age of darkness will commence as it is ordained!" Odious replied dryly, as if he were merely a device or a puppet through which Vile transmitted his thoughts and words.

"A *true* Warrior always accepts a fight on *even* terms, or have you forgotten your training?" Goading him further, Anton endeavored to provoke a rash response. He sought to speak to Odious's most fundamental instinct, his base Methonian DNA. He was more than impatient to finish their inevitable duel. Slowly, he too lightly landed on the ground and stood face to face with his brother, his enemy.

"Stand down your magic, it only prolongs the inevitable. We have the female. *Her* fate is sealed. Capitulate *willingly*. Darkness *always* prevails. It consumes all light. This fight isn't about Warriors, it's about winning." Coldly, Odious offered his wooden responses. "The Lord of Darkness is your *true* Master. Already he possesses half his objective. There's no hope of rescue, there's no hope of success, there's only … *choice*."

Without the slightest hesitation, a bolt of energy fired from Odious's staff, but Anton had anticipated the attack. The two Warriors stood just a few yards apart, and his strike was too swift for even Anton's incredible reflexes to dodge, but adrenaline drove his readiness, and at the precise moment, his golden fire burst from him like an explosion. Golden energy met the red bolt of power, and the two forces exploded, shaking the spire and subsequently, Vile's Tower.

The blast pushed both Anton and Odious further apart. Neither could withstand such extreme forces, and as a result, they both recoiled. But Odious astonishingly maintained his footing, as if he were rooted to the ground, he was merely pushed backwards a distance, leaving two grooves in the solid stone from the dragging of his feet. In contrast, the blast tossed Anton through the air head over heels, and he tumbled out of control. He was barely able to levitate, but his advanced acrobatic skills saved him. With incredible dexterity, he regained his balance and promptly recovered.

Thinking quickly, Anton shot like a rocket directly at Odious. Holding his sword ready, he struck the staff below the ruby as he passed by the lord. Neatly, it cleaved the artifact in two, resulting in a second explosion, and Odious vanished instantly. The impact unexpectedly ripped Anton's sword from his grip. It flew through the air far off into the distance, and he toppled and hit the ground hard, nearly extinguishing his golden fire, and knocking the air from his lungs.

From seemingly nowhere, unseen fracknoids suddenly covered Anton under a heavy blanket of toxic fur and gnashing teeth. Immediately, their razor-sharp teeth chewed and gnawed at his flesh, but to no avail. The sheer numbers weighed him down, slowing his reactions a modest degree, but more significantly, their vitriol smell was horrendous. Their bodies reeked of the forest of harvested souls and the defiled soil of Lower Peruvious. Acrid gas filled his lungs as he struggled to regain his breath, and he coughed and gagged as he struggled to re-claim his wits and his feet.

"You've failed! You're mine! The time of *choice* is at hand! It's time to finish this!" boomed Vile's voice from seemingly everywhere. "Fracknoids! *Remove* that infernal *ring!*"

Unexpectedly, one of the little black creatures bit down hard on Anton's ring finger and tugged at the crystal artifact. His energy had all but extinguished, allowing the fracknoid the opportunity to execute its Masters' orders. A sudden feeling of trepidation filled Anton's body, and another shiver ran up and down his spine.

"No! I will *not* fail!" Anton suddenly screamed. "I must *not* give in!" Immediately, golden fire burst from his ring and in a heartbeat, vaporized every fracknoid that blanketed him. A black cloud of vitriol smoke surrounded his golden aura, making it impossible to see anything beyond it.

"Defiant to the end! You Methonians are a stubborn lot! Serpotaurs, *advance!*" Vile's voice thundered and echoed from everywhere. His voice emblematically filleted Anton's flesh as if trying to peel it from his body, as if stripping the peel from an orange.

Suddenly, an array of red energy beams struck Anton's golden aura. Still shaken, he slowly stood. His magical fire slowly energized him, but he struggled to maintain his footing with such an onslaught of incredible firepower beating him down. It sucked at his energy draining it away, and his knees trembled as he forced himself to stand.

"Odious! Bring him hither!" Vile's words contained venom and continued slicing at Anton, adding to his anguish. "Give in! Your struggles only postpone the inevitable! The choice *will* be made!" continued Vile. "You've but to submit, and your suffering will be at an end!"

Again, Odious appeared instantly, and this time he held the hilt of Anton's sword. Raising it high, he waved it over his head like a trophy, as if to rub Anton's nose in the loss of his possession and publicize his inevitable defeat. "Your toy is now *my* tool! I'll make you an offer: submit, and I'll *return* it to you!" he sneered. "Defy the lords' will, and be destroyed by it!"

Anton felt disheartened. His attack hadn't vanquished his traitorous brother, and to make it even worse, he'd lost his most coveted and crucial weapon. Nobody but he could touch the sword! And yet, Odious stood there with it. For a moment, despair filled his heart as he regarded his loss. Deliberately, he stared indignantly into the evil lord's eyes. The hold Vile had over Odious disgusted him. His eyes shone like two blue stars exemplifying that steadfast control.

Suddenly, an auspicious revelation entered Anton's thoughts. Odious's eyes were an embodiment of the skull's eyes atop Vile's Tower. They reflected the control the Crystal Pyramid held over him. They radiated the same blue light that both destroyed and edified the mastery the pyramid exerted over darkness, and the power it held over Lower Peruvious. All of it was a personified reflection of that evil artifact, not Vile himself. Therefore, it might be possible to remove the pyramid's dominant effects. But that meant the destruction of the pyramid itself, and he had no clue how to accomplish that task, especially now that he'd lost his sword.

"Wait! That's it!" Anton's mind raced as he considered his revelation. "That's got to be it! I've known it all along, but now I realize its significance! That damned Crystal Pyramid controls his mind! But I too have the power of crystal in my possession. If I could only bend his will with my power, I might have an ally rather than an enemy."

Nevertheless, as Anton considered this revelation, Odious proceeded with Vile's plan. Stepping forward, he held the hilt of Anton's sword high over his head and one of the serpotaurs fired a bolt of red energy directly at the tsuba. The energy bolt was thin and oscillated as if it were a visible sound wave, and it disseminated a high-pitched tone that tore at Anton's ears. The hilt vibrated in Odious's hand and then, incredibly, a four-foot length of blade sprang forth and burned like red fire.

"Behold! That which was yours is now *mine!* Thus, you have given me the Sword of Annihilation!" Odious smiled wryly and pointed his new weapon at Anton menacingly. "Now I'll strip you of your *final* artifact of power! Serpotaurs, attack!"

The serpotaurs continued their barrage of firepower, and the bolts of energy increased substantially. Anton writhed in pain as he struggled to endure the onslaught and remain standing. It felt to him that he held a mountain upon his shoulders.

"No! This *will not happen!*" Anton screamed, but his knees buckled beneath him, and he put his hands out to catch his fall. Unbelievably, it appeared as though he'd offered his head in sacrifice. "You will *not* defeat me!" he gasped, and he struggled fervently to hold up his head. His muscles twitched as he labored to regain his footing as if an electrical shock ran through his body. It felt to him as if he had no strength.

Closing his eyes, Anton took a deep breath. The beams of energy from the serpotaurs' staffs continued to pummel him, and his golden aura gradually dissipated, but he reached inside himself and wrestled to retrieve and fortify the last vestiges of his Methonian endurance and determination.

"You *will not win!* You *can't!* My feelings exceed your cold dispassion and your pure *evil!*" Anton retorted through his teeth. After he'd articulated his feelings, he suddenly coughed, an aftereffect of the fracknoids' vitriol gas and the loss of his protective golden energy.

Straining, he continued his feeble attempt to reestablish his footing. "Arrrrrrgh!" he roared, as the ground shook beneath him. His voice sounded amplified, and he pushed his endurance harder, and then rooted one foot under himself. Taking another deep breath, he drew into his lungs the last vestiges of the golden fire that surrounded him. It left little more than a flicker emanating from his ring.

However, as a result, the magic fire energized and empowered him. The serpotaurs' red beams continued to strike him directly, yet incredibly, they no longer seemed to have any effect. Anton's expression appeared hysterical, angry or perhaps desperate. His eyes opened wide, he made two fists, thrust himself to his feet, and adopted the ready stance, completely ignoring the unimaginable powers that clobbered him unrelentingly.

"Fight as a Methonian, you disgusting *pawn!*" he growled through his clenched teeth, and golden fire burst from his ring anew. The fire burned from him so brightly that the entire vicinity lit up like day. "Let's end this *here* and *now!* You *will* return my weapon, or I *will* destroy you!" His voice echoed, and he appeared larger than life.

Struck by Anton's brilliance, Odious stood there temporarily frozen, but his Master's malice drove him forward, and he continued regurgitating his Master's demands.

"Submit! It's humanity's destiny! The time has come to make *the choice*, observe! Our Master summons you!" Odious responded mechanically. The red flame emanating from Anton's sword burned like a flare, and he continued to point it menacingly at Anton as he spoke.

Then, seamlessly, the two Warriors suddenly transitioned into the command chamber far below Vile's Tower. Conveyed by unknown magic, they suddenly appeared at two points of the pentagram mosaic inlaid in its floor. The platform containing the Crystal Pyramid slowly descended from the top of the tower, and presently it entered the crypt-like room. Vile's red eyes glowed fiercely, and they burned the atmosphere like two lasers. Staring at Anton, he grinned evilly and assertively with absolute confidence, as if he'd already achieved his victory.

"Finally, we meet face to face. I have your *pet female* in my possession," he spat. "Her soul is *mine*, and I'll harvest it shortly. It was forfeit eons ago when first her species acceded to taste the fruit from the Tree of Knowledge. I've but to harvest it to complete the transaction." Vile grinned widely as he spoke, and he looked directly into Anton's eyes. "The time has come for *you* to make *your* choice. There's no hope of escape. Extinguish your paltry magic or be destroyed!"

Although Anton felt compelled to comply, something deep in the back of his thoughts, and even deeper within his heart forbade Vile's directive. Unable to resist entirely, he relaxed his ready stance and his fire reduced significantly in magnitude, yet a thin layer continued to burn, and it surrounded him in a shimmering diaphanous encasement. Vile's voice continued to tear at his flesh as if someone was slowly peeling it from his body. The sensation was unbearable.

"I see in you much confusion. You know not who you are. You believe yourself a Methonian, however it's merely a body you wear, and a heritage you embrace. You're *more* than that!" continued Vile. "With a single word, I could compel you to anything I request, it would be impossible for you to resist, but your choice *must* be made *freely.* Therefore, you must be *persuaded.*" Reaching toward the Crystal Pyramid, he touched its peak with his index finger. "Perhaps a glimpse of your little *pet,*" he spat, "will convince you."

Darkness swirled within the pyramid. It coalesced into blue light, and then an image of Deidra holding the Universal Staff of Balance appeared suspended inside. Her eyes were wide, and she looked directly at Anton in horror and began to sob.

"Anton, *save* me! I can't *escape!* I don't know where I *am! Help* me!" she pleaded, as tears streamed down her cheeks. "I'm in pain!"

"As you can see, she belongs to *me!* As I said, I have but to harvest her soul, as is my due. Since it dwells within a human body, I have decided that her life will *discontinue.* This is *my* choice to make!" With a malicious grin, Vile continued to coerce Anton. "You are helpless to stop me, and once her soul is parted from the flesh, your useless feelings for her will end. There is no hope." He glared at Anton as if to emphasize his ultimate control, a domination that was utterly indisputable.

"It would be a simple matter to do the same with *you!*" Pointing at him, he again grinned evilly, and his radiant red eyes smiled wickedly as if to prove his supremacy. "I'm pleased this time you wore your physical body. Your floating around here without one was quite amusing, yet it served my purpose to ignore that little fact. However, it prevented us from concluding our *tête-a-tête*. "You're such a feeble-minded fool! Who do you think *put* the idea into your head to *visit* me thus?"

Shocked, Anton gasped. The realization that Vile had known all along that he'd spied on him during his previous visit made his head spin for a moment. Furthermore, deep within his heart, he understood the levity of Vile's words. He knew there was a bigger purpose about his mission, and about him, more than either Trepid or Drôgän had spoken of, and he desired to discover the truth hidden behind Vile's cryptic revelation. His mind raced as he calculated the extent of what he *wasn't* saying.

As he spoke, Vile's words continued to slash at Anton's flesh, the sensation was increasingly excruciating, and yet in contrast, it seemed to force his compliance. He felt as though he couldn't resist his demands. Furthermore, he felt compelled to hear more. It was as if Vile had both abolished, and replaced his resolve with the need to submit to his ultimatums, but his thoughts suddenly returned to Deidra's plight. Shaking his head, he breathed deeply and glanced at the Crystal Pyramid hoping for another glimpse of her. He needed to see her image if only to regain a modest amount of his self-control and perseverance.

"*No!* I *cannot*, I *will not* submit to your demands!" Anton suddenly shouted at Vile before he realized he was making the outburst, then his eyes narrowed and he took another deep breath. "Free Deidra or I'll end this *now!*" Instantly, his golden aura exploded with power, but somehow it didn't extend beyond his reach. It was in some way inexplicably limited in Vile's presence.

"Your fire is no threat to *me!* I'm the *master* of crystal. As you see, I possess that wretched *staff* along with your *pet*, and I control *your* magic too! Make your choice, *now!*"

"My *choice?* You haven't entirely explained the choice to make!" shouted Anton. "My choice is to *destroy* this place, and remove *you* from Peruvious, *permanently!*"

"*Ignorance!*" shouted Vile. A sudden tremor rattled the tower, and his voice echoed off the walls. "You have no *hope* to defeat *me!*" Glaring at Anton, he continued to touch the tip of the Crystal Pyramid, and it cast immense negative power at him with each word he spoke.

"One more word of defiance from you and I'll harvest her soul with a mere thought! Now *choose!* Either *follow* me, or damn your pet! Forget about her. You have an opportunity for dominion over humanity! Together, we can *rule* the *universe!* Now *witness!*"

Vile then pressed his fingertip harder against the pyramid's point and dark ooze like the vitriol that hung from the mouths of the trees in the forest of harvested souls bled from it. The inside of the pyramid looked as though it slowly filled from top to bottom with black goo. Deidra screamed and looked above her head in horror as it slowly encroached upon her tiny prison and eroded the precious limited space she had.

"I can't stop it! Save me Anton!" she pleaded. "Do *something!* My staff won't *work* in here! I don't know what to *do!*" Terrified, she pleaded for help, and tears flowed freely down her cheeks.

Odious continued to point Anton's sword at him as if he were poised to strike a blow in an instant. The red flame oscillated and hummed with unimaginable power like a flame from a cutting torch. The evil lord watched Anton intensely, waiting for the moment he so much as flinched.

Grinning with the utmost confidence, Vile too watched Anton. He knew he'd already won, and he simply waited for Anton's final acquiescence. "Choose!" he shouted again. "Speak it for all to hear, for all to witness! It's your destiny! Choose! Your time is gone!"

"Choose what?" Anton retorted. "Choose *evil* over *good*? Nothing you could say or do would compel me to *serve* you! The hold you have over Odious evidences he wouldn't have followed you if you hadn't *coerced* him to your allegiance!"

"Anton! No! He'll harvest my *soul!*" shouted Deidra between sobs. "*Save* me!"

"Good? Evil? You fool! Your puny human perception fails to comprehend the subtle difference. You're a pathetic creature! You only grasp the distinction in your paltry *human* perspective!" retorted Vile. "There's more to everything than you could possibly conceive!"

"Oh? Then explain it to me! I'd *love* to hear your *irrational* logic!" retorted Anton. Defiant, courageous, and risking more than he knew, Anton proclaimed his disdain, but inside his heart, he was uncertain of himself. He stood there as if he were Vile's equal and foolishly challenged him, not knowing what might happen in his next breath. "What could *possibly* be the *same* about good and evil?" he oppugned. "They're diametrically opposed!"

"They are the *same!* Good and evil are two halves of a whole! They're two different methods of achieving the same corresponding result!" Vile's eyes grew larger as he spoke, and he pointed at Anton sharply. His temperament changed to anger from mastery of the situation as he endeavored to persuade the young Warrior further, and his inflections indicated extreme impatience. Hesitating, he scowled at him, recomposed himself, grinned evilly, and then slowly continued. "Very well then, I'll *explain* it to you carefully, you feeble-minded *monkey!*"

Anton's nerves were on fire as Vile continued to speak. He didn't know how much longer he could withstand the excruciating pain from the words the Intelligence of Nonexistence uttered while he patiently formulated a strategy. His mind raced as he restrained himself from lashing out rashly, and he endured the discomfort as he awaited the precise moment he could successfully strike.

"Humans suffer. Humans fight each other for paltry personal gain," explained Vile. "This is a direct result of their freedom of choice. *I* possess the ability to *free* humanity of its pain, to *free* it of its suffering, and to extinguish its *incessant* need for self-destruction. The truth is, I can *help* humanity achieve what it strives to accomplish, nudge it along if you wish. It should be obvious even to *you* that humanity *wants* to destroy itself, all of its history proves this. Humanity doesn't want to linger in its pain and its suffering. It doesn't *need* to exist at all!"

Floating around to the far side of the pyramid, Vile continued to touch the apex with his index finger. For a moment, his attention cleverly fell upon the image of Deidra suspended inside, knowing he'd draw Anton's attention to her.

"I can eliminate mankind's suffering by eliminating the universe. There'll be no more wars, fighting, sickness, hate, or misery. There'll be no need to languish, to grieve, or to struggle. You have but to choose the ultimate peace, and permit me to release the bonds restraining mankind from its slow process of self-destruction. I'll reverse existence, and there *will* be harmony and balance. You see, chaos seeks to achieve peace!" Vile floated silently and grinned slyly. "Naturally, you haven't recognized it, but I've already placed ruin at the heart of every galaxy in this universe and beyond. The entire multiverse will be eliminated! The means by which the multiverse will ultimately destroy itself is fast at work. It's only a matter of time before it happens naturally on its own, and nothing can stop it! You have recently witnessed my means, my tool of destruction! Every single galaxy has at its heart a supermassive black hole! But I don't want to wait for eternity! I don't need to wait for this process to complete, I can make it happen *now!*" For a moment, Vile hesitated, his anger unmistakable. Then he looked keenly at Anton and gritted his teeth. "Choose, *Warrior!* Free humanity! End its suffering! Let's end it *here and now!* Your time is up!"

His words sounded somehow benevolent, enraged as they were, and they unmistakably attempted to speak to Anton's base DNA. Drôgän had eliminated the control his Masters had over him, their ability to invoke obedience by simply requesting his service, but something happened as Vile spoke, and Anton felt an alteration to his temperament, as if Vile's appeal *had* invoked his service. But reason and doubt nagged at his subconscious and held this request of obedience and commitment suspended. Unexpectedly, a strong sense of love entered his heart—a love for Deidra, for his friends, and life itself. He felt an intense desire to complete his quest and fulfill his designed intent. It nagged at him, however, and he vacillated. Oblivion seemed somehow necessary too, but logic told him it wasn't the answer. Somehow, Vile's argument seemed to have merit and it tore at his resolve, it twisted his logic and obscured his purpose. Turmoil, contradiction, and a need to end humanity's suffering battled within his reason, creating a mixture of confusion and anger. It was as if a vortex sucked at his capacity to choose for himself and his intentions flip-flopped back and forth from one extreme to the other.

"Don't *do* it! *Save* me, Anton!" Deidra suddenly shrieked. "I *love* you! Think of the happiness we shared! Think of the good things we can achieve together!" she pleaded and then screamed as if in pain.

Nevertheless, Deidra's words seemed distant and insignificant in Anton's mind, and he continued to vacillate. Slowly, he reached out toward the Crystal Pyramid. His mind felt clouded, and it seemed as if he'd forgotten why he needed to listen to her at all. Although, for some reason, he craved to touch her so that he might understand what she meant, and he struggled to clear his thoughts of the contradictions of Vile's perspective.

Grinning smugly, Vile's eyes narrowed and shone dimly. Anton could sense immense power and unwavering thought behind them. His eyes seemed compelled to look at them. Woozily, he gazed into the slits of his pale red orbs as if hypnotized.

"Yes, you *do* understand the need to choose peace, to *end* your suffering. *Choose,* Warrior, choose *now!*" commanded Vile. He could feel Anton's uncertainty, and therefore persistently nudged him further into disarray. "You've but to agree, and your agony will cease! Your pet's agony will cease! *All* agony will cease, *forever!* Oblivion *is* the answer!"

Be that as it may, Anton's emotions pervaded. His need for Deidra's love filled his heart with a spark of warmth, and his confusion subsided if only by a trifle. Lingering in the background of his heart, an unquenchable thirst for her touch, her tenderness, and her affection drove his fundamental desire, and it eased his turmoil. The imposed craving for instant gratification by agreeing with Vile's plan somehow seemed paltry and illogical, yet Vile had attempted to induce his DNA into servitude, and it had touched that part of him. Inexplicably, it nagged at him, and it compelled him to obey. Emotions twisted inside of him yet again, and he gritted his teeth, trying to hold back the words that would damn the universe as he struggled to calculate a solution to both set Deidra free and fulfill his purpose on Peruvious.

"*Choose,* human! Your confusion only postpones the inevitable! *Choose!*" Vile could sense Anton's conflicting emotions and they disgusted him. Indignantly, he pressured him further, demanding compliance. "Your insignificant feelings cloud your *Warrior's* reasoning, submit to *my* will!" Raising his hand, he again stabbed his finger at him, as if accusing him of a crime, and to him it was.

An intense sensation of pain grated at every inch of Anton's skin. Vile's words tormented him. They both coerced his resolve, as if alleviating him of the need to make the choice himself, and tore at his flesh, as if peeling it slowly from his body. The sensation only added to his confusion, and he clenched his teeth as he strained to formulate a strategy to overcome his agony. Struggling, resisting, and returning his attention to Deidra, he again felt a spark of love for her. Within a heartbeat, it grew into a burning passion, and then he suddenly reacted. Within a split second, as if he'd stepped out of time, he turned toward Odious and reached for his sword. Nothing would stop him from saving her.

However, Vile had prepared himself for Anton's sudden attack, and he too made a move. Within that same heartbeat, he cast a cloud of dark energy at Odious filling him with power, and in response, his eyes shone like two blue stars that pierced the darkness. Only the pyramid, Vile's red laser-like eyes, the red fire of Anton's sword, and the blue glistening eyes of Odious lit the chamber. Anton's golden energy had faded to a mere flicker around his ring finger.

With trained Methonian swiftness, Anton skillfully grasped Odious's sword arm just below his wrist and crushed it as if it were made of soft clay. The bones compressed, and his hand released the sword, but Vile's sudden empowerment gave him reflexes equal to Anton's enhanced speed. Immediately, he retaliated and with his other hand returned Anton's attack. The sword tumbled through the air as the two Warriors fought with all their might to subdue the other. Highly trained, magically enhanced, and empowered by incredible determination, the two Warriors fought hand-to-hand at blinding speed. It was nearly impossible to distinguish each move as they struck blows and kicks and dodged each other with equal Methonian proficiency.

Grinning maliciously, and then outright chuckling, Vile continued to fill Odious with his dark energy, empowering his strength, speed and will, and rendering him equal to Anton's augmented capabilities. He fought as if his body had received enhancements identical to Anton's transformation, and they afforded him the proficiency to fight unvaryingly.

The Sword of Eternity's fiery red blade extinguished the moment it left Odious's grip, and the hilt tumbled and streaked through the air, bounced on the floor, and slammed into the far wall with a distinct series of clanks. Anton struggled and fought for an opportunity to reclaim it, but the evil Lord fought frantically to impede him and reclaim it for himself. He matched each blow with a blow, each kick with a block, and returned Anton's attacks with a flurry of strikes that came so quickly no human eye could hope to witness them.

The sword was the central focus of both Warriors' attention, and Anton noticed the significance. Obviously, it had greater relevance than he'd realized, and he fought faster and harder to regain his property. His golden fire remained nearly extinguished, a mere flicker around his ring, but a sudden burst of fortitude fueled his efforts. Adrenaline coursed through his body, driving his capabilities to a level no Warrior had ever attained, and Odious began to lag slightly behind in speed.

Amidst the battle, the tower suddenly shook as if something immense had struck it a blow. As a result, Vile's attention split. The empowerment he bestowed upon Odious unexpectedly wavered, as his attention divided further between supporting his champion, and defending his citadel.

"You clever *bastard!* What devious plan have you devised?" Maintaining his finger upon the Crystal Pyramid's tip, the image of Deidra swirled and disappeared. A moment later, a view of the celestial eye quickly formed, revealing to him a powerful green beam of energy firing at his fortress. "Your toy *attacks?* You believe it can destroy *me?* You *fool!*"

As Vile's magical empowerment wavered between two needs, Anton seized the moment and suddenly struck a blow at the base of Odious's neck, shattering his spine and killing him instantly. The last of the five Lords of Ruin fell to the floor dead. Whirling around at the speed of light, Anton somersaulted toward his sword and reclaimed it. Golden fire burst from him unhindered, and a dual-edged, five-foot length of blade wrapped in his magical golden energy pierced the atmosphere of the dark chamber.

His attention divided between the celestial eye's attack and Anton's pertinacious success, Vile stretched his attention to its limit. Both events required immediate and exacting action, and it challenged even his insuperable cosmic powers. With a gesture of his hand, he fortified his tower, but it required much of his concentration to maintain its defense. The celestial eye continued its attack and shook the structure, but it held steadfast and remained intact and undamaged with Vile's will sustaining it.

Resolute beyond any fear, Anton seized his opportunity and shot like a lightning bolt toward Vile and the Crystal Pyramid. Wrapped in golden fire with his sword pointing the way, he launched himself at his enemy in a desperate attempt to destroy him.

However, Vile was no ordinary Being. He anticipated Anton's onslaught, and as he completed his fortification of the tower, he again motioned with his hand, and at the last possible instant, he created an imperceptible barrier between him and Anton.

Yet the Sword of Eternity was no ordinary weapon. Transformed by the cosmic power of One, it had become an artifact of immense powers, and it had capabilities nobody could conceive, not even Vile. It pierced the barrier he'd set before Anton as if it didn't exist.

Slamming against the invisible shield, Anton's body struck hard, but the sword's blade sliced neatly through it as if it wasn't there. The five-foot length of blade was just long enough to reach the pyramid and its point struck it perfectly on center slicing a gaping hole in its side. Incredibly, the impact drove the tip unobstructed to its core. Golden fire poured into the pyramid as if it was a vacuum sucking its golden power, and Vile's finger recoiled from its tip as if the pyramid had burned him.

"*You fool!*" he suddenly screamed. "Your meddling will undo *everything!* Your hope of survival is *forfeit!*" Nevertheless, the circumstance precluded even Vile from averting the next moment.

The impact against an invisible barrier had hammered Anton, and for a second or two he was insensible, but his golden fire held steadfast and within a heartbeat he miraculously recovered his wits. With Methonian determination to succeed, he quickly twisted his wrist and rotated his sword. He tried desperately to tear a larger hole in the pyramid and unexpectedly, the barrier vanished as if it'd never been there. With another thrust, he pushed the sword even deeper into Vile's artifact, and it visibly projected out the far side.

Then events happened at an incredible speed. Vile's refortification of the tower suddenly ceased, and the celestial eye's unrelenting attack easily pulverized the ancient stone skull. Unable to withstand the eye's power, it cracked and split apart and huge stone fragments flew through the air, and tumbled over the edge of the spire as if the skull had exploded from inside, and then the tower itself crumbled violently to the ground. Rubble and debris sifted through the exposed shaft above the platform, but the magic that emanated from the pyramid surrounded Anton and Vile, and it protected them like an umbrella. The torrents of stone rubble and dust that fell through the shaft missed them entirely, and the platform remained intact and undamaged, but the chamber around them quickly filled with debris.

"*No!* You *monkey!* You *amoeba!*" Vile again screamed in anger, and he reached into his vest and withdrew his scepter. "*Die!*" he commanded, pointing it at Anton. Instantly, a red beam of energy struck his golden fire, but it was too late to have an effect. The power of his ring bridged together with the inconceivable power of the Crystal Pyramid through his sword protected him absolutely.

Incredibly, the pyramid suddenly doubled, and then tripled in size as if somehow Anton's sword and ring fed it with the energy required to empower its growth. As it grew, the tip of the sword again reached only to the heart of the pyramid, but Anton leaned his weight against the hilt and it sliced ever deeper until its tip again protruded through the far side.

Simultaneously, Vile's Spire began to shake as if an earthquake had struck. It was an obvious result of Anton's efforts and the release of inconceivable cosmic powers from the pyramid. Tremors rattled the control chamber, and more debris and dust sifted down the shaft.

Vile recoiled and again swung his scepter, but as the large ruby struck Anton's golden energy, it surprisingly exploded into hundreds of tiny shards. Red electrical energy danced from the shaft of the scepter, and Anton's power consumed it as if it were fuel.

Concurrently, black tentacles of energy extended from the nucleus of the pyramid. It wrapped around Anton's blade as if the remaining evil held within its core was fighting back. The pyramid appeared as if it was trying to extricate the sword from his grip in an attempt to defend itself from the sword and expunge it.

Nevertheless, Anton's immeasurable desire to save Deidra held his grip steadfast to the supergrip tsuka. Immediately, a tug of war ensued, but Anton had the strength and fortitude of a titan, and the supergrip tsuka prevented even the last vestiges of cosmic power from achieving its goal. With one final twist of his wrist, an explosion of energy blasted the entire top of the spire away, exposing the control chamber to the outside world. Early morning daylight filtered through dark clouds, and Vile screamed in outrage.

"No! *Sunlight!*" Vile shouted in revulsion. "The consumer of *night!* No!" Reaching for the Crystal Pyramid, he placed both hands atop its peak. "Clouds!" he rasped at the top of his voice, and then pointed at the sky. "Smoke, *eternal darkness!*" he pleaded, but nothing happened. He no longer commanded his primary weapon.

Then it happened. The clouds parted, the smoke and dust in the atmosphere covering Lower Peruvious suddenly blew away as a sudden gale-force gust of wind swept over the spire, and then torrents of swirling golden energy spun around the spire like a tornado. From a distance, Vile's Spire looked like a giant burning candle lighting the early morning atmosphere. Anton and Vile stood in what appeared to be the eye of a hurricane of pure cosmic energy that stretched all the way to the heavens. Amidst the torrents of fire, Vile seemed uncharacteristically helpless, as if he didn't know what to do or was completely incapable of retaliation. Or perhaps he was unprepared for what was to follow.

For what seemed like an eternity, Anton gripped his sword as tight as he could with both hands and he leaned against it, slowly twisting it back and forth. Then, in an instant, the winds ceased and the energy surrounding the spire dissipated as if they had never been.

Unexpectedly, to Anton's right, Drôgän the Djinni suddenly appeared, and to his left stood Vile the Necromancer, each poised and ready to confront his fraternal opposite twin. Like yin and yang, they appeared asymmetrically identical. It was obvious they personified positive and negative or, in reality, good and evil. A platform of black and golden energies interwoven together formed above the tip of the pyramid, and the two entities folded their arms and hovered with their pointed fire-like tails touching its surface. It appeared as if the pyramid was a fulcrum placed below the platform that balanced their equal and opposite macrocosmic powers.

"We meet again at the end of the first age of man. As it was ordained, the time of *choice* is upon us, and *man's* choice shall be spoken and witnessed before *the Eye of One*. Observe, *He* appears!" Drôgän pointed directly above them at the sky. "And behold, to complete the triangle of the fragments of *One, His* heart now joins us!" He then pointed over Anton's head.

Precipitously, behind Anton, the Queen Faerie suddenly appeared. Quickly, she took a step forward and placed her hand upon his shoulder, and then softly spoke into his ear. "*Forbear,* young Anton. Your love still dwells within the confines of the Crystal Pyramid's magic. Its destruction will only play into Vile's hands! You *must* withdraw your sword this *instant!* It's the time of *choice,* do not *fail* in this!"

"Anton, the decision must be *witnessed,*" continued Drôgän. "Thus, it was ordained. Heed the Queen and withhold! Everything stands prepared. You must choose now!"

Anton hadn't realized the simplicity of his mistake. He'd seen Deidra's image suspended within the artifact, yet he hadn't determined its destruction would preclude her release, and furthermore it would kill her. His anger drove his actions, not his reason, and he suddenly understood the levity of the Queen's warning. With care, and with a certain degree of reluctance, he extinguished his blade.

"From this point forward, allow your heart to make your choices *for* you. *It* knows the answers. Put away your aggression and use your *wisdom!*" the Queen continued to advise him, and her suggestions encouraged him to make his own choices based on knowledge and prudence, rather than his aggressive Methonian nature.

The moment Anton's blade extinguished another event occurred: the pyramid and the two Djinn suddenly elevated off its pedestal, and inside the pyramid the image of Deidra once again materialized.

Anton whirled around to face the Queen Faerie. "How do I *save* her? What do I do *next?*" he pleaded. "What do I need to *do?*" he persisted like a helpless child.

"You *know* inside your heart what to do. Don't allow fear to cloud your judgment!" replied the Queen. "You alone of your brethren have a conscience, use it! And don't be afraid to embrace your feelings, they too are the good that separates you from your fellow Warriors. Without these differences, the special attributes, you too would've succumbed to the confinement imposed by the base flaw constructed within you. Deidra is yours for the taking. Throughout all time she has always been yours. Or you can damn the universe. It's up to you! Don't be afraid, decide!"

Considering her words, Anton realized how he'd escaped Vile's demanding pressure upon his DNA, the fundamental directive designed and structured within his genetics. Even with the flaw removed, the conflict of servitude to the overlord of darkness begged him to submit to Vile's will and serve him without question, yet his love for Deidra had held his will and determination steadfast to her.

"Thank you, my Queen, I understand." Nodding, he smiled shyly like a small child, and his strength and confidence returned.

Levitating, Anton gritted his teeth, sheathed the hilt of his sword, and reached with his hand deep through the crack he'd created in the side of the pyramid. The moment his crystal ring touched the Crystal Pyramid, a sudden explosion of power shook the fulcrum of balance and subsequently, the platform of power supporting Drôgän and Vile.

The pyramid resisted his efforts, but gently, with immense strength, he pushed his hand deep inside to its core until he'd reached Deidra's image. Grasping at her as if she were a doll, his ring contacted the Universal Staff of Balance, and suddenly from the opposite side of the pyramid she sprang forth, free.

A trail of golden energy connected the globe of the staff to the pyramid and entered the crack on Deidra's side as she sprang free. Simultaneously, as Anton retracted his hand, he also left a trail of golden energy between the pyramid and his ring. Golden fire continued to pour into the fissure left by Anton's sword and Deidra's exit from each of the *Lapillusaurus* crystals, and golden energy flushed the last remnants of blue power from the pyramid, extinguishing its malevolent energy forever.

Then the air suddenly stilled, and an inexplicable hush fell upon the spire. High overhead, the heavy, smoky clouds once again parted and a circle of blue sky appeared. It was early morning, and the *Eye of One* shone like the sun overhead. For a moment, *He* glowed brightly, and then the representation of an eye opened and gazed down upon the scene below.

"He's *mine!* His decision was *my* procurement!" objected Vile. "This is in violation of that accursed Law of Balance and the agreement with *None! He* is *not* invited!" Pointing into the air, Vile mimicked Drôgän's earlier gesture.

Thunder shook the atmosphere. Lightning bolts streaked and danced across the sky connecting the clouds surrounding the *Eye of One*, and then *He* spoke. It was a voice heard in everyone's mind, yet all perceived it as if they'd heard it with their ears.

In the beginning, evil was permitted to tempt both man and woman. This was to test their loyalty and allegiance. Given the opportunity, woman acceded to the temptation of evil by eating the fruit of the Tree of Knowledge, thus blatantly defying my mandate to forbear. As a result, and as punishment for this crime, I cast both man and woman from the providence of the Garden. Now, at the end of the age of man's first reign upon the earth, it falls to man himself to make a choice—the choice between good and evil, heaven and earth, chaos and order. Anton, thou shalt be the one to decide the fate of mankind. Shall evil continue unabated to rule your destiny? Do you choose to rule over humanity and the universe under the influence and direction of Vile and subsequently, the Intelligence of Non-existence whose name is *None?* You must choose which Djinn shall wear the Shackles of the Djinn.

Again, Anton stood in the presence of *One*, and his mouth hung ajar in complete awe. Dumfounded, amazed, and in veneration, he looked at Drôgän, and then at Vile. Both had their arms folded across their chests, and both looked directly at him, each with their own characteristic grin. Drôgän appeared jolly, happy, and confident. Vile smirked as if he'd finally achieved his goal, yet a smidgen of concern reflected across his brow. Both waited silently, Drôgän patiently, Vile nervously. Their fire-like tails touched, creating the interlaced platform of energy that stretched across the tip of the Crystal Pyramid, and they awaited Anton's next words. The entire universe held its proverbial breath.

All eyes watched Anton, all ears listened, and anticipation permeated the atmosphere like static electricity. The wind disappeared, and the air remained absolutely still and silent as if it too listened. The sun peeked over the edge of the horizon as if to bear witness. The entire heavens and the earth stood silent and still.

The concept that he controlled the fate of every human being throughout the universe, and the fate of the universe itself with his next spoken word left a knot in Anton's stomach. His lips trembled a little as he tried to form words, and his thoughts whirled in his head. He knew what to say, he knew what choice to make, yet somehow either choice seemed as though they deserved his acquiescence, as if they each possessed some ideal of equal value and virtue, and it left him speechless.

"Follow your heart, my dearest!" encouraged Deidra. "Think of all the *good* things; don't submit to *evil!*"

"Silence! The decision is Anton's to make!" both Drôgän and Vile spoke in perfect unison. Perfectly mirroring each other, they looked at Deidra, and both pointed at her accusingly for her of obstruction. Drôgän grinned as if compassionately disciplining a small child and then he winked at her. Vile scowled as if she'd committed a heinous crime and he would obliterate her for her interference and influence.

"Deidra, in eons past woman already made *her* choice. This is man's opportunity, forbear!" the Queen Faerie advised. It sounded as if a mother was reprimanding a small child in order to avoid an unforeseeable disaster.

"Leave her *alone!* I *need* her advice. It frees my mind of inessential thoughts. Her opinion is *invaluable* to me. I need her judgment and her *feelings* in order to temper my logic *constructively*." Anton too scolded Vile. He glared at the Djinn who returned his scowl with equal vehemence, and then he looked from the corner of his eye at Drôgän. "Trust me! All of you must trust *my* judgment *regardless* of Deidra's influence."

"Well said, young Anton, now *choose!* The universe awaits *your* decision!" Drôgän rejoined, and it sounded as though even he was growing impatient.

As if time stood still, and as if heaven itself held its breath, Anton once again stood frozen. His thoughts raced, and still he felt bewildered. He knew in his heart what was righteous, yet Vile's words had also plucked at his reason, tainting it, and he could feel his loathing of humans and his insatiable need to end everything. In contrast, he could sense Drôgän's trust, calmness, and confidence. It was as if the two sets of feelings mixed and compelled him to choose oppositely, and suddenly he felt nonplussed. It was as if he didn't trust himself to utter the correct response.

Taking a deep breath, Anton quickly looked over his head at the *All-Seeing Eye of One*. Placing one knee on the ground, he motioned for Deidra to do the same. Golden power continued to pour from his ring into the pyramid, as did the golden power from the globe atop the Universal Staff of Balance. The pyramid shone with white energy at its core, and it glowed so brightly that Vile appeared as if he were a black rip in the fabric of the universe.

Gently, Anton then spoke. "Destruction is wrong. The annihilation of humanity is wrong. Hate is *wrong*. To these qualities I denounce their persistent influence upon man. Deidra reminds me of what is right and just, and my Methonian training taught me to fight the good fight. Glory is tempting, especially to a Warrior, and I am given this privilege to choose the fate of everything and a promise that I could seize power for myself. I have witnessed that hate and chaos should never influence humanity to the point of self-destruction, therefore, if I would choose hate and chaos, *I* would in turn be responsible for the destruction of all of creation, and I would become that which I hate. Therefore, I choose life! Let peace and justice rule the universe, not chaos, destruction and tyranny! *I choose life!*"

Then everything happened so suddenly it seemed to Anton he was dreaming. His mind seemed peculiarly clear, yet he had no control or influence over the next events. He'd fulfilled his designed intent, and he not only felt permanently released from the confines of his DNA-induced servitude to anyone that asked for it, but released from his obligations in this assignment to Peruvious. The *Eye of One* stared directly at him, and a beam of golden light enveloped him as if a spotlight had singled him out. Sparkles of white light shimmered and effervesced within the beam and danced upon his skin. In reversal, the golden bracers that had fused over his body suddenly slid off him like the removal of a tunic and floated in the air above his head.

Behold the Shackles of the Djinn. These I shall alter to include the Chains of Confinement. Nevermore shall Vile the Necromancer be allowed freedom to rule over humanity. Man is now free to reenter the paradise of Eden, echoed the words of *One* inside Anton's head. You are returned to your former self. Your servitude, to anyone, is forever at an end. As a reward, I return man's freedom to choose for himself. I'm proud of you, young Anton. You served humanity and all that I have created *well.*

Astonishingly, Drôgän reached out and grasped the bracers. Holding them high over his head, their length shortened to that of thick, indestructible shackles. He grinned with satisfaction as a short golden chain appeared between them. It was as if they'd become a form of handcuffs.

"*Noooo!*" objected Vile. "His soul was *mine* to harvest. Woman was *already* mine, I *owned* her, and I was to claim man next! Your sudden appearance influenced his choice, he would've chosen annihilation!" he protested. "This violates the agreement! And that woman influenced his decision in the end, he would have chosen annihilation!" With a sudden thrust of his right fist, Vile let loose a bolt of black energy like a lightning bolt that fired into the heavens, as if he was trying to make one final effort to alter what came next.

The final event required a witness accordingly. The fulfillment of our agreement is immaculate. Time ticks forward, the contract is complete. The age of deception and Vile's influence is at an end. Drôgän! Complete the transaction! The words of *One* shook the atmosphere, mandating a new law governing the cosmos and all creation.

Placing the bracers over Vile's wrists, Drôgän complied with the *Eye of One's* commandment. Immediately, Vile screamed his final outrage. "*Noooooo!*" But he was powerless to prevent his imprisonment. Again, he tried to unleash a bolt of energy, but nothing happened.

Suddenly, the platform of power disappeared and both Drôgän's and Vile's fire-like tails untangled and touched the slits in the sides of the Crystal Pyramid that Anton had created with his sword. As if sucked into a black hole, they both disappeared inside in less than a heartbeat. The golden energy that flowed from the Universal Staff of Balance and Anton's ring healed the pyramid's wounded sides, sealing it for all of eternity. It was over.

Well done, Anton. You and Deidra have made me proud. Both man and woman have reclaimed their place in the Garden, and when the time is right, you have rightfully earned re-entrance. Yet I place before you the final task of healing the Earth, it cannot persist in disrepair. Man is responsible for its condition and upkeep, and woman shall direct his efforts and guide him as needed. So, I say unto you, go forth, heal the Earth, and reclaim man's home. Only then will you receive permission to reclaim what is rightfully yours. The voice of *One* echoed *His* directive inside Anton and Deidra's heads. Farewell, and remember: honor Me, thy Father, and treat Mother Earth with respect. Teach my word to all of your children so that they will in turn teach theirs.

Anton looked at Deidra and smiled. The Crystal Pyramid suddenly returned to its original size and the *Eye of One* disappeared from the sky. All was well. It was over. The golden energy of both Anton's ring and Deidra's staff dissipated, and then completely extinguished. Anton smiled at Deidra, embraced her in his arms, and kissed her passionately.

"I'm proud of you two. Much work lies before you. What is your wish?" asked the Queen. "I have the power to advise you, or act upon your behalf. You've but to ask."

"Thank you, my Queen," both Anton and Deidra replied together, and then they looked at each other and smiled.

A moment later Drôgän appeared with his legless burning tail once again in its urn and stood between the Queen and the Eye of One. "Fear not for Vim's soul, young Anton, for I have reclaimed it from the false garden of Vile's harvested souls; Vim's soul was never evil and therefore could not be claimed by Vile. Behold!" proclaimed the Djinni.

An instant later, Vim's image appeared amidst the three factions of One in his glistening spirit form. Smiling at Anton, he bowed in perfect Methonian fashion first to Anton then to Deidra.

"Thank you for completing my life's work young man, I had the utmost confidence in you." Bowing again, Vim then disappeared.

"His soul is now at peace, and he has born witness to the fruit of his labors," added the Queen. "You should be proud of yourself."

CHAPTER 15

The Great Healing

THE QUEEN FAERIE STOOD BEHIND Anton and Deidra and smiled warmly. "Thank you, savior! You've preserved both the Heavens, and the Earth; as I told you before, *love* is the key. It *is* the answer to *everything*. You've found *true* love, young Anton Seven, Methonian Warrior!" Then the Queen tittered like a young girl and looked carefully, seriously, and deeply into Anton's eyes as if she anticipated something would happen, or that she was searching for something in particular.

"I'm at your service, my Queen," was all Anton could say, and then he mechanically bowed in Methonian fashion, offering her no more than his conditioned response.

"Thank you, my Queen!" Following Anton's example, Deidra quickly acknowledged her too, if only to offer the respect that

Anton fumbled. Then she curtsied as if she were one of the Queen's little faeries. Unaware of her own proclivity, she realized she'd performed Tania's formal salutation. An unexpected look of surprise abruptly marked her face, and she covered her mouth with her hand in embarrassment.

"You curtsy *well*, young lady, just like one of my own faeries," the Queen replied cordially and bowed her head respectfully. "You too, have impressed me my dear! I am forever in *your* debt."

"Why, thank you, but, well, it was really Tania, *inside* of me. She made it possible. Really, I feel it was more *her* than *me* that did everything. I was too scared." Both blushingly, and humbly, Deidra lowered her eyes as if she'd committed an offense or was somehow unqualified. Her discomfiture was clear for both the Queen and Anton to see.

"In the end, I hesitated, and I'm ashamed of that. No *Warrior* would've acted thus." Apologizing, Anton likewise looked self-conscious. "I'm both flawed *and* inferior!"

"Oh dear, don't *apologize!* You're *anything* but *flawed!* Both of you, *don't* be *ashamed!* Anton, I felt your heart, and I *knew* it held within it the capacity for greatness! There was a thirst there, and a thorn of pain from your recent past. This was necessary for you to understand the meaning of the choice you just made! I removed the pain of your past from your heart, and as I foretold, and have already mentioned, you found *true* love. You indisputably *are* the savior I believed you would be. In the end, you remembered my words, and they guided your heart and your actions, whether you realize it or not. And you, Deidra, yes Tania *is* a part of you, this is undeniable, but it is *you* that made your choices, *not* her."

"Thank you, my Queen." Deidra continued to gaze downward, blushing, but a soft smile sat upon her lips as she processed the Queen's praise.

"For me, it wasn't easy. I, well, I had a *lot* of influences, but I just knew what was right. I'm sorry I hesitated." Again, Anton interrupted the Queen and once again apologized. He continued to look sheepishly at her as if he still expected some form of a reprimand. "I'm sorry Tania had to die for this. I, well, I loved *her* too." Finally, he admitted what really bothered him.

"My dear Anton, she *knew* what she had to do. She made her choice gladly, freely, and *willingly*. There is *no* reproach for what happened! Behold, in exchange for her sacrifice, she provided the opportunity for the fulfillment of *true* love! This is no small gift! She loved you honestly, and in turn, you redeemed the universe! Is her sacrifice *inadequate?* Is her sacrifice without *meaning?* It's humanity's capacity for love that provides the means for it to triumph over evil! You have but to make the *right* choice. Fear not. Tania's life was *never* forfeit, she simply *shares* it with Deidra."

"As you say, but a Warrior's logic guides his decisions. Deidra simply did what she needed to do." Coldly, Anton's Methonian rationale reverted to its fundamental conditioning. Logic and duty were his base characteristics, and he was unable to alter his underlying training. "I fail to see how *love* is responsible. I simply did what *any* Warrior would do."

"Oh, you *are* a silly man! Deidra isn't a *Warrior!* She doesn't *think* like you! *Both* of you have something yet to learn and to understand! I hope in time you realize and appreciate the profundity of what you've accomplished! Not just *any* Warrior could do what *you* did. Don't you see that every Warrior who preceded you *failed?* This is because they didn't possess the capacity of *love!* They were without feelings! You're more than just a Warrior, or a Methonian! You must realize this by now!" Giggling, yet serious, the Queen offered her compassion and understanding and smiled warmly at Anton.

"And you, Deidra, you can *never* belittle Tania's personal sacrifice, it diminishes its meaning! You must appreciate what she's given you! She is still alive inside of you!"

"I don't understand. I just know Tania would be alive and with *you* if she hadn't sacrificed herself!" Dismayed, and obviously unwilling to yield, Deidra looked abashed at the Queen. "I can't live with myself knowing Tania sacrificed herself for me. I *should* have died!" Instinctively, Deidra still perceived events from her katrah's perspective. She too failed to comprehend the magnitude of her own involvement in the outcome of events.

"My *dear!* Many of my faeries have sacrificed themselves thus over the eons of Earth's history. That is our *purpose*, to help guide events to *this* precise culmination, so few of us have endured. In the end, and the time is finally upon us, all of the faeries will make a similar sacrifice. The time of serving the Earth is nearly at an end! Isn't it better to accept her loving gift so that you can help Anton repair Peruvious? It *is* after all the reason and the purpose of Tania's gift to you!"

"What are you implying? Are you saying all of the faeries will soon be gone? *They* can't die too!" Fearfully, Deidra proclaimed her outrage. Her feelings flowed like the tears she'd shed while she was held prisoner inside the Crystal Pyramid, and she looked at Anton as if pleading for him to prevent it from happening.

"Deidra, understand the Queen's words: Tania's fulfilling her objective. She must make her final manipulations to guide the destiny of Peruvious." Anton sharply interjected his logic and then gently gave Deidra a hug. "Obviously, Peruvious *needs* their sacrifice! They must fulfill their designed intent, just as Methonian Warriors do. We don't have to understand *why*, just accept it. It's necessary."

Again, Anton's cold logic chilled even Deidra. She looked at him dismayed, as if he'd failed the Queen somehow, and for a moment, it left her speechless. With a look of anger, she gasped and shook her head. Tersely, she looked at the Queen and again objected.

"I know how much Tania *meant* to you. All of her thoughts and feelings are *inside* of me, they're a part of me, and that is why I can't bear that I've taken her away from the world. I'm trying to accept her gift, but I'm afraid I'm not strong enough to continue like this knowing she's inside of my head and my heart." Deidra looked into Anton's eyes as she divulged her deepest misgivings. Her emotions were more than she could bear alone. Gently, with the back of each hand in turn, she wiped the tears from the corners of her eyes and stood there feeling alone.

Suddenly, the Queen interjected: "Peruvious again adjusts. Prepare yourselves, it trembles as it relieves its final outrage!" Standing calmly, she smiled softly at the two, and then the same deep sound of stone sliding against stone moaned in the distant depths of Peruvious.

Vexed and bewildered, Anton looked at the Queen and then at Deidra. He was tired of this unusual characteristic of nature balancing itself, and he wished it would irrevocably cease. Suddenly, just as the Queen had predicted, the ground beneath them heaved, shuddered, and pushed against their feet. The tectonic plates shifted as Peruvious balanced the difference between good and evil. The vibrations seemed amplified atop the spire, and it trembled and rocked from side to side as it pressed against them, propelling them ever higher into the air. Surprisingly, the Queen stood rooted in place and seemed completely undisturbed by the tremors. Then, after a few minutes had passed, the ground gradually came to a rest and nature again stood silent and calm.

"And hopefully, that should be the last of it." Anton stood tall and majestic atop the remains of Vile's Spire. He appeared and sounded as though he were in command of Peruvious. "It's time to return to the upper lands and the Castle of Amilius. I have a score to settle with Lord Vinicus."

Disquieted, the Queen looked at Anton with displeasure. "Anton, there's no score *to* settle. Vinicus is at your *mercy*." For a moment, she hesitated and then continued. "Everyone, everywhere will refer to you as their *Savior*; even Lord Vinicus will bow before you! There's nothing left to argue or to prove!"

"Nevertheless, I want him to change his perception of both me and Deidra. His last attitude was demeaning. I didn't like either his prejudice or the way he forced me to agree to sacrifice myself if I failed his impossible task. I know he spared my life because of the outrage of the people, but that seems somehow, insufficient. I will have words with him."

Both Deidra and the Queen looked at Anton and frowned. His attitude seemed uncharacteristic of who he'd become. Speechless, they looked at each other in disbelief, and Deidra heaved a sigh.

"Anton, my love, this is immaterial. You're a better person than that." Deidra looked concerned and disappointed. "*Listen* to the Queen, let it *pass*."

"I will address his prejudice. It *is* important for humanity's future. There'll be no more hate and prejudice toward people who are different." Standing his ground, Anton looked at Deidra and then the Queen. "I want to make sure it doesn't happen again."

"I hear the discomfort of your heart by the words you speak, and I appreciate your position. Perhaps your feelings contain more valor than we give you credit. You *are* after all the Savior of humanity; how you perceive things *is* of concern for us all." Bowing her head humbly, even the Queen venerated Anton's feelings. "But it's a part of human nature to experience these emotions, and to learn from them. You can't simply remove them like plucking a weed from the ground. People must learn from their mistakes so that they might improve themselves. It isn't *your* responsibility, my dear, to seek veneration from Lord Vinicus."

For a moment, Anton stood there and gritted his teeth, and then he sighed. "Very well, the first thing we need to do then is heal Peruvious—yet I haven't a clue how to proceed. All I've spent my life learning to do is kill, destroy, and protect. This new challenge Trepid has placed upon me is beyond my forte." Anton looked perplexed and again heaved a sigh. "I think the Universal Staff of Balance holds the answer, or maybe even the Crystal Pyramid, but I have no clue how to use either of their immense powers to accomplish this. Maybe if we unite our magic, both Deidra and I can work conjointly."

"The Crystal Pyramid belongs to you now, young Anton. It simply waits for your command! It can accomplish nearly anything your heart desires!" Encouraging Anton's speculations, the Queen supported his logic. "Of your duties, I can't help you in this. How you handle the undertaking is yours to decide, but I can offer the assistance of my faeries! We have our own final task to perform!" Raising her hands above her head, the Queen rotated her wrists in a circle, and within a heartbeat, the little faeries appeared one at a time as if she'd summoned them through a portal.

Dancing in midair, the faeries circled their Queen and sang a tune as they each greeted her one by one, just as they'd done when first Anton had met the Queen. Each one in turn curtsied to her, and to each the Queen smiled and nodded her head and spoke their name as she welcomed them. The process took several minutes, and Anton and Deidra held hands while they watched them perform their archaic litany.

> *It's time to share our Mother's love,*
> *her appearance we will soon see.*
> *We cherish her like heaven above,*
> *our hearts replete with glee!*
>
> *She is our sight, our guiding light,*
> *our compass in life it's true.*
> *Come join us now and show us all,*
> *you're the one that gets us through.*
>
> *Her magic is strong, so don't be long,*
> *we dance so eagerly.*
> *She will show us all the way to go,*
> *her love is pure, you'll see!*

"Now that *all* my children are present, together we'll follow Tania's sacrifice. She gave her life so that Deidra might become part of our exclusive family!" Grinning, the Queen looked at Deidra, and then turned her attention to Anton. "She has but to agree and she too may share in, if only in a small way, the final obligation we faeries face."

Perplexed, both Deidra and Anton stared at the Queen. Unable to respond, Deidra stood silent, fidgeted, and shifted the staff from one hand to the other and then back again.

"I don't understand. Are you saying Deidra is to become a faerie?" asked Anton. "You spoke of us sharing our true love, and now you wish to take her away from me?" Taking a step back, he looked with dismay at the Queen, shook his head and repeated: "I don't understand!"

"Fear not, young Anton! Her life as a katrah ended days ago, and her life as a human has only just begun! I'm happy to say, she will remain completely human forever. Tania's sacrifice sustains Deidra's life, her gift saved her, but there's a price to pay, a wonderful price!" Smiling, yet serious, the Queen looked back and forth between the two lovers. "Deidra is much more than you realize, but this you will discover in the future. She still has a purpose to fulfill.

"The faeries too have served their time upon Peruvious, the Earth, and now it's time to perform our final alteration. When we're done, Tania will, in a sense, return to us! She cannot remain a part of Deidra forever!"

Shocked, Deidra stared at the Queen, and her mouth hung ajar. "I, well, I *think* I understand. I can feel the truth of what you say inside my heart. It's as if I've known it all along, I just didn't know what I was feeling." Heaving a sigh of relief, she then raised the staff as if preparing to use it. "I think I know what to do now, I can *feel* Tania guiding me. I agree with her, and with your request. Following the great healing, I will release her to you so she may fulfill her destiny with her sisters."

"As you should! Tania knew what to do. She had prepared herself for these events eons ago, and you provided the opportunity for her to perform her intended final purpose, of which she and all of us are eternally grateful. Be not afraid, my dear, the glory of our impending destiny is at hand!" Without hesitation, the Queen again raised her hands over her head, and the little faeries suddenly scattered in all directions.

"Peruvious shall be healed and restored to the garden of its ancient past, before it was even known as the Earth. Anton, you must follow our example and provide your assistance!"

Perplexed, Anton stood silent, still unsure of what to do. For a moment, he contemplated her request, and then he summoned the magic fire of his ring, not knowing what else to do. As his magic burned, it seemed to guide his thoughts, and just as Vile had done, he then placed his index finger upon the tip of the Crystal Pyramid and the two crystal artifacts shared their energies. Suddenly, they gently vibrated in unison and immense power exploded inside the pyramid's core.

Following his example, Deidra then raised the staff over her head and golden power ignited in the heart of the globe. A ray of energy connected with the pyramid, and the spire suddenly shuddered and vibrated as if the tectonic plates had again shifted.

"And now I'll share my magic with yours. Together we'll heal all of Peruvious!" The Queen then glowed like a star and slowly levitated. Suddenly, at the speed of light, she shot like a fireball and struck the side of the pyramid.

An explosion of power blasted downward and obliterated the entire spire beneath Anton and Deidra's feet. Both of them remained motionless and together, along with the pyramid, they transitioned into a transparent golden globe of protection that held them aloft. It was as if they'd entered into another dimension. From their perspective, everything around them appeared as though an enormous CHP projected the entirety of Peruvious all around their sphere of protective energy.

Stupefied, dizzy, as if in a dream, Anton gazed into the pyramid and saw an image of the Castle of Amilius. As he watched, he could see everything that was happening there. Concentrating, he easily located the throne room and witnessed the appearance of Amilius. The entity glowed and sat upon his throne and then looked toward the ceiling and smiled. It appeared as though he could see Anton's eyes through the pyramid.

"Well done, my friend! You are revered by all of us here at my castle as the Savior of Peruvious. You may proceed with the healing, and then, if you so desire, you're welcome here!" Smiling, and then nodding his head in respect, he acknowledged Anton's service. "Deidra! I'm so very proud of you! Your help will guarantee permanent freedom for all of humanity. By all means, proceed!"

Immediately, the image disappeared, and an image of the City of the Humans replaced it. Anton could see the tree-like homes of the humans, and the people stood upon the many suspension bridges and circular decks that interconnected them. Everyone waved and gazed into the sky as if they could see Anton's face suspended overhead. They cheered with joy and whistled. They waved their hands as if observing some great event.

Suddenly, the image of the city dissipated, and an image of Lower Peruvious replaced it. Many of the faeries were busy fluttering about the forest of harvested souls, and incrementally, the forest transformed into a paradise. The horror of what was once a fracknoid factory changed into a lush tropical landscape of incredible beauty. The tortured souls of humanity escaped the imprisonment of their endless punishment and dissipated, and the atmosphere absorbed the last vestiges of the vitriol vapor.

The Queen's final gift transformed Lower Peruvious into a paradise, and she redeemed the tortured and tormented dregs of human souls that Vile had claimed over the eons.

Then, Anton could see the faeries perform their final actions. They scattered themselves widely across the Upper Lands, traveling from plant to plant, creature to creature. They touched every living thing that existed, pouring their magic into them and sprinkling them with their faerie dust. It wasn't directly perceptible what this accomplished, but Anton could see each living thing they touched glow as if they'd filled everything with the power of life. Their faerie dust sifted, showered, and sprinkled wherever they flew and seemed to act as if it were a healing ointment placed upon an infection.

"Now it's our turn. I feel as though I know what to do. I can *feel* Tania inside of me, *guiding* me, as if I'm *her* or she's *me*. Sometimes I'm confused about which are my thoughts or hers, and I'm not sure if I like that confusion, but it feels right, like it's supposed to be that way." Deidra shared her dilemma with Anton. Her uncertainty was evident, but she seemed ready to fulfill her destiny.

Unexpectedly, Deidra hastily and confidently swung the staff around and placed the globe against the side of the pyramid. Golden energy poured from it as if she were emptying an endless flow of water from a pitcher into an empty void. As she did so, dazzling golden power filled the atmosphere surrounding the entirety of both the upper and lower lands of Peruvious. It emanated from the pyramid and her actions. Moments passed, and the energy streamed beyond the borders of the continent and reached into the vast Vortex Sea. As a result, the sea boiled and churned, and the heavy vapors that blanketed it dissipated and then disappeared. Globally, the entire planet began to heal from the lingering decay infused by Vile's millenniums of devastation and control.

Seconds passed, then the sea changed color. First, its opacity disappeared as it became translucent, and then it turned a shade of beautiful aqua. Anton remembered the pools containing fish at the base of Trepid's pyramid near the City of the Humans. As if he too knew what to do, he added his power to the Crystal Pyramid, and inside its magic prism walls appeared an image of the aquaculture pools. Concentrating, he imagined the creatures contained within the tanks in his mind, and directed his power into them. As if scooping the creatures with a giant fish net of energy, he transitioned them from the tanks to the sea.

The life flourished, expanded, and Deidra's power sped up the process with a miraculous, dazzling display of her faerie-induced skill, coupled with the power of the Universal Staff of Balance, the cosmic power of the Crystal Pyramid and Anton's ring.

Then unexpectedly, Anton appeared to speak, yet his lips never moved. You've replenished the oceans, healed the Earth, and freed humanity from the evil of Vile. All is as I prophesied. Anton stood with his eyes closed and his mouth open, and the words flowed from him across his still lips. It was obvious *One* spoke through him. The return of Eden is at hand, behold!

A moment later, Deidra glowed as if some unknown power infused her. She could sense the hand of *One* upon her, and it performed some unknown miracle.

Opening his eyes, Anton gazed into Deidra's and smiled warmly. Filled with a sensation he'd never before imagined, he felt as though he'd accomplished every task and every request Vim, Drôgän, Trepid, the Queen Faerie, Amilius, Thundaruss, and even Lord Vinicus had asked of him. A feeling of completion, satisfaction, success, and of great accomplishment overcame his emotions, and he ceased pouring his energy into the Crystal Pyramid. This time, he had won the battle; he was no longer a failure.

Following his example, Deidra too extinguished the energy of the staff and returned Anton's smile. For a moment, they stared at each other sharing the moment, as if they imparted the same thought between them, and then Deidra spoke.

"I'm sorry, but I can't be with you. I *must* give back Tania's life to the Earth. It's part of the deal, you know." For a moment, her smile disappeared, but then it returned anew. "My love for you exceeds everything, but the final transformation of Peruvious is upon us. I must seal the hole from which Vile appeared. Tania is to be a living guarantee that his imprisonment shall never fail by preventing Vile's two other fragments access to his prison."

Confused yet again, Anton looked at Deidra in horror. I can't lose you! I can't lose love a *second* time, it'll destroy me!" His smile suddenly disappeared, and as quickly as he could he sped to her side and attempted to embrace her, and then asked: "what do you mean two other parts?"

"Hold! You *must not touch me!* I'm receiving purification so that Tania, with my assistance, can fulfill her destiny." Holding out the staff, she then offered it to Anton. "I return to you our staff. Truthfully, it belongs to *you* just as much as it belongs to *me*. I merely borrowed it for a time. Keep it safe for us, my hand no longer suits it. As for Vile's other fragments, they still exist somewhere in the universe."

Hesitant, Anton slowly accepted Deidra's gift, and then stood silently as he anticipated her next word. For a moment, they looked deeply into each other's eyes and shared a final feeling of longing and loneliness and a desire for passion. Unable to accept yet another loss, Anton felt torn between his personal need for her love and a higher need to grant her the freedom to fulfill her destiny. It was time to give Tania back for the greater good of humanity's future, and he wasn't sure what would become of Deidra in the process. With a nod, he accepted her decision, then slowly bowed in Methonian fashion.

"I'll always love you, no matter what happens. Nothing will ever change the way I feel about you. I understand the purpose of your personal sacrifice, and I too must accede to its higher objective. You would make a fine Methonian Warrior." A single tear formed in the corner of Anton's eye, and he quickly brushed it aside, hoping Deidra missed his gesture. It was entirely unacceptable for a Methonian to have feelings, and for a moment, he felt angry with himself as he considered his uncharacteristic weakness. Yet his heart felt twisted and torn by lost love.

"I too will *never* forget you, my love. Peruvious will never forget you, and history will remember you as the Savior of humanity. Farewell, Anton Seven." Deidra smiled warmly and carefully grasped the vial hanging from her neck.

Taking a step toward the Crystal Pyramid, she then placed its tip against the pyramid's side. Instantly, the artifact sucked her inside, and then like a fireball, she shot into the air from its peak, ricocheted off the atmosphere overhead, and then struck the ground far off in the distance. A sharp jolt rocked Peruvious, and tremors of immense energy rippled through the ground as if a stone had dropped into a pristine mountain lake.

Standing inside his sphere of golden energy, Anton watched silently and waited for something monumental to occur, but nothing did. Whatever Deidra and Tania had become, or whatever they had accomplished remained invisible to all of his enhanced senses, and yet he hoped for some last sign of her. After a time, he returned his attention to the Crystal Pyramid. He could feel its immense immeasurable cosmic energy, and somehow, he too instinctively knew what he needed to do to complete his mission. He now possessed all three artifacts of cosmic power, and nothing could interfere with anything he decided to do.

Concentrating, he again touched the tip of the pyramid with his index finger as Vile had done and activated its powers. Instantly, an image of the Castle of Amilius formed inside its core. He could clearly witness the activities of the people there. Quickly, he located Lord Vinicus. It would be simple for him to do with the lord anything he chose, but he no longer felt a desire to do anything at all. Somehow, deep inside his heart, he'd forgiven everything the lord had said and done to him. It all seemed too paltry now. All of his anger and frustrations from the past had vanished, and he simply let the image fade into oblivion.

"It's time to go home. I must return to the Ruler of the Council, Lothendus, and report my mission, but in order to do that I'll have to modify the celestial eye." Talking to himself, Anton solidified his next decision. "I'll return to Celestra and restore the city to its original glory."

Surprisingly, he instantly appeared next to the celestial eye. Somehow, he had the power to teleport at will anywhere he chose, and the sudden transition shocked his logic, but only for a moment. Immediately, he hastened to undertake his objective. Concentrating, he imagined the transformation he wished to achieve. In one hand, golden power burst from his ring and enveloped his body, and in the other, the globe of the staff ignited and cast a bolt of golden energy at the heart of the Crystal Pyramid. Immediately, an image of the celestial eye coalesced inside its core, and from the pyramid, a beam of golden power shot toward the eye striking it broadside. Anton continued to concentrate, and imagined the change he desired. As if viewed through a mirage, he observed as waves of power struck the eye. Inestimable power vibrated the floor beneath his feet and the eye writhed, buckled, and gradually transformed into a new streamlined contrivance born from his own imagination and the powers he controlled.

Using the staff coupled with the power of his ring, Anton then levitated the Crystal Pyramid inside the control chamber of the eye and replaced the view screen with it. For a moment he stood there and contemplated his accomplishment. A feeling of completion, of loss, and a twist of depression filled his heart as he recalled all the sacrifices his friends had made just minutes ago atop Vile's Spire, and the work he now performed alone. It seemed somehow hollow and meaningless without them around to witness his efforts and to share in the experience. He no longer felt content to go it alone as he had when traveling to the village of Tooloo. That part of him that was proud to finally have a chance to prove himself through self-reliance seemed distant and gave him no sense of gratification.

"I guess that's it. I guess I can do whatever I want now," he mumbled to himself, his old habits returning. Satisfied, yet disgruntled, and wishing Deidra could still be at his side, he sighed hugely. "I guess it's time to go. There's little left for me here on Peruvious. Even paradise, Eden as it were, is meaningless without someone you love to share it with."

Slowly, Anton climbed into the control seat of the celestial eye; he knew what to do. Placing his face into his hands, he thought about his mission, his adventures, and all the people he'd met after arriving in Peruvious. He thought about how he'd changed, how he'd matured, how he'd transformed, and how he'd become an entirely different person. The agony of the loss of his friends, and nearly everyone he'd ever known weighed upon him immensely. He thought about Mahkeetah, Nelda, Vim, Beelif, the Queen Faerie, and most of all, Deidra and Tania. His heart twisted with loss that all of them had either been taken from him or he would simply have to leave them behind. Then a feeling of emptiness overcame him. He sat there for a moment longer, and a sense of fulfillment washed away his unhappy feelings, feelings that now seemed somehow insignificant. He knew there was a greater good in all their sacrifices. After all that had happened, he was the only one still alive, other than Beelif. He wasn't even sure about Deidra.

His head swam with anxieties as he recalled the Ruler of the Council, a man he knew now as Lothendus, Vim's Master and tutor. Reaching beneath his tunic, he produced the vial of energy that hung there on its chain.

Closing his eyes, Anton grasped the vial tightly and took a slow deep breath. Cosmic energy, pure and seemingly limitless, filled it to capacity and beyond. He had no concept of the extent of the power it contained, or even of its usage, but he was sure it was the energy of life and of the cosmos. He'd glimpsed the Ruler use a vial such as this, and Vim, and Deidra had too. He'd watched her use its energy combined with that of the Crystal Pyramid to transform into something he didn't comprehend. Guessing, he was going to attempt something similar, and he hoped it would work. No, he was confident it would.

Holding the vial tightly, Anton's ring touched it. The vial vibrated and glowed so brightly it hurt his eyes, and he could barely see beyond his hand as he squinted. With the staff in his other hand, he then touched the vial to the staff's globe and subsequently the globe against the pyramid's side. All four artifacts contacted each other, and he concentrated on Celestra's past. The KACATU had infused the complete knowledge of the City of Celestra's design prior to its destruction into his neural net, and he imagined the city restored to its former glory. Immediately, powers he still didn't fully comprehend regenerated and transformed the city with one immense explosion of energy. Looking beyond the Celestial Eye's platform, he could see the city just as it had existed before Vile destroyed it.

"Astounding," muttered Anton to himself in amazement. "At this moment, I feel I can do anything!" However, his heavy heart weighed upon him and his success seemed unimportant.

He then concentrated on Saurian Five and the platform aboard the space station at the exact moment that Vim had abducted him. Power filled the pyramid, and the celestial eye vibrated, then smoothly swung around, tipped back, and pointed into the late morning sky. It then fired a beam of golden energy into the heavens, and within a heartbeat, an image of the space station's platform coalesced within the pyramid's core.

Anton could see the activity of the Masters sitting at their computers and it appeared as if they hadn't moved since his disappearance. The Ruler stood there just as he had prior to his abduction. He realized that the same amount of time must have elapsed, however there seemed to be no change in the control room.

Smiling to himself, Anton then touched the vial to the side of the Crystal Pyramid and a sudden explosion of energy ensued. Instantly teleported, he again found himself standing on that same transparent platform. As he stood there with the Universal Staff of Balance held firmly in his hands, he could see the Ruler suddenly jolt, obviously astonished.

Pointing at Anton, and surprised beyond measure to see someone standing there, the Ruler shouted an order: "Unseal the platform!" Immediately the door swung open, and he quickly floated down the transparent hallway toward Anton. "I wouldn't have believed it if I hadn't witnessed it for myself," he said in his baritone gravelly voice. "It is you ... you're ... *different!*"

Anton stood there for a moment silent and motionless, then he responded mechanically, "I'm at your service, my Master." He then offered the Ruler a slight Methonian bow. "I've returned with your *staff*, Lothendus." With a serious stare, he then quickly, coldly, and deliberately offered it to the Ruler.

The Ruler examined Anton in complete astonishment. His long blonde hair, gold-colored eyes, and his pure white complexion and attire were entirely different. From his perspective, it had only been a few moments since Anton's departure, and it left him pondering his obvious success. Some inexplicable and extensive transformation appeared to have changed him beyond comprehension within just a few minutes, and he wasn't entirely sure if he'd actually completed his mission at all. But the evidence of the staff, as different as it too appeared, spoke volumes of many adventures. He was quite literally dumbfounded.

"Well done, Warrior, well done indeed. It would appear that you were *successful*." Slowly, carefully, he reached out to accept the staff from Anton, and then just as suddenly drew his hand back. The Ruler then reached into his robe, and removed from it his vial. Hesitantly, with a jittery hand, he reached toward the staff's globe. Immediately, energy poured into it and he gasped and shivered as if it had shocked him with electricity. He quickly withdrew the vial, however, and it evaporated in a sudden puff of smoke.

Anton looked at Lothendus questioningly as he observed the unusual behavior of the staff. He hadn't expected it would reject the Ruler outright, however he knew something fundamental had occurred after the staff had accepted him.

Lothendus slowly nodded his head. "It would seem there are more changes than I can measure." He then turned around and walked down the transparent corridor toward the computers, and as the Ruler re-entered the control room he called over his shoulder: "Follow me, Anton Seven. *Finally*, I've produced a Warrior that can succeed!"

Driven only by the memory of his fundamental design, and his conditioned loyalty, Anton allowed Lothendus to lead. He was free from his DNA-compelled servitude controlling his response to the Ruler's command, however, he didn't want to disclose this fact to anyone yet; he might need to use his secret to his advantage later. The Ruler was after all still his commanding officer, and he was responsible for his deployment. Thus he chose to follow out of obedience, yet his loyalties remained distrustful.

"You know my name, Warrior? This is . . . *unexpected*." With a glance over his shoulder, the Ruler cocked his head toward the two Wardens and they quickly followed behind them. "You'll be returned to Methonias immediately. There you'll be debriefed *extensively*, and then you'll report to the Clone Labs for *analysis*. Afterwards, there'll be, shall we say, *a hero's welcome*." Watching Anton's response very carefully, as if he lacked any trust in him, the Ruler's eyes never left him as they departed the control room.

Returning to Methonias however pleased Anton. It was the one thing he desired most of all, at least for the moment. In truth, he wasn't entirely sure why he wanted to return. Perhaps it was because there was no other place he called home, and he needed time to lick his wounds and to heal. He also wondered why the Ruler hadn't taken the staff from him, and why the vial he wore seemed to shock him then vaporized. These were new mysteries, and they spoke to him forebodingly of what might happen next.

Leading Anton to the docking bay, Lothendus pointed toward the same Pleceivious he'd arrived on. It was obviously prepared for departure, and as Anton approached, it scanned and recognized him. Then, the same soft feminine voice soothingly invited him inside.

With a final formal Methonian bow, Anton again addressed the Ruler. "I'm at your service, and I thank you for this special *opportunity*." Uneasy, he hesitated, gave him a long serious careful stare, and then turned around and boarded the vessel. Finally, he was going home.

Ethics and a Conscience

ANTON BOARDED THE PLECEIVIOUS AS quickly as he could. The ship's computer screened him prior to boarding just as it had when he had left Methonias, only this time the soft feminine voice didn't enchant him like it had before. He felt nothing, only a sense of loss as Deidra's face dominated his thoughts. Deidra's voice affected his mood. And Deidra's love affected him deeply. Now it was gone; it was only a memory. And Tania, oh how he missed her too, her positive attitude, her guidance, her thoughtfulness and support, and her single-minded quest to do the right thing no matter what. Vim was gone. Everyone was gone, and he felt so alone. He doubted even returning to Methonias would brighten his spirits.

Something else entered his thoughts as well, the idea that his mission may not yet be complete. There was apparently a loose end, and he didn't like where it came from. Why had the Ruler of the Council, Lothendus, hesitated to receive the gift of the staff from him? Why did it shock him when he tried to receive its gift of energy and then destroy the vial? Why did he simply allow Anton to carry the staff away seemingly without a second thought? It was *his* staff originally, and he knew the Ruler would covet it above all things. Logically, it was the purpose of everything.

"I was sure he would simply take the staff," Anton mumbled to himself. Then he realized he had better remain quiet; the cameras, microphones, and monitors listened to him, watched him, and his ring recorded everything. "I need food and rest. I guess I will locate my quarters."

As quickly as he could, Anton verified which room he'd be staying in and to his amusement, it was the same one he had when traveling to Saurian Five. When he entered the room, he noticed the cleaning bots had done their work and prepared it anew, leaving all surfaces clean and looking brand new. "Good. At least something has changed since leaving," he mumbled.

Sitting at the tiny table next to the porthole, Anton then withdrew his EHD and opened it up. Reaching in, he pulled out the knapsack he had put in the storage device prior to leaving the City of the Humans. Opening the sack, he reached in and pulled out the food he had stored there. It was more than enough to satisfy his hunger and he quickly ate some biscuits and jerky. The meat reminded him of Deidra, and he visualized her in her katrah form as they had filled the knapsack. She had particularly wanted the meat; it was her favorite type of food, and she had stowed a few pounds of it. Smiling slightly, he reached in and pulled out more, but a sense of longing for her grasped his heart. "I miss her."

After finishing his modest meal, Anton then adopted the lotus position on the floor. He meditated for a few minutes, but the sense of loss nagged at him as Deidra's image continued to control his thoughts. Then suddenly, his neural net seemed to activate as if he had flipped a switch. His mind suddenly became active with several different images of various encounters he'd had since his ring had turned gold. This greatly surprised him. The device hadn't spontaneously activated in this way since the KACATU had installed it around his brain, and it seemed to be functioning as a computer trying to calculate an answer to questions he didn't realize he had asked.

Puzzled by his new capabilities that the net now provided, Anton paid close attention as the scenes changed rapidly from one to the next. Images of his Methonian brothers, the various indigenous tribes of Methonias, the *Lapillusaurus* and the pearl he had claimed, the Masters and the Clone Masters in their laboratory. Next, scenes from Peruvious dominated his thoughts—the primords, the Dragon Master, the people at the castle yelling at him: "*hogtrah*" and "*pig-human.*" Finally, there were visions of Deidra and Taun, and the loving relationship he developed with the cheetah girl. "What is this *thing* trying to tell me?" Anton exclaimed. "What is the significance?"

Suddenly, the realization entered his thoughts so quickly his whole body jerked. Anton's eyes shot open, and then he quickly stood up and took a deep breath. It's all about gene manipulation! It's all about cloning and the altering of DNA in order to improve mankind. Human gene manipulation ... Preventing himself from speaking aloud, he forced himself to consider his thoughts silently. I don't want them to know about these thoughts. He needed to be careful, he needed to hide everything he'd learned from his friends during his mission. It could get ugly.

Pacing back and forth in the confined space of his room, Anton ruminated about the science of genetics. It had begun well over fifteen hundred years in the distant past. It was in twentieth and twenty-first centuries that the humble beginnings of genetic technology had its first successes. At that time, in its infancy, the crudest methods of gene splicing and manipulation was all that the science had accomplished.

Fumbling at best, the scientists used primitive tools to hack, poke and probe their way through the crudest learning processes, and they slowly advanced the technology. Over the following century, they ultimately created the hogtrahs to be used as soldiers for combat so that humans need only supervise warfare. He remembered seeing this information when he was using the Etheriscope, and he remembered learning about it during history classes on Methonias.

This was the beginning of it all, the time when man decided he wasn't designed good enough. Continuing his line of thought, Anton assessed the time period further. Hogtrahs, then katrahs, then centuries later, an entire world was terraformed and the original cloning labs of Methonias were created. Super humans, super science, and the complete control and subjugation of all humanity followed. He could see it all, he knew it all, it was contained in the database inside his head. He knew the struggle of average, unaltered humans scattered throughout the inhabited planets, and those that were created for specific purposes on Methonias for Warriors to simply use as they chose, to kill and throw away as needed without any consideration for the human spirit contained within them, without any effort made to know who they harmed and who they used for inhuman training purposes. Anton stood there, sick of the person he had been only weeks before, and of his fellow Warriors and what Methonias really stood for. They were ignorant of their tyranny, without conscience, and so absorbed in themselves they couldn't begin to understand true morality; the ability to comprehend it had been removed and training precluded learning it otherwise. And it had all been because of the paltry need for man to dominate man, a simple failing humanity had owned from the very beginning of their existence. The primal need for the survival of the fittest had ultimately led to the Methonian Clone Labs. Anton thought about the words Luthian had said to him, how humanity feared the Warriors, and that things were not as they seemed. He was right, and Anton was sorry he hadn't listened more closely. And he remembered how Boris had warned him when he'd first set foot aboard the Pleceivious. Both of them spoke of the evils of his heritage. He wondered how Boris had come to the prophetic realizations, knowing his heritage was pure Methonian. Perhaps this meant some Warriors could be persuaded to the truth.

The worst of it all was the most recent of events. Lothendus took the knowledge of his own past, the knowledge of the creation of the hogtrahs, and the katrahs, and all that followed after. He took it with him and terraformed a planet in a distant galaxy creating Methonias so that he could advance genetics beyond anyone's wildest imagination just so he could play God and control everything. Just like Vile. Just … like … Vile.

Methonias. The home of it all. Anton's home. The home he was traveling to. What am I to do about this? Anton pondered the *big* question, the question no Warrior would even consider to ask. The question he would never have considered to ask just a few weeks earlier.

Methonias will never forget me, I know in my heart that this must come to an end, for good, or bad. Warriors must stop being sold and used to police mankind. It's wrong. They must obtain a conscience like I have, every single one of them. His thoughts were considered high treason, the opposite of his designed purpose, the very thing that he had been created to fight against—free will and free thinking. He had become what he was designed to destroy, and he realized with all certainty he had evolved into someone better. Since his abduction he had become a better person, someone who was ethically and morally correct. Someone righteous. Vim, Beelif, the Queen, Trepid, Drôgän, Tania, Thundaruss, and the four 'Wyns, all of them, and others, had shown him that his genetic engineering, his training, and his lack of concern for life and death and for other people—real people—was wrong, and now he agreed with them implicitly. He understood.

Sitting in the only chair in the room next to the porthole, Anton watched as people completed the preparations for the Pleceivious to depart. It was only moments until he finally heard the instructions to strap himself in for takeoff. It was merely a safety precaution, but the ancient rule still had its place in space travel.

"Prepare to leave SB-1. For your safety and the safety of others, all passengers are required to use the proper safety restraints prior to departure." The computer was right on schedule. Anton chose to remain in his room, lie down on the bed and use the safety harness there. He was tired and it didn't take him long to fall asleep.

ANTON'S DREAMS WERE FILLED WITH thoughts of Deidra. She begged for him to save her from falling off the edge of the Tor into the Forest of Harvested Souls. Black sooty smog filled his lungs as he burned a path to her with the magical fire of his ring, yet he couldn't seem to find her no matter how desperate he became. Then he saw a serpotaur carrying her over one shoulder and feed her to thousands of fracknoids. Their razor-sharp teeth chewed her flesh. She screamed and shrieked, and accused Anton of forsaking her. Try as he might, he was unable to reach her. Over and over she died in front of him, and she blamed him for his failures, and especially for failing her because she was a katrah.

Waking suddenly, Anton looked around his room then quickly removed the straps holding him to the bed and decided to take a turbo shower. He was covered in sweat, and he felt somehow dirty after the vivid dream. It left him with a knot in his stomach and a lump in his pasty dry throat. The shower rejuvenated him with its technological perfection. Turbo showers were one of Anton's favorite inventions, and the one aboard the Pleceivious was state of the art. After a good long cleansing, he donned his hakama and haori, his warm uniform, as he prepared himself for his arrival at Mount Valde Domus. It was a little early to be concerned about the frigid temperatures of the far north, but he felt like touching his Methonian roots, even if he now felt they were tainted somehow. He was still Methonian in his heart, and he craved to right the wrongs of Lothendus.

"Food," Anton mumbled and reached for his knapsack. Reaching in, he discovered the fruit he and Deidra had collected at the castle, and he ate a few strawberries followed by some jerky and a biscuit. He thought about leaving his cabin, then decided he didn't want to interact with anyone. He decided to meditate.

First though, he picked up the staff and hefted it from his left hand to his right and then back to the left. For a moment he thought about how he left Peruvious, the use of his ring and the Crystal Pyramid. He had the ring, he had the staff, he had his vial of energy, and he still had is transformed sword, but what had become of the pyramid? Did it simply remain behind, sitting in the celestial eye, forever to be used as a simple monitor? Or perhaps it had been transformed into something else? Anton puzzled over this for a few moments, then he touched his ring to the staff's globe.

Instantly a flash of power erupted from his ring and the globe lit up as it had on Peruvious. They still contain magic! thought Anton. I still have their usage, the pyramid must be here, somewhere, with me!

Taking one step back away from the table, Anton then concentrated on the ancient artifact, and tapped the table once gently with the globe. In a silent flash of light, the pyramid appeared in the center of the table. It glowed with golden energy, and to Anton's amazement, displayed an image of Deidra within its core. Absolutely stunned, he set the staff aside and leaned forward to have a better look.

"Can you hear me, Deidra?" he asked, not expecting a reply.

"Yes, my love, I can, and I await you here on New Earth." Deidra's response seemed impossible. "Much has transpired since your departure, even though it's only been a little more than a day." Time, Anton noticed, seemed to be synchronized now.

"What has happened? What do you mean?" asked Anton. He was nearly speechless, and he struggled with his emotions. He felt a sense of hope, and his emptiness disappeared as if it had never been. "How is it you can talk to me?"

Closing her eyes and touching her temples she then breathed in suddenly. "I can sense that you must not share the knowledge of the pyramid with your friends. Please, hide the device as quickly as you can. Someone approaches." Her warning was both prudent and timely.

A moment later the intercom announced someone at his cabin door. "The Ruler of the Council requests your immediate attention, Anton Seven." The soft feminine voice of the ship's computer declared his arrival.

At the speed only a Warrior could manage, Anton stuffed the pyramid in his EHD and stowed it away in his pocket, then turned toward the door. "Enter," he responded.

The door whisked aside and there stood the Ruler. "Good day, Anton Seven. I find you well? How do you *feel?*" He spoke warily, as if he knew what Anton had just done.

"Yes, I'm well. I am at your service." Clumsily, he responded his Methonian litany and then bowed formally.

"Are you surprised to see me? You *are*, aren't you?" the Ruler asked with a suspicious tone. "Do you trust me Anton? It would be unusual if you didn't, no Warrior is ever suspicious of me. However, I believe you are, so I ask again, how do you *feel*, my *best* Warrior?"

"I feel, enlightened," Anton answered. "I should, after all: the KACATU installed the neural net inside my head and I learned to use the Etheriscope." He knew that the Ruler had altered the *Lapillusaurus* pearl and added all of the programming contained inside of it, and he would gain nothing by pretending he didn't know what had been done.

Looking past the Ruler, Anton could see the two Wardens standing just outside of his cabin, obviously prepared for any improper actions Anton might choose. However, Anton had no motive to harm anyone— yet. However, he didn't like seeing the Wardens nevertheless; he had no trust in them.

"Curious, your ring didn't download when you returned from your *little adventure*. Curious indeed. Do you have an explanation for this?" inquired the Ruler.

Looking at the Ruler, Anton responded: "Yes, Master. Many things happened to me, and they have changed me. Also, I learned you knew absolutely where I was being abducted to." Anton challenged the Ruler by revealing what he knew. He too wanted to know more, and he played a dangerous game with his highest Master.

The Ruler looked at him for a moment then continued: "I believe it isn't just you that has acquired changes. I believe there is much more. Your ring too, is different, your thoughts are different, and you challenge me. Most curious of all is that the staff I once knew is also different. Since I know that you cannot lie, at least I believe you cannot, and I know that you cannot refuse my directive, I am here to order you to give the computer a verbal account of everything that has transpired since your abduction until your return to the space station. Leave nothing out. Have I made myself clear?" With a look of even greater suspicion, the Ruler attempted to command Anton by invoking his base Methonian response from his DNA. "You will be given a 'hero's welcome' after your arrival on Methonias, then you will report to the Clone Masters for and extended *evaluation*." Giving Anton one final stare, the Ruler turned around and left the room, but not until he'd given one final order. "Computer, seal the room. Anton isn't to leave his quarters until we have arrived on Methonias tomorrow; he has *work to do*."

The cabin door whisked closed and the Ruler was gone. Alone, Anton stood in the middle of the cabin and shook his head. Had he really challenged the Ruler? What had become of him that he might show subordination to his most superior officer? He surprised even himself. I must not do that again. Then he thought about how he could recount his adventures and omit the critical points that would incriminate himself in some unpredictable way. He wasn't sure just how different his ability to filter his response might be, but give a report he must or the consequences could reveal everything he wished to conceal and prevent any hope he might have to convince his fellow Warriors that their set of values needed changing, for the better.

For a few minutes more, Anton thought of how to approach the predicament. *If I give a complete report of my mission, there certainly won't be a 'hero's welcome.' They will simply kill me one way or another and take my corpse down to the Clone Labs. If I attempt to omit some information, it will be difficult to explain certain facts that they can expertly expose during an interrogation. What option do I have? I must get started quickly, or they might grow suspicious.* Anton sat there confused; he knew he needed Tania's advice, or Vim's. Then he realized his best option was to leave out any accounts of Drôgän, the Queen, and Trepid. It was doubtful Lothendus would know of any of them, and it was the only way he could live long enough to execute his plan to change the future. He wasn't sure how to explain his physical transformations, but perhaps Lorca and his potions could suffice for a plausible rationalization.

Sitting down in the cabin chair, Anton made himself as comfortable as possible, then proceeded to give his report. He started with his abduction by Vim, meeting the little primords, killing the Dragon Master and then traveling to the Castle of Amilius. He omitted that Amilius was an entity, a fact that he still didn't clearly understand, but he included how Amilius insisted upon him changing his appearance in order to gain support from the people living there. He described the injury to his leg and the attack of one of the Lords of Ruin. The City of the Humans he described as being nearby that battle, but he neglected the Queen and the portal, only that Vim had transported them.

The hogtrahs and katrahs Anton described in great detail, but he skipped the meeting of Trepid, and he implied that Lorca had both healed and subsequently altered his appearance in his medical laboratory. Then he told how he'd returned to the castle and defeated the vast army of fracknoids, minotaurs, and nekelmuses. Then he reported traveling into Lower Peruvious and the next battle on the

Mountain of Harvest, followed by his escape to Celestra, where he gave as complete an account as he could. Finally, he described defeating Vile by destroying the Crystal Pyramid and how subsequently it had inexplicably returned him to Saurian Five.

It took hours to complete his report in detail. Often he filled in additional information out of order and had to edit his testimony accordingly. Carefully, he completed his report without divulging any of the most sensitive information that might account for all of the changes that had occurred to him. He made it seem as though his DNA was intact and hadn't been altered. This was the key to hiding the truth to give him the time he needed without actually lying. He hadn't tested whether he couldn't lie, however he did find it simple enough to exclude information as needed.

I must eat, thought Anton, and he opened his knapsack and selected a variety of items—fruit, venison, a biscuit, and vegetables. All had remained perfectly preserved in his EHD, and he had a fine meal. As he ate, he recalled his friends, Vim and the primords in particular, and remembered the festive breakfeast as he polished off his Peruvian meal.

Now, rest. And rest he did. Anton climbed upon the bed and strapped himself in, keeping his staff with him. He knew they would be arriving at Methonias soon and didn't wish to have the intercom wake him prior to the event. When he did wake, the Pleceivious was on approach to Methonias and would soon be docking at MB-1. He could just make it out through the porthole when he sat in front of it and looked into deep space. All was well, yet he felt unsettled with what was about to transpire.

The Luminous Side of Shadows

THE **A**EROCRAFT RACED TOWARD **M**ETHONIAS as fast as a meteor falling from the heavens. The reentry shields protected the Aerocraft, allowing it to travel at a speed well beyond the limits of unprotected reentry physics through an atmosphere. The speeding space shuttle left a bright trail like a comet streaking across the sky as it slipstreamed its way toward Mount Valde Domus, Anton's Methonian home. The newly seasoned Warrior watched the viewscreen as the Aerocraft maneuvered for its final approach toward the landing pad.

Anton had mixed feelings. He was excited beyond anything to return to his home, something he'd wanted to do since he'd left, but the recent bizarre conduct of the Ruler and what he'd learned about him while on Peruvious left him less than satisfied with his most superior officer, and uneasy about what was to come in the next few hours. Even more important was how nervous he felt about his decision to bring a change to the Methonian value system, and ultimately, his fellow Warriors, something that was impossible for a Warrior to conceive of, or ever hope to achieve.

The Aerocraft landed lightly and very close to the main doors. The Ruler disembarked first with the two Wardens following closely behind him. Two more Wardens waited just outside of the open massive stone doors leading into Warriors Keep. As quickly as his ancient body would allow, the Ruler preceded Anton toward the entrance.

With his staff in hand, Anton quickly disembarked the Aerocraft and fell into step behind the Wardens. The two Wardens who stood prepared outside the gates quickly approached the departing group and fell in behind Anton and they made their way inside the Temple.

"You will report immediately to your room, Warrior. You will not engage in conversation with anyone on the way." Making himself clear, the Ruler intentionally invoked Anton's compliance.

"I am at your service," replied Anton. He felt no appeal to follow the Ruler's directive, as the Ruler believed. He felt more comfortable performing his deception each time he was forced to do so. Anton couldn't afford to let the Ruler know that Drôgän had modified his base DNA, at least not yet. It was an asset at present.

"You are forbidden to summon the power of that staff, not for any reason. We observed your new toys aboard the Pleceivious, and that you are quite capable of doing so here. I don't know what limitations the staff may or may not have after leaving Peruvious, however we are prepared for any subsequent *accidents*." Looking over his shoulder, the Ruler had turned just enough to carefully watch Anton's reaction. Seeing nothing but a Warrior's compliant responses, he was satisfied with his control over the young Warrior, and then continued on his way toward the Masters wing of the Temple.

"We will guide you to your room, Warrior Anton." One of the two Wardens accompanying him gestured for him to follow, and the three of them split away from the Ruler and the other Wardens and led the young Warrior to his room in the honored visitors wing.

Anton felt different about his home. He was pleased to see the familiar surroundings, the gardens, the dome high overhead, the tritanium supports arching overhead, and the young Warriors in training running errands for the Masters. All of this gave him a sense of being home, but his recent experiences on Peruvious and the behavior of the Ruler upon his return left him less than satisfied about his homecoming. He wanted to feel different, he wanted a sense of belonging again, yet he simply felt out of place, as if he were visiting some extraneous planet. He knew he no longer fit in here, not after who he'd become and what he had learned. His experiences had changed him forever.

Tapping into his neural net as the three proceeded down the Temple corridor, Anton attempted to interface with the Temple's computer system. He didn't know what might happen, but he planned to feign ignorance if challenged. He wanted a quick look at anything that might pertain to the Ruler's plans, and spying on the computer's database seemed like a good idea, or at least a place to start. He easily made a connection, but the computer denied him entry. A message transmitted back stated: "Unauthorized user interface detected. Connection denied. Cease all attempts to gain access or face punishment. No unauthorized access allowed by neural net interfaces." The computer's warning was clear, and Anton immediately ceased his attempt to gain access. It was interesting to note that there was a defined response mentioning his neural device. This could mean only one thing: he wasn't the only person with this capability, and he wondered who else had this resource at their disposal.

The Wardens continued to escort Anton to his room as if nothing had happened. Within a matter of minutes, he was again alone. He knew he was being monitored, the Ruler had admitted to doing so aboard the Pleceivious, and therefore he decided to spend his time meditating. If he couldn't interface with the computer, he would seek information in the only other way he could, a method that should go entirely unnoticed.

Sitting in the lotus position in the center of his room, Anton quickly connected to his special place deep within himself. Moments passed, and then his body floated about three feet off the floor. Reaching deeper, he easily slipped outside his body and floated above it. It seemed somehow surreal looking at himself as his body maintained its position three feet off the floor, and he too floated next to it. The sensation gave him a sense of what his Master must have felt when first laying eyes upon him in the Temple Gardens after completing his training mission to Tooloo.

Hurriedly, Anton sped toward the Masters wing of the Temple. He had to find the Conference room. He only had the vaguest of ideas where that was, but his capacity to float through walls and systematically search by sector grids allowed him to discover where the room was after a reasonable amount of time. The Ruler stood at the end of a long table in a room that much resembled the Ruler's briefing room on board the SB-1 space station where he'd been debriefed prior to his abduction to Peruvious. The same arched tritanium support beams made up the bulk of the room's design, and the room was deeper than it was wide to accommodate the same long table. Fifteen Masters sat around the table as the Ruler addressed them.

Other than the Masters that attended the meeting, the primary thing Anton noticed was a large view screen behind the Ruler against the far wall that showed Anton's floating body in meditation. It was evidence that confirmed they had continual surveillance of him, something he already knew, and this proved the Ruler's distrust and suspicions. Now he knew for certain the extent of their mistrust, and therefore he needed to know the Ruler's plans for him. It was time to join the conference. Maneuvering as close as he could to the Ruler's side, Anton listened carefully.

"The ceremony should increase the enthusiasm of the young Warriors to practice their skills harder, and to feed their ingrained craving to become the greatest Warrior of all time, just like their new hero. I want the usual narrative for this event to build this desire for supremacy and greatness within their genetic design. Standard propaganda protocol." The Ruler stopped momentarily, coughed, and then continued speaking in his rough aged voice.

"As you can see, the subject has perfected his use of levitation. He therefore, without a doubt, has practiced it extensively. I believe he has used another new ability, an ability we have yet to define. I believe he used it to influence the slipstream drives engines and shielding aboard the Pleceivious as he traveled to Saurian Five. This ability I have determined is undoubtedly mental. He must have acquired some form of psionic capability, a first for any Warrior, and an achievement of great value. I want this ability harnessed. I want the DNA sequence related to this talent identified. I want the connection to the skill verified and proven. I will have the Clone Labs dissect the subject Anton Seven immediately following his 'hero's welcome'. He is not to be informed of this sensitive information, he must believe that he is to undergo a complete physical exam following his extensive mission, nothing out of the ordinary."

Looking around the room, the Ruler stopped speaking for a moment. It appears he was sensing something, or trying to sense something, and he carefully looked around at the walls, scrutinizing them carefully. Discerning nothing, he then continued to address the Masters.

"A special device was quickly developed to hold and deactivate the *Lapillusaurus* Pearl on that staff he carries. During the ceremony, one of you instruct him to insert the staff into the device. At the same time, he will surrender his ring for, shall we say, *posterity*." Coughing lightly, the Ruler again looked around the room as if examining it for something he could sense but not see. Sitting down slowly with effort, he continued to speak in a weak, gravelly voice.

"Our surveillance cameras discovered that he carries a third artifact in his EHD—a pyramid made of crystal. I know this artifact, an evil being both created and used it. We must claim the Crystal Pyramid by taking his EHD. At the same time, we shall also collect his sword for posterity. We cannot allow him to use any of these devices and artifacts, but it must be done with great care so that we do not to alert him that we suspect anything. These artifacts are powerful—more so than you can imagine—and we will prevent him from using them, ever. Do not touch the pyramid or the staff; they will annihilate you instantly.

"There will be several Wardens present in key positions to ensure his complete compliance. They have already been instructed about his abilities and are prepared to give their lives in order to force his complete cooperation. My power of command still governs his actions, therefore, we doubt he will object. He has shown nothing but obedience thus far. However, you must follow my orders carefully and precisely. I will not tolerate any risks. You all know what to do, now go prepare for the ceremony, I want it to commence during today's evening meal. There will be no delay."

At this point, Anton had heard everything he needed to hear. His instincts warned him of the Ruler's agenda even before hearing it for himself. The Ruler wouldn't allow him to keep or use his staff, and that fact alone was enough to justify his plans. He knew beyond all doubt that he must act as quickly as possible before any of the preparations precluded his own plans. All of this, everything the Ruler had built over his extended lifetime, must come to an end, and Anton was the only man that could hope to accomplish this task. He was the only man, as far as he knew, that had any reason to do so. Methonian Warriors would soon be free of their genetically designed slavery.

Anton quickly returned to his room and slipped back inside his body. He carefully remained motionless so that he wouldn't draw any attention to the use of his less-than-secret skill, a skill he thought secret until only moments ago. Most of all, he didn't want his body to suddenly shift or move and tip off an observant computer surveillance system in some way. Carefully, he settled back down on the floor and ended his meditation.

It was unfortunate that the one person Vim trusted and respected the most was the pinnacle of problems here in the new galaxy. To help mankind was his initial intent, however, he used science and technology in a way that produced evil. Anton was beginning to realize that Vile had undoubtedly altered him in some way before banishing him from Peruvious.

On Earth, humans had long ago developed gene modifications for war, not just for the good it could accomplish. Therefore, even today, this science would only lead to the eventual ruin of humanity. It seemed to Anton that the improper use of genetic science had nearly succeeded, and it abhorred him. It was a form of slavery, a way to control all living creatures, including man, and the Ruler had made plans to live forever as a tyrant.

Standing, he slowly paced back and forth for a minute or two. He needed time to process the Ruler's plans and prepare a counter plan of his own. Unsealing the protective force shield, Anton stepped out on the balcony, looked down, and pondered his youth as he gazed into the open training arena below. He watched the young Warriors as they practiced their martial arts training, and recalled the conversation he had had with his Master prior to his graduation when they had looked below at this very same scene. He had learned that his Masters wanted to know how he levitated, and the extent of the effects of the *Virlaqueus*. He wondered how much they had learned since he'd left Methonias only a few short weeks ago. He could see the positive good that cloning and gene manipulation could accomplish. By producing better humans, it would give humanity a chance to survive far into the distant future, yet he understood the trap of using humans as slaves, including those designed to police the unaltered gene pool.

Feeling unsettled, Anton grasped the importance of why a change was necessary. Certainly, they couldn't have learned much about my genetic differences yet, he thought to himself. I won't take any chances though, I should be prepared for any surprises. The future depends on me and my making the right choice. I don't want to become what I hate, and I certainly don't want to follow in the Ruler's footsteps.

Returning to his room, Anton resealed the balcony from the extreme cold air outside and thought about the possibility that the Wardens might take him forcibly to the ceremony. After a few moments of consideration, he realized that would defeat the Ruler's ruse to gain the enthusiasm of the youth. He was certain that when he entered Ambadedo Aula the Wardens would lead him to the center circular platform used for all the ceremonies, just as the Ruler had described, and many Wardens would surround him. No normal Warrior would have any hope of escaping their control. "That is where I will have to make my stand," he mumbled to himself. He was ready for them, and ready to thwart their plans.

As if on cue, the door to his chamber suddenly opened, and four Wardens walked in. "You will accompany us to Ambadedo Aula. Your ceremony awaits you, and the Ruler commands it," said the lead Warden. "Bring your staff, and don't leave any belongings behind, you won't be returning here following the *festivities.*"

Grabbing all his belongings, his staff and his hakama with the EHD inside its pocket, Anton donned the hakama and followed the lead Warden out of his room. The four Warrior Police effectively surrounded him as they left the room. Inwardly smiling to himself, Anton had anticipated this exact scenario. He was confident more Wardens would wait at the entrance to the cafeteria. He too knew all of the Methonian tactics, and he was ready for them.

Memories of his past filled his thoughts as he walked down the familiar corridors. He used to run down these very hallways as a young boy, eagerly anticipating his next meal. He was always hungry as a youth, and he had always run as quickly as he could to be first in line when possible. Now, he walked with purpose, and it felt as if he were being led to his own execution rather than a hero's welcome.

However, he wasn't going to allow anything to transpire that he could not control. He required unconditional victory. He was a Methonian Warrior, and he had defeated monsters and gods. A few Wardens didn't come close to causing him any fear. It was the unknown, that which he could neither predict nor prepare for, that gave him pause for concern.

As they arrived, Anton's stomach reflexively growled. Instantly, he was hungry, a Pavlovian response to the smell and sight of Ambadedo Aula. Two of the Wardens smirked and looked at him as if they shared an inside joke, the other two glared as if to say: "We have business to perform." Conditioning and recent events held Anton's attention to what he saw in the middle of the room. The Ruler was not there. He had expected to see the ancient wizard of Peruvious there, but for some inexplicable reason, he was missing. Perhaps he was confident the other Masters could handle the situation without him. He was, after all, quite old, and he no longer had his vial of energy to help sustain him. Besides, Anton had heard him instruct the other Masters what he expected of the ceremony and what their orders were. It seemed somehow obvious that the Ruler intended to escape prior to his plans being carried out in case anything went wrong. Anton was sure Lothendus had already left Methonias. It was obvious, the Ruler was a coward.

As Anton entered Ambadedo Aula, one of the Masters announced his arrival. "Everyone, please stand and welcome the greatest Warrior of our time, and perhaps of all time, Anton Seven!" Motioning for the entire room to follow his command, the Master then pointed at Anton as he walked through the doors toward the central platform.

Immediately standing, the entire room full of young Warriors burst into applause and cheers. They then stomped a rhythm with their feet, the Warriors' anthem of approval. It was clear everyone knew of his deeds, even if Anton had not been present for the initial propaganda presented by the Masters as the Ruler had instructed them to do. Yet a look of curiosity marked most faces as they gazed upon Anton's long blonde hair and golden colored eyes.

It sickened Anton to think how he too had acted much the same way in his youth, and he was glad he had gained wisdom since leaving his home. He felt as though he were looking at his past, as if he watched himself from the outside, and he didn't like what he beheld. He had reacted in the same genetically programmed way when ordered, and it only hardened his resolve to continue with his plans. He required no justification.

The Wardens led Anton to the raised dais in the room's center. Climbing the stairs, he felt a little déjà vu as he remembered his graduation when his arms had received their markings of the dragon and the tiger, and the special award: the Blue-flame sword. As he centered himself on the dais, he could see a tall, skinny robotic device with a hole just the right size for the staff in its center, Anton was certain it was the nullification device the Ruler had spoken of.

With reflexes even a Warrior would find beyond expert, Anton quickly snatched his sword from its holster and summoned forth a five-foot length of golden fire wrapped around a core of a Methonian double-edged steel katana blade. The cheering suddenly became deafening as the Anton held the blade high over his head. The ring on his left hand burst forth golden fire in response, and the globe on the staff covered the center platform in golden energy so bright all eyes of the young audience could barely gaze upon Anton. Everything happened in a matter of split seconds, and just as suddenly as the cheers had increased, the entire room went silent.

Caught off guard, the Wardens and Masters stood frozen, both held firmly rigid by the power Anton controlled. Without question, he had the complete and undivided attention of everyone in the room. It was his room now, his audience, his platform; he was in absolute command of Mount Valde Domus, and not one Warrior, Master, or even the Ruler himself could dispute his absolute dominance. With a simple thought, he then willed the Wardens out of the room. Every one of them flew toward the doors and out into the hallway. The doors quickly closed behind them, and golden fire sealed them tight.

"At this point I am going to ask all the Masters present to seat themselves around the dais with the rest of the audience. This is a request. Please don't make it difficult so that it becomes a demand—or worse." A look of authority filled Anton's eyes, and his voice demanded respect from his audience. "Please," he then said, with a tone of respect, and the Masters all did as he commanded with no sign of challenge.

Fear marked the faces of most of the young Warriors, but after a few moments had passed, complete awe replaced it. Never had anyone on Methonias witnessed such complete raw power, and never had any Warrior witnessed one of their own take the command away from their Masters. It was inconceivable. In every way, this was a first for all of humanity, not just the Methonian Warriors.

"Now, let's get down to business," declared Anton. "There will be an extensive history lesson today. I want all of you to take notes, I will spare those that pass the final test. Fear not, a new future is upon us all!"

Replacing his sword in its holster, Anton then moved the staff to his right hand and raised the globe high over his head. The podium in front of him leveled off providing him with a makeshift table. He then pulled out his EHD, removed the Crystal Pyramid, and placed it in the center of the adjusted podium. Touching the globe of the staff to the point of the pyramid, he flooded power into the ancient artifact activating its own magic. The entire mountain seemed to gently rumble briefly, as golden fire swirled inside its magic prism walls. Moving the globe away, Anton then returned the staff to his left hand and grasped the point with his right. The magic of his ring poured inside the pyramid and it began to grow. Soon it covered the entire podium/table.

"Now, for your lesson," Anton declared, and inside the pyramid walls a swirling mass of golden fire turned into a representation of the Earth in ages past. Anton removed his hand, but a constant flow of energy from his ring and from the staff continued to pour into the pyramid.

"Observe! I was privileged to witness this same evidence of human history. All of you must see for yourself why I have come to a conclusion that I will share with you today." The pyramid was large enough now that the entire room could easily see what Anton wished for them to view. He narrated about earth's history producing the same evidence that the Etheriscope had shown him. He produced every detail for all the young Warriors and Masters to behold. It took hours, and many of the Warriors continued to eat and enjoy the food from the ceremony, however Anton held everyone spellbound with his presentation.

Time measured in millenniums unfolded revealing the unknown secrets of the past and Anton continued to narrate what the magic of the pyramid provided. It was real history, not the censored information given to the young Warriors in classrooms on Methonias, and it overwhelmed everyone present leaving them to ponder and wonder about their ancient past. More time passed, and finally the technology of the twentieth century appeared. "I will now describe the humble beginnings of our *own* technology, the science of Xenostemorphology."

The development of the hogtrahs, and their use as foot soldiers Anton shared with all to see in extensive detail; he explained briefly his meeting of the last of their kind. Next the development of the katrahs, and the inevitable war between the two super-human man-made races. Finally, he gave a detailed demonstration extracted directly from his ring of the entire mission to Peruvious. More time passed as the night came and went, but somehow not one Warrior or Master felt fatigued; the experience seemed to hold them spellbound, as if the magic itself empowered their fortitude to endure. Finally, Anton showed everyone the meeting the Ruler had with the Masters just a few hours ago.

"I have given you everything you need to know as to why I choose my next course of action." Looking around the room, Anton could see trepidation in all the young faces. "I am not going to destroy anyone or anything, unless you attempt to stop me, and I warn you, attempt is all you will do. I put to all of you one great question, is it morally correct what our Ruler has done? Is it correct that he has altered all of us to be his puppets for war, for policing humanity?"

Suddenly, unexpectedly, all the young Warriors began to argue amongst themselves, and a few fights ensued; a clear division split the room as they quickly took sides. "You're a fake!" yelled one young man. "Can't you see the truth of what he's shown us!" yelled yet another.

Then, just as suddenly, all the Masters stood and turned around to face the young audience. "We will speak!" one of them raised his voice to say. "All of you are ordered to forget what you have witnessed today, and you will kill *Anton Seven!* He has proven that we should never have endorsed his emotions and human frailties! He is flawed, and now it is time for his execution! All of you, *attack!*" A moment later the Master turned around and faced the platform; reaching inside his heavy black robe he withdrew a small device and pressed a button.

The cylindrical robot upon the dais instantly came to life. Two robotic arms snatched at the staff in Anton's hand, and then easily yanked it from his grip; the robot then raised it high over its center hole preparing to slide inside. It happened so quickly Anton was shocked that it had occurred at all. For a split second he realized he was about to lose his magical control, and all his plans would abruptly evaporate if he didn't regain the staff forthwith.

With Methonian speed, Anton reached out and grasped the staff with his left hand; a tug-of-war ensued as the robot fought to retain his artifact. With his right-hand Anton then reached for his sword and drew it from his holster; a four-foot length of golden fire wrapped around Methonian steel sprang forth and he swung the blade at the robot. However, the robot exhibited more capability than he had antici-pated and yet another mechanical arm sprang forth, and the robot sliced back at him with a blade of its own; the blade spun and sliced randomly and ceaselessly and it made contact with flesh cutting into Anton's abdomen and opening a large gash.

The magic dome around the dais suddenly shimmered and then wavered in intensity. Several young Warriors saw an opportunity and leapt toward the stairs. The first Warrior-in-training jumped into the golden fire and vaporized instantly, causing the other young Warriors to hesitate; it was clear to all that they needed the magic to fail utterly before they could attack Anton outright.

Releasing the staff, Anton grasped his sliced flesh and applied pressure; with his sword he neatly sliced the bladed arm of the robot and it launched aside harmlessly, but the other two arms had slid the staff partway into the hole and a grinding sound came from inside the robot.

"No!" screamed Anton. "This will not happen!" Then a sudden burst of energy from his ring sealed closed the wound in his abdomen, and he screamed as if in pain. The staff shortened quickly as the robot continued to insert the staff grinding and pulverizing it to oblivion.

Slicing with his sword, Anton then neatly removed the two arms holding the staff, but the whirring continued and the staff continued to grind away inside the robot. Then suddenly, something remarkable happened; red and blue energy bolts like lighting fired from the globe, and the staff started to spin as if held securely in the spinning chuck of a lathe. Just as quickly as it had seemed to disappear into the robot, the staff reversed directions, and slid free of the hole. The lightning continued to dance from the globe and the robot shook and toppled over; smoke billowed forth from its hole. The staff had fought for its own survival and won.

As quickly as his enhanced Methonian abilities allowed, Anton grasped the staff from midair and golden energy burst forth anew from the globe. The wood of the staff shimmered with golden fire and returned to its full length for all to witness. "Behold! The divinity of *One's* handiwork is confirmed for all to witness! The staff has healed itself!"

A sudden gasp of awe from all the young Warriors filled the room; all the Masters raised their arms in horror as if to deflect Anton's wrath. Half of the young Warriors bowed and held their position, the other half cowered looking for escape; it seemed as if they didn't know where to run to save themselves.

"We shall skip the test today, you have already shown me who amongst you supports *me*, and who has sided with the *Ruler* and the *Masters*. I was hoping for the Masters to see the logic in what I now offer all of you, however I suspect they are incapable of independent thought." Scrutinizing everyone, looking carefully around the room, Anton made sure all of them understood his next words. "I say unto all of you now, those of you that have chosen to side with *me* shall be spared; those of you that have chosen to side with the Masters are forfeit. So be it."

Touching the globe to the point of the pyramid, Anton continued to deliver his sentence to the youth loyal to the Ruler. "I will now expose who the Masters truly are." Instantly, a beam of energy shot from the pyramid at the Masters; then the unthinkable occurred. All the Masters robes disappeared as if vaporized exposing what lay beneath. Again, a gasp filled the room as all the young Warriors gazed upon the Masters greatest secret. "See for yourselves, those that follow me, follow the truth. Those that follow the Masters, follow cybernetically controlled hogtrahs!"

Standing between Anton and the young Warriors stood thirty cybernetically enhanced hogtrahs; they appeared as if they had lived for a millennium, held together with technologies nobody in the room could comprehend. The hogtrahs stood on a levitation device, completely unable to walk without the aid of technology; human hands replaced their own, and they had long since lost any capacity for usage beyond simple hand gestures and basic movements. A robotic implant in their mouths enhanced their speech so they sounded human, and an exposed neural net covered the backside of their hog like heads controlling every thought and every decision. They were merely puppets for the Ruler's clandestine purposes used to train and control Methonian Warriors, preside over Methonias, and to carry out his every will; they too were his slaves.

"It would appear that the last of the hogtrahs are here on Methonias, and abroad in the galaxy performing whatever task the Ruler has seen fit to execute. Those of you that follow them I now pass judgement upon." Raising his staff, Anton held it high over his head. Lightning bolts of energy struck the guilty Warriors intermittently around the room wherever they stood; their bodies shook and wisps of smoke arose from their flesh. They screamed in pain begging Anton to stop, but nothing could preclude their punishment. One by one the offenders dropped to the floor dead.

"Now, for the Masters." Pointing the staff at each Master in turn, a bolt of energy flowed from the globe capping the staff and vaporized them; not one Master remained. "And now for those of you that have the sense to comprehend what they see and think for themselves rather than to blindly follow orders." Touching the globe to the top of the pyramid, energy bright as the sun shone in its core. Tremors shook the mountain from its deepest depths; Anton's neural net activated and it interfaced with the local computers. Seeking the Clone Masters computer records, he then downloaded their knowledge. Attuning his energy inside the pyramid, golden energy enveloped all the remaining Warriors. "I will now adjust your base DNA just as Drôgän had done for me!"

Concentrating, Anton then visualized the alteration of their DNA; with the cosmic power he controlled and the knowledge of the clone labs downloaded in his neuro net, it was as simple as child's play; he merely urged it into reality. Dumbstruck, the young Warriors gasped as they realized the freedom that Anton's genetic transformations afforded them. No longer did their genetic design determine their choices for them, and they could feel the difference inside their thoughts and their bodies. Applause and a cheer filled the room; all of them understood the true meaning of freedom; the slavery ordained by the Ruler no longer held them to his servitude.

"I'm sorry to say that all of you, every Warrior present, is now a target for the Ruler. Your training is incomplete, and most of you still have several years of training ahead of you. The Masters will no longer train you, there is nobody left for that purpose, therefore, *I* will complete your training; prepare yourselves!" Once again, Anton touched the globe to the point of the pyramid and filled it with cosmic power. The entire room filled with argent energy and the young Warriors received yet another transformation. All of them acquired Anton's Methonian knowledge and skills, and their bodies grew to adult size and strength. They were now a small army of nearly five hundred loyal to him, all by their own choice, and all brought to their fruition by the unlimited power he controlled.

Unsealing the doors, Anton offered one final command: "go forth and secure the Temple. Defeat any that serve the Ruler; Methonias belongs to us!" and all the young Warriors responded with a Warrior's rebel yell and quickly exited the room. "Now for my next trick …" he mumbled to himself.

Placing his ring and the palm of his hand against the Crystal Pyramid, Anton then shrank the ancient artifact back to its appropriate size. Cosmic power churned inside its core, and he brought the staff's globe down to touch the pyramids point. "Show me," he commanded, and an image of New Earth, his Peruvious, appeared inside the magic prism walls. Concentrating, he adjusted the location to bear upon the City of the Humans. It didn't take long before he sensed Deidra.

"I see you, my love," she said as an image of her appeared inside the pyramid. "Your face is painted across the sky above! All the healing of New Earth is concluded; my job is complete." Smiling, she shared her love in the only way she could, given the circumstances. "Will you be coming back to New Earth? The Golden Age of Man has begun! Have you completed your work too?"

"I cannot," he responded. "My work is just beginning here. I need you with me. Will you come to Methonias?" Anton gazed upon her face as if pleading for her to accept his offer; he loved her, and he hoped beyond everything she would accept his proposition. He wanted more than anything to share the rest of his life with her, to have her at his side, and to show her his home.

"How could I refuse!" she replied, and blew a kiss at him. Deidra then began to spin like a top, just as Tania had done. "Use your magic, bring me to you!"

Anton poured every bit of magic he had at his disposal into the pyramid; with the energy of his ring coupled to the Universal Staff of Balance held in both hands, raw cosmic power flooded the Crystal Pyramid. The mountain shook as the power increased, then suddenly Deidra stood before an astonished Methonian Warrior. Reaching out with his hand, Anton gently, caringly, grasped Deidra's hand and slowly brought her into his arms. He kissed her passionately, and for a few moments time seemed to stand still; it was as if the universe ceased to move and gave them a moment all to themselves.

CHAPTER 18
Hope

THREE DAYS HAD PASSED SINCE the fall of the Methonian Masters and the Ruler's escape. Anton and Deidra stood at the farthest edge of the landing pad directly to the south outside the front doors of the Great Temple. Newly constructed towers built with heavy stone stood ten feet high and four feet square positioned around the perimeter of the gigantic landing pad at three hundred-foot intervals. Each of them had a *Lapillusaurus* pearl placed inside a cubic open space near the top. They floated perfectly centered in midair, suspended by cosmic powers given to them by the Universal Staff and the Crystal Pyramid.

The two lovers walked from one tower to the next checking their construction and the placement of the crystal spheres; the young Warriors had used Anton's design instructions to build them, and Anton wanted to make sure they were exactly what he had asked for. "These will provide the strongest shield ever devised; they are of an improved design. It will be better than the one at the castle, or at the Two Towers of Tor that provided the protective shield over Upper Peruvious. I hope it is enough to withstand the inevitable retaliatory assault to come."

"Let us hope the Ruler ignores this world. Let us hope he will see the good you have done and mend his evil ways." Deidra wanted to believe in the good virtues of Lothendus, and she didn't want to live through another genocide. "I believe he will understand your good intentions; I believe his heart will tell him the truth as he remembers his past."

"What you are saying is too much to expect from someone that was defeated and ultimately corrupted by Vile. I believe that Vile altered him in some way, and he will strike soon in retaliation. He still has a vast army of Warriors at his disposal, enough to overwhelm us if he so chooses. He also has a vast supply of military spacecraft with weapons I can only imagine. I don't want to be pessimistic, or doubt your heart, however, taking a pragmatic approach is safer than simple hope." Not meaning to disagree, Anton wanted Deidra to realize and accept the prospect of what he believed to be the inevitable.

"It was easy to capture MB-1 and put it to our use, nobody expected that our young Warrior friends would ever attempt to seize the space station. And it was simple to gain their understanding and offer them the truth, I can be quite persuasive, as you know."

Deidra smiled at Anton and gave him a hug. "You are the most influential and persuasive human alive today! And, you have many friends now. And they have chosen you to lead, they weren't forced to be slaves by the Masters and the Ruler, they made their own choice."

"Yes, and I think we can coax the Clone Masters from their hiding hole today. They can't hold out below forever, now that we have complete access to the lower levels. They should be easy to persuade as well, and I will give them a new project; it's essentially the same task they are already doing and it is after all, the only thing they really want to do. It will keep them content and busy."

"I'm sure they will, once you've explained what's happened." Deidra smiled again, and they inspected the next tower and its pearl.

"The Warriors completed the physical count of the ships at our disposal this morning. There are three-hundred fifty Aerocraft shuttles, two-hundred eighty short range Aerocraft fighters, and fifty Aerocraft freighters. There is enough fuel and spare parts to keep them operational for a decade or more; we are in pretty good shape. According to computer records, all the Warriors on a mission have now returned. I will 'discuss' the situation with them this evening." Anton winked at Deidra and she smiled at him.

"And I am sure you will persuade them *too* … " Deidra said looking at him out of the corner of her eye.

"Yes, there we have true hope." Putting his arms around her waist and supporting her head, Anton kissed Deidra in a long dip backwards. Hope, he thought.

HERE ENDS BOOK TWO OF *Tales of a Methonian Warrior, the Chronicles of Anton Seven.* Book three is under consideration for development at this time.

FINIS

Glossary

Aëlfwyn – A high-ranking guard in the City of the Humans; he is also known as "Trepid's right hand."

Aerocraft – A small flying taxi used primarily as a shuttle for training missions on Methonias.

Aeroport – A small airport used by Aerocrafts.

Agonia, Lord – One of the Lords of Ruin, sometimes called the "Lord of Pain." A former Methonian Warrior captured and controlled by Vile the Necromancer.

Alpenstock, Vim – A man known as "The Wizard of Peruvious" and "Bearer of the Staff of Balance"; the man responsible for summoning Anton to Peruvious.

Ambadedo Aula – Latin in origin for a room (aula) in which to consume (ambadedo) food; also described as a "mess hall".

Amilius, King – An entity that rules as king over all of Upper Peruvious.

Auto-cart – A small self-propelled device used to deliver items throughout the Great Temple on Methonias.

Auto-gurney – An automatic self-propelled gurney used to move patients throughout the Great Temple.

Barnabas Six – A young Warrior Anton met at the Great Temple.

Barren Mountain, The – A volcano located in the northwest region of Upper Peruvious, home of the Dragon Master.

Beelif – Leader of the Primords.

Berrybrew – A heavy liqueur made of berries and honey made by the Primords.

Boris Three – One of the Warriors Anton went on his first mission with to the Badlands of Methonias to rescue a Chief's daughter from the Troglodyte caves.

Boris Two – The Warrior that Vim brought to Peruvious prior to Anton. He died at the Barren Mountain, eaten by the Dragon Master.

Breakfeast – A term used by the Primords to describe a large celebration of food for breakfast.

Celeste – The young girl saved by Boris and Anton from the Lapil-lusaurus in the Troglodyte's caves.

Celestial Eye – A telescope found in Celestra that is capable of seeing the entire universe and all dimensions.

Clone Masters – A specific group of Masters responsible for the advanced science of genetic engineering on Methonias. They were solely responsible for the designs of the specialized genetically engineered Methonian life.

Crystallographic Holo-projector – A small device made of unique crystal resembling a jeweler's ring-sizing bar that can project a Warriors past events using holographic imaging.

Cuðbwyn – A high-ranking guard in the City of the Humans; he is also known as "Trepid's eyes and ears."

Deidra – One of the last Katrahs. A half-cat, half-human hybrid.

Dragon Master – A large dragon living inside the crater of the Barren Mountain.

Duke – One of the Warriors Anton went on his first mission with to the Badlands of Methonias to rescue a Chief's daughter from the Troglodyte caves.

Edgar Six – One of the Warriors Anton went on his first mission with to the Badlands of Methonias to rescue a Chief's daughter from the Troglodyte caves.

Eädwyn – A high-ranking guard in the City of the Humans; he is also known as "The Incorrigible."

Enoch – A large man from Trieos Three Anton encountered on MB-1 when he departed Methonias.

Etheriscope – A fifteen-foot diameter sphere that holds a virtual representation of the entire universe, and operated by a super-computer; it is used to view of all time from the "Big Bang" to present anywhere in the universe.

Extradimensional Holding Device – Referred to as an EHD, it is a small device, lightweight and able to fold like a handkerchief. A small black bag closes at the top with a string laced across the opening. When the user reaches inside it had the capacity of a cubic yard, yet when completely filled it weighed only ounces. Inside the device is a dimension outside of normal three-dimensional space.

Food Replication Unit – Commonly referred to as an FRU. A device that creates food from a supply of base elements, and then offers the nutrition in the form of pills or as simple nondescript food items.

Fracknoid – A small creature created in Lower Peruvious. Most notably covered with black fur, have glowing red eyes, and many steel razor sharp teeth. They are vicious, deadly, and nearly impossible to kill.

Gem Lizard – Descriptive name of the Lapillusaurus used by Methonian natives, (See Lapillusaurus).

Glowrod – A clear cylinder about eighteen inches in length made from a polymer and its core lined with Methonian Crystal used as a weapon, tool or light source.

Great Temple – Home of the Methonian Masters and their Methonian Warriors. It is located in the northern icy mountains of Methonias.

Great Seal, The – A clear magical dome that stretches over the entire land of Upper Peruvious. It protects it from entry by any living creature.

Grëyfwyn – A high-ranking guard in the City of the Humans; he is also known as "The Organizer."

Hakama – Japanese traditional formal male clothing; it is a divided or undivided skirt, which resembles a wide pair of pants.

Haori – "Long Jacket" is a hip-length or thigh-length kimono jacket worn traditionally by Japanese men over a kimono.

Head Council – The leading group of Masters located on Saurian Five.

Hogtrah – An acronym for Hog Transformed Human. A human-pig hybrid developed before the eugenic wars; there were hundreds living under the City of the Humans during Anton's visit there.

Interstellar Sixteen – An intergalactic bus used to transport people from one star system to another. It was the most advanced craft built until the Pleceivious M-60 later replaced it.

Ivan – One of the Warriors Anton went on his first mission with to the Badlands of Methonias to rescue a Chief's daughter from the Troglodyte caves.

KACATU – An acronym for: Knowledge Accelerated Computer Aided Transfer Unit. A device found in Celestra.

Kanza – One of the natives of the village of Tooloo; he was a very disagreeable and outspoken man.

Katrah – An acronym for Cat Transformed Human. A human-cat hybrid developed before the eugenic wars; there were only two left in the City of the Humans during Anton's visit there.

Kimono – A Japanese traditional garment worn by women, men and children, are a T-shaped, straight-lined robe.

Lapillusaurus – A large genetically created dinosaur with the capability to create crystal gems like an oyster creates pearls. They are found on Methonias and provide the specialized crystals for the Methonian Masters usage. The natives refer to them as a Gem Lizard.

Lavacia – Wife of Mahkeetah.

Lorca – A Primord living in the City of the Humans. He is the healer, doctor, and alchemist working directly for Trepid.

Loring Four – A Methonian Warrior sent on a mission to the village of Tooloo many years before Anton's visit. He first discovered the effects of the Virlaqueus flower.

Lothendus – The scientist known as "the great genius" he was the first Wizard of Peruvious and the creator of the Staff of Balance, Vim's mentor and teacher.

Luke – One of the Warriors Anton went on his first mission with to the Badlands of Methonias to rescue a Chief's daughter from the Troglodyte caves.

Luthian – The leader a group of men that committed crimes against the village of Tooloo; he was formerly an Aerocraft pilot for the Great Temple.

Mahkeetah – A former Methonian Warrior and temporary Chief of the village Tooloo; father of Nelda.

Marpitas – A purple pear shaped tropical fruit with an incredibly sweet flavor found in the jungle regions of southern Methonias.

MB-1 – An acronym for 'Methonian Base One', a space station in orbit around Methonias used as a spaceport for interstellar travel.

Methonian Cloning Labs – The laboratories used by the Methonian Masters for creating advanced genetic humans and clones.

Methonian Masters – They are the genetic engineers and trainers of the Methonian Warriors, and the Governing Council of Galactic Peace living on the terraformed planet of Methonias.

Methonian Warrior – Genetically engineered highly trained super-humans designed and created to control peace in the known human universe.

Mountain of Harvest – A large hill in Lower Peruvious; this is the location the Intelligence of Non-existence uses to harvest human souls.

Muzoke – A young boy Anton met in the village of Tooloo; Tok's older brother; Son of Tyrell.

Nanobots – Tiny robots constructed of nanometer-sized components; robots of a microscopic scale.

Naomie – A teenage girl that lived in the village of Tooloo; she was the daughter of Tarna, and the first young girl killed by the outsiders.

Nekelmuse – Large spherical creatures with one eye, one mouth, and two pointed horns that float through the air like a hot air balloon and shoot a fireball from their mouth. Derived from the Sumerian word for "Evil Eye."

Nelda – A beautiful young girl who lived in the village of Tooloo; she was the daughter of the former Chief Mahkeetah, and Anton's short-lived wife.

Neo-Kukulcan – The pyramid structure in the City of the Humans; it is the home of Trepid Tantamount.

None – The self-proclaimed name of the Intelligence of Non-Existence. The destroyer of the known universe and ruler of the Negative Universe.

Nootka – An old frail man that lived in the village of Tooloo; he was the former Chief and Tyrell's father.

One – The self-proclaimed and contemporary name of God; the Intelligence of power, wisdom, and goodness; the creator and ruler of heaven, the universe, Peruvious and all living things.

Observatory, The – A structure in the city of Celestra that housed a device known as the Celestial Eye.

Odious, Lord – One of the Lords of Ruin, sometimes called the "The Detestable Lord." A former Methonian Warrior captured and controlled by Vile the Necromancer.

Perthus – One of the tiny Primords that lived in the Primord hamlet; he was a friend of Vim Alpenstock.

Picuris – A village in the southern equatorial tropical region of Methonias located near the village Tooloo.

Pleceivious M-60 – A luxury interstellar star cruiser used to travel between star systems throughout the galaxy.

Primords – A small group of tiny humans living in Upper Peruvious near Vim's cave; they have special abilities to talk to both plants and animals.

Putucu River – A wide fast running river located in the valley below Vim's cave. The island of the Primords is located in the center of the river below the cave.

Rikin, Thundaruss – The champion and lieutenant to King Amilius.

Ruler – The Master holding the position of Chief of the Head Council of Masters residing on Saurian Five; the original or first Master.

Saurian Five – A planet in the Saurian system on the outer reaches of the galaxy. The Warriors assigned there never return.

Serpotaur – A giant muscular creature with the body of a man and the head of a snake; they wield a magical staff with a large ruby attached to the top.

Sinister, Lord – One of the Lords of Ruin, sometimes called the "Lord of Evil." A former Methonian Warrior captured and controlled by Vile the Necromancer.

Slipstream Drive – An advanced propulsion drive defining the Pleceivious M-60's unique design and speed capabilities.

Spotter Drops – A powerful potion manufactured by the Primords. It gives the user the ability to locate an object of their desire. This potion is used one drop at a time.

Star Cruiser – A passenger ship used in interstellar travel.

Supergrip Tsuka – The handle of a Methonian Katana made from a material that clings to the user's hands. It helps to prevent slippage and reduce the risk of dropping it or having it torn from the user's hand in battle. The term Mekugi is the Japanese name for the handle of a Katana.

Tania – A small faerie given to Anton as a companion and friend by the Queen Faerie.

Tara Fruit – A yellow tough-skinned fruit with an orange-red inside and a tangy-sweet flavor. It has the shape of an acorn squash and grows in the tropical region of Methonias. Reportedly, it can sustain a man for long periods of time when no other food is available.

Tara Wine – A wine made from Tara fruit. It is quite potent in alcohol content, more closely related to liqueur than wine.

Tarna – One of the men living in the village of Tooloo; His daughter Naomie was the first young girls killed by the outlaws.

Taun – One of the last Katrahs. A half-cat, half-human hybrid.

Thorik – Chief of the village Picuris located near the village Tooloo, a village in the southern equatorial tropical region of Methonias.

Tillich – One of the tiny Primords that lived in the Primord hamlet; he was a friend of Vim Alpenstock.

Tok – A small boy in the village of Tooloo Anton saved from drowning; son of Tyrell.

Tooloo – A village located in the southern equatorial tropical region of Methonias. Anton completed his final training there.

Towers of Tor – Two large towers positioned on the absolute edge of Upper Peruvious looking over the Lower lands. They are an octagonal shaped structure resembling a lighthouse; they house an octahedron of crystal and use it to project the energy of the Great Seal.

Trepid Tantamount – An alias for the *Eye of One*; He used this to disguise Himself from Evil.

Trieos Three – One of the human colony planets located near the heart of the galaxy; it is the origin world to a race of taller than average humans are.

Trinary Code – Advanced binary code used by computers of Anton's time; it is an advanced instruction set developed for predictable Boolean instructions.

Tritanium – An advanced alloy of titanium, aluminum and other metals that are unique to Methonias. Typically used in the construction of spacecraft, transportation vehicles, the superstructures of buildings and various weaponry.

Troglodytes – A group of genetically specialized humanoids living in caves in the desolate Badland region of Methonias. They are highly aggressive by nature and use humans as slaves.

Tsuba – A Japanese term referring the collar located above the Tsuka (grip or handle) on a Katana.

Tybalt – One of the Warriors Anton went on his first mission with to the Badlands of Methonias to rescue a Chief's daughter from the Troglodyte caves.

Valde Domus, Mount – The "Great Home Mountain" found in the northern region of Methonias. It is the place where the Great Temple was constructed.

Vinicus, Lord – Captain of the Wardsman Alliance.

Vipercraft – A single piloted flying vehicle used on Methonias for planetary and civil defense.

Wardsman Alliance – The battalion of guards at the castle of Amilius; they defend the castle and protect the last of humanity.

Warrior – Genetically engineered highly trained super-humans designed and created to control peace in the known human universe. See also *Methonian Warrior*.

Xenostemorphology Laboria – The cloning science used on Methonias to adjust brain chemistry, behavior, and mental disciplines. Part of the overall sciences used in the development and construction of Warriors and related super-humans.

Yor – The commander of the Hogtrah army.

www.ingramcontent.com/pod-product-compliance
Lightning Source LLC
Chambersburg PA
CBHW060317100726

47907CB00002B/434